FROM HUMBLE BEGINNINGS

WENDY SUE ELLIOTT

To Anita

With Love & All
Good Wishes

Wendy Sue
Elliott

Foxdale Publishing

© Wendy Sue Elliott 2006
From Humble Beginnings

ISBN   0-9553535-0-5
        978-0-9553535-0-5

Published by:
Foxdale Publishing
27 Cove Road
Rustington
West Sussex
England
BN16 2QW

A CIP catalogue record of this book
can be obtained from the British Library.

Designed and produced by:
The Better Book Company Ltd
Forum House
Sterling Road
Chichester
West Sussex
PO19 7DN

Printed in England

DEDICATION

My grateful thanks to my dear husband Chris, my son Stephen, my daughter Sue, granddaughter Emma and grandson James for all their support and encouragement in helping me to achieve a life-long dream.

Thank you, also, to all other members of my family including Mike and Lin, Pam and Barry, Ann and Don, Hilda and Chalky and my late parents Margaret and Frank Love, together with Pat and Pete and all my friends, for helping me to sustain that dream.

Chapter 1

'There goes that 'igh and mighty Anna Briggs with 'er 'ead in the air. There's some say she's got the blood of the gentry in 'er. I've heard tell that 'er mother was …'

At times such as this I would hurry on through the village and ignore the woman's malicious tongue. I'd learned to ignore the whispers of others over the years, but there were times when I couldn't avoid overhearing the local gossip as she passed on the information to a newcomer with a certain amount of intrigue and, dare I say it, pleasure in her voice. Little did she know that I held my head high, not because of a feeling of superiority, but more from the need to convince myself that I was a worthwhile human being. I refused to believe that I was just a mass of unintelligent flesh and bones put on this earth to eke out a soul-destroying existence in poverty and squalour until, ultimately, my life came to an end somewhere out on the open moors with no one to care or even to wonder what had happened to me.

I entered this world on a bleak and windy October night. We lived in a shack – it couldn't be described as anything more – on the edge of the Devonshire moors in a time when people were either rich, or they were poor. We were poor – very poor indeed.

Born the sixth child in a family of eight, I had four brothers and one sister older than myself and two younger sisters, all of us born within the space of ten short years. My father worked fourteen hours a day for a pittance on a nearby farm, the owner of which also staked a claim on the hovel we dared to call home.

From a very early age it was impressed on me that I was different from my brothers and sisters. This was largely down to my father who made no secret of his feelings towards me. He hated me – there was little doubt of it. Had it not been for my mother's protection he would have drowned me at birth, of that I am quite sure. He always claimed that I was not his child but the outcome of an attack on my mother one evening when she returned alone from the farm with a jug of milk. It was rumoured that the farmer's wealthy brother had been staying with him for a short while and had found her very attractive. He saw her leave the farmhouse alone that evening and followed her across the fields. Somehow he persuaded her to go into an old barn with him where, against her will, he took his pleasure then left her to find her own way home, sobbing and crying; too terrified of what her husband might do to tell him what had happened. Inevitably, my father learned of that tragic encounter and when I made my presence known a few months later he had vehemently declared that the child she carried was not of his blood. My mother always disputed this emphatically, but deep within me I sensed the truth in such accusations. Although I bore a certain resemblance to my brothers and sisters there was nothing of my father in me, and many said that I had an almost aristocratic air, which was not apparent in any other member of the family. I could neither read nor write and my grammar left a lot to be desired, but I always felt that life held something more for me and, one day, I was sure, things would be different. If only I could read and write. I was certain that these two things were the key to my future but who was there to teach me? My family was as illiterate as I, and when I expressed my wish on one occasion, my father mocked me cruelly and laughed openly in my face.

'You? Learn t' read an' write? Who are you kiddin'? Yer 'ead's too full of such fanciful ideas. Reckon yer too good for us, do yer? Well, you can forget them notions, and fast. You'll learn t' scrub floors and wash dishes then you can go as scullery maid in some Lord an' Ladies 'ome and earn some shillings. Just you remember yer station in life an' don't go gettin' any big ideas. Read an' write? Whoever 'eard of such a thing for the likes of us?'

Despite my father's harsh words I wasn't discouraged. One day I would learn, though how I was to set about it I had no idea. For a while my hopes were raised. My mother knew how very much I wanted to have an education and she somehow persuaded my father to allow me to go to the village school. But my joy was short-lived. More often than not I was told that I was needed at home to help with the chores, so what little schooling I had was really of no use to me although it did give me the opportunity to make friends and get to know some of the other children in the village.

Life was hard for all of us but we were tough; we had to be. There were times when we had nothing to eat but soup made from dandelions which our mother had sent us into the fields to collect. But we were thankful even for that. At least we had a roof over our heads, such as it was, unlike some poor creatures who had neither job nor home and were reduced to sleeping out on the moors in all weathers.

The place we lived in was a mixture of flint stones and wood, roughly thrown together to form three small, inadequate rooms which housed the ten of us. The four boys, Joey the eldest, Harry, Jimmy and Benje, all slept in one room; Megan, who was three years older than I, Mary, Cathy and I shared the other room and our parents slept in the main room where we spent most of our time. There was little furniture: a couple of coarsely made benches, a table, some stools, an old chest of drawers and a few well worn mats scattered on the floor. We had no beds. At night we slept on the cold stone floor, huddled together for warmth on an old rug with one blanket to cover four of us. My mother worked hard to keep the place clean, but it was a thankless task with ten of us living in such confined space. Our clothes, despite the fact that they were thin and worn from constant wear, were washed regularly and our mother took a pride in the fact that neither us, nor our home, smelt as did so many others.

As soon as they were old enough, the boys were sent to work on local farms. Mr Gatsby, my father's employer, took Joey on but he said that father would have to make other arrangements for Harry, Jimmy and Benje. The few shillings a week they each brought home, together with the occasional eggs or bread, helped to raise our living standards just a little, though not very much. When Megan was ten she went to work as a scullery maid in a big house about three miles away. She lived there with one full day off every two weeks. On that day she would walk home, bringing with her a bag of food which the housekeeper had been kind enough to send us. Now and again she would also bring some old clothes or pieces of material which had been thrown away and, when she did, mother would sit busily with her scissors, needle and thread and produce something new for us to wear.

Tragedy struck when I was nine years old. Megan had been at the big house for almost two years and was due home as usual for her day off. It was Sunday and father and the boys were also there which meant that we would all be together for a short while. We always looked forward to Megan's visits with excitement because she never failed to bring something with her. Cathy, the youngest of us, sat on the doorstep eagerly awaiting her arrival which was always a little after nine o'clock in the morning.

The time came and went and eventually I could see that mother was becoming anxious.

'Maybe they ain't given 'er the day off,' I said after a while, hoping to ease her concern.

'She'd 'ave let us know,' was all she replied.

'P'raps she couldn't. One of them other maids might 'ave gone sick or somethin' at last minute and Megan might 'ave 'ad to stay an' do 'er work. She'd only be able to let us know if someone was passing this way to give a message.'

She pondered on this thought as she carried on with her mending but after a while I could see the uneasy doubts creeping back into her mind.

'I'm sure she'd 'ave got a message to us somehow,' she said eventually. 'Something's 'appened to 'er. I know it 'as. I can feel it in me bones.'

Two hours passed and there was still no sign of Megan. At last my father left what he was doing and said he'd take a walk to see if she was coming. He took the boys with him.

Never in all my days will I forget that moment when they returned. I saw them as they trudged across the fields; the boys with their heads bowed and my father carrying the wet, lifeless body of my sister Megan. They'd found her in the stream not half a mile away.

It appears she must have slipped as she took her usual route along the water's edge. There was a deep bruise on the side of her head, probably caused by contact with a large boulder as she slipped on the mossy stones. The water wasn't deep at most two or three feet – but in an unconscious state she had remained beneath the water, with no one nearby to come to her rescue, and she'd drowned.

My mother never recovered from her death. In some way her grief affected her mind and her sense of reasoning. The result was that she became both mentally and physically ill so that, instead of going out to work as I would have done, I, now the eldest girl, had to remain at home and help her.

The years passed and eventually Mary, and Cathy too, had a job to go to. Little Cathy, with her violent temper, her big brown eyes, her thick crop of dark, curly hair so different from my own fair waves. She seemed such a baby. It just wasn't possible that she was now old enough to contribute to the family's income. I have to admit that Cathy, despite her temper, had a special place in my heart. I loved all my brothers and sisters, but the others were always so independent while I felt that Cathy needed someone to lean on occasionally. Invariably, I was that someone.

My mother's health became steadily worse until eventually she was little more than a vegetable and I took over her responsibilities completely. This didn't enhance me at all in my father's eyes. In fact he showed his hatred for me even more, sometimes picking up one of the cooking pots and throwing it violently in my direction if I had done something which displeased him. He often spent nights away from home and I very soon learnt that he was friendly with a young woman in the village nearby. Rumour had it that she was carrying his child but I chose to ignore such gossip.

The turning point came in my life when I was just eighteen. Joey and Harry were both married and fortunate enough to be living in houses which were owned by the farmers they worked for. Jimmy and Benje still lived at home and Mary and Cathy lived at the big houses where they worked, returning home only when they had a day off. My mother lay all day in a make-shift bed, stirring only to take a small amount of food. Most of the time she just stared, unseeingly, at whatever was directly in front of her. Occasionally, she went through bouts of extreme violence and when this happened it was best to get out of her sight and leave her to exhaust herself as she threw her body and any available object around the room. I soon learned that the one thing that brought on these attacks quicker than anything was the sight of muddy or dirty clothes. It occurred to me that it could be connected to the tragic day when Megan was brought home, her clothes wringing wet and caked with mud.

* * * * *

One morning I was walking along the road on my way back from the nearby village of Thursledown. There had been a heavy rainstorm the night before and puddles and mud were thick on the ground. Without warning, a carriage suddenly appeared. The driver gave no thought or care for anyone who might be on foot and it was upon me before I had time to think. I had no alternative but to jump out of the way and into the ditch. When I picked myself up I was covered from head to foot in thick, clinging mud. My fair hair was more like dark brown and the hem of my dress clung to my ankles. Whatever was I to do? If I went home looking like this my mother would, without a doubt, throw one of her fits. Desperately, I tried to remove some of the filth. It was a useless task.

I was agonising over my predicament when a thought occurred to me. I was very near to Foxdale, a large country mansion not far from where I lived. I knew that in its vast acres of land there was a beautiful lake; I had seen it as a child when my brothers had dared me to climb the high boundary wall and walk along it. If I could only get inside the grounds I could bathe in the lake and wash my dress. It was a warm day and it would soon dry. I would be late home, but my mother was oblivious of time so she would be none the wiser. The other members of my family weren't due to return until evening, so I had plenty of time.

I decided that this was my best course of action and set out along the road until I came to the high wall which formed the southern boundary of the estate. First checking to make sure that I wasn't being watched, I managed to get a foothold in the uneven flints and once at the top, dropped silently into the bushes on the other side. My heart was pounding. What if someone should catch me? I dared not think of it. I just had to get to the lake and clean myself up.

I stood very still and listened for sounds of anyone approaching. I could hear nothing. When I was certain that there were no gardeners or gamekeepers around I crept slowly towards the edge of the lake which was through a small glade of trees about two hundred yards away. Every few feet I stopped to listen. There was complete silence. All I could hear were birds singing happily above me in the trees and the soft rustle of the leaves blowing gently in the breeze. I had almost arrived at the lake when a pair of red squirrels suddenly darted out ahead. I let out a frightened gasp and for some seconds stood shaking nervously until I'd recovered sufficiently to continue.

When I arrived at the lake I was so enthralled by the sheer beauty of the scene that I quite forgot my fear. The clear blue water stretched before me for a distance of about one hundred yards, dotted here and there with colourful clusters of red, yellow and orange water lilies. At regular intervals, weeping willows rose sturdily from the bank and dipped their swaying, lush green foliage to gently caress the ripples on the surface and dance with the sparkling rays of sunlight which came from the clear, blue sky to play like gold dust on the water. Four beautiful, white, long-necked swans glided gracefully round a clump of bulrushes at the far end. They were oblivious to my presence and quite unaware that they were being watched and admired. Peace and tranquillity surrounded me.

Beyond the lake were a few trees then a large expanse of grass, which rolled towards the manor. It was an imposing Elizabethan structure rising majestically out of the ground in the distance. From where I stood the back of the house was fully visible and I could just make out the stables and coach house to the right. French windows opened onto a wide terrace where there were a number of fine statues and enormous pots of flowering shrubs. A broad, curved flight of steps led down to the well-kept gardens below.

I stood in awe of the view, quite forgetting the purpose of my visit and the fact that I shouldn't be there at all. The sudden cry of a pheasant close by brought me to my senses and reminded me of the urgency of my task. I was satisfied that I couldn't be seen by anyone walking on the terrace. The trees shielded me from the house and gardens. I slipped out of my dress and washed it quickly in the lake. When it was clean I hung it over a bush to dry and set about removing the mud from my shoes, face, arms and hair. At first I tried to get it off with a few large leaves which I dipped into the water, but this only spread the mud around my arms and face and made me look worse than ever. Eventually I decided that I had no choice but to remove my undergarments and go for a swim. That way it was also easier to wash my hair.

I'd almost taken off my bodice when I heard a sound close by. I froze with fear. What was that? I listened hard. There it was again. It was the sound of a horse blowing restlessly through its nose. Panic caught hold of me and my first instinct was to hide. A horse wouldn't be wandering around on its own. It had to have a rider. Hurriedly I gathered my clothes and made for the nearest clump of bushes. I crouched down, terrified and trembling. With bated breath I waited as the sound of hooves came nearer and nearer and finally stopped.

'Come out! I know you're in there.' The voice was commanding and well educated.

I didn't move.

'Will you come out, you little brat, or do I have to come in and horse-whip you?'

I knew from his tone that he meant what he said. There was no choice but to reveal myself. Escape was impossible. Clutching my dress to my half-naked body, I slowly left the protection of the bushes and stood up. It was then that I realised there were two men on horseback not one, as I'd first thought. Immediately, I knew who they were. I'd often seen them from a distance riding across the moors. They were the sons of Sir Mortimer Tremayne, Squire of the district and owner of Foxdale.

'Well! Well! Well! What have we here?'

It was the older of the two who spoke. He dismounted and walked arrogantly towards me. There was a touch of cruelty in his twisted smile and I knew that it was unlikely he'd show much mercy. His smirking, leering gaze took in my half-clothed, dishevelled appearance.

'So – it's one of the village sluts.' The colour rose to my cheeks, not just because of my scantily clad appearance but in indignation and anger at being referred to as a slut. I was on the point of telling him just what I thought of his insulting remark but then I thought better of it. I clamped my jaw shut and glared defiantly into his hard, grey eyes.

'What are you doing here, girl? This is private property – as well you must know.'

I said nothing. A sudden feeling of panic and fear churned my inside. Words stuck in my throat. What would he do? Let me go? I doubted it.

He came nearer. My heart was pounding furiously and I clutched my dress closer to me.

'I can see we shall have to teach you a lesson.' He caught hold of my left arm with hard, brutal fingers. I felt his nails dig into my flesh.

'Please! P–please. Let me go,' I begged.

He laughed cruelly.

'Let you go? Indeed, not! You must take the consequences of trespassing in private grounds, my girl. Filthy, you may be, but you've a fair body under those garments, I'll be bound. It's been some time since I've had the pleasure of lying in the grass with the likes of you.'

He left no doubt in my mind as to what he intended to do. My legs were weak and I was panic-stricken as he pulled me closer and clutched at my dress to throw it aside. At the same time, his face was so close to mine that I could smell his stale breath and feel his wet lips as he tried to kiss me.

'No! No!' I screamed, and struggled furiously to free myself from his hold.

'No?' he questioned. 'Why ever not? I don't doubt that I'm probably one of many.' Then he paused, as another thought dawned on him. 'Or could it be that you've not yet known the pleasure that a man can give.' He laughed, arrogantly. 'If that is so, then my enjoyment of you will be all the greater. You should consider it an honour that I will have initiated you into such matters.'

He threw me, none too gently, to the ground. His heavy body was pressed hard against me as he clawed at the clothes I still had on.

Tears blinded my eyes. 'No!' I screamed again. He was a big man. I didn't have the strength to push him away.

Then he was gone and I was free of him. In amazement and relief I stared as he rolled in the grass some ten feet away. He was clutching at his groin which had felt the hard tip of his brother's riding boot. I'd forgotten the other man who was with him and it was he who had come to my rescue. Or had he? Perhaps I was relieved of one attacker, only to find myself faced with another. Gratitude swept over me as I realised that this was not so. He stood firmly between the older man and me.

'What in God's name has got into you, Nigel?' he roared. 'Have you so little feeling of self-respect that you can take this girl with me, you own brother, looking on?'

Nigel Tremayne rose, slowly, to his feet and brushed the dirt and leaves from his breeches. His face was a black as thunder.

'I wasn't aware that you were asked to stay and watch,' he snapped. 'Why don't you just take a ride back to the house and mind your own business?'

'I consider it is my business. This girl is terrified. If I go back and leave her with you I'd be something less than a human being.'

'My dear Adrian, don't make me laugh. Do you mean to stand there and tell me that this girl's virtue is of any importance to you? You know as well as I do that these village sluts are only good for one thing. Or could it be that you wish to claim her for yourself the minute I'm out of sight?'

Once again, very slowly, he cast his hard, grey eyes over me in critical appraisal. 'On second thoughts,' he added, 'you're welcome to her. There are plenty more where she comes from.' With this he strode over to his horse and almost threw himself into the saddle before riding off at speed.

I waited, unsure of what to expect.

When he was positive that his brother was well out of sight, Adrian Tremayne turned to me and I was able to see him clearly for the first time. A man in his early twenties, he was tall and thick-set with a mop of dark hair which fell carelessly across his forehead. Though reasonably good-looking, one couldn't call him a handsome man. Even so, there was a strength of character in the firm line of his jaw, his long nose and his deep blue eyes which were set evenly apart. He smiled kindly at me. When he spoke the line of his mouth bore a gentle quality, unlike the thin, hard, cruel lips his brother had.

'Stand up,' he said. 'You've nothing to fear from me.'

'I rose to my feet, still clutching at my dress. My fear had lessened although I was still weak from the effect of it.

'What's your name?'

'Me name's Anna, sir,' I replied. 'I didn't mean no 'arm, really I didn't. Yer see, me mother's ill and goes mad at the sight of mud. A carriage nearly ran me down on the road and I 'ad to throw meself into the ditch else I'd 'ave been under the 'orse's 'ooves. I knew there was a lake in 'ere, so I thought no one would notice if I came and cleaned meself up. I didn't mean no 'arm, sir. I was going to leave as soon as I'd done. Truly, I was.'

He smiled, a gentle, understanding smile. 'I believe you,' he reassured me, 'but you're lucky that my brother wasn't alone or that one of the gamekeepers didn't catch you.'

12

'I – I don't know 'ow to thank you for comin' to me rescue just now, sir. There can't be no better gentleman than you. Not many would 'ave done as you did.' Of a sudden I felt embarrassed. Perhaps he would think I was being a little too outspoken. I dropped my gaze to the ground.

'You have nothing to thank me for,' he said, after a moment's silence. 'But take care, you'll not keep your virtue long if you take more than a passing glance at men with those beautiful, hazel eyes.'

Colour warmed my cheeks. I was touched by his compliment. Nobody, in my life before, had ever told me that there was anything pretty about me, let alone beautiful.

He called his horse and it trotted forward, obediently. I watched as he lifted himself into the saddle, wishing that it were possible for him to stay just a little longer. He was so kind, so gentle. Never before had I met anyone who had treated me in such a way.

'Don't linger here,' he warned, as he turned his horse's head. 'Be gone as soon as possible or my brother may return.'

As he rode around the lake I watched him go with an unexplainable sense of loss at his going. I was drawn to him, almost as if I knew him well; as if we had known each other long, long before this day. So long before, that it could even have been another lifetime.

The moment passed and I was quickly reminded of the fact that I had to get away from the grounds of Foxdale as soon as I could. My hair was still thick with mud, my body dirty. Hastily, I washed myself in the lake. I put on my dress even though it was still damp and ran as fast as my feet would carry me to the boundary wall. Once on the other side I was able to breathe more freely and contemplate my lucky escape.

I didn't return home immediately. Instead, I walked across the moors until the sun had dried my clothes and hair. My mind was full of the events of the past hour and I found it difficult not to dwell on those few short moments with Adrian Tremayne. The incident with his brother was temporarily blotted from my memory as I recalled, with pleasure, his benign good looks and gentle voice. He stirred in me something, which until now, I'd not felt for another human being. It was a strange, new feeling; one that I wasn't altogether sure I understood.

After that, it became almost impossible to get him out of my mind. Occasionally, I caught sight of him riding across the moors and my heart would pound but I knew that it was fruitless to hope that I might talk with him again. He never saw me, and had he done so I doubt that he would have recognised me. My hair was clean and fair and my face was no longer masked with dirt. A complete contrast to the girl he'd met by the lake.

It came to my ears some time later that a scullery maid was needed at Foxdale. Sadly, I contemplated the fact that, had my mother been in good health, I could have applied for the position with the chance of living closer to him. I might even have had the opportunity of speaking with him now and again, if only just to say, 'Good morning, sir.'

Time passed and I settled into a hopeless acceptance of my situation. He had been born into the wealthy classes, whereas my family couldn't have been poorer. The two just didn't mix unless, of course, it was as master and servant. As there was no possibility of me securing a position in the Tremayne household in the near future, I resigned myself to the fact that I had to put him out of my mind. But my thoughts would often wander to that day by the lake when, for the first time in my life, another human being had shown true concern for my feelings.

CHAPTER 2

It was late autumn when my mother passed away and more than a year had gone by since my encounter with Adrian Tremayne. After years of battling with ill health, both mental and physical, it seemed that her body just gave up the struggle and life slowly petered out one night as we all slept peacefully on.

I rose early that morning and set about my usual chores. Father, Jimmy and Benje went off to work and, as always, I left my mother to wake naturally. She was less trouble asleep so the longer it was before she woke the better because it allowed me to get on with my jobs undisturbed. The time passed and it was whilst I was washing the dirty clothes that I realised she'd slept rather longer than usual.

I crossed the stone floor to where she lay and gently pulled the covers back from her face. She was on her side. Her skin was very pale and just a hint of a smile softened her expression. When I put out a hand to touch her cheek I was startled to find that she was stone cold.

'Ma!' I cried, 'Ma! Wake up!'

I took her hand in mine and patted it in an effort to get some response. She didn't stir. Slowly the truth dawned. She was dead and I realised that never again would she open her eyes.

For a time I knelt beside her lifeless body and let the tears run freely. I thought of the hard, difficult life she had led and the pitiful way in which she had spent her last years. It all seemed so pointless and sadly, in many ways, her death was a happy release from a gruelling existence.

After a time, I dried my eyes and walked to the farm to tell my father. He took the news calmly but there was a sadness in his eyes as we returned to the house. This surprised me. He hadn't given her a great deal of his time lately; not since she'd become ill shortly after Megan's death. But maybe their years together had counted for something after all.

* * * * *

Her burial was simple. We had only a few late-flowering blooms, picked from the fields, to place on the soil which covered her. It was the best we could do; headstones for a grave cost money and we had none.

Silently, we all walked along the road towards home. Cathy was the first to speak.

'What'll you do now, Anna? I suppose you'll stay an' keep 'ouse fer Dad and the boys?'

Before I had time to reply my father answered for me. 'Oh, no she won't,' he said decisively. All the hate he had ever felt for me showed now as he turned to look in my direction. 'I've put up with you all these years for yer mother's sake, but I'll not 'ave you in me 'ouse any longer. Yer mother 'ad never been touched by another man until that swine took 'er against 'er will that evening. Then you was born. And there's no one can tell me you weren't 'is child. It wasn't 'er fault; she was a good woman. But I'll not 'ave you around to remind me of that one blight on what was a good marriage up until then. You was useful while she was ill, but now she's gone you can pack yer things and go too.'

I was shocked; hurt. I knew that he'd always hated me, but I never thought for one moment that he'd turn me out at the earliest possible opportunity without so much as a word of gratitude for the years I'd spent looking after mother and him and the rest of the family. I could do nothing except stare at him in wide-eyed astonishment. It was Mary who opened her mouth first.

'But Dad, what'll you do? You can't just turn 'er out like that. Who'll do the washing fer you an' the boys? And, anyway, where will she go?'

'I don't care a damn where she goes,' he growled. 'That's up to 'er. As fer me an' the boys, Bess can come and live with us now. She'll do all that's needed.'

Bess was the woman he'd spent so much of his time with over the past few years; the mother of his child.

My brothers and sisters protested strongly against his harsh decision, but it was of no use. Clearly, all the hatred, all the blame which he'd harboured against me for so many years was now unleashed. It was more than my life was worth to remain under the same roof with him. He totally ignored their pleas. With his hands slung deep into his trouser pockets, he strode off across the moors to be alone with his own private thoughts.

My brothers and sisters were all sympathetic but I told them not to worry.

'There's an 'ouse a few miles away that wants a kitchen maid,' I lied. 'I'll go there tomorrow and see if they'll take me on. Don't you worry about me. I shall be alright.'

They appeared satisfied and we went on to talk of other things. Only Cathy mentioned the subject again. It was as she left to return to Satchfield House, the place where she worked. With tears in her eyes she looked at me with concern.

'What'll you do if yer can't get set up in that job you was talkin' about?' she queried.

I tried hard to sound nonchalant.

'There's plenty more places I can go to. I'm bound to find a job somewhere.'

She thought hard. 'Take me with you, Anna,' she begged. 'I can give up the job I 'ave at the moment and we can look for something together.'

'Don't be a little fool,' I chided, gently. 'You've got a good position and they feed yer well, don't they? They're not unkind to you, are they?'

She shook her head, silently.

'Then stay where you are. Work's not that easy to come by an' it could be even 'arder for the two of us.'

Her lips quivered slightly. Eventually she swallowed hard and agreed that it was a foolhardy thing to do. I promised that, if I could, I'd let her know where I was and how I was getting on.

When I thought about it later I was touched by that small display of loyalty. All the others had been quite ready to accept the fact that I'd be able to take care of myself. Even Harry and Joey, who had homes of their own, hadn't suggested that I should go to them for a short while if I had no other place to sleep.

* * * * *

Early next morning I put together my few possessions and left that shack on the edge of the moors which had been my only home for the past nineteen years. My father didn't return that night and I never saw him again. Jimmy and Benje wished me luck as they rushed off to work but neither seemed bothered that I might never pass that way again.

The cold morning air found its way through my thin clothes as I walked along the muddy road. Even the shawl I wore around my shoulders didn't serve to protect me from the biting wind. Everything I owned in the world was bundled into an old cloth bag which I carried at my side. I had no idea where I was going or what tomorrow might bring.

As I passed the flint wall which formed the boundary of Foxdale, my thoughts turned to Adrian, second son of Sir Mortimer Tremayne. Even though so much time had passed, on the rare occasions when I'd seen him from a distance he had still caused my heart to flutter. I wondered whether or not I should go to the house and enquire if they were in need of a kitchen maid; but no, I was sure that I would have heard of such a vacancy. I was always interested in the comings and goings of the servants and I'd heard of nothing. Even if there was such a job, would it do me any good? Far better, I thought, to go far away from the Tremayne household, however much it saddened me. Far better to try and forget completely that son of a nobleman whose way of life was a world apart from my own.

I walked on. After a while I realised that I was on the road which led to the coast about twenty miles away. I had no preference in which direction I travelled, so I continued along the rough uneven track and met up with no other travellers on the way. I had with me a piece of dry bread and some old cheese which I ate late into the afternoon, not because I was hungry but more from the need to keep my strength up. I gave little thought as to what would become of my life but I knew there was a large town near the sea and I guessed my chances of finding work would be better if I went there. Eventually, night came. Feeling deeply sad and totally exhausted, I found shelter in an old, disused barn where I lay down and fell sound asleep.

When I awoke it was very early morning. I was stiff with cold and a mist hung low over the fields like a damp blanket. I stood up and wrapped my shawl about my shoulders. The best way to get any warmth into my body was by walking, so I started out along the road again, shivering with cold, my bones and limbs aching.

I must have travelled for about half an hour when, quite by chance, I came upon an overturned trap. The mist was slowly rising and I could just make out a dark shape in the road ahead. There was no horse; presumably it had broken free and cantered off. As I drew near it I could see that a man was slumped over the side of the up-turned trap. It became clear that there had been a dreadful accident. At first I thought he might be dead but this fear was soon dispersed when I saw a movement of his hand. I hurried to his side and his eyes flickered open. There was a vague, shocked expression on his face. He was an elderly man with greying hair which was thinning on top. He was well dressed and wore fine clothes although they were now rather dirty and torn.

'What 'appened?' I asked him.

'I – I don't know. I – ,' vaguely he searched his memory for an explanation. 'My head – .' He placed his hand to the side of his face which was bruised and swollen.

'Can you get up?' I enquired.

He lifted himself to his feet with great difficulty. He didn't appear to have any broken bones but it was clear he was suffering from shock and exposure.

'Do yer know 'ow long you've been 'ere?' I asked.

'I – last night – I think – . It was dark.'

'Can you walk?'

'Yes – I think so.'

I noticed a church spire not far away. If we could make it to there I was sure the vicar would take care of him. Leaning heavily on my shoulders, he took a few painstaking steps along the road. Then he stopped. His breathing was laboured and it was obvious he couldn't go much further.

'I'll tell you what,' I said, gently, 'you sit 'ere on the grass an' I'll run to the vicarage an' get 'elp. Will you be alright?'

He nodded gratefully and I ran as fast as my legs would carry me in the direction of the tall spire.

Breathless and exhausted from running so fast I knocked on the door of the vicarage. It was opened a few minutes later by a very startled maid wearing a neat black dress and starched white apron.

''Ere, what d'you you mean by banging on the front door like that? Who d'you think you are, a member of the gentry or somethin'? Be off with you or I'll call the master.'

There was no time to argue. I placed my foot in the door just as she was about to shut it.

'Please,' I begged, 'fetch yer master. There's been an accident. A man needs 'elp.'

She eyed me with suspicion as if she doubted my words. For a brief moment I was afraid she would force the door shut. Then a man's voice came from behind her.

'What is it Belle? Who's there?'

'I don't know, sir,' the maid replied, courteously. 'There's a girl 'ere who says there's been an accident.'

He came to the door and I saw that it was the vicar himself. Before he was able to ask who I was, I told him what had happened and that the man I'd found needed help. Within minutes we were in his horse and trap, returning speedily to the place from whence I'd come. We found the old gentleman still sitting at the side of the road; his head cupped in his hands. Carefully, we helped him into the trap and set off again at a jog-trot back to the vicar's home. Once there, I left the elderly man in capable hands and slipped quietly away. I had almost reached the gate when the maid came running after me.

'Heh! Miss! The master says you've to be given some breakfast if you'd like it?'

Never was I more grateful for food in my life. I followed her to the kitchen where I was given a mug of steaming hot tea. It tasted so good. Far better than the cheap stuff we'd just about been able to afford on occasions at home. I sipped it slowly; savouring every mouthful and feeling the hot liquid slip gently into my stomach. It seemed to warm every cold, aching bone in my body. When it was gone I ate a huge piece of home-made bread, still warm from the oven and smothered with butter and fresh blackberry jam. I was quite at liberty to eat as much as I pleased and I did so, since I was unsure when I'd have my next meal. The cook asked where I was going and, kind soul that she was, packed up some bread and cheese with a few cakes 'to keep me going on my way'. I thanked her, gratefully, and set out again feeling all the better for the food and hot drink inside me.

I learned, much later, that the gentleman whom I'd helped, was ill for a number of days and suffered from a chill and mild concussion. When he eventually regained his senses he wanted to know who it was who had saved his life, for I had, indeed, done just that. The doctor claimed that, had he been allowed to remain by the road-side much longer, he would most certainly have died. When he learned of this he expressed his desire to repay me in some way for my good deed, but I'd long since gone on my way. The cook, however, was able to tell him that I was making for the coast. Beyond that, they knew nothing.

It appeared that luck was with me. As soon as he was fit to travel, a day or so later, the old gentleman resumed his journey. His horse had been found wandering in a field not far away. It wasn't his intention to look for me but it so happened that I was on the same road which would take him to his home town of Lynhead.

When I look back now I'm so thankful that I hadn't yet reached the town before he caught up with me. My journey had been made longer by stopping to run errands and do odd jobs on the way in order to earn a few coppers with which to buy food. By the time we met again I was just two miles from the coast. I was cold and tired, and the clothes I wore must have appeared shabbier than ever, if that was at all possible. My hair was dirty and uncombed and I looked and felt a mess.

The clip-clop of a horse's hooves coming up from behind made me step aside, but I kept on walking. The trap went slowly by, then came to a stop. An elderly man turned to look at me and I recognised him at once as the gentleman whom I'd helped. The bruising on his face had lessened considerably and he now looked clean and well groomed, but there was no mistaking who he was. I smiled up at his kind face.

'Hello, sir. You feelin' better now?'

'It is you,' he remarked, joyfully. 'For a moment I couldn't be sure. Everything was so hazy the other day that I didn't really get a good look at you. Yes, I'm much better now, thank you. But, tell me, where are you going?'

'Nowhere in particular, sir. I'm looking for work and I thought I'd try me luck in the town near the coast.'

'Well, as it happens, I'm going there myself. I live there. Jump in, my dear, you must be weary. I've no doubt you'd be glad not to have to walk the last few miles.'

How kind he is, I thought as I climbed up to sit in the seat next to him. He was obviously a well-educated man and from the fine quality of his clothes and the gold watch and chain attached to his silk waistcoat he was certainly not short of money. But despite these trappings of wealth it didn't seem to matter to him that I was of a different class. He treated me almost as an equal, which in some ways embarrassed me. I had always been taught to show deference to the upper classes.

With a gentle, 'On you go, Bess,' to his horse, we began the last part of the journey. I was so thankful to rest my weary legs.

'I have a lot to thank you for young woman,' he said, as we trotted along. You may not be aware of the fact, but you saved my life the other day.'

'I only did what anybody else would 'ave done, sir.'

'I'm afraid I have to disagree with you there ...' he paused. 'What is your name, young miss?'

'Anna, sir. Anna Briggs.'

'Well, Anna, there are many who would have relieved

me of all my valuable possessions and left me to die in that ditch. I don't doubt it. But you gave me help and saved my life. I must find some way in which to repay you for your kindness.'

'You don't need to repay me in any way, sir. Thank you is quite enough and you've already said that. I'm only glad that I came along when I did.'

We travelled in silence for a while, then he turned and looked at me closely. A broad smile lit up his face. 'You say you're looking for work?' he asked.

'Yes, sir. Anything I can get, really.'

'Then this could be a very providential day for both of us, my dear. It so happens that my daughter and I – we live together in a cottage just outside the town – have been discussing recently the idea of having a live-in maid to help her with all the chores. She's been a wonderful daughter to me but she isn't getting any younger and our house-keeper is quite elderly. An extra pair of hands would be most welcome, I'm sure. What do you say? Would you like the job? We'll give you a roof over your head and three good meals a day along with a small amount of money each week which will be your wages.'

I was speechless. This was more than I could ever have hoped for.

'Do you mean it, sir? Do you really mean it?' I managed, when I was at last able to check the tears that welled into my eyes.

'My dear child,' he laughed, 'of course I do. Would I ask you if I didn't?'

'But you don't know me, sir. And I don't have no references.'

'I'm a very good judge of character, Anna, and I think your character has spoken for you during our short acquaintance. Do I take it your answer is yes?'

'Oh, yes, sir, yes. Thank you. Thank you from the bottom of me 'eart. I've been 'aving nightmares wondering what I shall do. I had visions of me tramping the streets, starving and penniless, looking for work. An', without references, 'ho'd take me on?'

'Well, I will, so from now on you have no need to worry. But, tell me, how did you come to be in this predicament?'

So it was that, as we trotted through the countryside towards the place which was to be my new home, I poured out to him the events of my relatively short life and told him how I had come to be so far from home, wandering towards the coast.

'Have you a big 'ouse, sir?' I finished by asking.

'No, it's not very large. I'm not a wealthy man by any means, but I am able to afford a few of the finer things of life. I used to teach at one of the great Universities of Cambridge but I gave that up long ago to retire to a more peaceful way of living.'

'You mean you taught people to read an' write, sir?'

'Oh, far more than that,' he smiled.

'I've always wanted to read an' write,' I admitted, quietly.

He looked at me with interest. 'In that case we shall have to see what we can do. Perhaps we can teach you.'

Right then I could have willingly thrown caution to the wind and flung my arms around his neck to plant a grateful kiss on his dear, kind face. In the past I'd been laughed at for having such ideas, and yet here was a man who was prepared to teach me. Suddenly my life had a purpose after all. I'd been offered a job with a roof over my head and I was to learn to read and write. What more could I ask for? My good fortune seemed unbelievable.

CHAPTER 3

Professor Joseph Argyle lived just outside Lynhead with his daughter Lucille, whom he told me was thirty-three years old. It was a source of great sadness to him that she'd never married and given him the grandchildren he and his late wife had so longed for. But it wasn't to be and when her mother died, from a severe chest infection, Lucille had remained with her father to take care of him in his fading years. He also had a son, Richard, who was a little younger than Lucille. He was, by all accounts, a successful architect who spent most of his time away from home.

The thatched roof of Cherry Tree cottage was visible in the distance long before we arrived. A thin spiral of smoke rose steadily into the clear, blue sky from the old, and slightly crooked, chimney stack. As we drew nearer I noticed that the cottage itself stood on its own in a large garden with a small orchard to one side. A few late-flowering summer roses clung loyally to the arched trellis around the small, wooden gate. The garden was beautiful. Each border was neatly turned and cleared of weeds and dead blooms; each section of grass cut to perfection and laid out like a length of velvet.

The horse, knowing it was home, came to a halt by the gate. I'd barely stepped down from the trap when the cottage door was flung wide and a young woman came hurrying to greet us. I guessed she could only be Lucille. Slim and graceful, she had dark hair pinned neatly to the crown of her head and the same expression on her pretty face that her father possessed.

'Father! I'm so pleased to see you. Where have you been?' she enquired as she embraced him affectionately. 'I expected you home before now. I was becoming quite anxious.'

Gently, he placed a kiss on her brow. 'I'm so sorry I've caused you such concern, my dear. I'll tell you all about it whilst we have tea. In the meantime, I'd like you to meet someone very special.' He turned to me. 'This young person, here, is Anna. Anna, this is my daughter, Lucille.'

'Pleased to meet you, miss.' I dipped my knees in deference to her position in society. She then did something which totally surprised me. She took hold of my hand and with a warm 'hello' she greeted me like an old friend. The fact that I was dishevelled and, most certainly, could do with a wash didn't seem to bother her at all. I liked her immediately. She had a sweet, kindly disposition and a natural gift for treating people as her equal, whatever their station in life.

'I'm sure you'd both like to wash and freshen up,' she said. 'Come inside and I'll tell Mrs Fairs to put the kettle on.'

Mrs Fairs, I soon learnt, was a lady who had lived with them for more than twenty years as their cook and house-keeper. She was getting on in years and was finding the work increasingly difficult to cope with. It had, apparently, taken quite a bit of persuasion on the part of the Professor and his daughter to make her see that an extra person to help with the chores would benefit them all. They hadn't wanted to hurt her feelings by telling her that she was becoming too old, so they'd been in no hurry to advertise the post. Fortunately for me, my path had crossed with the Professor's at just the right time. He saw it as a way of introducing me into his household as a much-needed extra pair of hands without upsetting the old lady.

The house was beautiful. To me it was like a palace. The hall was large and airy, made lighter by the big lattice windows either side of the oak front door. A thick, patterned carpet covered most of the highly polished, wooden floor. I slipped my shoes off, afraid to step on it or touch the brilliant white paintwork all around. A grandfather clock ticked softly in one corner, adding a peaceful tranquillity to the feeling of contentment which pervaded the whole house. Four Georgian-style doors led to rooms off the hall and a narrow passageway disappeared behind the staircase, no doubt to the kitchen and scullery beyond.

Lucille led me up the stairs to a bedroom on the second floor. It was under the eaves and wasn't large but to me it was absolutely wonderful. Never in my life before had I slept in a room that I could call my own. It was so bright and airy, with the same pretty latticed windows and sparkling white woodwork which characterised the house. A neat little kidney-shaped dressing table, with a very pretty, cotton floral surround, stood under the window. Against the wall to my left was a small white wardrobe. To my right a single bed, with a counterpane to match the surround of the dressing table, stood out from the wall into the centre of the room. The curtains were of the same, pretty floral design and contrasted beautifully with the plain, pink rug which covered the floor. I was lost for words. I couldn't believe that this was to be my room. There must be a mistake. Any moment now Lucille would take me to another, more stark, less cosy and very basic room somewhere at the back of the house. Her next words brought a thrill of excitement to my stomach.

'This is to be your room, dear. I hope you'll be comfortable enough.'

'Oh, Miss.' Tears came to my eyes. I was speechless. All I could do was stand and stare at this beautiful room, knowing that it was for me. She watched my expression with interest, a gentle, understanding smile on her face. 'Life's not been easy for you, dear, has it?'

I shook my head, crushing, immediately, any feeling of self-pity which might have arisen.

'Well, perhaps one day you'll tell me about it,' she said, not prying any further, 'but for now, come downstairs to the kitchen and fetch a pitcher of hot water so that you can wash and freshen up. Afterwards we'll talk about your daily routine and what will be expected of you. Mrs Fairs is in total charge of all matters concerning the cooking and the up-keep of the house so it will be she who tells you what needs to be done.'

'Thank you, Miss. Thank you so much,' I said, as we returned down the stairs. 'I won't let you down, I promise you, I won't.'

'I know that, dear,' she said with a smile. 'My father is a very good judge of character. He wouldn't have brought you into our household if he hadn't thought you were trustworthy.'

In the kitchen, Mrs Fairs was preparing the evening meal. She was a plump, motherly looking person who regarded me with a little bit of suspicion, but her greeting was cheery and she had a kind face. She wasn't surprised to see me and I guessed that the Professor had already spoken with her about my arrival. I felt sure we would grow to like each other.

'Water's on the hob,' she said, after Lucille introduced us. 'There's a jug and bowl you can use in the cupboard over there,' she pointed to a corner of the room. 'Mind you don't scald yourself as you take it upstairs.' I nodded and thanked her before leaving the two of them to discuss the change in household arrangements.

Upstairs, and back in my room, I placed the green and white pitcher, with its matching bowl, on the edge of the dressing table, then sat down on the side of the bed to marvel at my good fortune. The mattress was unbelievably soft. If I could have lain down right then and there I would surely have fallen asleep, possibly for the rest of the day. It was a luxury I'd never had. After a time, I stood up and crossed to the window. Beyond the picturesque, cottage garden, almost devoid of colour now because of the onset of winter, lush green hills rolled gently towards the sea. I knew that, because I could just see the glint of sunshine on the blue surf in the distance. I'd never been to the sea before. A thrill of excitement ran through me. All I wanted to do was to stand in awe of my surroundings. It was a dream; it had to be. Any moment now I would wake to find myself cold, hungry and miserable, tucked under some hedge in the middle of nowhere. But it didn't happen. This was real. I truly had been brought home by Professor Argyle and given a job and a beautiful place to live.

I took a fresh dress from my bag. It was worn and frayed at the cuffs but it was cleaner than the one I had on. I washed and changed and did what I could with my hair, then prepared to go downstairs to the sitting room, as Lucille had instructed me. I was all but ready when my attention was drawn to my heavy, dirty shoes. I couldn't possibly put them on, but I had no others. There was nothing for it; I would have to go barefooted. This I did, feeling the soft carpet beneath my feet. With every step I revelled in the luxury of it.

Downstairs in the spacious hall I looked at each of the four closed doors. I wasn't sure which one led into the sitting room. After a moment I heard voices coming from behind the one to the left of the front door. Tentatively, I knocked and waited. There was no response. I knocked again, this time a little louder.

'Come in,' came the Professor's bright and cheery voice. 'Ah, Anna,' he said, as I entered, 'I've just been telling Lucille how you saved my life and how grateful I am to you.' He sat in a big, comfortable armchair, a cup and saucer of delicate bone china in his hands. I smiled, nervously twisting my fingers together, then became aware that they were both looking at my feet.

'My dear child, where are your shoes?' It was Professor Argyle who asked the question.

'I took them off, sir. They was far too dirty to wear in your fine 'ome, and I 'aven't any others.'

'Then we must do something about that.' He turned to his daughter. 'Perhaps, tomorrow my dear, you'd like to take her into town and buy some new clothes and shoes. She'll need a grey dress with a starched white cap and apron for when she's working and a couple of day dresses along with some shoes.'

'Yes, of course, father. It'll be my pleasure,' Lucille agreed.

I couldn't believe my ears. 'Oh – thank you sir.'

'Not at all,' he replied. 'If you're to live here and work for us you must be clean and respectably dressed. I've a number of influential friends who frequently call. I can't imagine what they'd think if I permitted you to remain here clothed as you are.' He paused, a little embarrassed. 'I'm so sorry. I didn't mean to sound rude.'

'That's alright, sir. It's only the truth after all.' I was amazed to think that a person of his standing would show such concern for the feelings of one such as I. He truly was a gentleman.

Lucille offered me tea, but I was nervous and ill at ease in such surroundings. The chairs and sofa, with their big, puffy cushions, were covered in a pretty chintz material. The heavy, lined curtains which draped the wide, latticed windows were of the same exquisite design; all of which were complemented by a thick green carpet that felt like velvet beneath my feet. A nest of highly polished tables stood to one side of the white, marble fireplace where a shining, brass companion set had been placed on the hearth. Around the room were one or two other items of highly polished furniture and some fine ornaments, which, even to my inexperienced eye, were clearly valuable. A smell of lavender and beeswax permeated throughout the whole room, gently wafted around by a soft breeze coming in through the open window. Everything was so new to me, and vastly different from that which I'd known all my life. I was far more at ease, later, when I sat in the kitchen with Mrs Fairs.

* * * * *

The day that Lucille and I went into Lynhead to buy my new shoes and clothes is one I shall never forget in all my life. We took the trap and left early in the day so that, as Lucille put it, 'we could spend the maximum of time browsing round the shops.' It was an entirely new adventure for me. All I had ever worn were 'hand-me-downs' and other people's cast-offs. I'd never so much as set foot in a dress shop before.

The first place we entered made me feel very uneasy. I could see that the assistant regarded me with a certain amount of disdain mingled with unchecked amusement.

'What you doin' in 'ere?' she giggled, at first unaware that I was with Lucille. Before I could reply Lucille turned away from a dress that had caught her eye and answered for me.

'This young lady is with me. If you'd be so kind, I'd like you to take her measurements then show me a selection of day dresses which will fit her.' The assistant's mouth all but fell open. I could see what was going through her mind and her astonishment was clearly undisguised. 'Young lady, eh!' she sniggered under her breath as she showed me into a small room. I chose to ignore her. It was easier that way. Besides, it was none of her business how I came to be in such a fortunate position. After a number of attempts to try and get me to talk about myself, she finally gave up and concentrated on the task of accurately measuring me for my new clothes. When this was done she went off in search of Lucille who had already made a selection for me to try on. Of these, there was only one which met fully with her approval.

'That's the one,' she said, as I slipped the pale lemon gown over my head and waited for the assistant to button up the back. 'My word, it totally transforms you, dear. That certainly is your colour. We'll take it,' she said, to the girl. 'No, leave it on,' she added as I began to unhook the buttons.

I turned and caught sight of myself in a long mirror. The dress was beautiful; very simple, but skilfully made to enhance every curve of my figure. Tiny blue flowers dotted here and there took the plainness from its appearance and the delicate cream lace at collar and cuffs enhanced it still further. I turned to Lucille.

'Thank you. Oh, thank you,' was all I could say, tears momentarily clouding my vision.

'We're not finished yet, dear,' she told me. 'I can't tell you how much I'm enjoying myself. By the end of the day you'll have everything you need – including new undergarments,' she said with a smile. I blushed. Clearly, it hadn't escaped her notice that, although clean, my underclothes were old and well worn with a number of repairs where I'd stitched up the holes.

Lucille was true to her word. By the time we returned home, weary and longing for a cup of tea, I had everything I could have wished for and a great deal more. But it concerned me that so much money had been spent. To me it was a small fortune. I voiced this to her as we neared the cottage. What would the Professor say? Surely, he'd be cross at such extravagance.

'Not at all,' Lucille reassured me. 'He left you in my hands to ensure that you have what you need in the way of clothes, as befits you living with us. It's a very small acknowledgement of the fact that you saved his life.'

I stared down at my shiny, new shoes, once again rendered speechless by their kindness. 'B-but, the Professor said two day dresses – you bought me three. And – and I have two uniforms, not one. Then there are all the other things. The shoes, the undergarments; oh, miss, surely 'e won't be pleased with all that.'

'He most certainly will,' she laughed. 'As I said to you earlier, he left you in my hands. Believe me, he'll be more than happy with our purchases. Now, don't look so concerned. Enjoy it all.'

'I've never, in all me life, spent so much,' I said, half to myself. 'Well, I didn't spend it, you did. But you know what I mean, don't you? I feel guilty; when I think of all them that's got nothing.'

As we arrived at the back of the cottage where the horse was stabled in a small field, she gently placed her hand over mine. 'You have a very caring nature, Anna,' she said, kindly. 'You, clearly, know what poverty is and what it's like to have very little in the way of material things. But we are each responsible for our own lives and our own happiness. If God chooses to place us in a fortunate position, we should be grateful for that fact and, wherever possible, help those who are less fortunate than we are ourselves. Don't feel guilty. Just appreciate what you have and where you now find yourself.'

I recalled her words often in the weeks that followed. I had so much for which to be grateful. I was sure I'd wake one day and find myself back in my childhood home; that it was all a dream and nothing of what had happened was real. I was living and working in a beautiful house with lovely people who treated me with such kindness. As well as my board and keep I received a very generous allowance of three shillings a week to spend on my own personal needs. Never had I been so well off. If only my brothers and sisters could see me now.

It was whilst I pondered on this thought one day that Cathy came to my mind. I was reminded of my promise to let her know, if I possibly could, that I was alright and had found myself suitable employment. I smiled inwardly at the expression which would, no doubt, cross her face when I told her of my good fortune. I would never put it past her to arrive on the doorstep hoping that she, too, could be employed by the Professor. That worried me a little, but I had promised to get a message to her in some way, and I was never one to break a promise, so I spoke with Mrs Fairs and asked her what I should do.

'Well, my dear, we could send her a letter. You know the address of the place where she works, don't you?' she answered.

'Yes, I do. It's called Satchfield House. But I don't think her employers would take too kindly to her receiving a message in this way. Besides, she can't read so someone would 'ave to read it to 'er. In any case, I can't write.'

'But I can, so that would be no problem. What we really need, though, is someone who might be passing that way and could, perhaps, call in and see her.'

'Do you know of anyone?' I asked, hopefully.

'Well, I do know that my son sometimes travels in that direction on business. He sells and buys property for people, you know? At least for them that can afford it. Doing nicely for himself, he is. He works for a man in the town but one day, he told me, he's going to start up on his own.' She said this with obvious pride. 'Anyway, we'll see what we can do. If I learn that he's going anywhere near your sister's place of work I'll ask him if he wouldn't mind taking a message.'

'Oh, thank you Mrs Fairs. Thank you, so much. You're very kind.'

* * * * *

It turned out to be more than a month later before Mrs Fairs' son, Graham, called to see her. It was the first time

I'd met him and I took to him straight away. He was a very likeable person with a quiet disposition which belied his ability to take control of any situation with an air of authority. I could see why Mrs Fairs was so very proud of him. Curiously though, at the same time, I had a feeling of deep unease, as if some inner instinct was warning me to be careful of him.

After we were introduced, he sat down at the kitchen table and eagerly tucked into his mother's home-made scones along with at least three cups of tea. As I carried on with my kitchen chores I watched him from the corner of my eye. He talked, animatedly, with his mother, excitement lighting up and giving expression to his whole face. It wasn't a handsome face, far from it, but when he smiled his whole character shone through and it stirred in me a desire to know him better. Why, I couldn't say, but I was drawn to him.

He glanced up and caught me staring at him. I felt my cheeks turn warm. He couldn't fail to see that I was blushing. Although he was still talking to his mother, he looked at me with interest and his smile broadened. I turned my back on him, not just to cover my confusion but in case Mrs Fairs looked round to see what it was that had drawn his attention. Thankfully, they carried on talking without a pause, so perhaps she hadn't noticed. From then on I kept my eyes well away from where he sat but I listened intently to what he was saying.

'So you see, Ma, I may have my own business sooner than I thought. There's a shop in Nether Wilmslow which would be ideal. I went to see it a week or so back and I'm off there again today. The rent's a bit steep, but I've spoken with my Bank Manager and if I can come to an agreement with the owner I'm sure I can manage it. He's asking too much anyway. That's why he hasn't found anyone to take it on. I thought I'd …'

'Nether Wilmslow?'

They both turned to look at me. 'Nether Wilmslow?' I repeated.

'Yes, why do you ask?'

'My sister works a mile or so from there,' I told him. At the same time my eyes pleaded for help from Mrs Fairs.

'Oh, yes, my dear, it clean went out of my mind,' she said after a second. 'Graham, I wonder if you could do Anna, here, a very great favour.' She went on to explain to him just what I'd told her and how important to me it was to get a message to Cathy.'

'Of course, I'll see what I can do,' he said, this time looking me straight in the eyes. 'Give me the name of the place and I'll try and see her after I've completed my own business.'

I was so grateful to him. My only wish was that I could have accompanied him on his journey but I knew that he wouldn't return for at least two days. They were the longest two days I can recall. Every time a visitor called at the door or I heard a horse in the lane, I wondered if he'd returned.

Eventually, there came a knock at the kitchen door, not two but three days later. I was so anxious to have news of Cathy that I barely gave Graham time to say hello to his mother. Mrs Fairs was a kind, understanding soul and allowed him to tell me all he had found out before he embarked on telling her his own news. She was well aware that the extra day of waiting had caused me great anxiety.

'Did you see Cathy?' I asked of him before he had time to sit down. There was a long pause.

'I'm afraid not,' he admitted.

'But, why? Wouldn't they allow you to see her? Did you pass a message on for her?'

'I'm sorry to tell you, but it would seem that Cathy no longer works at Satchfield House. I was able to speak to the house-keeper who told me that she left her job quite suddenly. When I asked why she didn't seem to know – or didn't want to tell me. I had the distinct impression that she was anxious for me to leave. I did manage to speak with two of the maids and a gardener but none of them had any idea where she might have gone.'

Disappointment engulfed me. For the first time in weeks I felt really, really sad. Whatever had become of Cathy? I was truly concerned for my little sister's well-being.

* * * * *

CHAPTER 4

Six months went by. Six wonderful months during which I became accustomed to a life which, before, I could only have dreamed of.

'It's time we began your lessons,' Professor Argyle said to me one day. 'It's time for you to learn to read and write.'

I was thrilled and excited. I couldn't wait for my tuition to begin. Often, I'd thought about his promise to teach me but because he'd said no more about it I assumed he'd forgotten. I didn't like to remind him because he'd already been so kind.

'Lucille and I are very pleased with the way in which you've settled down here,' he told me. 'You've adjusted very quickly to your new way of life and you work very hard and very conscientiously. Only the other day, Mrs Fairs was singing your praises. She, I know, is very glad to have you with us, despite her initial reticence at having an extra pair of hands to help with all the chores.'

'I'm very 'appy 'ere, sir,' I said. ' I can't thank you enough for all you've done for me.'

'I'm the one who has to be thankful, Anna. You saved my life, remember? Lucille will agree with me when I say that there is nothing that can repay that debt. What I can do, though, is give you an education which will, hopefully, help to improve your life so that you need, never again, experience the hopelessness of your impoverished beginnings. Now that you're well settled here I suggest we spend an hour a day on your lessons. If you wish to do any extra work in your free time, that is entirely up to you.'

'Oh, I will, sir, I will. Thank you. Thank you so much.' I wanted to hug him, I was so grateful for this opportunity, but I kept my emotions in check. Instead I gave him a beaming smile and asked when it would be convenient to begin my tuition.

'Why not now?' he replied. 'Mrs Fairs tells me she can do without you for an hour, so we'll make it at this time each day, shall we?' He glanced at the clock. 'Half past two. I shall expect you in my study on the dot. Now, let's get started.'

I followed him across the hall to his study, a small, cosy room lined with books and smelling of polished wood and leather. He placed himself behind the desk. 'Sit over there,' he said, pointing to a table and chair which had been arranged for my benefit. I did as I was told. The excitement of it all almost overwhelmed me. I knew that this moment heralded the beginning of my future. A future far removed from my humble beginnings.

'Today, we shall start with the letters of the alphabet,' began my mentor.

* * * * *

He found me a keen and willing student and I made rapid progress. Within a year I was reading and writing quite fluently, largely due to the fact that I spent all my free time reading any available books and practising my letters over and over again. I would even sit in bed until late at night reading by the light of one small candle.

I was doing just that, one evening, when I became aware that the handle of my door was moving very slowly. I watched as it turned fully. Whoever was on the other side tried to push the door open. Thankfully, it was locked. I didn't always lock myself in my room but, on this occasion, I had done so. I remained quiet, waiting for the intruder to leave, but a sick feeling of disgust lined my stomach. There was only one person who could be on the other side of that door; Richard Argyle, the Professor's son and Lucille's brother. He'd recently returned home on a visit, the first since my arrival, and I have to admit that I took an instant dislike to him. He was quite unlike his father and his sister. He had a harsh, arrogant nature and once or twice I'd caught him looking at me in a very unsavoury fashion. I didn't trust him.

I watched, now, as he tried the handle again. 'Damn the girl!' I heard him mutter. After a moment I heard him walk away. A few seconds later, Mrs Fairs' voice came to my ears. Her room was next to mine and it was plain that she had also been aware of his presence. In a raised whisper I heard her say:

'If I ever catch you near Anna's room again, I shall tell your father.'

I didn't hear his response to her rebuke but I could well imagine that he just shrugged his shoulders and ignored her. I smiled to myself. How like a child she treated him, probably because she'd known him since he was a small boy. I could just envisage him slinking off to his own room like a scalded cat with its tail between its legs. He made no attempt to come to my room again, but on more than one occasion I caught him looking at me. I made sure that my door was locked each and every night from then on. When he left a short time later, saying that it would probably be another year before he could visit again, I was more than a little relieved.

* * * * *

The years went by. With each passing month my knowledge increased and I became more educated. A whole new world of information opened up for me and Professor Argyle took immense delight in my progress. So much so, that he insisted on devoting not one, but three hours of his time to me each afternoon. History, geography, English, French and arithmetic; I revelled in all of these and strove for perfection in all that I did, sometimes working late into the night. I was often tired, but I was happy in the knowledge that I was becoming far removed from the poor wretch I'd once been. The coarse inflexion in my voice slowly lessened until, in time, it had gone completely and my grammar was as perfect as it ever would be.

Lucille and I became very close, more like sisters even though she was so much older than I. My position in the household slowly underwent a subtle change as I grew older. Both Lucille and her father began to treat me almost like a member of their own family and although I still helped with all the household chores, it was more as a family member than as a servant. The grey dress and starched white apron I'd worn as their maid were, on their request, eventually discarded. Even Mrs Fairs, who herself was treated like an old friend, not just the cook and house-keeper, accepted the transition in my status.

Graham, Mrs Fairs' son, was a regular visitor to the house. At first, several weeks would go by before he came to see his mother. But then I noticed that he was calling more and more frequently and it was very rare for a month to pass without her seeing him. I liked Graham. He gave the impression of having a kind disposition and he knew where he was going in life. He worked hard and was eventually successful in acquiring his own premises in the village near to Satchfield House.

'I only rent it,' he told me one day, 'but I've found a niche in the market in that neck of the woods. There are a lot of properties owned by wealthy people round about there and I'm the only local property dealer. Of course, there are those who insist on calling in the big agents from London and the like, but one day they'll all be calling at my door. You wait and see. My business is expanding all the time and I'm making quite a name for myself. In time I shall make an offer and buy the shop where I am at the moment, then I can think of renting another place in one of the larger towns.'

I was intrigued. He knew exactly what he wanted and had his life mapped out in order to achieve his goals. But it did occur to me that there seemed no room in his life for women. He never mentioned anyone special although I felt sure that an eligible young man such as he would, surely, have many young ladies anxious to make his acquaintance.

'Do you have much of a social life?' I asked him out of curiosity.

He stared down into his cup with a smile on his face and I heard Mrs Fairs cough as she took a batch of scones from the oven.

'Do you mean, have I got any girlfriends, Anna'?'

'Well, yes, if you like to put it that way.' I felt the colour coming to my cheeks. It had, I suppose been rather a personal question. 'I-I'm sorry, I shouldn't have asked. It's none of my business. Forgive me.'

'I think you and I have known each other long enough for you to ask such a question,' he answered. 'And I really don't mind. Yes, I do have a "social life", as you put it. But most of my time, at the moment, is taken up with my work and all the book-keeping. I have two assistants in the shop but I could certainly do with more help. Since starting out on my own I've gone from days which were very quiet to days where I don't have a moment to spare. When I do have the time I go out with friends and occasionally I have been known to escort some very beautiful young ladies to the theatre or to dinner, when I'm in London – always chaperoned, of course.' He grinned. I felt he was making fun of me. 'However, I have yet to find a woman whose company I would prefer to ...' He stopped. Prefer to whom? Had there been a lost love in his life? 'Whose company I would prefer to that of you and my mother,' he said with a laugh. 'Where else could I go for a cosy chat and the best home-made scones in all the county?'

'Get away with you,' Mrs Fairs laughed. She gave him an affectionate nudge. We both know you come here to fill your stomach with a decent meal every now and again. You'd waste away otherwise.'

'Mother, dear, you know I come to see you. You're the dearest mother a man could have,' he said, rising to his feet. 'Now, I must be off. Business calls and it's a long journey home.' He kissed her warmly on the cheek and with barely a look in my direction, called out 'cheerio' over his shoulder and disappeared through the back door and into the lane where his horse was tethered. I picked up his cup and saucer and turned to take it to the sink, just in time to catch a curious smile on Mrs Fairs' face. She quickly looked away and pretended to check the timing of the next batch of scones in the oven, leaving me to wonder what had been going through her mind.

* * * * *

It was almost five years since my departure from the house on the moors. One day Lucille and I decided to take advantage of a quiet afternoon in town, shopping for new curtain material and a few other things. Periodically, we enjoyed a day in each other's company, either shopping or going for a long country walk. Over the years we'd grown very close, almost like sisters, and it was hard to believe that, when I first met her, our worlds had been so far apart. I never ceased to wonder at my good fortune in meeting up with the Professor, even though it had been in somewhat dire circumstances. And I never ceased to be grateful for all that he and Lucille had done for me, even though they both insisted, still, that it was they who were grateful that I'd chanced to come along on that fateful morning.

We wandered in and out of the shops in Lynhead until, finally, after about two hours and with our arms laden with parcels, we decided to take a break and stop for tea. We made our way to a small tearooms in the centre of town which we often frequented on our shopping trips.

We both lowered our heads and held on to our bonnets as we went through the small door and down two or three steps into the room which had a low, beamed ceiling. Narrow shelves lined the walls upon which there were all types of copper kettles and china ornaments. A welcoming fire crackled in the hearth. We were glad of its warmth; autumn was upon us and there was a cold nip in the air.

Lucille and I were never lost for words. We stopped talking only briefly to order our tea and scones before continuing with our appraisal of the afternoon's shopping. I heard the bell tinkle over the door as another customer came in but I didn't look in that direction until I heard the man's voice. He was talking to his companion, a beautiful young woman who sat down gracefully, on the chair he extended for her, and elegantly removed her gloves. My whole attention was drawn to them. They were a handsome couple, clearly well suited.

'Anna – are you alright?' Lucille's concerned question drew my attention back to her. I found my hand was shaking.

'Yes – yes, I'm fine, thank you,' I lied. 'Why do you ask?'

'Well, dear, you've become very pale. And you did stop in the middle of a sentence. Do you know that couple?' she asked in a whisper.

'I'll tell you later,' I said, quietly. Now, wasn't the time to explain to her that this man was Adrian Tremayne and that once, many years before, he'd saved me from his lecherous brother. I wondered if he would remember me. Apparently not. He looked across the room at me on several occasions but there was no hint of recognition in his eyes. This wasn't surprising in view of the fact that my appearance and whole demeanour had changed quite dramatically since our last meeting.

It was strange to be sitting so close to him. I was intrigued by both him and his companion and almost forgot I was with Lucille in my efforts to catch a few words of their conversation. Although we continued to make small talk, Lucille could see I was distracted and I knew she was intrigued to know why. We at last finished our tea and scones and left the little tearooms. As we passed by their table I was almost tempted to tell Adrian who I was, but I thought better of it.

Outside, I took a deep breath and realised that, although it had briefly crossed my mind to introduce myself, I was actually glad that he hadn't recognised me. When I considered the incident later, I realised, with a moment of shock, that he still had the power to make my heart skip a beat. I had come to believe that my feelings for him all those years ago had been prompted by the chivalrous way in which he'd rescued me from his brother. Being young and impressionable I'd immediately taken him to my heart. But now that I'd seen him again I knew that it hadn't been just a passing attraction prompted by his kindness. There was something about him that stirred my heart. Something I knew would be with me forever.

* * * * *

There were few men in my life. On occasions, one or two of the local young men showed an interest in me and either asked me to accompany them to the annual fair in Lynhead or to some other popular event. But as I grew older and became more educated, I also became more discerning as to whom I wished to spend my time with. Both Mrs Fairs and Lucille anxiously warned me against some of the local lads but I pointed out to them that, having grown up with four brothers, I was well able to look after myself. I was wary of them all and I certainly wasn't going to allow one of them to take me down. George, the Blacksmith's son, found this out to his cost one day when he allowed his hand to stray inside my jacket to the buttons of my blouse. I hit him so hard he reeled.

'You do that again, George West, and the tip of my boot'll find its mark somewhere that will put you out of action for many a day,' I told him. When I told Mrs Fairs what had happened, she laughed so much I could see tears in her eyes.

'Well, he won't be bothering you again,' she commented. 'You've certainly got some spunk, lass, I'll say that for you.'

As I grew older I found I was drawing attention from a number of the young men who visited Professor Argyle for private tuition. By this time I had long since discarded my grey uniform and was treated very much like a member of the family, although I never presumed as much. Graham, Mrs Fairs' son, visited frequently and always had a kind word for me. I looked upon him as one would an older brother. We got on so well and he could certainly make me laugh.

'Right, whose coming courting you today?' he'd ask, with a twinkle in his eye.

'No one,' I'd tell him, 'no one that matters, anyway.'

Then one afternoon he said something that quite puzzled me. 'I'm glad to hear it, Anna, cos there's no one here-abouts whose good enough for you.' He said it in all seriousness, and the smile had slipped from his face. He stared at the grouts in the bottom of his teacup and I couldn't think what to say. I wasn't usually lost for words with him. Only then did it occur to me that his feelings in my direction might be more than just a type of brotherly affection. The colour touched my cheeks. In all the years I'd known him, I'd never,

ever, regarded him as a possible suitor, although I was well aware that he was single and doing very well in the property market. He wasn't a young man. He was all of ten, maybe fifteen years older than I.

He looked up, now. No doubt from the expression in my eyes, he realised that something had dawned on me. 'I must be off,' he said, in a hurry. 'I'll see you both in a week or two's time,' and with a quick peck on his mother's cheek, he was gone.

Mrs Fairs carried on with the preparation of the vegetables for our evening meal. She appeared to be concentrating extremely hard on the job in hand and, very pointedly, didn't look up at me. On a cheerful note I made some excuse to leave the kitchen and hurried to my room. From there I could just see Graham's back as his horse galloped down the lane. Surely, I must be wrong. But what if I wasn't? If he had grown to love me over the years as something more than a friend, then how did I feel about that? My mind was in turmoil. I'd become so used to Graham's presence that the idea of being romantically involved with him took me completely by surprise. Was it so out of the question, though? There was no doubt that I cared for him deeply but I'd always regarded him as a very good friend – Mrs Fairs' son.

From then on I looked forward to his visits. I began to see him in an entirely different light. It was as if my eyes were suddenly opened and for the first time I realised how much he meant to me. This affection for him had grown so slowly over the years that I hadn't even recognised it. I was so used to his regular visits and the affectionate banter which had grown up between us that, until now, I hadn't given any thought as to how I would feel if he were no longer there.

'Mrs Fairs, why has Graham never married?' I asked her one day.

She studied me thoughtfully for a few seconds. 'That's

something you'd have to ask him yourself, my dear,' she replied at last. 'It's not for me to say.'

There was no telling how long it would be until his next visit but I found myself hoping that it would be soon. More and more he was in my thoughts. Then one morning, about three weeks later, I was upstairs in my room when I caught sight of his horse tethered in the lane. My heart began to pound uncontrollably. I hurried down to the kitchen, eager to find out how he would respond to me.

I was in for a bitter disappointment. He was alone, I could hear his mother in the pantry, but he barely glanced in my direction. In fact, it was I who said 'good-morning', to draw his attention to the fact that I was there.

'Oh, hello, Anna.' That was it – his only response. He was quite indifferent to my presence. I don't know what I'd expected. After all, he was hardly likely to come and throw his arms around me. But I did hope for some sign that I wasn't wrong in assuming that his affections towards me were something more than just that of a casual friendship. My hopes were like a balloon which has been pierced by a pin and slowly shrivels to nothing. My excitement, on becoming aware that he was in the house, was suddenly deflated. Clearly, he wasn't bothered in the least as to whether I was there or not. He'd come to see his mother. I turned and hurried into the hall, anxious that he shouldn't see my confusion. The colour rose to my cheeks and I was at a complete loss for words. How foolish I was. Why, in heaven's name, would he take a second look at me when he could, quite possibly, have the pick of many beautiful women nearer his own age? I chided myself for allowing my feelings, and my imagination, to run away with me. Thank God his back had been turned in the kitchen and he hadn't seen the look of anticipation on my face. I hurried back to my room where I needed time to compose myself before I faced him again.

A short time later I was once more in control of my emotions. But it would seem that the floodgates were open and that, for me at any rate, there was no going back to the easygoing friendship we'd always enjoyed.

After a while I felt calm enough to return downstairs. Graham was seated at the table, a cup of tea to his lips. 'Where did you disappear to?' he asked, casually.

'I – I suddenly remembered something I had to do upstairs,' I lied. 'How are things with you, Graham?' Even to my own ears my voice seemed reserved and stilted despite the fact that I tried to sound casual and relaxed. If he noticed, he chose to ignore it.

'Busy, as always,' he smiled.

Mrs Fairs appeared from the pantry. I noticed her glance at us both before crossing to a big basket of washing which sat by the sink. She busied herself, silently, for a while before saying, 'Wasn't there something you wanted to tell Anna, Graham?'

He looked at me for a second or two – a trifle embarrassed, I thought – then brushed aside his mother's question. 'No – it'll wait. I haven't really got time to go into it now. I'll talk with you some other time,' he said, turning to me. This left me wondering what on earth it was that he had in mind. Surely, it couldn't be that he was plucking up the courage to ask me out? I felt, again, a thrill of hope and excitement. Perhaps, after all, he did have feelings for me. Perhaps, with his mother present, he didn't want to risk a rejection from me.

'I must go,' he said, rising to his feet.

'But you've only just arrived,' I blurted out. 'Can't you stay a while longer?'

'I'm afraid not. I have business in Lynhead. I must be going or I'll be late for an appointment. If it's not too late in the day I'll call in on my way back,' he said to his mother, 'otherwise I'll be passing this way again next week, so I'll see you then.'

Even Mrs Fairs couldn't disguise her disappointment. She left what she was doing and followed him into the yard. 'Bye, Anna,' he called back over his shoulder as he went through the door. I watched him go. It was as if a huge great cloud of disappointment and depression descended upon me. I returned to my room and watched as he and his mother talked for a while before he mounted his horse and, with a backward wave of his hand, took off at speed in the direction of Lynhead. I didn't see him again that day, nor did I see him for many weeks to come.

* * * * *

CHAPTER 5

It came as a tremendous shock to us all to learn that the Professor was terminally ill. For a long while he kept the secret, even from Lucille. Only when he could no longer hide the fact that he was a very sick man did he finally tell her that he had but a few short months to live. From that moment on it seemed that he went rapidly downhill. He became more and more frail and lacked interest in the things which he had so loved to do. It was like watching a light slowly dim. In his final weeks he rarely left the house and, ultimately, was confined to his bed where Lucille remained constantly at his side. She wore herself out looking after him, refusing all offers of additional help to give her a rest.

On the day that he died a great hush descended upon the house. We'd all been expecting, and waiting for that saddest of days but it did nothing to lessen our grief at his passing. To all of us, in different ways and for different reasons, he'd been a special person, a true friend. Now he was gone.

In the days that followed a great many people called to express their condolences. Dozens attended his funeral to show their respect for this learned man whom, it became apparent, had touched the lives of many. Hundreds of letters and flowers were delivered to the house, each one bearing a fond and touching message of farewell. I knew from my own experience what a good, kind and generous man he was. But this overwhelming display of heartfelt sympathy and sense of loss from people whose lives he'd touched over the years proved that he was also a very modest man who had never shouted of his achievements.

It was very late in the afternoon when the last of the mourners took their leave and the house became unnaturally quiet. Only the Professor's solicitor remained, presumably to discuss the contents of his Will with Lucille and Richard.

Close as I had become to Lucille, I didn't feel it was my place to remain in the sitting room with them. I found my way to the kitchen where Mrs Fairs and Graham were discussing the events of the day and the people who had attended. Mrs Fairs had slipped off her shoes and was seated on a kitchen chair with her feet up on a stool. All around them, dirty cups and saucers and plates were piled high.

'I'll give you a hand with these,' I said, pouring hot water into the sink. I was tired and very weary but it gave me an excuse not to sit too closely to Graham. I was almost afraid that he would see the affection I had for him in my eyes. I still didn't know if he returned that affection. He gave no indication that this was the case. Maybe it was because the Professor had been so ill, or maybe because he'd thought it inappropriate in the circumstance but, for whatever reason, he'd never enlightened me as to what it was he had wished to discuss with me so many weeks before. He appeared to be a very sensitive person. With all the sadness of Professor Argyle's illness and, ultimately, his death, it was quite possible that he felt it necessary to keep his affection for me hidden for the time being – or so I told myself. When he felt the time was right he would no doubt let his feelings be known. In the meantime, I could only wait – and hope.

'Leave that for the time being, my dear,' Mrs Fairs told me. 'It doesn't have to be done immediately. I think we all deserve a rest for five minutes.' She pushed a cup of tea towards me and I was obliged to sit next to Graham whether I wanted to or not. Still, I reasoned, it was better than sitting opposite him. At least he couldn't see every fleeting expression that crossed my face. 'This house won't seem the same without the Professor,' his mother continued after a moment's silence.

'No, it won't. You're right,' I agreed. 'I wonder what Lucille will do.'

'Marry me, I hope.'

The room fell silent. It was as if the roof had come crashing down on me. I stared at Graham. Was he joking? No, he wasn't joking. I could see from the expression in his eyes that he was deadly serious. It felt as if every drop of blood in my body left me and drained out through the bottom of my feet in that one short moment. His words left me in a state of total shock. He took a sideways glance at me and grinned.

'Close your mouth, Anna. It's not so astonishing, is it? Lucille and I have known each other since we were small children, ever since my mother first came to work for the Professor as his house-keeper. We grew up together and we've always been very close.' He held up a hand as if to stem any flow of words I may be considering. 'I know what you're thinking,' he said, 'you're wondering why we didn't marry years ago if that was the case. Well, I'll tell you why. The Professor was a dear old man but, you may be surprised to learn, he wouldn't have condoned his daughter marrying the house-keeper's son. In our younger days, we did hint at the possibility. He merely dismissed it out of hand and made some reference to the fact that he'd be very sad to have to replace my mother. So you see, marriage for Lucille and me was out of the question. What would my mother have done without her job here? Where would she have gone? Besides, it would have caused a rift between him and Lucille and it was around that time that his wife died. Lucille was needed here to look after him. You've seen for yourself how close they were. I couldn't take her away from him under those circumstances. It would have broken her heart.'

I was stunned. So many questions crossed my mind. How could I ever have so foolishly imagined he was in love with me; that it was only a matter of time before he would ask me to go out with him? I had to say something, before he wondered at my silence. I swallowed hard.

'So – so, do you think she'll accept your proposal?'

'I sincerely hope so. All along we've planned for the day when it might happen. I've worked hard. I now own a business, which is prospering, and I can tell you now, Lucille has gone a long way to help me finance it, without her father's knowledge, of course. The old boy would have gone mad, had he known. I now have an income that will allow me to give her everything she has ever wanted. No longer is there a financial divide between us. We're equals in every way so no one can say that I'm marrying her for any money she may inherit from her father.'

'I – I'm amazed,' I stammered. 'In all the years that I've lived and worked here I've never so much as suspected that you and Lucille were so close.'

'It had to be that way. We had no choice. Only my mother, here, knew of our plans. For years now Lucille and I have been meeting whenever it was possible to do so without the Professor being aware of it. Sometimes, weeks have gone by before an opportunity has arisen. In fact,' he admitted, with a half smile at his mother, 'I was on the point of enlisting your help a few months ago. You're a good friend to Lucille and – I like to think that you're a good friend to me as well. We were on the point of letting you in on our little secret and asking for your help in arranging a few days together. We had hoped to arrange for her to take you back to the village in which you were born – which, of course, is very close to Nether Wilmslow where I have my business and where I now live. But it wasn't to be.' He sighed. 'As you know, circumstances changed with the sudden knowledge that the Professor was so very ill. It didn't seem appropriate to go ahead with those plans.'

So that was it. That was what he'd wanted to discuss with me all those weeks ago. I'd let my imagination run away with me and now I felt so foolish. Pray God that he wasn't aware of my feelings towards him. I nodded silently; at a loss for words. I was hurting inwardly. He regarded me as nothing more than a friend. That was how he'd always thought of me. It also hurt to realise that even though Lucille and I had become very close companions over the years, she had never once indicated that Graham was anything to her, other than Mrs Fairs' son. I was spared any further revelations by Richard who suddenly appeared from the hall.

'Would you come through to the sitting room, please,' he said, holding the door ajar. We all glanced at each other, our previous conversation momentarily forgotten. What could the Professor's solicitor possibly want with us? We passed into the hall and through to the sitting room where Lucille stood at the window. She turned as we entered and I couldn't deny my feeling of emotional pain as I witnessed the close, knowing look she gave Graham. Why had I never noticed, before, such looks which, surely, must have passed between them over the years?

'This is Mr Gilbrady, father's solicitor.' She introduced the man standing by the fireplace. He was a rotund, little man wearing a pin-striped suit and spectacles which slipped to the end of his nose. He appeared arrogant and officious. I didn't like him. But then, I didn't have to. I was, however, curious to know what he had to say.

'Well, now,' he began, 'I'll not beat about the bush. My time is precious and I have to return to Lynhead before five. This has nothing to do with you, Mr Fairs,' he said, looking over his spectacles at Graham, 'but I'm assured by Miss Argyle and her brother, here, that they wish you to be present.' He immediately looked very pointedly at Mrs Fairs and myself. ' It would appear that your employer has been most generous to you.' For the first time in years I felt like a servant again. All I needed was a starched cap and apron. It was as if this revolting little man expected us to bob a curtsey in deference to him. I lifted my chin and held his gaze – defiantly. He hesitated for only a second.

'Mrs Fairs – you are to inherit the princely sum of one thousand pounds, in appreciation for your many years of devoted and loyal service.' Graham's mother gasped, her hand flew to her mouth and I saw that there were tears in her eyes. 'Miss Briggs,' he paused, just long enough to cast a calculating glance at me. No doubt he was wondering just what my position in the household was. 'I am to inform you that you are to inherit whatever books you so wish to take from the library.' He waited for my reaction. I was thrilled. I hadn't expected anything from the Professor, but in giving me a choice of his books he must surely have known that it was the one thing I would treasure most. My delight was obvious. Mr Gilbrady, on the other hand, gave the impression of being a little chagrined. Clearly, he'd expected me to be disappointed. He coughed and cleared his throat. 'You, also, inherit the sum of one thousand pounds,' he added in a much lower tone. No doubt he hoped that I wouldn't hear.

For a moment I was speechless. One thousand pounds? It was a small fortune. I turned, first to Lucille and then to Richard. Surely there must be some mistake. Lucille came towards me and took both my hands. 'My father was very, very fond of you, Anna, and I can well understand why. You saved his life and have made an immense contribution, in many ways, to the happiness of this household since you've been here. Richard and I are well provided for and both agree that you are very deserving – both of you,' she placed an arm around Mrs Fairs, 'of this inheritance. Take it with our love, but most of all, take it with the love of our father.'

Mrs Fairs and I looked at each other in disbelief. Never in a million years could we have hoped for such a generous gift. We were well aware that Professor Argyle had been financially 'comfortable'. But it would seem that he was far more wealthy than either of us had ever imagined.

'I must be off,' Mr Gilbrady said, brusquely, as he closed his case. 'I'll be in touch to sort out the finer details of the arrangements. He completely ignored Graham, Mrs Fairs and myself. With a brief shake of the hand and barely a backward glance he said goodbye to Lucille and Richard and hurried through the front door to his horse and trap which awaited him by the gate.

In silence, Mrs Fairs and I went through to the kitchen. I noticed that Graham held back, no doubt hoping to speak privately with Lucille. To say I was stunned would probably have been an understatement. I felt totally dazed. So much money! Why, I could even afford to find a small cottage of my own in which to live. But what of Lucille? I couldn't just abandon her now that I'd come into this small fortune. We'd become close friends but my position in the household was, to an outsider, something of a curious one. I'd started out as a servant and, as such, had always done all the tasks expected of me. But gradually it was as if I'd become more a part of the family, although I was careful not to abuse my elevated position. Lucille and I had become the best of friends and companions whilst, at the same time, I worked diligently with Mrs Fairs to clean and maintain the house. I looked at Mrs Fairs, now. She seemed of a sudden to have become very old. She was old when I first came here, I mused. She, too, appeared a little dazed as she filled the kettle with water and placed it on the hob. She kept shaking her head as if unable to believe what she'd just heard.

'What will you do now?' I asked her.

'That will depend on Graham, my dear. If Lucille agrees to marry him – and I don't doubt that she will – then I shall no longer be needed here. They'll probably move to his home in Nether Wilmslow. I certainly wouldn't go with them. I've earned my rest. It's time for me to retire. All my friends are in this area and now that I won't have to worry about earning a bob or two to live on, I can rent a little cottage in Lynhead and see out my days there. What will you do?'

'I really don't know. It's all too much to take in at this moment.'

She thought for a second. 'Well, if Lucille marries Graham I wouldn't be surprised if Richard were to take over this house. I would imagine it's been left to the pair of them. The Professor, being the man he was, would have insisted that both Lucille and Richard benefited equally from his Will. Of course, they may sell it. But they both grew up here so I would imagine Richard will probably give Lucille the money for her half. He doesn't own a home of his own so it makes sense really. He's away a lot so he won't live here very much but he will need someone to look after it. You could stay on as his house-keeper.'

'I don't think that would be a good option,' I told her. There was no way I wanted to live under the same roof as Richard, even if he was away a great deal. The thought of being alone in the house with him, even now, filled me with horror. My experience of his philandering ways all those years ago, had left me very wary of him and to this day I didn't trust him to act as a gentleman if we were alone together.

Just then Graham came hurrying through the door. 'Well, have you asked her?' his mother prompted. He shook his head. 'It isn't the right time,' he said 'We've only just buried the Professor. Give her time to mourn. It would be insensitive of me to talk of marriage on a day like today.'

'I thought that's what you were going to speak to her about.'

He shook his head again. 'No, I just wanted her to know that I'm here if she needs to talk or could do with a shoulder to cry on. She was very close to her father.'

'You're right, son. I don't know what I'm thinking of.

It would be insensitive to bring up the subject, today of all days. You have all the time in the world ahead of you both now.'

I rose to my feet and was about to go to my room. All this talk of marriage between Lucille and Graham churned up the sick feeling of sadness which had washed over me prior to learning of my inheritance. I wanted to get away; be on my own; give myself time to think. It wasn't to be.

'Sit down, Anna,' Graham demanded. 'You can't leave us now. Surely, you'd like to sit and talk with us over a cup of tea. It's not every day you learn that you've inherited such a princely sum of money.'

'I have to admit, I am rather tired.' I tried, lamely, to excuse myself. 'It's been a long day.'

'Well, just you drink this cup of tea I've poured for you,' Mrs Fairs said, as she pushed a cup and saucer towards me. 'It'll perk you up a bit. It's all been something of a shock, hasn't it, dear, what with one thing and another?'

For a moment I thought she suspected my feelings towards Graham and was alluding to that as well as to the day's events. But I soon realised she was completely unaware of how I felt about him. She went on to talk of future plans and asked whether Lucille would move to his present house when they were married or if he proposed buying something larger. He could well afford it. In the years since I'd known him, he had not only started his own business but had made such a success of it that he now owned two other offices. One was in Lynhead, the other in Castleford, and he employed a manager and staff in each of them. He'd started life very modestly, moving into Professor Argyle's home when his mother had become widowed and needed the job as house-keeper for them to survive. But the Professor's influence had taught him that the basis of all successful men is a sound knowledge of reading, writing, and arithmetic. From his early days in the Argyle household he set about making himself successful. Without doubt, he'd achieved that aim. So why had Professor Argyle been so against his marriage to Lucille? Particularly as he'd so wanted her to marry and give him grandchildren. It was a mystery, but one I had neither the desire nor the inclination to think about at the moment.

The conversation continued in a light-hearted vein, although I didn't feel light-hearted. As soon as I could, I escaped to my room where I was glad just to be alone with my thoughts. Today's events had cast a completely new light on my future. What now? Six months ago it had seemed that my life would continue forever in this cottage which had become my home. Not so, any more.

I lay on my bed and looked up at the ceiling, as I had done so many times before. For the first time, I began to contemplate what it was that I really wanted from life. My inheritance now gave me a choice. I'd always visualised meeting a man, one day, whom I could love and who would love me in return. Graham sprang to mind. Instantly, I shut him out of my thoughts and quashed the sad feelings which threatened to bring tears to my eyes. I turned my thoughts to the future. I hoped to have a nice home – one far removed from that which I'd grown up in – and children, several children. This thought of children prompted me to reflect on my upbringing and I began to wonder what had happened to all my brothers and sisters. After my initial, fruitless, effort to contact Cathy I'd put them all to the back of my mind. I'd neither seen nor heard of any of them since. I took the view that, as they'd shown so little concern for my welfare on the day my father had cast me out, they would be totally disinterested in what had become of me since. But I couldn't help wondering where they were and what they were doing. Joey, Harry, Jimmy and Benje; and Mary and Cathy; had life been as kind to them as it had been to me? I had a sudden desire to know. With the money Professor Argyle had left me

I could return, now, to the place of my birth and, perhaps, seek them out. The more I thought of it, the greater my need became to see them all again. Perhaps it had something to do with going back to my roots in order to start afresh and go forward into yet another new and challenging part of my life. Quite what that challenge would be, I didn't know. What I knew, beyond doubt, though, was the fact that my life would never be the same again.

* * * * *

Chapter 6

When Lucille and Graham announced their intentions to marry, I somehow managed to express a feeling of genuine delight. It would have done no good to show the disappointment and sadness I felt knowing that he'd never had any romantic notions about me. I'd always been a friend to both of them and I wanted it to remain that way. I kissed Lucille warmly on the cheek.

'I do hope I may come to the wedding,' I said.

She squeezed my hand. 'But of course, Anna. You've become a very dear friend over the years. How could I not include you in the happiest day of my life?' She left my side and went to take hold of Graham's hand. He looked down at her with so much love. How lucky she was. Maybe one day I would be fortunate enough to find such happiness. 'We will, of course, acknowledge a year of mourning for my father,' she went on, with a tinge of sadness in her voice. 'After that, Graham and I will live at Nether Wilmslow. He's found a beautiful house, larger than the one he owns now. It does need a lot of alteration to bring it to the standard we would like, so the next few months are going to be very busy for us. I hope you'll come with me to choose all the furnishings and drapes for the windows. I'm really so excited,' she said, brightening again.

It was a great compliment that she wanted to share, with me, such an important event in her life. I could hardly say no, although it did cross my mind to tactfully refuse. My love for Graham would, somehow, make helping her to choose the décor and furnishings for their home together seem a little bizarre. But I had no choice. I had to hide my feelings and go along with her plans. Anything else would have made them question why I wasn't happy to be involved. Next moment, thankfully, she changed the subject.

'Now that the details of father's estate are almost complete, I can tell you what our arrangements will be. Richard will take over this house. Obviously, I won't need to live here once I'm married to Graham. Mrs Fairs tells me that she has found a little cottage in Lynhead and intends to retire there where she'll be amongst her friends. We'll see her regularly, of course, because Graham has one of his offices in the town. That only leaves you, Anna. The money my father has left you will be placed into a bank account for you. Mr Gilbrady will shortly want to see you in order to arrange this. You'll need to see the bank manager and give him a sample of your signature so that you can withdraw the money as and when you please. No doubt, as it's such a large amount, he'll wish to discuss with you any plans you may have to invest it.' She paused. 'Are you happy with that arrangement?'

For a moment I didn't know what to say. Me, with a bank account? It seemed unreal. Never had I visualised having enough money to warrant a bank account. 'Oh, yes – yes, of course,' I said, at last. 'Thank you, thank you very much.' I was stunned. I was still reeling from the knowledge that Professor Argyle had left me anything at all, let alone such a large sum. Now it was becoming reality and I couldn't believe it.

'What will you do?' Lucille drew me away from my inner thoughts.

'I – I really don't know. Well – yes, yes, I do. I'd like to return to Thursledown and see if I can trace any of my family.'

Lucille smiled and nodded. 'Well if you're in no hurry, you can come and stay with Graham and me for a while after we're married and when we've moved into our new home. Can't she Graham?' she said, looking lovingly into his face. 'That way she'll be very close to where she used to live and it will make it that much easier to search for her brothers and sister.'

'Yes, indeed,' he acknowledged. 'You'll be very welcome in our home, Anna, any time you wish to visit,' he said, turning towards me. I thanked him, thanked them both, hoping that the warm glow I could feel coming to my cheeks wasn't too obvious.

'Meanwhile, what will you do when your bank account has been arranged and your inheritance has been transferred to you?' Lucille asked. 'I hope you'll stay on here for a while, at least until I move away. Of course, I should imagine that Richard would be more than happy for you to stay here permanently if you so wish. He'll need someone to look after the house whilst he's away, which seems to be all too often.'

I couldn't tell her why that wasn't such a good idea. 'I'll have to think about it,' I said with a smile, knowing all too well that I had absolutely no intention of living under the same roof as her brother at any time or under any circumstances. 'I might buy a little cottage of my own,' I added.

'It may be that I could help you with that,' Graham put in. 'I have a number of suitable properties which you could afford to buy or rent. One in particular isn't far from Nether Wilmslow.'

'Thank you, Graham, I'll bear it in mind,' I said, at the same time wondering if that would be such a good idea. We changed the subject and they returned to their plans for the wedding and the purchase of their new house. I made my excuses and left them to it, wrapped in a world of their own where only the two of them existed.

As I closed the door behind me I was still pondering on my plans for the future. I really couldn't make up my mind what I wanted to do with my life. Circumstances around me had changed so quickly that I found it difficult to absorb the implications of it all. As it happened, a decision was very soon made for me. A week or so later I was shopping in Lynhead with Lucille when I received one of the biggest shocks of my life. It was this which prompted me to go in search of my family and, in particular, my sister Cathy.

* * * * *

As usual we were weighed down with bags, parcels and boxes from our morning spent shopping. This, though, was only a fraction of the purchases we'd made. Lucille had arranged for the remainder of the goods that we'd bought to be delivered the following day. I'd had a wonderful time. Now a woman of considerable means, I was able to purchase some of the clothes and undergarments which, hitherto, I'd only dreamed of wearing. It was difficult to refrain from constantly pinching myself to confirm that I wasn't just caught up in some wonderful dream from which I was about to awake.

We were both very tired. A pot of tea, home-made scones, jam and cream, were very appealing as we made our way to the quaint, little tearooms which we knew so well. The bell tinkled above the door and we stepped down into the small, cosy room. There was a table free by the bay window with its mullioned glass panes and wide sill. A number of brass and china ornaments decorated the sill and in the centre was a beautiful vase of mixed flowers. I couldn't resist putting my nose to them.

'Oh, they smell wonderful,' I told Lucille. 'One day I shall have a garden of my own full of all the flowers imaginable.'

'I'm sure you will,' she laughed. 'I don't doubt it for one moment.'

As I smelled the flowers I looked about me and took in the ambience of the little tearoom. 'You know, I'd love a tiny place like this,' I told her. 'It's got such character and charm and such a warm, cosy feeling.'

'Well, it's always a possibility.'

'What do you mean?'

'A tearooms. Your own tearooms. There's really no reason why you shouldn't consider the idea if it's what you really want. In fact ...' she pondered on an idea for a moment, 'I'm quite certain there's a premises available in Thursledown Graham knows of. It would lend itself wonderfully to such an idea. There isn't another in the village so I'm sure it would be most acceptable to the local people. Would you like me to have a word with him about it?'

A thrill of excitement ran through me. It was a wonderful idea. Why hadn't I thought of it sooner? I'd be working for myself and it would give me an income on which to live. Not only that, it would enable me to return to the village where I was born; possibly find my brothers and sisters again. My enthusiasm mounted. Lucille and I talked and talked for more than an hour. When our teapot became empty we ordered another and were unaware of the people who came and went in the course of that time. Lucille was as excited as I. Together we planned and imagined what could be done with the shell of an empty old cottage that Graham had been commissioned to sell. Our ideas grew along with our excitement until, finally, we fell silent. I sat day-dreaming, looking through the window panes out onto the street beyond.

I was so happy and so full of wild anticipation at the dream of things to come that I didn't see her at first. She was a small child about five years of age. Her clothes were immaculate; made of beautiful, deep emerald green velvet and silk ribbons. Her dark, shining hair dropped in ringlets down her back and she wore a matching emerald green velvet bonnet which was tied in a pretty bow beneath her chin. Her white stockings were also of silk and her shoes were of the finest black leather. They shone to perfection. It was plain for all to see that her parents were moneyed people and that she was a privileged member of the gentry. The lady with her, on the other hand, was in complete contrast, wearing only a simple, plain, navy gown with a white collar and a navy blue and white bonnet to match. Clearly, she was the child's governess.

When I first became aware of them they were looking in a shop window. I was about to turn away, acutely conscious that I was staring at this beautiful child, when they turned towards me. My heart missed a beat. I found it impossible not to stare at the little girl as she walked towards me on the other side of the road.

'Are you alright?' I heard Lucille ask.

I nodded but I was unable to say a word. I knew the colour had drained from my face and my hands were trembling. I couldn't draw my eyes away from the child's face. Every feature, every expression, even the tilt of her pretty little nose reminded me of my sister Cathy when she had been that age. A lump came to my throat and tears began to well into my eyes. It was difficult for me to maintain my dignity.

Then she was gone from sight. I wanted to run after her and ask who she was but no doubt such an approach would not have been appreciated. It was some time before I managed to regain my decorum. Only then was I able to give Lucille an explanation for my behaviour. She was so sympathetic and understood completely how I must have felt. She was such a good friend. It was difficult to imagine that we had ever been anything other than close friends. It seemed almost impossible to believe that all those years ago when her father had brought me home in his trap – a dirty, unkempt and uneducated girl – she had been my mistress and I her servant. What wonderful people it had been my good fortune to meet up with. I thanked God for the day on which they had come into my life because I knew it was rare for anyone to be as fortunate as I had been.

We gathered together our belongings and returned home. My mind was so full of the child I'd seen that it was a little while before I was able to regain enthusiasm for my future plans and the tearooms I so hoped to invest in. But as the journey progressed, the gentle sound of the horse's hooves as it clip-clopped along the country lanes calmed me down. Lucille and I, once again, began to discuss the possibilities of such an investment. My excitement returned and by the time we arrived back at the cottage I'd almost forgotten the incident with the child; almost, but not entirely.

* * * * *

Lucille was so excited. 'Just think,' she said, 'if you open a tearooms in Thursledown we shall live very close to each other. You'll only be in the next village to Nether Wilmslow.' When I told her I was still contemplating the idea, she would have none of it. Before I had time to take a deep breath she'd spoken with Graham who quickly produced all the details of the premises she'd told me about.

'It's an old cottage in the village centre,' he told me. 'It's in an ideal situation for a tearooms. It's double fronted, made of old flint stone. The previous owner converted the downstairs into a shop so that she could sell silks and cottons and materials. You know the sort of thing, all the bits and bobs that women so like to browse through. Unfortunately, she died a few months ago and her family is now looking to sell the place. None of them wants it, they all live too far away. There's a good-sized kitchen at the back of the cottage with a scullery which leads into the garden. Upstairs there are three rooms – a sitting room and two bedrooms. It's absolutely perfect for your needs.'

I thought for a moment and tried to recall the village as I'd known it. There was an old flint cottage that I remembered. It stood back from the road, next door to the church and a short distance from the butcher's shop. It came to mind because, as a child, I'd always admired it. In particular I recalled the thatched roof. It had a straw peacock perched near the chimney pot and a weather vane which swung in the wind. I used to dream that, one day, I would own such a cottage but at that time it was nothing more than a pipe dream. Surely, this couldn't be the same place. I described it to Graham and told him the exact location.

'Why, yes, that's the one. You know it then, so I don't need to tell you what an ideal position it has in the village.'

A bubble of excitement touched my stomach. Not only did this give me the opportunity to return home to my birthplace, I would also own the very property I had so loved as a child. It seemed that my wildest dreams were about to come true. In that instant, all doubts concerning my plans for a tearooms were dismissed to the back of my mind. I knew that it was the right thing to do and I couldn't wait to go ahead with the arrangements.

'Surely you want to see it?' Graham asked.

I shook my head. 'I already know the property and the village Graham, so, providing you can assure me that it isn't tumbling to the ground, I'm quite happy for you to go ahead with the purchase on my behalf. I'm sure I can trust your judgement.'

Lucille laughed. 'That must be the easiest afternoon's work you've done in a long while,' she told him.

He agreed with her and we went on to discuss the price and other related matters. By the end of the day I was dreaming of the moment when I'd take possession of my very own property. I couldn't believe it. If my family could only see me now. Who would have guessed, in my childhood years, that I would one day be a lady of means with a home and a business of my own. These thoughts led me into wondering how long it would be before I saw any of my family again. Would they recognise me? Would they want to know me, or would they, in view of my education, consider me too stuck-up for the likes of them? Of one thing I was very sure; my father would never, under any circumstances, accept me back into the fold. This was something I was prepared for and I knew there was nothing I could do to change his view.

From then on the weeks and months flew by. There was so much to be done. As well as helping me with all the plans for my tearooms, Lucille and Graham were in the midst of purchasing their new home and also making plans for their wedding which was fast approaching. The anniversary of Professor Argyle's death came and went and I was still living at Cherry Tree Cottage, an arrangement I was happy to continue with all the while that Lucille was there with me. Mrs Fairs had long since found her little retirement home in Lynhead and had taken up residence several months before. This left Lucille and I to maintain the cottage for Richard and we shared the chores equally. He, it must be said, rarely put in an appearance. I was more than grateful that he didn't. I always felt so uneasy in his presence.

As it turned out, my new home was available to me long before Lucille was ready for her move to Nether Wilmslow. I didn't want to leave her alone at Cherry Tree Cottage, especially as her marriage was imminent and she had a great deal of packing up to do in order to transfer her belongings to her new home. I agreed to stay on but only until there was no point in me remaining there any longer. This, in fact, was far longer than I imagined. I was desperate to get on with my own plans by the time Graham made arrangements for Lucille's possessions to be transferred to the house at Nether Wilmslow where he'd taken up residence. By that time, with just one week to go to the wedding, there was little point in me travelling the long distance back to my childhood home, only to return a few days later for their marriage in Lynhead.

'You could remain here until I return from my honeymoon,' Lucille suggested. 'You've been so kind to me and given me so much help. I was hoping that you'd allow me to do the same for you. When we get back, Graham and I can help you settle into your new home. You can't do it all by yourself.'

I knew she was being kind but she, clearly, didn't know how very much I wanted to see the house that I'd bought. From the moment she and Graham had told me about it, to this very day, I hadn't been to take a look. There were many times when I could have gone. Lucille had travelled the distance on a number of occasions with Graham. But they had relied on the kind generosity of friends in the area who invited them to stay. I didn't feel that I, too, could impose on such kindness, least of all because I was not acquainted with them.

I had no qualms about buying the property without first going to see it. I felt I knew it well. So many times I'd stood, as a young girl, and gazed at the pretty chintz curtains and marvelled at the work of the thatchers. Even though I'd never passed through the door I could well imagine what it would be like inside . I trusted Graham's judgement and he assured me that I'd be very pleased with my purchase.

'I think I should like to move into my new home as soon as possible,' I told her. 'You're very kind Lucille but you will be away for a month and in that time I can do so much. After you and Graham are married I'll stay with Mrs Fairs overnight. She has already invited me to do so. The following morning I shall be up bright and early so that I can take the stage-coach to Thursledown where I shall stay at the inn for a day or so until I've got myself organised. By the time you return my little tearooms will be almost ready to open.'

Lucille seemed just a little disappointed. 'I was looking forward to seeing it all take shape,' she said, 'but I mustn't be selfish. I've taken up so much of your time just lately. It wouldn't be fair to ask you to wait for my return.' She gave me a hug. 'How will you feel, going back there after so long away?' she asked.

I thought hard before answering. 'I don't know. I'll have to tell you when you come home from your honeymoon,' I told her. It was a question I'd asked myself many times in recent weeks. Very soon, now, I would have the answer.

* * * * *

Chapter 7

I stepped down from the stage and looked about me. I felt myself trembling as I waited for my possessions to be unstrapped from the back.

The village was just as I remembered; nothing had changed. Even the people were the same, which was to be expected. There were one or two unfamiliar faces but, on the whole, I recognised most of those who passed me by. They were older, of course, but still the same people from my childhood. No one recognised me.

Across the street and a little to my right was the butcher's shop. Further along, a pretty lych-gate led to St Mary's church, the place of my christening, which lay back in its own vast acreage of trees, shrubbery and gravestones, some of which had been there for centuries. Between the two sat the cottage of my dreams, the property I now owned. I couldn't suppress my excitement. Instinctively, my hands clutched at the old, cloth travelling bag which hadn't left my side. I could feel the keys, safely tucked away in the bottom. At the very first opportunity I'd go over there to take a look. Meanwhile, I needed to wash and freshen up after my long journey.

We were outside The Laughing White Rabbit inn, known affectionately by local people as 'the Bunny Burrow'. I smiled at this recollection and glanced up at the sign swinging in the breeze – a big fat, white rabbit with its paws to its rounded belly, laughing for all it was worth.

'Can I take yer bags, Miss?' This question came from a member of the staff who had rushed from the Inn to help me with my luggage. I was led inside and taken up the stairs to a room which overlooked the main street. It was comfortable and well furnished and had small, latticed windows enhanced by a pretty pair of floral curtains. I removed my bonnet and lay down on the bed. What a welcome relief it was from the jostling and shaking of the stage-coach as it had travelled along the bumpy uneven roads.

My mind drifted back to the events of the previous day. Lucille and Graham were married in the early afternoon. Everything had been perfect. She looked truly beautiful as they made their vows in the little church of St Peter's on the outskirts of Lynhead. She had only one regret, which I knew she felt deeply. That was the fact that her father, Professor Argyle, wasn't there to give her away – so making her happiness complete. Instead, the task fell upon Richard's shoulders who, it must be said, would have made his father very proud indeed. He exuded warmth and affection for his sister and a genuine delight in welcoming Graham as his brother-in-law and a member of their family. It was one of those very rare occasions when I actually felt I liked him. I still didn't trust him though, and nothing would have induced me to stay at Cherry Tree Cottage any longer than was necessary.

My eyes focused on the ceiling and I was brought back to the present. A knock on the door brought me to my feet. I opened it to find a young girl standing outside. She was holding a tray which had on it a pot of tea and a plate of home-made biscuits. She smiled as she brought it in and placed it on a small table by the window. There was something vaguely familiar about her face but I couldn't place her. Clearly, she didn't recognise me but then she was very young and would have been no more than ten or eleven when I'd left the village. As she went out she bobbed a curtsey and closed the door softly behind her. How strange it was to be shown such deference by a member of my own class. It was something I couldn't get used to. I wanted to say: 'you don't have to curtsey to me. I'm Anna Briggs. I grew up here and lived in that old hovel on the farm just outside the village on the Nether Wilmslow road,' but I remained silent. The quality of my clothes and luggage, although not terribly expensive, belied my upbringing. I sat down by the window and poured my tea into the china cup. It was very welcome. On the street below, I watched as the people went about their daily business. What would most of them think when they came to realise who I really was? Would they accept this new, middle-class Anna Briggs into their midst? Maybe I should change my name. The thought did cross my mind. I had nothing to hide, but wanted to be accepted for the person I'd become and not be constantly reminded of my past by those who had known me in my younger days. I considered the idea for a while and even contemplated what alternative name I should take. In the end I came to the conclusion that it was a fruitless idea. Whatever name I came to be known by there would come a time, undoubtedly, when my true identity would be discovered. It wasn't something I could hide forever, especially from the older members of the village who had known me for the best part of my life.

* * * * *

My evening meal was brought to my room, at my request, as I thought it inappropriate for me to dine alone downstairs. The hot meal was very tasty and most welcome. By the time I'd finished it, I was refreshed from my journey.

With little else to do, it was very tempting to wander up the road and take a closer look at what was to be my new home. But the light was fading so I decided it would be more prudent to get up early next morning. After a good night's sleep I'd be prepared for a busy day ahead. There was a lot to be done although, thankfully, I didn't have to worry too much about furnishing the cottage. The previous owner had left all the contents to her family as well as the cottage itself. They weren't interested in keeping any of the furniture and would otherwise have had the task of removing and disposing of it. They were only too happy to sell me various items which I was in need of. Graham had assured me that it was of good quality and would certainly tide me over until I felt I wanted something new.

*****

The following morning I awoke to the soft patter of Spring rain on the latticed windows. It didn't dampen my enthusiasm. I couldn't wait to be up and about. By the time breakfast was brought to me I was dressed and almost ready to leave.

It was a little after eight o'clock when I slipped a cloak around my shoulders and took the short walk across to the cottage. One or two people were about and wished me 'good-morning' as they went on their way. I was so excited that I didn't even notice the puddle I walked through as I drew nearer to the small, wooden gate.

I looked up at the thatched roof. The ornamental peacock was still there, perched high on the gable end. Admittedly, it did look a little worse for wear, but if it was the same one that I remembered so well, it had been there many, many years. The weather vane, too, was just the same. It squeaked, softly, as it blew gently in the breeze.

The cottage itself appeared smaller than I recalled but, then, the whole world tends to appear larger through the eyes of a child. I opened the gate and walked the short distance up the path to the heavy, oak front door. My hands trembled as I found the keys and placed the appropriate one in the lock. It turned easily.

For just one moment I felt a pang of apprehension. For the first time I doubted my good sense in buying this property without first taking a look at it. But then circumstances had made it impossible for me to make the journey to see it for myself. Besides, it wasn't as if I'd never seen it before. It was the one property in the village I'd so loved as a child. In any case, Graham assured me that I was most definitely doing the right thing. Lucille, too, added her own enthusiasm to my plans. I suspect that she was especially keen to have me living within a few miles of Nether Wilmslow where she and Graham had their home.

I opened the door and peered into the hall. It was of average size with a staircase up the middle. To the left, a door led into a good sized room which, clearly, had been used as a small shop selling haberdashery items. The wooden floor had been swept but wasn't particularly clean. There were one or two boxes of cottons and ribbon lying about and a few old knitting needles that nobody had wanted. At the far end was an old wooden counter and several empty boxes were stacked in the corner. Apart from that, there was nothing else. I stood in the doorway and saw my dreams coming true.

Opposite me, in the centre of the outside wall, was a very attractive brick fireplace. I could see, in my mind's eye, the fine ornaments I'd place on the mantle and the large vase of flowers which would stand in the hearth. I'd scrub and clean and polish the wooden floor until it shone to perfection then I'd cover the centre with a pretty, floral carpet. The room was large enough to take at least a dozen tables and chairs. I could see these laid out with fine white linen, silver cutlery, delicate bone china and a small vase of fresh flowers on each. At the far end I could place a sideboard which would accommodate all the necessary accoutrements.

To my left was a sweeping bay window with leaded lights and the occasional mullioned pane of glass. I imagined it with a lace curtain that arched in the centre to allow those seated nearby to watch the world go by outside. The heavier curtains with a deep, gathered pelmet to match would be of a pretty, floral design to complement the cushions on the chairs.

It was some time before I drew myself away from the room. It was so perfect. If I'd had any misgivings as I entered the cottage, they were now dispelled. My plans for a tearooms were about to come true. It had everything I could wish for. The rest of the house didn't really matter so long as I had somewhere to live and sleep and a decent kitchen in which to work. I turned back into the hall and crossed to the door opposite. Here was the kitchen. It was a smaller room and had a big open range with two comfortable armchairs placed either side of it. There was a substantial scrubbed, wooden table in the centre with six chairs placed around it. A door at the back of the room led into a scullery where I found an old kitchen sink with no plug and brown marks in the bottom. I'd soon clean that up. A rusting, green mangle was tucked away in the corner. At least I wouldn't have to wring out my wet clothes by hand after washing them. Across the ceiling, two ropes were fixed to the walls at either end for airing clothes on a wet day. To my left there was a walk-in pantry. I took a peek inside. It was empty except for a bucket on the floor. Three shelves lined the walls either side and along the back. That would certainly be very useful.

I found my keys and opened the back door into the garden. It was larger than I imagined. The grass was long and the borders over grown, but that didn't pose a problem. I looked forward to the time when I'd be able to spend a few hours tidying it up and planting all my favourite flowers and shrubs. Towards the back there was a small shed and a few gardening tools had been left scattered around along with some pots. At the far end was a building tucked away in the corner. I presumed it was the midden. After a quick glance around I went back inside and locked the door behind me.

Upstairs there were just two main rooms and a small box room. The largest, which was immediately above what would become the tearooms, was a sitting room. Pleasantly furnished, it was bright and airy and had a warm cosy feel about it. I was well pleased with the fact that I'd purchased the furniture. Graham was right; it was in excellent condition and would certainly tide me over until I felt I wanted a change. Against one wall was a very attractive red, velvet covered chaise-longue and either side of the fireplace were two comfortable armchairs in a pretty floral pattern which also matched the material used for the curtains. The lady who had owned the cottage before me clearly loved flowers. A good quality rug covered the highly polished floorboards right to the far end of the room where there was a table and four dining chairs These, too, were polished to perfection as were the occasional tables to my left, in the bay window. To my right, and to one side of the fireplace, there was a beautiful carved sideboard. When I opened the doors I was pleasantly surprised to see that a considerable amount of china, cutlery and glasses had been left along with it.

I returned to the landing and crossed to the room opposite. This was the bedroom. It, too, had curtains made of a pretty floral material and a large wardrobe stood in the recess beside the fireplace. A matching dressing-table had been placed in front of the window. To one side, against the internal wall, there was a small, green velvet chair with highly polished wooden arms and legs. There was no bed. This, I had asked to be removed as the lady concerned had died in it and I felt more at ease with the idea of buying a new one. The flooring was of plain polished boards. I would have to buy a few rugs as well as a new bed and a number of other items that I required. Other than that, I could almost move in straight away. The small box room was completely empty, an ideal place in which to store all the linen and necessary items for my tearooms whilst they were not in use.

It had been my intention to stay at the Inn for a few days until I was able to have various items, such as the new bed, delivered. But having seen the cottage I was now eager to take up residence in my new home. What did it matter that

I didn't have a bed in which to sleep? It wouldn't be the first time I'd slept on the floor. This thought drew me back over the years to my childhood and the cramped conditions in which ten of us had lived. This cottage was a palace compared to the hovel we'd all lived in then. Naturally, my thoughts turned to my family and I wondered what had become of them. At the earliest opportunity I'd seek them out. What would they think of me now? Would they be happy to see me? My father wouldn't, I knew that. It went without saying. But Cathy, Mary, Joey, Harry, Jimmy and Benje – what sort of welcome would I receive from them? I was eager to find out. But first things first, my priority right now was to return to the Inn, collect my luggage and have it brought to the cottage. My mind was made up. I wouldn't waste another moment.

I hurried downstairs and across the street. As I did so, a carriage passed by. It bore the crest of the Tremayne family and I was, not unnaturally, curious as to whom its occupants were. I wasn't prepared, however, for the surprise I received. Sitting very demurely, looking from the window, was the little girl I'd first seen in Lynhead. Once again I was struck by her resemblance to my sister Cathy. The carriage passed by very quickly and when it was gone I suddenly became aware that I'd stopped in my tracks and was staring after it. Who was the child? Why was she travelling in a carriage which bore the Tremayne family crest? No doubt in time I'd find out, but it puzzled me greatly. An unexplainable feeling of uneasiness washed over me. All the excitement of taking possession of my new home momentarily disappeared.

*****

It took only a few days to establish exactly what was needed in order for me to open my tearooms. I made a list of everything I should need, both for my business and personal use. I'd never been so excited in all my life. It was wonderful being able to list down the items I wished to purchase, knowing all the while that I had ample money to buy them.

When the list was complete I took the stage and found my way into Castleford, a large town some seven or eight miles away. Lucille had expressed a wish to join me on this shopping trip but she was away and would be for another three weeks or more. I was anxious to purchase all my goods and I couldn't wait for her to return from her honeymoon. By the time she and Graham came back to their new home in Nether Wilmslow I'd have everything at the cottage just as I wanted it.

I returned home later that afternoon, very, very tired. With me were a number of packages, smaller items that I was able to carry. The larger items were to be delivered a day or so later. It was a wonderful feeling, opening my own front door; knowing that the cottage was mine. Every time I walked into the hall I couldn't contain a bubble of excitement inside me. I still couldn't believe it. Dear, dear Professor Argyle. It was all down to his generosity and kindness. Where would I be now if I hadn't come across him that day on my way to Lynhead? I didn't dare to imagine.

Casting my mind back to that particular time in my life reminded me, again, of my desire to trace my family. At the earliest opportunity I'd go in search of them. This opportunity came a few days before Lucille's return when, for the first time since my arrival, I found I had an hour or two to spare. Everything in my new home was just as I wanted it. My bed, along with other items of furniture and all the tables and chairs for the tearooms were delivered as requested. I spent hours re-arranging everything until I was happy with it all. Then I spent hours more polishing and cleaning until everything shone and sparkled. It was my intention to buy some brass and china ornaments for the tearooms, along with a few framed pictures to hang on the walls around the cottage. This was something I knew Lucille would enjoy helping me with so I decided to leave it until her return. I was in no hurry to open for business – I knew Lucille wanted to be a part of that exciting moment – so I decided to take a few days in which to sit back, relax and enjoy everything I'd achieved.

It was a little over three weeks since my return to the village. In that time I'd been so busy I'd had very little opportunity to talk to anyone other than to pass the time of day if I went to the grocery shop or to the butchers. No one, it seemed, recognised me. They were curious to know who I was, I was well aware of that. Even though they didn't ask me to my face I knew they talked about me when I was out of earshot. Nothing had changed in the village. Life went on just as it had in my childhood days. There were many people whom I remembered. They were older, of course, but I still recognised them. For some perverse reason I was loathe to admit that I was Anna Briggs – the girl they had once known as the daughter of the Gatsby's farmhand who lived in a hovel on the Nether Wilmslow road. I took a certain delight in allowing them to regard me with a modicum of respect, for I did own my own property and my clothes indicated that I was a woman of means. How I should love to see their faces when the truth became known; for known it would be – eventually. In the meantime, it was unlikely they'd link me with that child of so long ago.

* * * * *

It was a bright morning in early May. With little else to do I decided to take a walk to Gatsby's Farm and visit my old home. It was warm but not yet warm enough to discard my cloak so I wrapped it around me and set off.

As I ambled along the Nether Wilmslow road it was as if I was slowly drawn back into another world. Once again I became the poor, shabbily dressed child of years gone by.

I recalled the times when I had, so often, run barefoot across the moors feeling the prickle of bracken beneath my feet. I remembered happy moments from my childhood, because despite our poverty and my father's dislike of me, there had been many of these. I thought, too, of the sad times; in particular the day when Megan had been found dead; of the years during which I'd nursed my sick mother and, finally, I recalled the day when I'd packed together my few belongings and left.

I found myself walking past the Tremayne Estate. A cold chill ran through me at the sight of the boundary wall over which I'd climbed on the day I was spattered with mud from a recklessly driven carriage. Nigel Tremayne sprang to mind and once again I thanked God for Adrian's intervention. I didn't care what had happened to Nigel but I did wonder about Adrian. I would always be grateful to him for rescuing me from his brother. Was he married? Maybe he had children. This thought brought to mind, again, the child who so looked like my sister Cathy. Who was she?

I walked on slowly. I was so pre-occupied that I came upon Gatsby's Farm before I realised it. What had once been a large field of wheat was now laid to grass with cattle grazing peacefully in the lush green pasture. I skirted round them and looked into the distance, expecting to find my old home. It wasn't there.

For a moment I wondered if I was in the wrong place. But, no, I'd crossed this field so many times. I wasn't in the wrong place. Even so, my old home was no longer where it used to stand. A strange mixture of sadness and regret came over me. Instead of an old hovel of flint and wood there remained only a mass of stones and rubble, quite clearly destroyed by fire. I moved closer in order to get a better look but there was really nothing to see. Where was my father? What had happened to him? And the girl, Bess, who had borne his child? What had become of her?

I wanted to know what had happened to them; more from curiosity than anything else. I returned to the village and went straight to the vicarage. I could have enquired at the farm but I'd never liked the man Gatsby. I was also afraid that I might meet with my father; an encounter which I felt would do neither of us any good.

At the vicarage I gave my name and asked if I might see the vicar on a matter of urgency. I was shown into the drawing room. I remembered, so clearly, standing there as a small child, too fearful to go near or touch any of the fine things which to me, now, appeared so very ordinary.

I heard footsteps coming across the hall. Reverend Mead paused at the door. For a moment he stared across the room at me, then pushed his spectacles further up his long nose in order to see more clearly.

'Good gracious me! It can't be! Surely, it can't be …'

I laughed at his astonishment then moved forward and extended my hand. 'Yes, it is,' I enlightened him. 'Anna Briggs. I'm so pleased to see you, Reverend Mead.'

He took both my hands in his own and studied me for a long, long moment. 'I really am astonished, my child,' he said, at last. 'I've never seen such a marked change in any one person in the whole of my life. Sit down and tell me all that has happened to you.' He indicated a chair by the window and waited for me to be seated. When I looked up he was staring at me. There was a deep furrow on his brow.

'But, wait a minute – surely I've seen you in old Nellie Sanders' cottage next door. I've been meaning to pay you a visit but you always look so very busy I thought it better to give you time to settle in.' He shook his head, repeatedly, in amazement 'I had absolutely no idea it was you, Anna.' He crossed to the bell pull by the fire. 'You have time for tea, I hope?' he asked.

'That would be very nice, thank you,' I nodded, and smiled at him. How lovely to feel so welcome.

'Let me take your cloak, my dear.' He took it from me and handed it to the maid who came in. 'Bring us a pot of tea and a plate of biscuits, will you Agnes?' When she was gone he turned to me again and sat down in a chair nearby. 'This really is amazing. Tell me all that has happened to you.'

Briefly, I told him how my change of fortune had come about. I told him how I'd met Professor Argyle and how, through him, I'd become educated. We spoke of my life at Cherry Tree Cottage and of my friendship with Lucille. Finally I told him of the Professor's death and how he had so kindly left me a sum of money which had enabled me to buy the cottage next door. I also told him of my plans for a tearooms. He was delighted.

'Splendid! Splendid! That's just what the village can do with, Anna. I'm sure it'll be a popular success.'

'I went for a walk today,' I told him. 'I thought I'd take a look at my old home, but when I got there it had gone; nothing but a pile of burnt out rubble. I've really come to see if you know what happened. Are any of my brothers and sisters still living in the area?'

The smile left his kind face 'You mean to tell me that you don't know?' he asked. 'You have no idea what has happened to your family?'

I shook my head. 'I haven't seen or heard of them since I left. I did try, many years ago to contact Cathy but the person who kindly went to see her for me said she had left the place where she used to work. I've no idea where she went.'

Reverend Mead shook his head sadly. For a long time he thought very carefully, as if cautiously working out what he would say next. His words came as a shock.

'I'm afraid, my dear, I have some very sad news for you.' He cleared his throat. 'Your father, the girl Bess and their small child were all killed in the fire which destroyed your family home. There was nothing anyone could do to save them.'

Shocked and in silence, I contemplated their terrible end. Had they really deserved such a tragic death? I had no tears to shed for them, only deep regret at the unnecessary loss of their lives.

After a while, Reverend Mead went on to tell me that Jimmy and Benje had, long ago, left for London to seek better lives. 'Joey and Harry,' he told me, 'were both married some years back. When I last saw them they each had two children. Joey has a son and a daughter and Harry has two sons. But they and their families have all moved away. As far as I know they're no longer in the district.'

My head drooped. I was so disappointed. 'And what of Mary and Cathy?' I asked. 'Do you have any news of them?'

He placed a hand over mine. 'I'm afraid that Mary met a travelling gypsy and, in her own words, "went off to see the world".'

To Reverend Mead's surprise I burst out laughing. How very like Mary that sounded. She'd always been somewhat irresponsible and a wanderer as a child. It didn't surprise me in the least that she had married someone who would take her to see all the places she dreamed of. The smile left my face and I fell silent again. Each one of my brothers and sisters filled my thoughts. Sadly, I wondered if our paths would ever meet again.

'But what of Cathy?' I asked, hopefully. He hadn't mentioned her yet. Perhaps he knew of her whereabouts.

He placed a sympathetic hand on my shoulder. 'I'm afraid that she, too, is dead, Anna.'

A lump found its way into my throat. This time the tears did come freely to my eyes. 'Dead?' It was hard to believe. I couldn't – didn't want – to believe it.

'I'm afraid so.'

Cathy, my little sister, dead? It couldn't be. She was so young. I recalled the time when she'd begged me to take her with me. 'We can look for work together,' she'd said. Now, more than at any other time, I regretted my decision not to take her with me.

'How did she die?' Even as I asked the question, something told me that I wouldn't want to know the answer.

He rose to his feet and crossed to the window where, for some moments, he stood with his back to me. With his hands clasped behind him he twirled his thumbs nervously. Then, as if coming to a sudden decision, he spun round and studied my face for a full five seconds before answering.

'I think it would be better if you were to speak to my sister,' he told me. 'She'll be able to tell you far more than I can. If you have time to spare I could take you there now.'

He led me across the road and down a narrow lane until we came to a small group of cottages standing alone. In the garden of the second one an elderly lady was busy planting out spring flowers. I recognised her immediately. As a child she had always shown me such kindness. She stood up and glanced over the old flint wall to see who was coming. With a smile for her brother she then went on to turn her attention to me. For a moment she didn't seem to recognise who I was, then with a look of sheer amazement on her face, she hurried out to greet us.

'Why, Anna. It is Anna. Isn't it?'

I nodded with a smile.

'My dear, I hardly recognise you. Come in. Come in. What a wonderful surprise.' She laid down her fork and trowel and took off her gardening gloves. 'You've time for a cup of tea, I hope?' she asked, as she placed an arm round my shoulder. 'We've so much to catch up on.'

'That would be very nice, Mrs Gilmore,' I said, as I followed her through the low cottage door and into a small sitting room.

'Anna has returned to live in the village,' Reverend Mead enlightened his sister. 'I felt sure you'd be pleased to see her.'

'Why, yes, of course,' she said with obvious sincerity. 'Take a seat, my dear. I'll just pop the kettle on then we can have a long chat. I want to know all that has happened to you.'

Reverend Mead followed his sister into the kitchen and I heard him say that he had to get back to his sermon for the coming Sunday. He then lowered his voice and I was aware that they were talking to each other but I couldn't make out what was being said. A few minutes later he put his head round the sitting room door.

'Duty calls,' he said, with a smile. 'I must be off but I look forward to seeing you. You know where I am if you need my help.'

I thanked him and wished him goodbye, then watched as he walked slowly down the path and back along the lane. He'd barely left when Mrs Gilmore appeared carrying a large tea tray. On it, were two plates, one piled high with home-made cakes, the other with biscuits; enough to feed an army. She placed the tray on a small, highly polished occasional table, then sat herself down in an armchair close by.

'My, my!' she said, as she looked at me, almost in disbelief. 'I'd never have accepted that there could be such a dramatic change in any one person, but for the fact that I've seen you with my own eyes. Tell me all that has happened to you, my dear.'

I was anxious to hear what she knew of Cathy but she was a kind person and her interest in me was genuine. Briefly I told her what had happened over the past six years and how, through Professor Argyle's generosity, I'd come by the means to buy my cottage in the village, part of which I also planned to open as a tearooms.

'Why, that's wonderful,' she commented. 'I'm sure you'll make a great success of it all.'

'I was hoping you could give me some news of my family,' I prompted her.

Her expression was one of great sadness. 'Yes – I believe my brother has already explained to you the tragic circumstances surrounding your father's death.'

I nodded.

'And he also mentioned what has become of your brothers and sisters?'

I nodded again. There was a long silence before she went on. 'There is no easy way to tell you this,' she said, after a while. 'Your sister Cathy died in a very tragic event but ...' she chose her next words very carefully, 'perhaps I shouldn't say it but it's my belief that her death was – shall we say – arranged.'

I stared at her, allowing her words to sink slowly into my mind. I could barely speak. Tears came to my eyes. Surely, she couldn't mean ..? 'Are ... are you saying that you think Cathy may have been murdered?' I managed, at last.

She drew her chair closer to me and placed a gentle hand over my own trembling fingers. 'Of course, I can prove nothing, my dear, and it's only supposition on my part, but there are so many things which don't add up.' She settled herself back into her chair and waited for me to ask the obvious question.

'What happened, Mrs Gilmore? Please – tell me everything you know.'

She drew in a deep breath and thought long and hard. 'It was about six months after you left the village, Anna. As you are aware, Cathy was employed as a kitchen maid at Satchfield House. A new cook was taken on and, I'm afraid, she made your little sister's life a misery; so much so that she couldn't stand it any longer. With nowhere to go she left her job in the hope of finding a position elsewhere. She had no idea where you had gone or I think she would have followed you.'

My eyes once again welled up with tears. If only I'd been able to contact her sooner. When Graham had made enquiries on my behalf she could only just have left Satchfield House.

'She was out on the road, day and night, for nearly two weeks looking for work,' Mrs Gilmore continued. 'The weather at that time was atrocious. Day after day – we had – of gales and torrential rain. It wasn't fit for the animals to be out in let alone a human being. She tried everywhere to get a job but as time went by her appearance became worse and worse and her health began to suffer, too. She was so hungry she actually ate the grass off the fields and scrounged around the pig bins on a farm at night. Eventually, she became very ill and, against her better judgement, somehow made her way back to her father's house. Sadly, his new wife wouldn't have anything to do with her. She turned her away and told her never to come back. Your father wasn't there at the time. I sometimes wonder if he was ever aware that she'd gone to him in her time of need.'

'So, how did you come to learn of these events?' I asked.

She stared out of the window for a long time. Her mouth was set in a firm line as if she was, inwardly, rebuking my father and his wife. 'Cathy told me herself,' she went on. 'After her encounter with Bess she felt so sad and rejected. She lost all will to live. It occurred to her to make her way to the church and she was on her way there when she collapsed by the roadside. It was there that I found her. By some stroke of good luck it so happened that I went to visit my brother that evening. I was returning home when I saw her crumpled body lying in the ditch. Had I not done so, it's unlikely she'd have survived the night. It's a quiet little lane and few people wander along it after dark. I brought her home and nursed her back to good health.'

At this point Mrs Gilmore paused as if to be sure of recalling her memories correctly. What she told me next turned my heart to stone.

'When Cathy was well enough she decided to seek work at Foxdale. I told her she was welcome to stay with me for as long as she wished, but she was very aware that she needed to earn money to pay for her keep. I have only a small income, not enough to support two of us. When she learned that they were in need of a house-maid at the manor she went there straight away. She didn't hold much hope that she'd get the position because, until then, she'd only ever worked in the kitchens but she was so determined to find employment. "Its worth a try," she told me, as she walked out the door. "They can only turn me down." I watched her almost skip down the path. She had on a dress which had been in my cupboard for years. I cut it down to her size so that it would fit her. We altered it a bit and she looked a real cut above a kitchen maid. I can tell you, it didn't surprise me in the least when she came back and told me she'd got the job.'

'So what happened then?'

'Well, everything went along splendidly for a while. She lived with me here and went off to work at Foxdale each day. I really enjoyed her company. It was lovely to have a young person in the house even though she went to work early and came home very late some evenings. She was a good girl. I became very fond of her. She had a temper on her, I'll say that, but all in all she was a pleasure to have around.'

I smiled. Cathy had always been very volatile, but at the same time I recalled she could be very lovable. It didn't surprise me that Mrs Gilmore had become so fond of her.

The smile slipped from my face when I noticed she'd closed her eyes and there was a dark frown on her face. I waited. After a moment she continued.

'One evening I was sitting where you are sitting now.' She looked towards me then let her gaze wander over my shoulder and out through the cottage window to the lane beyond. 'Cathy was late. I was used to her coming home at different hours but on this occasion she was far later than usual. I was concerned, so I went to the gate to see if she was coming. When I reached it I saw her further down the lane. She was struggling to get home, her clothes were torn and her hair was in a dishevelled mess.'

My hand went to my mouth and I fought back the tears. A cold chill ran up my spine. Even before she told me, I knew what had happened to my little sister.

'I could see she'd been crying,' the old lady told me, 'but by the time she arrived home there were no tears, just a glazed unreal expression in her eyes. She seemed to go into a trance, poor child. It was at least two or three days before she would even talk of it but, of course, I knew straight away what had happened to her.'

I felt sick. If only I could have been there to comfort my little Cathy. During her childhood years I was the only person she'd been able to lean on and when she'd needed me most I hadn't been there. Grief and guilt crowded in on me. But there was worse to come.

Fearfully, I asked the question that was foremost in my mind; dreading the answer yet at the same time knowing that my suspicions were, probably, correct.

'Who did this dreadful thing to her, Mrs Gilmore?'

It was as if she took on the appearance of someone even older than her years as she looked at me steadily. 'It was Nigel Tremayne,' she answered.

I wanted to be physically sick. When I think of the disgust, the hatred, the repulsion he aroused in me on that day when he'd tried, unsuccessfully, to claim my own body, I wondered what sort of anguish, what torment must have been in Cathy's mind after he'd taken her against her will. Unlike me, clearly, no one had come to her rescue. Had she taken her own life because of it?

'What happened after that?' I asked, quietly.

Mrs Gilmore's voice was kind and gentle. She could see, very clearly, that I was shocked and disturbed by what she'd told me.

'Are you quite sure you wish to know, my dear?'

'Yes. Please go on. I want to know it all.'

'Well, Anna, she never returned to Foxdale but a few weeks later she found she was going to have a child – his child.'

I gasped. The little girl – the child I'd seen in Lynhead and then again in the Tremayne carriage as it passed through the village – no, surely not. But then she had reminded me so much of Cathy. Now it was all falling into place. I felt all colour drain from my face. After a moment I explained what I'd seen and how the child had looked so much like my little sister.

Mrs Gilmore nodded slowly. 'That is Annabelle, my dear, – your sister's child and your niece. Cathy gave her that name because it was similar to your own. She was always talking about you, wondering where you were and what you were doing. It's a curious thing, but when the baby was born she made me promise that if anything ever happened to her, I would make enquiries and try to find you. She said,

"Ask her to see that no harm comes to Annabelle." I told her not to be so silly; not to think of such morbid things as dying at her young age. But, looking back now, I think she must have had some kind of premonition that she wouldn't be around for Annabelle. Anyway, she was so insistent I promised to do as she asked and I kept that promise. When she died I tried very hard to find you, my dear, but it was a fruitless task. So much time had gone by and no one had any idea where you had gone.'

It was hard to fight back the tears. 'If only I'd returned to Thursledown before now. If only I had been able to. 'So, how did Cathy die?' I asked, almost dreading the answer. Before she told me what I wanted to know she went to a small cabinet and poured out two large glasses of home-made elderberry wine.

'Take this,' she said,' I think we both need it. In any case, the tea has gone cold.' She settled herself down again in her armchair and drew in a deep breath. After a large sip of wine she continued, mulling over her words carefully. 'Shortly after Cathy learned that she was to have a child, Nigel Tremayne had a fierce quarrel with his father. He went off to London and became quite a society man. He even dabbled in politics. Then one day, quite by accident, I happened to see something in the newspaper about him. The article mentioned him and a Gentleman's club where he went quite frequently. I tried to keep it from Cathy but she came across it and from then on she became obsessed with the idea that the child should have a good home and be brought up properly in a way that she, herself, could never hope to do. She went straight to Foxdale and demanded to see Sir Mortimer.' Mrs Gilmore drew in a deep breath and bit on her lip before carrying on.

'What did he say to her?'

'Oh, he was very sympathetic at first but he told her that what his son – particularly that son – did, was none of his business; and in any case, she had no proof that the child she carried was a Tremayne. She told me that he'd sneered at her and asked if she really thought the child she carried was the only one ever to have been fathered by a Tremayne. He'd laughed, amused at the idea. Then he told her to go away and not bother him again since she had no more proof that Nigel was the father of her unborn baby than any other man in the district. As it turned out, he was proved wrong. The day Annabelle made her appearance into the world she presented Cathy with undeniable proof herself. On the back of her neck, just behind her right ear, was a very distinctive birthmark; identical to the one that her father possessed in the very same place. Cathy had seen it quite clearly as he lay in the grass beside her on the day he raped her.'

'So what did she do then?'

'As soon as she was fit enough she went straight to Sir Mortimer and took Annabelle with her. What she did next was a very brave thing to do but Annabelle's future was always first and foremost in her mind. There was another young lad in the village who would have willingly married her and given Annabelle his name but, even though she cared for him, she was determined that Annabelle should have a better life. She was determined that the child's father would take responsibility for what he'd done. She confronted Sir Mortimer and told him that if Nigel didn't give the child a decent home she would bring disgrace on him and his family and ruin his political career by publicly denouncing him.'

I sat quietly; inwardly digesting all the information Mrs Gilmore had given me. It didn't surprise me at all that Cathy had confronted Sir Mortimer. She had a terrible temper but she also had a great deal of courage. If she believed in something she would fight tooth and nail to achieve her aim.

'So Annabelle was accepted into the Tremayne household?'

'Not immediately, no, my dear. Cathy's threats had the desired effect. Sir Mortimer did sit up and take notice. He didn't much care what his son did but his family name and its honour were another matter. He wrote to his son saying that there was absolutely no doubt of the child's parentage. He told him he was to marry Cathy immediately. No doubt the thought of his son marrying a poor, uneducated girl from the village didn't appeal to him. At any other time he would have been appalled by the very idea. But Nigel had long since lost any place in his father's heart and Sir Mortimer saw it as a form of punishment that he should have to marry and contend with someone less refined and well educated than himself. To add to his son's punishment he threatened to alter his will. He stipulated that very little of the estate would pass to Nigel, only to be squandered after his death, unless his wishes were carried out.

The thought of marrying Nigel Tremayne never entered Cathy's head. In fact it was the last thing she wanted. She loathed the man. All she wanted was to ensure that the child would be brought up at Foxdale but Sir Mortimer was a crafty and malicious old devil. Not only did he want to bring his son down, he also wanted to make Cathy suffer for daring to be so impudent. He was well aware that neither of them would be happy with the marriage but they both had so much to lose. His son's future political career hung in the balance and, as for Cathy, he was well aware that she wouldn't jeopardise her daughter's future by refusing to marry Nigel.'

'But why did he hate his son so much that he wanted to bring him down and tie him into a disastrous marriage?' I asked. 'I can understand people not liking the man. He's loathsome, totally unlike his brother Adrian. But, when all is said and done, Sir Mortimer was his father.'

'I have no idea, Anna. It's something Sir Mortimer Tremayne took to the grave with him.'

'He's dead then?'

'Yes, he's dead. But there came about a change of heart in him, towards Annabelle, before that happened.

Nigel responded to his father's demands by saying that, after much consideration, he would marry Cathy when he returned home. Cathy accepted the decision, reluctantly, and saw it as a way of improving her own life as well as that of her baby.

The months passed and she waited for his return but it seemed that he was determined to stay away as long as possible. During those months no one, not even the servants at the manor, knew a thing about Sir Mortimer's grandchild. He became a frequent visitor to the cottage so that he could see her; usually at night when it was less likely that anyone would notice. In time it became obvious, to me and to Cathy that he was growing very fond of Annabelle. So much so that eventually, realising that his son might not comply with his wishes, he did change his will. He stipulated that if, at the time of his death, Nigel hadn't married Cathy, Foxdale would automatically pass into Adrian's hands. At the same time, a very large sum of money was to be placed in trust for Annabelle until she became of age. She and her mother were to receive an allowance on which to live. This money, in point of fact, was a considerable proportion of what Nigel, himself, should have inherited. However, according to the terms of the Will, if he married Cathy and acknowledged his responsibilities towards the child then he would receive the allowance – which would otherwise go to them – along with a considerable annual income from the estate. If he refused to acknowledge the child and her mother legally Sir Mortimer declared that he would be totally excluded and would receive nothing of the estate whatsoever. All of it would go to Adrian with the exception of Annabelle's inheritance. There was just one proviso. If Annabelle were to die before coming of age all the monies which had been placed in trust for her would go to charity with the exception of a third which, it was stipulated, should go to her mother. Sir Mortimer, at that time, was a relatively young man and it seemed unlikely that this would have any immediate effect. He wrote to Nigel, telling him of his action, in the hope that he'd return home straight away. Sadly, Sir Mortimer died soon after in a tragic riding accident.'

Mrs Gilmore paused to pour another glass of elderberry wine. I was anxious to hear what came next but she took her time before continuing.

'Of course, Nigel had to return for his father's funeral,' she said, at last. 'It was obvious that he suspected it was all just a bluff which he regarded as a huge joke. However, when the Will was read and he discovered that his father had been deadly serious, he was absolutely furious to say the least. He was trapped and he knew it. He had no alternative but to marry Cathy. He was desperately in need of money and couldn't do without his share of the estate, albeit less than he had hoped for as the eldest son. Reluctantly, he agreed to the marriage.

It was arranged that his carriage would call for both Cathy and Annabelle and take them to a place in London. There, he would marry Cathy in secret. When they returned it was agreed that they would tell everyone they had married in London shortly after he had gone to live there, before Sir Mortimer had died. It would then appear that the child had been born in wedlock. Of course, many of the staff at Foxdale knew Cathy from when she worked there and they were also aware that she was living with me, so a story was concocted to dispel any doubts the gossips might have. You quite possibly remember that I was once a governess?'

I nodded. There had been many times in my childhood when I'd envied the children in her care. She was such a lovely person. They must have had a wonderful time. 'So, you were to become Annabelle's nanny?' I asked.

'Yes, at least, that is how it was supposed to look. Everyone was to be told that life in London hadn't suited Cathy's health and, because of the rift between Nigel and his father, she had been unable to live at Foxdale. We knew that no one would be surprised to learn that I'd been asked to look after them both because I was once nanny to Nigel and Adrian at Foxdale; hence their reason for living with me in the village. If anyone queried the fact that Nigel hadn't been seen visiting his wife and child they were to be told that he hadn't wanted his father to know he was in the vicinity of the manor and that occasional meetings had been arranged between him and Cathy several miles away. I'm sure there were many who would have accepted this story but there were also those who would have questioned its validity.' She paused for a moment or two then continued to unravel the facts. 'On the day that Nigel Tremayne's carriage called here to collect her, Cathy suddenly decided to leave Annabelle behind, despite his request that the child should accompany her. She wouldn't explain why but she was quite adamant that Annabelle was not to go with her. After she'd gone I remember feeling terribly anxious. Time passed but I couldn't settle myself to anything. I just had this most terrible feeling of gloom. As it turned out I was right to feel so uneasy. I never saw your dear sister alive again. Within hours we learnt that there had been a terrible tragedy. The coach in which she was travelling was held up by two notorious masked robbers some twenty miles from here. Both she and the coachman were shot and killed. Cathy was dead.'

Here, Mrs Gilmore stopped and took a handkerchief from her pocket. She blew her nose and wiped the tears from her eyes. It was plain for anyone to see that she had been extremely fond of my little sister and I was so thankful that she'd been there for Cathy to turn to when I had not been able to help her.

'I'm so very grateful to you for all you did for Cathy,' I told her.

She smiled, sadly. 'I only wish I could have done more, my dear. It's always been my one regret that I couldn't find you before I handed Annabelle over to her father. He didn't want her then and I'm convinced that he doesn't want her now. The only good thing about it is that she has her inheritance and is well cared for at Foxdale. She has all that she needs including a decent up-bringing. I'd have kept her myself and done my best to give her a good home but I'm not as young as I was and I thought it only right that she should go to him. Mind you, he didn't want to know at first. He paid for a proper funeral for Cathy but he never mentioned the child. In the end I took her to him and told him I was too old to cope with young babies at my age and that she was his responsibility. I said that if he didn't look after her I'd see to it that all his influential friends knew what he had done. He looked frightened then. I think it was that which made me suspect Cathy's death hadn't been just an unfortunate tragedy after all. Of course, I have no proof and it happened too long ago for anything to be done about it now, but I've always had my suspicions. It wasn't until I returned home on that occasion that I remembered how insistent he'd been that Cathy should take Annabelle with her. For a while I was gravely concerned for the child's safety because it crossed my mind that he might have had something to do with Cathy's death. I wondered if it had been his intention for them both to die on that tragic day.' But then I realised that it certainly wasn't the money he was trying to get his hands on because if Annabelle had also died that night, all her inheritance would have gone to charity and Nigel wouldn't have benefited in any way. The only explanation could have been that he wanted both Cathy and Annabelle dead because they had, effectively, deprived him of his true inheritance. He didn't want to marry Cathy and he certainly didn't want the responsibility of a child. His anger at being placed in such a predicament held no bounds and even if it meant that he inherited nothing, he wanted to be rid of them.

I looked at her in horror. Was she saying that she thought Nigel Tremayne might have been responsible, in some way, for my sister's death? I waited for her to continue.

Eventually, she said, 'He is such an arrogant man. It occurred to me that he probably thought that if they both died before he married Cathy the terms of his father's Will would be null and void; he would still inherit Foxdale and his share of the estate. But as I've said before, Sir Mortimer was a very crafty and clever old man. I've since learnt that the solicitor acting on his behalf was told to carry out the Will to the letter. Nigel had to be married to Cathy in order to receive anything. If her death was just a tragic twist of fate, then he must have been incensed by the turn of events. All he received was a nominal income. I believe that Adrian, out of the kindness of his heart, increased the sum paid to his brother from the estate each month by quite a considerable amount. The only way Nigel could obtain his rightful inheritance from Annabelle would be if she dies after she reaches the age of twenty-one and the terms of her grandfather's Will have been executed. As her father and her next of kin he would be able to claim everything she owns, providing, of course, that he can prevent her from marrying in the meantime. Since she would have to have his permission to enter into a marriage, I can't see that it would be a problem for him. So you see, my dear, I don't think we have any cause to worry where Annabelle's safety is concerned at the present time even if my suspicions about her mother's death are correct. He would have little to gain by trying to rid himself of her before she reaches twenty-one. At least, that is what I keep telling myself. But I do have a terrible uneasy feeling. I'm concerned for her and I would put nothing past him. He is a devious man and quite capable, I'm sure, of finding a way round the terms of his father's Will so that the money would eventually come to him.' She paused. 'I don't know what to think,' she said, at last. 'Annabelle has been at Foxdale, apparently quite safe ever since, so perhaps he doesn't have it in him to harm her. Maybe I am wrong to even consider that he could kill someone. Anyway, it's not for me to judge and he is giving her the life her mother wanted her to have. For that, at least, I'm thankful.'

As Mrs Gilmore came to the end of her story I sat in silence. A cold chill ran through me. Cathy murdered? Could it be? It was a terrible thing to contemplate; yet I didn't put it past that brutal man with the steely grey eyes and cruel mouth. But how was I to prove it? I knew one thing though – if there were any truth in Mrs Gilmore's suspicions, I would make him pay for my little sister's death. I wouldn't rest until I got to the bottom of it.

We changed the subject then. For some time we talked of my life with Professor Argyle and of Lucille and my plans for the tearooms in the village. It was quite late when the time finally came for me to say goodbye. As I left she took both my hands in her own.

'You will come and see me as often as you can, won't you Anna,' she said. 'And, my dear, – please, do take care.'

I promised faithfully that I would visit her again very soon and hurried back along the narrow lane, turning only once to wave goodbye as she stood at the garden gate and watched me go.

As I hurried home I thought about what she had told me. A strange, uneasy feeling came over me when I recalled her warning just before we parted. I knew that, unless it could be proved without a shadow of a doubt that my sister's death had been a sad case of being in the wrong place at the wrong time, I had good cause to be wary of Nigel Tremayne, especially if he ever learned that I was Cathy's sister. I was also deeply concerned for Annabelle.

* * * * *

CHAPTER 8

By the time Lucille and Graham returned from their honeymoon I was well established in my new home. Very briefly, Lucille was a little piqued that I hadn't waited for her return before embarking on all the purchases for my new venture. When I explained to her that I was anxious not to waste any more time than was necessary, she saw my point of view and embarked on an excited inspection of all that I'd bought. For almost a week we were hardly out of each other's company. Either we were at the cottage putting the final touches to the tearooms; or we were at her new home which she'd been eager to show me. It was a beautiful house in the centre of Nether Wilmslow village but for all its charm and spaciousness I wouldn't have exchanged it for my cottage in Thursledown.

For quite some time I was well aware that I aroused curiosity in the village. No one, it seemed, had connected me with the poor, barefooted child of years gone by. I knew that eventually my secret would be known but, for the time being, I took an unprecedented delight in keeping them all guessing. One or two of the older members of the community stared hard at me on occasions, as if they vaguely recognised me but couldn't quite place where they'd seen me before.

It was Mabel Gutheridge, the village gossip, who eventually revealed what everyone was eager to know. She was the woman who had spoken so disparagingly of me over the years and informed all newcomers at the earliest possible opportunity that I was the product of my mother having been raped by farmer Gatsby's younger brother. She was much older now. The years hadn't been kind to her; or perhaps it was that she hadn't been kind to herself, just as she hadn't been kind to others. Every malicious thought, every derogatory word, every jealous feeling of hatred and discontent was etched on her face in the form of a network of fine lines and furrows surrounding her steely eyes and thin, cruel mouth. It gave her the appearance of being far older than she actually was. Nature had paid her back for her lack of compassion and understanding for her fellow human beings.

It was my misfortune to be in the butcher's shop one morning when Mabel Gutheridge happened to be there. I took very little notice of her, having no desire to enter into any conversation with such a hateful woman who would have my business spread around the village before I had time to return home.

'Ah, good morning, Miss Briggs.' Arthur Tibbit welcomed me as I entered the shop. He was a portly man with a lovely twinkle in his eyes when he smiled. I knew, too, that he kept his own counsel and never discussed his customers one with the other. He was the height of discretion and for this reason I'd been able to talk with him, when there were no other customers around, and tell him of my plans for the cottage. He was fairly new to the village and had no idea of my previous connections.

At the name of 'Briggs', Mabel Gutheridge shuffled over to me. She had an old wicker shopping basket in one hand – the very same one I'd seen her with in years gone by – and a bent, gnarled stick, to help her walk, in the other. She peered up at me. She was all of six inches shorter than I.

'Briggs! So that's yer name, is it?' She peered at me closely through narrowed eyes. 'I knew I'd seen yer somewhere else. You're Anna Briggs ain't yer? That 'igh and mighty madam from old Gatsby's farm.'

I refused to be drawn by her derogatory tone.

'Why, Mrs Gutheridge, how very ...' I was about to say 'how very nice to see you,' but it wasn't nice to see her. She was the last person in the village I wanted to stand about chatting to. Fortunately, I didn't have to finish my sentence.

'I might 'ave guessed you'd come back looking like that,' she said, casting her gaze slowly up from my feet to the tip of my head in what can only be described as an offensive manner. If I hadn't known better I'd have thought she was spoiling for a fight. But I knew her of old and was well aware that she knew no other way of talking to people.

'Miss Briggs looks very nice indeed,' Arthur Tibbit put in. 'Any man would be proud to be seen with her.'

'And no doubt they 'ave. Lots o' them. That's probably 'ow she came by 'er money,' the old bitch sneered.

I was tempted to put her right; to tell her how my good fortune had come about because of the kind and caring generosity of a fine, upstanding old gentleman. But I thought better of it. No doubt she would twist my words and hurt me deeply by denigrating Professor Argyle and his family. I chose to ignore her completely.

'I'd like a pound of mutton, please Mr Tibbit.'

Arthur Tibbit followed my example and weighed out the meat without saying a word. I noticed that he kindly gave me several ounces more than I'd asked for but still only charged me the same as for a pound. There were other items I wanted but I had a deep desire to escape from the shop and Mabel Gutheridge. I decided to return later when she'd gone. Without a passing glance in her direction, I went out into the street and took a deep breath of clean, fresh air.

* * * * *

My tearooms opened on the following Monday. To my surprise I was almost rushed off my feet. So many old and familiar faces called in to wish me well and express their surprise at learning who I was. They all said the same thing: 'Your face was vaguely familiar but I had no idea, Anna, that it was you. You've changed beyond recognition.' It was reassuring to have their support and, although I suspected that Mabel Gutheridge had spread the word of my return, it was apparent that all of them were unimpressed by her malicious tongue. Without exception they were all delighted to know of my good fortune and pleased to see me back in the village. Many, as a matter of courtesy, expressed their condolences at the tragic death of my father. But I suspected that it was merely out of politeness, not because they held him in any great regard.

After an initial flurry of activity my life settled down to a more leisurely routine. On learning the true nature of my identity there were, of course, many people who called in for afternoon tea with the express idea of quenching their curiosity. Some didn't know me and had only heard, second-hand, of my childhood and the squalid conditions in which I'd been brought up. Others just wanted to see and find out for themselves how such a remarkable change had come about in my life.

I told them very little. Only that I'd been fortunate enough to be taken in by a family who had educated me, so giving me the means by which to better my life. It was none of their business how I had come by enough money to buy my own home and start my own business.

My cooking skills held me in good stead. I had Mrs Fairs to thank for that. She had taught me all I knew and I'd learnt well, which was borne out by all the compliments I received.

I saw less of Lucille and Graham because I was always so busy but we did spend the occasional evening together. I found myself working seven days a week. My little tearooms became a meeting place for many people from far and wide and I soon became known for my hospitality throughout the district. People from all walks of life stopped by to indulge in a light lunch or afternoon tea and to meet their friends for a cosy chat.

At first I loved the thrill of it all, the novelty of being my own boss and watching it succeed. I worked long into the night making bread and cakes, biscuits and pies for the following day. There was little time for a social life and I was too busy, and too happy, to worry myself about it.

It was Lucille who suggested it was time for me to slow down.

'You look so tired,' she said to me, one day about six months after the Cottage Tearooms opened. 'You must take a rest or you'll become ill. You work so hard. We rarely have time to see each other these days. Why don't you employ someone to help you? You can't go on like this.'

She was right, of course. Even I acknowledged that I couldn't keep up such a pace indefinitely, much as I enjoyed it. There would come a time when it would all be too much and I should have to close the doors and take a rest to preserve my health. I didn't want that to happen. If I thought about it carefully, now, and planned for the future then there was no reason why my business shouldn't continue to thrive. I'd never considered the idea of taking on staff. The thought of having people working for me was quite alien. I'd grown up in a culture of subservience, where it was my place in life to be beholden to others and do their bidding. Professor Argyle and Lucille had changed all that. Even so, the idea of paying other people to work for me left me with a curious feeling of unreality. Had I really come so far? One thing was certain; I would never treat anyone in my employ as anything but an equal. I had no delusions of grandeur and no desire to make others feel less worthy than myself.

Within the week I had advertised for, and found, two young girls to help wait at table. This left me free to remain in the kitchen where I was able to do much of the baking and cooking during the day whilst at the same time overseeing the day-to-day running of the business. During quieter moments, Jenny and Maevis, my two young helpers, took it in turns to wash up the dishes and help me in the kitchen. I insisted that at least one of them was in the tearooms at all times – even when it was empty – to welcome the customers as they came in.

I have to admit that it wasn't until I had more free time in the evenings that I became aware of the extent of my tiredness. For the first few weeks I was in bed at an early hour and didn't wake until well after dawn. On one particular morning I was still in my night-clothes when Jenny knocked at the door, all ready to start her day. But as the weeks went by I settled into a more natural routine with plenty of time to take up more leisurely pursuits.

At first there was little I wanted to do which didn't involve my business plans but I soon became aware that Lucille was increasingly anxious to draw me into her circle of newfound friends. Most of them were married couples but on occasions I found myself seated at the dining table with an unattached gentleman and I became highly suspicious of Lucille's motives. It became increasingly obvious that she was trying to find me a suitable husband.

'Lucille,' I said to her one day, 'I know you mean well, but don't imagine that I'm not well aware of your very kind intentions.'

She looked at me sheepishly. 'I can see my little plan didn't go unnoticed,' she laughed. 'But you're twenty-five Anna, wouldn't you like to be married; have someone to share life with?'

'At the moment, no,' I told her firmly. 'I'm quite happy as I am. I have my home and my tearooms which keep me busy for most of my waking hours. There isn't room in my life for romance at the moment.' I saw disappointment cross her pretty face. 'I'm very happy, truly I am. I'm also very lucky because I have the means by which to look after myself. So many women are dependent on marrying well in order to have someone to care for them and a roof over their head. Thanks to your father I don't have to marry for such reasons. For the time being I'm more than happy with my life.'

'You're so independent. The man you marry will have to be very understanding.'

'My independence is borne of the fact that I had to take care of my brothers and sisters from a very early age. I had to make decisions for them and for myself. My mother was ill and I received no support from my father. Most of the time he wasn't there.'

'Yes, I know,' she said, 'but surely there'll come a time when you will want children of your own.'

I thought long and hard. Until now the idea had never so much as entered my head. I supposed that most young women of my age were consumed with the idea of marriage and babies. But I was really too busy to think of it seriously. For the time being I was enjoying being a woman of independent means and having to answer to no one with regard to my business affairs. A man would quite possibly only complicate my life and I told Lucille this.

'You amaze me,' she said. 'When I think of the young girl who arrived at Cherry Tree Cottage with my father all those years ago it's hard to imagine you're the same person. You've come a long way Anna.'

I smiled. 'All of it is due to your dear father and to yourself, Lucille. If I had never met you both and been given the opportunities to read and write and become educated in all ways, I should not be here now.'

She came closer and gave me a hug. 'I, for one, am so pleased that it was you who found my father on the road that day. You saved his life, Anna. Nothing I do can repay you for that. He was very proud at the way you worked so hard to change your life from its poor and humble beginnings to what it is now. If he were here today he would wholeheartedly agree with what you have done with the money he left you. As for me, I've come to regard you as more of a sister over the years and I hope, so much, that you feel you can look upon yourself as part of my family.'

I was so touched. It was true; we had become very close over the course of time, but never would I have presumed to be included, openly, as a member of her family. I nodded, trying hard to swallow back the lump which suddenly came to my throat. Nothing more was said and we changed the conversation. Diplomatically, she didn't mention again the subject of me finding a husband but I knew that it wasn't far from her mind. She worried about me living alone and a husband would have allayed her fears in that respect. The answer to her concern for me came in the form of a very bedraggled, half-starved, black and white mongrel dog a few days later.

* * * * *

I was standing in the scullery, up to my elbows in hot water and soap, when I looked from the window to see a poor excuse for a dog limping along the narrow lane which took its route beside my cottage and up around the back of the church. It stopped when it came to a few bags of rubbish containing stale bread. They were just inside the small, wooden gate which was half open. Normally I threw any scraps out for the birds. I hated wasting food and, where possible, gave it to anyone or anything I thought would appreciate it. Most of the time this meant the birds or the animals in the fields, but occasionally I had some poor soul call at my door asking for any scraps that might be left over. I was only too happy to help those less fortunate than myself for hadn't I, too, been in that very same position in my childhood years. I knew what it was to be penniless and without food.

The dog looked wary, almost afraid yet, clearly, at the same time it was starving and desperate for food. I watched

111

as it tore open the paper bag with its teeth then paused to make sure there was no one in sight. It gulped down the few scraps and sniffed hungrily at the other bags in case it had missed any tiny morsel. My heart was touched. He was so thin, so frightened and so terribly in need of food and a little love and care.

I went to the larder and took out the remains of a leg of mutton I had sitting there. It was almost gone and I'd eaten several good meals from it. Quietly, I opened the door into the back garden and crept out. He was so busy scrounging that he didn't notice me there. I threw the bone across the garden. It was pointless trying to get closer in order to give it to him. He would have just run away.

He ran anyway. His little eyes turned on me in fear as he jumped up on to the low flint wall and ran a few yards along it before disappearing down the other side. I hurried back indoors and watched from the window. Just as I thought, a few moments later, when he was quite sure that the coast was clear, he returned for his much needed meal.

From then on he became a regular visitor and I made sure that there was always something waiting for him, whatever time of day or night he might choose to come. I suspected that at times the odd fox or two benefited from this arrangement but, on the whole, it was he who benefited the most. Several weeks passed and there grew up between us a certain trust. I found him watching me once or twice when I went out to leave a bone for him. He didn't run away as on the first occasion and there came a time when I found him sitting in the garden and he allowed me to move to within three feet of him. I crouched down and extended my arm to give him a juicy beef knuckle but before I could do so he jumped to his feet and dashed across the garden. At the gate he stopped. He watched me, then his eyes went to the bone and back to me again. There was no fear in his gaze any more, just a wariness borne of distrust for the human race. I spoke gently to him then took a few steps backwards towards the scullery door. From there I watched as, with one eye on me, he moved closer to the bone and took it in his jaws. I expected him to leap the wall with it and be gone as on other occasions but this time he only went as far as the gate. Still glancing in my direction every now and then, he sat down and gnawed away at it with obvious pleasure.

'Good boy,' I said to him, gently. 'You enjoy that.' Then I left him and went indoors to continue my work.

The next morning I looked from the scullery window to see if he was about. There was no sign. He had come to learn that I always put out food for him in the early morning and last thing at night. Once he was aware of this routine he never missed a day but this morning I couldn't see him anywhere. All sorts of fearful things rushed through my head as I imagined him being attacked by predators. It seemed unlikely but he was still only a little dog and would quite likely have made easy prey for a large male fox. I had no idea where he went when he wasn't waiting at my door, but he always returned as regular as clockwork. The warm, summer nights were upon us and I guessed that he slept somewhere out in the open. I had already made up my mind that if I couldn't encourage him to come into the house by winter I would make a bed for him in the shed at the bottom of my garden.

I gathered up a few scraps from the previous day. No doubt he wouldn't be long in coming. I would leave them by the gate as usual.

It was a warm morning and a soft breeze ruffled my hair as I opened the back door. I stepped outside with the bowl of scraps and took a deep breath of the clear, early morning air. Then I saw him.

He was lying down by the cottage wall, to my right. His little eyes stared at me in anticipation of his coming meal and his little pink tongue flopped lazily from his mouth as he panted in the warmth of the sun. I smiled and spoke to him softly, afraid that he might jump up and run away. But it seemed that he had at long last chosen to trust me. He stood up slowly and waited for me to put his breakfast on the paved stones in front of him, then he golloped it down greedily. Whilst he did this I went inside and found a large oval dish. I filled it with water from a pitcher and took it out to him. To my surprise he was still there. The food, however, had gone.

Not wishing to risk the loss of this newfound friendship I put the dish down and retreated into the scullery. I left the door open and went about my usual morning chores. Much as I wanted to spend more time with this little fellow, I had a business to run. There was a lot of work to be done for the day ahead and Jenny and Maevis would be arriving shortly.

*****

In all the weeks the little dog had been calling on me I had never thought to give him a name. It was quite by accident that I discovered one day that he adored my home-made muffins. It was also the first time that he ever set foot inside the cottage.

I put the newly baked muffins to cool on the kitchen table and left the room for only a few moments. When I returned I found the baking tray, and the muffins, scattered across the floor with one very guilty looking little dog peering round the back door at me with a half-eaten muffin in his mouth. Of course I couldn't be angry. It was such an amusing sight and at the foremost of my mind was the fact that he must have plucked up the courage to come in the back door, through the scullery and into the kitchen. For the first time he had dared to enter the cottage. I was delighted. It was then that his appropriate name came to me.

'Muffin!' I said to him. 'Muffin! I shall call you Muffin.' He seemed to know that he now had a name and wagged his tail in approval. From then on our relationship grew, based on trust and affection and loyalty. He soon became my closest companion and never left my side, not even at night when, much to Lucille's disapproval, he bounded up the stairs with me at the words, 'Bed time,' and slept the whole night long stretched out on the bed beside me. I soon learned that he was a little dog with a very big heart. His loyalty to me held no bounds and he watched my every move. I began to feel I had everything I could wish for: a lovely home, a thriving business, a loyal and lovable dog who was both a companion and a friend; people all around me who were kind and friendly and, of course, Lucille and Graham who were the closest and dearest of everyone I knew.

There was only one thing that marred my happiness at this time. I couldn't get out of my head the fact that my sister Cathy may well have been murdered. Of course, I had no proof but the thought niggled away in my mind until eventually I had to do something about it. For my own sanity and for Cathy's sake I felt compelled to discover the truth. Somehow I would find out exactly what had happened on that fateful day.

In the dusky light of dawn I tossed and turned. The more I thought of Cathy, the more determined I became to discover the truth. Of one thing I was absolutely certain; if Nigel Tremayne had anything to do with my little sister's death I swore that I would see him punished. I wouldn't rest until justice had been done.

*****

CHAPTER 9

A situation presented itself to me in late August which, unbeknown to me at the time, set in motion a train of events which would ultimately help me solve the mystery of Cathy's death. Until then I could see no way of setting about proving my suspicions.

It was a Saturday afternoon. I was happily settled in my new home and things were going well. On occasions I'd seen Annabelle pass through the village in the Tremayne family carriage but my sightings of her until then had been only brief. On this particular afternoon I left my baking in the kitchen to wander into the tearooms in order to talk with a few of my more regular customers. I tried not to spend all of my time in the kitchen because I knew how important it was for me to be seen and to maintain contact with all the people who helped my business to thrive. Many came from the village and the surrounding district; some were just travellers passing through. All of them received the same cheerful and friendly welcome.

I closed the kitchen door behind me, crossed the hall and entered the room opposite through the open door.

I saw them immediately and for a second hesitated before continuing into the room. Annabelle, Adrian Tremayne and a woman, unknown to me, were seated at the table by the bay window. They had already been served with tea and fresh home-made cakes and were undoubtedly enjoying each other's company. He looked straight at me but there was no glimmer of recognition in his eyes. Instead, he continued with his conversation and turned his attention to the lady with him. I found myself trembling. Thank goodness I wasn't carrying anything. Quickly, I gathered together my senses and walked up the room where I could see a group of ladies who frequently stopped by for afternoon tea and a chat. As always, they liked to pass the time of day with me and enlighten me as to the goings-on in the village. On this occasion, however, their attention was drawn to the group in the bay window. They said very little but their eyes were constantly drawn in the direction of Adrian Tremayne, Annabelle and the lady with them.

'You're honoured, Miss Briggs,' one of them whispered to me as I checked the cutlery drawer and rearranged the napkins on the dresser. 'Your reputation has clearly gone before you. Those people are the Tremaynes. Landed gentry from the big estate on the Nether Wilmslow road. Foxdale.' Her voice was so low she almost mouthed the last words. I gave her no indication that I was fully aware of who they were and where they had come from.

'Really?' was all I replied, raising my eyebrows in mock surprise.

'Well, aren't you going to speak to them?' she asked after a moment.

'All in good time, Mrs Babcock. All in good time.' I could see that several of my other customers were taking an interest in our unexpected visitors but, clearly, I wasn't as impressed by the small group in the window as they might have expected.

I passed the time of day with one or two of them and then decided to return to my work in the kitchen. As I walked by the bay window I caught Adrian Tremayne's eyes as he glanced in my direction. I smiled and inclined my head very slightly. 'Good morning. I trust everything is to your satisfaction?' If he, or anyone else present, expected a more subservient attitude from me, then they were disappointed. Landed gentry or not, I had no intention of grovelling to him as some would have done.

'Very nice indeed,' he replied, with a broad grin and no hint of any airs or graces. His companion was an entirely different matter. She looked at me as if I had just crawled out of the floorboards. Her whole attitude challenged the fact that I had dared to have the audacity to speak to them. I held her gaze as she cast a brief but disparaging look at me from head to toe.

'You must be Miss Briggs,' Adrian said, his tone warm and friendly. I had the vaguest notion that he was trying to draw my attention away from the cool, hoity toity air of the lady with him.

'Yes, indeed.'

'Then it's a pleasure to meet you.' His manners were impeccable and he rose from his chair as he spoke. 'This delightful tearooms was recommended to me by a mutual acquaintance,' he went on.

I was puzzled. Who on earth could I know who would be acquainted with a family such as the Tremaynes?

'Mr Graham Fairs,' he enlightened me. 'I believe you and his wife are close friends.'

'Why, yes.' I smiled and nodded, trying hard to contain my surprise. Certainly, Graham had gone up in the world. He had a thriving business and owned a very beautiful house in an elite area of Nether Wilmslow, but I was unaware that he and Lucille socialised with the likes of Adrian Tremayne.

'I met Mr Fairs at a Gentleman's club in London about a year ago,' Adrian continued. 'He was introduced to me by a family friend. At the time I was contemplating selling some land and cottages on the estate and Mr Fairs was instrumental in executing a very good business deal for me. It was quite a stroke of luck that I happened to meet him. The fact that he lives in Nether Wilmslow, just a few miles from the estate, made our business arrangement very much easier.'

So, that was it. Graham had come to know Adrian Tremayne through a business deal. 'Well, I'm very pleased, and very flattered, that you decided to take up his recommendation and pay us a visit, Mr Tremayne. I do hope you'll come again.' I could see that his companion was far from pleased at the attention he was giving me. I couldn't imagine that she would be returning. Everything in her manner denoted that she considered my small but cosy cottage tearooms as far beneath her. If she were to raise her very straight, rather large nose any higher into the air it would disappear beneath the brim of her hat. Annabelle was quite different. She was relaxed but well behaved and was thoroughly enjoying her iced lemonade and toasted tea-cake.

'Oh, can we come again? Please, Uncle Adrian. Please say we can come again. It's such a pretty little cottage. I just love all the things on the shelves,' she said, looking around the room at all the ornaments, china animals and miniature teapots. Oh, how she reminded me of Cathy in that moment: her expressions; the sound of her voice, albeit far more educated than my sister's had been. I had to contain the lump of emotion which came to my throat.

'We shall have to see,' was all Adrian replied. Clearly, he was only too well aware of his lady companion's disapproval.

I could see that my continued presence was creating a certain amount of tension between them. I was about to wish them 'good afternoon,' and retreat to the kitchen when a man, whom I'd never seen before, almost bowled me over as he rushed in through the doorway. He gave me only the briefest of apologies as he turned to Adrian Tremayne with a broad grin on his face.

'It is you. My dear chap. I was passing and I saw you through the window. How are you?'

Adrian, who had returned to his seat, rose to his feet again. 'Simon! How good to see you. Please, won't you join us? Sit down,' he said, indicating an empty chair.

The newcomer suddenly remembered his manners and acknowledged the other members of the group before he sat down. He appeared to know them well. Even Adrian's poker-faced companion managed a smile and appeared genuinely pleased to see him. I was completely forgotten in that moment – which was just as well. As I left the room I indicated, silently, for Jenny to attend to them.

I was glad to return to the kitchen. I was so full of mixed emotion. Adrian had been so charming. I could well understand why I'd fallen for him all those years ago. And then there was Annabelle. How lovely it was to be so close to my sister's child. Whatever would she think if she knew that I was her aunt? Whatever would any of them think? Especially the rather snooty lady who was with them. I wondered who she was. Perhaps she was Adrian's wife. The thought caused me to stop what I was doing. Surely not. If she was, then a more unsuitable match I couldn't imagine.

Finally, there was the late arrival; the man whom Adrian had referred to as Simon. What part did he play in their lives?

It never occurred to me that my curiosity had been unduly aroused until a frantic scratching at the scullery door, and a soft 'woof, woof' drew my attention to Muffin. I opened the door and left it open. It was a warm day and he was at liberty to come and go into the garden as he pleased. He wagged his tail and brushed past me into the scullery, but that's as far as he went. Whenever I was cooking or preparing food for my customers he seemed to know that the kitchen was not the place for him. He often sat in the scullery and watched me at work through the open door but he would never come any further until I gave him permission. I filled his water bowl and set about making a batch of scones and the dough for bread and rolls.

The door into the hallway, although pushed to, was not entirely shut. About twenty minutes or so later I heard

Adrian Tremayne and his party leave. They were laughing and talking amongst themselves and, once again, I wondered about his lady companion. Who was she? And what part did she play in Annabelle's life?

I was to find out a lot sooner than I imagined.

*****

It was a week or so later when I next saw Lucille. She and Graham called in to see me one Sunday morning when they knew I'd have a little spare time to sit and chat with them. Time was a precious commodity by now. All my waking hours seemed to be taken up with my business. The Cottage Tearooms was very popular and it was all I could do to maintain a freshly baked supply of all the bread and cakes and pies needed to satisfy my customers. At times I felt almost guilty where Muffin was concerned. I took him for a walk only when my busy working day allowed it, which wasn't as frequently as both he and I would have liked.

'You're looking tired,' was Lucille's first comment.

I was touched by her concern. She always treated me like the younger sister she'd never had and it gave me a warm feeling to know that there was someone who genuinely cared for my well-being. Graham did, too, of course but in a different sort of way.

'Time to take on more staff,' he added to Lucille's remark. 'You could do with some help in the kitchen.

'But I've got Jenny and Maevis who help me,' I pointed out. 'They're good workers and always so cheerful to my customers.'

'Do they do any of the cooking?'

'Well, no. I like to do all that myself.'

'That's very admirable, dear, but you won't be any use to anyone if you work yourself into the ground. Why don't you consider taking on a kitchen assistant, someone who can help you with the preparation of the food.' This suggestion came from Lucille.

I have to admit that she was right although at the time I was stubbornly determined that only I would do the cooking and baking. Maybe it was because I'd received so many very flattering comments on my cakes and pies that I was afraid someone else wouldn't make them to the same high standard. We talked over the idea for some while during which time I came up with every excuse possible as to why I didn't need any extra help. Eventually, they wore down my resolve and I, at last, saw the reasoning behind their suggestion. It made sense after all.

Before we parted company later that afternoon I promised faithfully that I'd make enquiries regarding a cook-cum-housekeeper who could clean my living accommodation upstairs as well as help me in the kitchen. The lady, whoever she was, would have to come on a daily basis. I wasn't in a position to have anyone living in. There were just not enough bedrooms. Even if there had been I should not have liked the idea. Muffin and I were happy living on our own with each other for company.

Once Lucille and Graham were convinced that I would carry out their wishes we changed the topic of conversation. We took Muffin out for a short walk along the lane that went up beside my cottage and skirted around the back of the church. It was a beautiful day and we could see for miles across the fields and countryside to the wooded hills in the distance. It was so quiet and peaceful. The merest hint of a breeze softly rustled the grass and the leaves on the trees. None of us spoke; almost as if we were afraid to break the wonderful feeling of tranquillity. One or two dragonflies floated around some short distance from the stream which skirted round the village and meandered up through the countryside towards Nether Wilmslow. A gentle sound of crickets came to our ears from the meadows where buttercups and daisies were growing in profusion; and all around us there were bees, humming away happily amongst the wild roses and bramble bushes laden with blackberries almost ripe enough to eat. I felt so content. How lucky I was.

And then, in an instant, my sense of well-being was taken from me. Her name stared back at me from the neglected headstone on the other side of the flint wall that bordered the church and the graveyard. Tears sprang unchecked to my eyes. It had never occurred to me to wonder where Cathy was buried, perhaps because I didn't want to believe that she was really dead. Yet here was the evidence. A very plain slab of dark grey stone with the inscription: 'Catherine Briggs. Died 5th January 1857'. The final part of the inscription was almost worn away making the seven of the year 1857 only just visible. Whoever had placed it there had used the cheapest of stone so that the elements, or maybe naughty children, had found no difficulty in erasing her memory. How much longer would it be, I wondered, before there was no obvious wording on the stone and she would become just a mention in the church records and a number indicating the plot where she was buried. They hadn't even remembered her by her full name which was Catherine Agnes Briggs, nor had they put her date of birth.

My legs felt heavy. I couldn't move as I stared at the headstone. Graham had gone on ahead with Muffin but Lucille stopped when she realised I was no longer with them. She came hurrying back and put an arm round my shoulder. 'What is it, dear? Are you hurt?'

With a trembling finger I pointed to Cathy's grave. I had no need to tell her who it was. She knew everything about my family and I'd told her that Cathy was dead. The only thing I hadn't mentioned to her were my fears about the suspicious circumstances surrounding my sister's death and the events which led up to it. At any other time I would have spoken with her about it, but for some reason – instinct, premonition, call it what you will – for the time being, at any rate, I preferred to keep that information to myself.

'I had no idea she was lying so close to me,' I blurted out. 'She's only yards from the cottage. It never crossed my mind to see if she was buried here.' Now guilt took over as I stumbled through a break in the wall and made my way around the other graves. When I reached the spot where she lay I dropped to my knees. It didn't matter that my dress would become dirty. I wanted to be as close to her as I could. Lucille didn't follow me. Instead, she called to Graham and I heard her tell him that I'd found my sister's grave. They said nothing as I sobbed silently into my hands.

After a while I stood up and dried my eyes. 'Do you think your father might be buried here also?' Graham asked, as I walked back to them. I saw Lucille give him a long hard stare. She knew how it had been between my father and I. No doubt she suspected that I might not be interested in where he had been laid to rest after the tragic fire that had destroyed both him and his new young family. But I was interested. Despite everything I held no grudge against him. We searched the nearby stones but there was no sign until I thought to look at my mother's grave. A different headstone had been erected and his name had been added beneath hers. I later learned from Reverend Mead that this was his dying wish, made clear to my brother Joey in his last moments after he'd been dragged from his burning home. The woman he'd lived with, Bess, and their young child had been nothing more than charred remains by the time the fire had been doused enough for anyone to get to them. What was left of them had been placed in a small grave not far from where my parents lay. How sad. What a waste of life. It seemed pointless, now, not to find it in my heart to feel sorry for that poor young woman and her small child. It was curious, though, that my father hadn't wished to be buried with them. I half wondered if my brother, Joey, had determined of his own accord that my parents should be buried together. It was something I would never know.

There was just one last grave that I was shocked to find. It was that of a small child, a little boy aged one year and four months. His name had been William, my father's name – son of Joe and Martha Briggs. Was this a little nephew I'd never known? Quite possibly so. There was so much I didn't know about my brothers and sister's lives after that sad day when I left Thursledown and travelled to Lynhead. I knew that Joey had been keen on a girl called Martha Skillet. It was more than possible they had married and that this little boy, William, had been their child.

What had started out as a happy, carefree afternoon saw me arrive home in a more sombre frame of mind. Lucille and Graham said they would stay longer to keep me company but I wanted to be on my own. There was so much on my mind, so much to think about, and I didn't want to drag them down into the depths of my unhappy thoughts.

'We're having a dinner party next Saturday evening,' Lucille told me as they left to return home. 'It's to celebrate Graham's birthday. Please say you'll come. It will do you good to get away from the cottage for a while. Your life is all work at the moment. You need a break.'

'Why not come until Sunday,' Graham put in. 'You can bring Muffin with you.'

I thought about it. It certainly was a lovely idea. 'But I should have to be back by Sunday lunch time,' I told them. 'We open for afternoon teas at half past two.'

Lucille, I could see, was disappointed. 'Couldn't you close up just for this one Sunday? I'm sure Jenny and Maevis would jump at the chance of an extra half a day off.'

She was right, of course. On this one occasion it probably wouldn't matter too much and the idea of waking up on

Sunday morning without the thought of how many muffins, tea-cakes or scones I should need to bake for the day was very appealing. 'You could place a notice in the window telling your more regular customers that the Cottage Tearooms won't be open this coming Sunday afternoon but that you'll be open for business as usual on Monday.' She said, persuasively. 'You work so hard Anna, I'm sure no one will begrudge you a few hours to yourself.'

How could I refuse? particularly as I had no real wish to refuse anyway. 'Very well, we should love to come, wouldn't we?' I said, smiling down at Muffin whose little ears were pricked up sharply with his head on one side as he tried to understand just what we were talking about. He wagged his tail as if in approval and gave a soft 'woof' which could almost have been a 'yes'. Lucille and Graham laughed.

'This dog's more human than some people I know,' Graham commented as he stroked my adored companion and rubbed him behind his ears. 'It's nice to know you have him around. It makes us feel more easy about you living on your own.' For the first time since his marriage to Lucille I detected a note of real affection in his voice. I'd begun to think that the close friendship we had once shared was gone forever. Had he been aware, I wondered, of my love for him? Had he known that I'd foolishly hoped he might ask me to marry him in the mistaken belief that he loved me too? Perhaps he had, and the embarrassment of it all had caused him to keep his distance. I hoped, with all my heart, that my feelings for him hadn't been too obvious and that I had managed to cover up the pain and confusion I'd experienced on learning of his plans to marry Lucille. I thought I had. In fact I was quite proud of the way in which I'd coped with that awful sense of grief and rejection, never allowing him or Lucille to know my true thoughts and emotions. Now he was looking at me with a warmth in his eyes that I hadn't seen in a long while. Lucille, too, regarded me in the same way and I was so pleased that the friendship between us all hadn't suffered in any way because of my own foolish stupidity.

'I'll send someone to collect you,' he said, as they waved goodbye. 'In fact, I'll call for you myself,' he added, 'I'm sure Lucille will be pleased to have me out of the way while she's putting the finishing touches to the preparations.' They both laughed. They were so happy together. I just hoped that nothing would happen in the future to mar that happiness.

As the horse trotted on and the brougham went out of sight, I had an overwhelming sense of premonition. But why should anything happen to mar their happiness? What could happen? They were a devoted couple. Even so, as I shut the cottage gate behind me, I had an unexplainable sense of unreality as if all the cosy, well-structured events in our lives were about to change and nothing would ever be the same again.

It was a warm day but I shivered as I went indoors and a cool chill ran down my spine.

* * * * *

CHAPTER 10

Early Saturday evening I was ready when Graham called to collect me. It had been a rush to close the tearooms and make sure everything was ready for Monday morning, but the two girls were very good and only too glad to stay an extra half an hour if it meant they could have an additional day off.

I was well pleased with my appearance. I'd paid much attention to my hair and to what I should wear, deciding finally on a pale lemon gown which complimented my figure and fell gracefully to my ankles in multiple flounces decorated with tiny ribbon bows of pale blue silk. It had been my greatest extravagance. I'd never owned such a beautiful gown; never before had I been able to afford it. Lucille and I had been out shopping shortly after I was in receipt of my inheritance and it was she who persuaded me that it would be a very necessary addition to my wardrobe. At the time I couldn't see that I should have an occasion to wear it but it was such a beautiful gown that it didn't take a lot of persuasion on Lucille's part for me to make the purchase. When I was told what it would cost me I almost hesitated but then I decided it was a small luxury I could well afford just for once in my life. When I saw the look on Graham's face as I opened the door to him, I was almost embarrassed by his admiration. At the same time I was secretly pleased that he obviously approved of my appearance.

'I've never seen you look more beautiful,' he commented. There was a huskiness in his voice and a depth to his eyes which should have warned me to beware. But I was unused to such flattery – unused to the ways of men – and regarded it as nothing more than a kind observation from a very dear friend. Then he did something which took me completely by surprise. He leaned forward and was about to kiss me on the lips. I withdrew quickly from him. I was shocked and amazed. How could he do such a thing? How could he abuse my friendship in such a way? He shrugged his shoulders with a smile on his face. 'Sorry,' he said, when he realised I wasn't at all impressed by his behaviour. He took it all so lightly. Obviously he didn't appreciate just how much his action had disturbed me.

'I think we'd better go,' I told him, frostily.

We left immediately. My overnight luggage was all ready and I'd been round the cottage twice to make sure that everything was locked up and safe. Muffin waited patiently at my feet half wondering, I suspected, whether or not I was going to take him with me. When I picked him up his delight was obvious and I had to put him down again lest he spoiled my gown. I took his lead and led him to the waiting brougham whilst Graham put my bags on the back.

The journey, thankfully, passed quickly. It was the first time that we'd been alone together for many months. Not since before Professor Argyle's death had we been able to talk together without others being around. But things had changed. I was beginning to see him in a different light. I acknowledged that I certainly didn't love him any more and his actions made me wonder if I hadn't had a lucky escape. Poor Lucille. I felt so sorry for her if, indeed, he had a roving eye.

I tried to forget that he'd just attempted to kiss me. I didn't want it to spoil our friendship. Perhaps it was purely a moment of madness. In all events I'd made it clear to him what I thought of his action. As we travelled to Nether Wilmslow I slowly relaxed in his company again and we actually slipped back into the easygoing friendship we'd once known. The light banter and cajoling which used to exist between us returned. It was short-lived, however. As soon as he stepped into the spacious hall of the house he shared with his wife he became quite different. It was as if any closeness between us evaporated as he called to Lucille and marched resolutely towards the drawing room.

Lucille came hurrying to greet me. She was eager to show me to my room before her other guests arrived. She kissed me briefly on both cheeks then in a flurry of excitement led me up the stairs to a beautiful room overlooking the village green. I was enchanted by it. It was spacious and decorated in soft pastel colours. A canopy of delicate white lace framed the four poster bed. A pale pink, velvet chaise longue had been placed at the foot of the bed and a matching chair stood in front of a highly polished mahogany dressing table in front of the bay window. A large mahogany wardrobe and chest of drawers completed the suite. It was all set out on a pretty floral carpet bordered by wooden floorboards which shone to perfection.

I had visited Lucille in her new home on a number of occasions but never before seen the upper part of the house. 'This is beautiful,' I said, as my eyes wandered round the room. I was holding Muffin in my arms and was almost loathe to put him down.

'I wouldn't expect him to be anywhere other than with you,' Lucille told me when I voiced my feelings. 'He's as welcome as you are in this house,' she added, stroking my beloved pet under the chin. 'Anyway, I'm sure that if his paws get wet and dirty when you take him out, you'll dry them before he comes in just as you would at home.'

I nodded in agreement. She was so easy to get on with and such a good friend. As we talked a young girl brought in a pitcher of hot water and placed it next to a matching bowl on the chest of drawers. She left two clean white towels with it and respectfully told me that if there was anything else I required she'd happily get it for me. With a smile and a dip of her knee she left the room.

'Jane is my live-in maid,' Lucille enlightened me. 'She's a little treasure and such a hard worker. I'm lucky to have her.

As you know, we have a cook also, Mrs Braid, and in time Graham tells me he'd like a man servant to attend to him and do the heavier jobs.'

I raised my eyebrows with a smile. 'My word! Graham's real estate business must be thriving.'

'Yes, it is. In fact he's talking about opening another two offices in larger towns locally and even possibly a third in the city. He has friends and contacts in London and there are several who would give him the financial backing he would need. He regularly travels up there and stays at a Gentleman's club in Kensington. In fact, one of the gentlemen he met is a guest this evening. Simon Pendleton.'

'He wouldn't happen to be an acquaintance of Adrian Tremayne of Foxdale?' I asked, thinking of the man who had hurried into the tearooms not so very long ago. 'Mr Tremayne and his daughter and another lady visited the cottage one Saturday afternoon. The gentleman I'm thinking of saw them through the window and came rushing in. I gather he and Adrian Tremayne are good friends. Which reminds me, I must thank Graham for recommending my tearooms to Mr Tremayne. He told me they'd met through a business arrangement.'

'Yes, that's correct and I believe Simon and Adrian Tremayne are well acquainted. Graham is certainly coming into contact with some very wealthy clients these days. Through his business he meets with people from all walks of life. But whether they be poor or very wealthy he treats them all with the same regard. Which is why, I think, he is so successful. He appears to be liked by everyone he meets.' Her love for Graham shone from her eyes and in that moment I was reminded of the way in which he had looked at me earlier in the evening. I hoped desperately that I'd been right in presuming that his obvious admiration of me was nothing more than the kind observation of a good friend.

'Simon Pendleton is a very nice man,' she went on as she walked to the door. 'He and Graham have known each other for some time. They became firm friends from the moment they met but he spends most of his time in London so it's not often he pays us a visit. This evening is special though, being Graham's birthday.' There was a twinkle in her eye as she turned to leave. 'I'll see you downstairs in the drawing room in a little while,' she said, as she closed the door softly behind her. I had the distinct feeling that she was up to something.

* * * * *

There were ten of us in all at the dining table that evening. I was seated next to Simon Pendleton whom I had met earlier in the drawing room when he first arrived. He recognised me immediately and I found him to be very courteous and a good listener. We had much in common – apart from our social background, that is. Whilst I had spent my childhood days running barefoot across the moors, he had been brought up in the luxury and comfort of a large manor house. I didn't tell him of my squalid beginnings, or of my subsequent good fortune. I merely said that I'd grown up in a small cottage on the other side of Thursledown village.

Inevitably, our conversation came round to the day when I first saw him. The day on which he'd rushed into my tearooms to speak with Adrian Tremayne.

'Have you known Mr Tremayne long?' I asked.

Simon cast his thoughts back. 'I suppose you could say that it is his brother Nigel and I who are friends although, of course, I've known Adrian for many years. Nigel and I first met at university. We shared the same room and have remained friends ever since. Our backgrounds are a little different, of course. My family could be considered to be reasonably well off where money is concerned, but in no way on the same scale as the Tremaynes. They are very wealthy landowners. But – he paused and smiled, 'Adrian doesn't hold it against me. Sometimes I feel that he doesn't approve of me but we get on well enough. He's certainly no snob. He's a nice chap and a true gentleman – which is more than can be said for his brother, at times.'

Silently, I agreed. 'Who was the lady with Mr Tremayne and his niece that afternoon?' I ventured to ask. It was a bold question but my curiosity was aroused and got the better of me.

'Oh, that was Lady Charlotte Grieves, Adrian and Nigel's cousin. There's a stuck-up madam if ever you came across one. Struts around like lady of the manor when in fact she has nothing. That's why she's living with them.'

'She lives at Foxdale, then?'

'Yes. Has done for a little over a year now.'

I waited for him to continue.

'She's the daughter of Adrian and Nigel's' uncle. Their mother's brother,' he went on. 'He was a gambler, so the story goes. He lost all his money at the tables and when he died his estate had to be sold to pay his debts. There wasn't a penny left. Lady Charlotte's mother ran off with her long-term lover and she was left homeless which is how she came to Foxdale. She and her mother never hit it off very well. There was no love lost between them so both went their separate ways. I don't like the woman but I have to feel sorry for her in some respects. She was to have been married the summer after her father died in the spring. When her fiancé learned of the family's misfortune he dropped her like a stone. The wedding was cancelled with such haste that it became clear he'd only wanted her for what he hoped to inherit. His family owned the land which adjoined the Grieves' estate and, when he realised there was no land and no money coming his way via Lady Charlotte, he was quick to withdraw his affections for her.

I've since heard that he married one of the daughters of the people who subsequently bought the estate.'

'Poor lady,' I mumbled, 'she must have felt terribly rejected.'

'Not only rejected but destitute. It was fortunate for her that Nigel needed a governess and someone to look after Annabelle. The previous one had only just left – in rather a hurry I might add. Lady Charlotte has much for which to be thankful. Her plight could have been much worse if her cousin hadn't offered her the job but she's full of resentment and refuses to be treated like a governess or, indeed, as a member of the staff. A number of the servants at Foxdale have left because of her high-handed treatment of them. What makes it worse is that Nigel spends a lot of his time in London. She's desperate to marry him in order to maintain her position in society but he's never there. When he is, he tends to drink a lot. If you ask me, he's going the same way as his uncle. He's often seen at the gambling tables in London. It's just as well that old Sir Mortimer had the good sense to leave the vast majority of his estate to Adrian. I think all the family wealth would have long since been frittered away in Nigel's hands.'

'But if Lady Charlotte is aware that everything went to Adrian Tremayne, why does she want to marry Nigel?' It was an obvious question and one I had to ask.

'The short answer to that is, I don't think she does know that the younger brother inherited almost everything. Besides, put simply and plainly, Adrian doesn't like her. He keeps her very much at arm's length, whereas Nigel, when he's about, flirts with her outrageously. I think he just does it to keep her happy. He's frightened that he might lose the only person he's been able to hang on to as governess and nanny to Annabelle. Every now and again he buys her gifts and hints that one day he might settle down with her. But in reality I don't think he has any intention of marrying his cousin. She, unfortunately, appears to have taken quite a shine to him though heaven only knows what she sees in him especially as it would appear that he's becoming a replica of her father. Having said that, I think if Adrian were interested in her she'd accept him as a husband. It's my opinion that she'll do anything to regain her position in society.

At this point I felt it was an appropriate moment to enquire after Annabelle's mother.

'To be honest, I don't know a lot about her,' he answered, in reply to my question. 'All I know is that she died soon after Annabelle was born. She was one of the servant girls he got entangled with. Word has it that she proved to Sir Mortimer that Annabelle was his grand-daughter and demanded that she be brought up as Nigel's rightful daughter. The old man was so incensed by his wayward son's indiscretions he vowed to teach him a lesson and told him that if he didn't marry Annabelle's mother and give the child his name he would be cut out of his will.'

'And did he marry her?'

'Apparently not. One thing seems certain, though. The child found her way into her grandfather's heart and the majority of what should have gone to Nigel was put in trust for Annabelle instead, with a clause which stated that if anything happened to her before the age of twenty-one, all her inheritance was to be placed with a charity known only to the solicitor who deals with her finances.'

I gasped inwardly. Could it be that Sir Mortimer, too, suspected that his son was evil enough to harm his own daughter? Did he dare to believe that his eldest son might just be capable of murder? In any event, Annabelle's safety was assured until she reached adulthood. For the time being, at least, Nigel would be a fool to contemplate doing her any sort of harm, knowing full well that anything she had inherited from her grandfather – money which, by rights, should have come to him – would be passed on to a charity if she died. No doubt he had already planned how he could retrieve it. In the meantime, my mind was set at rest, knowing that my sister's child was safe, albeit temporarily, from his evil, scheming ways.

I decided it was time to change the subject. I didn't want Simon to become curious about me. He had no idea that Annabelle was my niece and to show an undue interest in her and her family would give rise to suspicion.

'So how did you meet Graham?' I asked.

'Well, as you quite probably know, I'm a Solicitor,' he volunteered. I shook my head. Lucille and Graham had told me nothing of him. 'Well, anyway,' he went on, 'Graham and I met some years ago through business connections. We've since become firm friends. We have a lot in common. It was when I took him to my club in London on one occasion that I introduced him to Adrian. As it happened, Adrian was thinking about selling off some of the land on the estate. That was another bone in Nigel's throat,' he said, as an aside. 'Nigel, as the eldest son, should have become lord and master of the whole estate. As it turned out, Adrian inherited almost everything. Believe me, his brother was not pleased. Even now he gives everyone the impression that Foxdale belongs entirely to him. As I said just now, I think Lady Charlotte believes him to be the rightful heir which is probably why she's so keen to marry him. Adrian has told me that it's in his best interest not to tell her the truth. She would probably seriously set her sights at him if she knew and he really doesn't like her.'

'Then I promise not to say a word if I'm ever invited up to the manor,' I said, conspiratorially, with an amused smile. The very possibility of me ever receiving an invitation to Foxdale seemed a million miles away. His next words proved me wrong.

'Actually, you've just given me an idea.' He placed a hand on my upper arm. 'I've been invited to attend a party for Adrian's thirtieth birthday. Would you come with me? I'm sure he wouldn't mind.'

I didn't know what to say. I was both flattered by his invitation and apprehensive at the same time. 'You're very kind,' I said, at last, 'but I really don't think I would – it would – be appropriate for me to attend a function at Foxdale. I'm sure I should feel completely out of place.'

'Nonsense! It won't be so daunting as you imagine. I'm quite certain that if I can feel at ease there, you will as well.' It was clear that he wasn't going to take 'no' for an answer. It was alright for him, he'd known Adrian and his family for many years. The fact that the Tremaynes had far more land and property, and quite possibly money, than Simon's family made no difference to their friendship. But from what I could gather, Simon had grown up in one of the more elite families in the area who, by no means, could be considered anything but wealthy in their own right. If he knew of my own humble beginnings he would perhaps begin to understand my apprehension. I decided that this was not the time to give him an account of my life history.

'Please say you'll come,' he pressed further.

All manner of thoughts passed through my mind in a matter of seconds. Part of me thrilled with excitement at the idea. Another made me anxious that I would, socially, feel terribly out of my depth. In the end it was the thought of Annabelle which prompted me to accept his invitation. She was, after all, my niece and there was always the possibility that I might learn something about Cathy and the mystery surrounding her death. It was a vague hope and I had to be very careful not to arouse suspicion by asking questions, but it was the only way possible I could see of discovering the truth of how and why my sister had died. Simon was delighted when I agreed to go with him and his expression of pleasure brought all eyes around the table upon us. It was only then that I realised we'd spent most of the meal engrossed in each other, paying little attention to the other guests. I caught the smile on Lucille's face. She, at least, was not disappointed by our joint lack of attention to everyone else. In fact, I had the distinct feeling that I was right and it had been her aim all along to bring Simon and me together.

From then on I made a special effort to pay attention to everyone else around the table. Initially I felt a little embarrassed that Simon had distracted me so singularly but the moment soon passed and the rest of the evening was most enjoyable. I found all of Graham and Lucille's friends easy to get on with. With the exception of one couple, Barbara and Peter Smithson, they were all new acquaintances. Mr and Mrs Smithson were very old friends of Graham and had visited Cherry Cottage in Lynhead on one or two occasions. The other two couples, Stella and Gordon Braithwaite and Lucy and William Richardson were more recent acquaintances and lived nearby in Nether Wilmslow. It did cross my mind to wonder why Mrs Fairs hadn't been invited for the weekend, but then I remembered that she'd been unwell recently and would probably have found the journey too much.

After much eating, drinking and a great deal of laughter we all adjourned to the drawing room where, once again, I found myself next to Simon. He perched himself on the arm of the sofa, there being no vacant seat beside me. I glanced up just in time to see the frown on Graham's face. There were plenty of other chairs around so perhaps he objected to Simon sitting on the arm. I could think of no other reason for the look of disapproval on his face.

'Perhaps you would find it more comfortable to sit on one of the other chairs,' I suggested to Simon with a smile.

'Leave the poor man alone,' Lucille intercepted with a laugh. 'He can sit just wherever he wishes.'

I have to admit I was more than a little annoyed by this attitude from her. She was so anxious to ensure that Simon and I were almost within touching distance of each other that it was embarrassing to say the least. It never occurred to her that I might not want his attentions and would have been grateful to have him sit elsewhere. Simon remained where he was.

*****

I was glad when the evening came to an end. Even more glad when, after lunch the following day, I returned to my little home with Muffin by my side. Throughout our stay at Nether Wilmslow he'd been confined to my room at all times except when I took him for a walk so that he could do what was necessary. He wasn't impressed by this arrangement and stared at me with forlorn eyes every time I left the room without him. Overnight he slept with me on the bed, as he always did. I'm quite certain that Lucille and Graham would have been horror stricken – had they known.

Simon insisted on taking me home. He said that he was on his way to Foxdale and, since he had to pass near the village, it would be a pleasure to see that I returned to my cottage safely. I caught a brief frown on Graham's face which was quickly replaced by a smile and words of thanks to Simon for his kindness. Nevertheless, I had a vague, uneasy feeling that he wasn't pleased. Why should that be so? I wondered.

At my cottage door Simon gave the impression of being a perfect gentleman. He carried my bag in and then said goodbye without any assumption that he might be invited in.

'I look forward to taking you to the ball at Foxdale.' He smiled, then paused, 'You will still come?' he asked, anxiously. 'You haven't changed your mind overnight?'

'Not at all,' I assured him. 'I'm looking forward to it.' Which wasn't strictly true. I wanted to go for my own personal reasons but I was, undeniably, apprehensive.

He squeezed my hand in a warm gesture and turned to walk back down the path. I watched as he got into his brougham and with a tilt of his hat, gave me a wave and set the horse at a trot through the village in the direction of Foxdale. He appeared to be a very nice man. I felt at ease in his company. He had the manners of a gentleman and I was sure that he'd do nothing which would disturb my peace of mind.

Which was more than I could say for Graham. Several times his eyes had been on me during the weekend and there was something in them which began to make me feel uneasy. He was Lucille's husband. Why then did he regard me with such interest? Not so long ago, before his marriage to Lucille, I would have thrilled at the idea of him acknowledging my presence and taking an interest in me. But time had passed and I'd long since ceased to think of him in romantic terms. Lucille was my very dear friend and he was her husband. To be honest, there were times when I came to wonder how and why I'd fallen in love with him when I'd lived at Cherry Tree Cottage. Clearly, it wasn't love. It had been nothing more than an infatuation brought about by my naiveté and lack of experience with men. He meant nothing to me now, other than just as a friend. But something inside me warned me to be on my guard. Perhaps I should voice my concerns to Lucille. A small voice inside me said, 'no'. She was so very much in love with him. Quite possibly she would refuse to believe my suspicions and, if she did, it would hurt her terribly. Quite possibly, too, it would spoil the close friendship which she and I shared.

I closed the cottage door behind me. It was so good to be back in my own little haven of tranquillity with Muffin to share it all with. Even he seemed to have changed in mood from the moment we returned home. Excitedly, he raced up the stairs, as if he'd been away for weeks, and appeared a minute or so later with a small toy which I'd given to him as his own. I knew how he felt. I'd enjoyed my stay with Lucille and Graham and their friends were all very pleasant people, but I was grateful that it had been for no longer than just one night.

Humming softly to myself, I unpacked and hung up my beautiful gown then wandered down to the kitchen. Before long I was immersed in baking cakes and bread and biscuits for the week ahead. I was in my element. Truly I'd found my niche in life. I was undeniably happy. I thought about Lucille's idea of me hiring a cook-cum-housekeeper. Despite my promise to her I dismissed the idea once and for all. I had my own little tearooms, my cottage and my constant companion, Muffin. I had Jenny and Maevis to help me and I was content with things just as they were. None of this, I appreciated, would have come about without the kindness and generosity of Lucille's father, Professor Argyle to whom, I knew, I would be eternally grateful. I should never forget him.

* * * * *

Chapter 11

'Don't look so nervous, they won't eat you.' Simon laughed at my anxious expression as the carriage turned in through the gates of Foxdale and made its way sedately up the long, tree-lined drive to the front entrance of the house. There was no way he could know the true extent of my feelings or the real reason behind my anxiety. How could he? I'd told him nothing.

I suppose what really lay behind my fear was the rather ludicrous thought that Nigel might just recognise me from our encounter so many years before. Or that he might, possibly, see something of Cathy in me which would trigger his curiosity.

I had no need to worry on either of these counts.

Adrian, of course, knew me from his visit to my tearooms with Annabelle. Simon was his friend and a regular visitor to Foxdale so he was more than delighted to welcome me as his companion and guest for the evening. When Simon introduced me to Nigel I saw no flicker of recognition in his eyes, much to my relief. What I did catch in his expression, though, was a lustful approval of my appearance which he did little to disguise. I felt a cold chill pass through me. Even now, the memory of his smooth, groping hands on my skin left me with a sense of repulsion. It was all I could do to remain polite to him and not turn and walk away.

There were people everywhere, two hundred guests at least. Some I liked, some I didn't like. Most of them, it appeared, had travelled quite a distance, but there were those whom I recognised as more local people. All were very wealthy, or so it would seem, and keen to impress. My experience of people had taught me to look beyond the trappings of wealth and false platitudes. I suspected that quite a number of those present were deeply in debt and there purely in the hope of meeting a possible benefactor who would help them out of their financial difficulties. Many had brought their unmarried daughters with them, in the hope no doubt of obtaining an introduction to some wealthy bachelor who could be enticed into marriage.

I found myself studying those around me and listening discreetly to their conversations – that is, when I was able to. Much of the time I found my card full with requests from one man or another to have the next dance.

Simon was quite happy with this arrangement. He partnered me through a number of dances, having staked his claim at the very beginning of the evening by signing my card before anyone else had a chance to do so. I noticed that on other occasions, when he wasn't with me, he was by no means short of partners. He was a good looking man and so handsome in his evening attire. I could quite believe that he was eagerly sought after by many of the mothers of unattached daughters in the room. From what I could see he very deftly escaped their clutches on a number of occasions and found his way back to me. I was beginning to see his reason for asking me to accompany him to the ball. Far from being because he was attracted to me in any way, it was more so that he had a refuge, someone he could escape to if he found the attentions of the husband-seeking mothers too overwhelming.

Time seemed to fly past. Unexpectedly, I found I was enjoying myself and the evening was almost at an end before I remembered that I was hoping to learn something about the circumstances under which Cathy had died. Quite by chance, I was fortunate to overhear a conversation by two elderly ladies gossiping quietly in a corner.

'Of course, the child's mother was nothing more than a peasant girl, or so rumour has it.' I heard one say. My attention was immediately taken.

'Re-e-ealy?' her astonished companion replied in wide-eyed disbelief.

'Oh, yes, my dear. If the stories are true, the girl took young Annabelle to old Sir Mortimer with proof of her parentage and demanded her child's birthright. Of course, at first he would have none of it. But it appears that the baby weedled her way into the old man's heart and he then made it almost impossible for Nigel to reject her.'

'So where is the mother now? Did she just abandon her child?'

'No, no. From what I can gather, Sir Mortimer chose to punish his son for his gambling, his drinking and his wayward ways by insisting that he marry the girl or be totally disinherited from the estate. Of course it was all kept very, very quiet. But these things have a way of coming out.'

'But you still haven't said what happened to the mother.'

'Oh, that was sad, very sad. She died in the most appalling tragedy. I believe she was on her way to London to meet with her husband. He married her in secret you know, or so the story goes.' The lady's voice dropped to a whisper in a very conspiratorial manner. 'It wasn't until after the mother died that the whole story came out. Mother and baby were being looked after by a nanny in the village – the vicar's sister would you believe? – because, by all accounts, they weren't welcome here at Foxdale. Whether that was Sir Mortimer's decision or his son's I don't know. After the mother died the nanny said she couldn't look after the child any more and that she was her father's responsibility.'

'So she came to live here?'

'That's right. They had nanny after nanny and no end of governesses to look after her. I don't think it was the child's fault. More likely her father, with his roving eye, had more to do with it. Then that Lady Charlotte Grieves came here to look after the child. She can't have been here more than eighteen months. She's related to the family you know? Down on her luck, so rumour has it.' This last piece of information was said in an even lower whisper to her companion from behind her open fan. I only just caught what she said. 'She's a poor relation. Father lost all his money and estates at the gambling tables.'

The conversation, what I could hear of it, turned to gossiping about Lady Charlotte Grieves and her side of the family. Nothing more was said about Cathy until some time later when, after several minutes silence, the lady who had first imparted all the information about my sister suddenly said, 'She was unrecognisable, you know?'

'Who?'

'The child's mother. She was shot then burnt to cinders by two masked robbers. I don't think they even found enough of her in the wreckage to give her a decent burial.' I stifled a gasp at her words. I felt myself trembling. Mrs Gilmore had said Cathy had been shot, nothing more. Of course she'd been found. I'd seen her grave in the churchyard with my very own eyes. What was this lady talking about? What did she mean, 'the wreckage'? Obviously, she was just repeating hearsay and taking great delight in the horrified expression on her companion's face as she gossiped about the tragedy, no doubt adding her own embellishments and gruesome details to the story she'd heard. 'There was something strange about the whole affair,' she went on. 'Let us just say that if any of my daughters were still unmarried I'd keep them well away from Nigel Tremayne. I like his brother Adrian but there is definitely something about that other one that I don't trust.'

I knew exactly what she meant and I had to agree with her on this point. Clearly, I wasn't the only person to regard him with caution. I was desperate to know more but it would have been rude to break into their conversation. Besides, to tell them who I really was would have achieved nothing. Instead I sat quietly, hoping that more information would come my way without them realising that I was eavesdropping. Unfortunately, before many more minutes had passed Simon appeared to claim yet another dance and there was no further opportunity to hear what else they had to say. However, before the evening came to a close and the time arrived for Simon to take me home, something else very significant happened.

* * * * *

'Well, I'll be blowed! Anna?'

I froze inside. I was making my way across the hall when I heard the man's voice just behind me. I turned, wondering whom it was that had recognised me. A smartly dressed man in the livery of head footman stood staring at me, a look of pure astonishment on his face. He was about my own age and he seemed familiar but I couldn't place him.

'It is Anna, Anna Briggs, isn't it?' he ventured, boldly – boldly, because for a footman to speak to one of the guests in such a way was decidedly out of order. 'I am right, aren't I?' he persisted. 'We went to school together in the village.'

I searched my memory for my childhood companions. Of course, he was Jamie Bilbrook. How could I forget? In my younger years, before I'd been taken out of school to look after my ailing mother and the rest of the family, he'd taken great delight in pulling my hair and had teased me mercilessly. There was little point in denying all knowledge of him.

'Why, Jamie. How nice to see you again.' This wasn't strictly true. I'd never liked him at school and I was far from happy to have met him again under such circumstances.

'James. I'm called James now,' he corrected me, a broad grin on his face.

'Yes, of course. I'm sorry. For a moment I was recalling us back in the school classroom.'

'You've come up in the world.' For a brief instant his eyes moved swiftly over my gown. The same beautiful lemon gown I'd worn to Graham's weekend birthday celebration. I had considered buying another for this occasion, then thought better of it. It was an unnecessary expense. I doubted there would be very many opportunities to wear such a gown in the future. 'But then, of course, you're Miss Annabelle's aunt, aren't you?' he added, in sudden realisation.

My mouth became dry. I was unable to respond immediately. The last thing I wanted was for it to become common knowledge that I was related to Annabelle. For the time being, at any rate, it had to remain a secret. It was the only way I would discover the truth about Cathy's death. I glanced around me, hoping that no one had heard his comment. There were only a few other guests in the hall and most of them were too engrossed in their own conversations to have noted what he'd said. I forced myself to smile warmly at him. Lowering my voice a little, I said quietly, 'No one here knows of that, James.' He was silenced for a moment and stared into my face, a question in his own eyes. 'For the time being, I wish it to remain that way,' I continued. 'Were you employed here when my sister Cathy worked here?'

'Yes, I was.'

'Then you know the whole story?'

He hesitated, then surprised me with his next remark. 'Does anyone?' he asked. There was a gentle kindness in his voice and an unspoken sympathy in his eyes. This was not the Jamie I'd known at school. I warmed to him and inexplicably, felt I could trust him.

At that moment I caught sight of Simon coming down the stairs. 'Please James, don't say a word of this to anyone. Perhaps we could talk. I own the tearooms in the village.'

Before I had time to say more or receive any reassurance from him Simon was by my side. James took on the respectful air of his position in the household.

'I was just coming in search of you, sir,' he addressed Simon. 'I believe the young lady was looking for you.'

'Thank you, James.' Simon smiled warmly at him. He obviously knew him well from the many visits he'd made to Foxdale Manor. 'Are you ready to go?' he asked, turning to me. I nodded with a smile. 'Then we'll take our leave of our hosts and I'll see you home. Would you have my carriage brought round please, James?' James disappeared and there was no further opportunity to speak with him. I only hoped that he would contact me at some later date. Until then I could only hope and pray that he would keep our conversation to himself and not be tempted to talk to anyone about it.

Deep inside, I was confident that this would be so.

* * * * *

CHAPTER 12

To my surprise, Simon called on me the following morning. It was fairly early in the day and I wasn't expecting him. In fact I'd made no arrangement to see him again after he'd escorted me home the previous evening.

'Nigel and Adrian send their apologies,' he said, almost before he'd set foot in the door. I was puzzled.

'Whatever for?'

'Apparently, they feel that they didn't pay you enough attention last evening.'

'But there were a great many people there. I certainly didn't expect to be singled out for any exceptional attention from our hosts.' In truth, undue attention from Nigel Tremayne was the last thing that I'd wanted but I couldn't tell Simon that.

'All the same, as my guest they felt they should have danced and spoken to you a little more.'

'Tell them not to worry,' I responded.

'You can tell them yourself, if you'd like to? You're invited to the Manor for tea this afternoon. I do hope you'll come.' At this point he took hold of my hand. 'I shall only be there a few more days and then I must return to London. If you're agreeable I should like to spend as much time with you as I possibly can before I go back.' There was a sparkle in his eyes which made him very attractive. I liked him but there was no question of any romantic involvement with him. Pleasant though he was, I had no desire to regard him as anything other than a friend. Clearly, he had other ideas.

'You're so very pretty, Anna,' he told me. As he did so he moved closer but I had no wish to encourage him. I turned away.

'You're a kind man, Simon, but ...' As I shifted away he took hold of my arm.

'Anna, please. At least, give me some hope. Don't disregard my attention without giving it any consideration. After all, you're not getting any younger. Many women of your age without a husband would regard themselves as on the shelf.'

How dare he! Anger flared in me. After all, I was only twenty-five. In my eyes, at least, I was by no means past a respectable marrying age. Even if I was, I most certainly wouldn't be tempted to welcome the advances of just anyone purely in order to get a wedding ring on my finger. Without a doubt I would have to love my future husband. I most certainly wasn't desperate enough to marry the first person who came along.

He saw the anger on my face and realised he'd overstepped the mark. 'I – I'm sorry. That was a very tasteless thing to say.'

'Yes, indeed. And not one that endears you to me.'

Again, he put out both hands and held me by the shoulders. I tried to shrug him off but he held fast. He really was far too tactile and I didn't like it. 'I am so sorry,' he began, 'I hope you'll ...' Before he could finish there was a low rumble from behind me as Muffin came to the kitchen door and realised that I was far from pleased with my visitor. The low rumble in his throat became louder and louder until eventually he barked menacingly at Simon and forgot all the training I'd given him never to enter the kitchen unless I said he could. In his desire to protect me he shot forward and took hold of Simon's breeches between his teeth. Simon was so taken aback he let go of me. Then he did something quite unforgivable.

With language, which no lady should be subjected to, he kicked out and sent Muffin sprawling across the floor, yelping and whining. I was incensed. I rushed over to my dear little pet and took him in my arms. If anger had been in my eyes at Simon's earlier insensitive remark it was nothing compared with the expression in them now. I turned a look of full hatred on the man whom, until this point, I thought I liked. Clearly, because I hadn't fallen into his arms in the way he'd expected, he had abandoned all his social graces and here was the true man beneath the refined and flattering exterior, angry because he couldn't get his own way. How ever could I have imagined that I liked him?

'I think you'd better go,' I muttered, carefully controlling my own anger. He was about to say something more but thought better of it. He turned on his heels and left. As he went through the door I had the deepest urge to pick up the nearest object to hand and throw it at his back. I never wanted to see the man again. How in heaven's name Lucille and Graham had considered him to be an appropriate suitor for me I shall never know, for clearly, it was they who had set about bringing us together.

I sat down and cuddled Muffin in my arms. He licked my face and seemed none the worse for his experience. I was touched by his loyalty to me. This little dog whom I'd taken in had, clearly, made it his mission in life to protect me from harm. What better companion could I have? It was only then that I stopped to think of my future and realised how much my business had engulfed my life. I'd been so busy that I'd given little or no thought to any romantic notions or the possibility of one day finding a husband. I was happy with Muffin, my little cottage and my tearooms which kept me busy from morning till night. There was no room in my life for a man, much less someone like Simon Pendleton.

I made myself a cup of tea and slowly regained my composure. At first I felt angry and unsettled but as time went by the needs of the tearooms overtook my thoughts and I began baking bread and preparing cakes and scones for the following day. The mere act of beating and kneading the dough for the bread helped to dissipate my anger. A few hours later I'd put the incident behind me, hoping emphatically that I would never see Simon Pendleton again.

* * * * *

CHAPTER 13

James Bilbrook did come to see me – eventually. I was beginning to think that he wouldn't when, one busy afternoon, he walked through the open door. He was casually but smartly dressed and looked quite different out of his working uniform. He was taller than I remembered from our brief meeting and when he smiled at me his velvet brown eyes lit up with a sparkle which I'd never been aware of in his childhood years.

'I'm sorry I couldn't come before,' he apologised. 'I've been looking forward to seeing you again.'

I looked around the crowded tearoom. 'Well, as you can see, I'm very busy at the moment. Perhaps you'd like to come through and talk with me while I'm working in the kitchen.'

This idea seemed to appeal to him and he followed me willingly across the hall. Muffin took an instant liking to him. He wasn't allowed into the kitchen whilst I was working but it didn't stop him standing at the back door wagging his tail in a frenzy of excitement at the sight of our new visitor. James crossed over to him and, stepping outside into the garden, scooped him into his arms and treated him like a long lost friend. Clearly he loved animals and Muffin was well aware of this. His little pink tongue moved almost as fast as his tail as he greeted his new-found friend with a barrage of wet sloppy kisses. He licked his face from ear to ear. James was the only person I can ever remember Muffin reacting to in such a way

When all the greetings were over and Muffin had quietened down somewhat, James sat himself in an armchair in the corner of the kitchen as if it was home from home. Muffin crept in and flopped adoringly at his feet. I didn't have the heart to tell my little pet dog that he shouldn't be there and to banish him to the garden. He looked so content and so pleased to be in the company of our visitor.

'I can see he's taken to you,' I told James. 'He obviously likes you.'

'And I like him,' James responded. He tickled Muffin under his chin which prompted him to roll over onto his back and wag his tail furiously with pleasure, his lips drawn back to reveal what can only be described as a big toothy grin. I laughed. It was wonderful to see the rapport between them.

'You realise you're responsible for making him break all the rules,' I said. 'The kitchen is out of bounds to him whilst the tearooms are open.'

James looked up into my face with a wonderful sparkle in his eyes. 'Then perhaps I'd better take him into the garden.'

'No, he can stay. Just so long as none of the customers see him. Some of them wouldn't be too happy to know he was around me whilst I'm preparing the food.' I walked over to the door leading into the hall and made sure it was firmly closed, then turned with a smile on my face and a mock note of sternness in my voice as I wagged a finger at Muffin. 'Just this once,' I told him. 'You're not allowed to make a habit of it.' Muffin responded with a delighted whimper and licked James' hand.

I hope you won't mind if we talk while I work,' I said to James as I took a batch of hot scones from the oven.

'Not at all,' he leaned back in a relaxed easy fashion, almost as if he was quite accustomed to sitting with me in my kitchen whilst I did my baking. I felt perfectly at ease with him, as if I'd known him all my life which of course, in some ways, I had. But he was far removed from the little boy I recalled having been at school with.

I poured him a cup of tea and placed two of the hot scones onto a plate with jam and cream for him then set about preparing the dough for the following day's batch of loaves.

'What can you tell me of Cathy,' I asked, on a more serious note.

He stared into his cup and thought for a moment, a deep frown on his face.

'To be honest, not a great deal.' This response disappointed me somewhat. I had hoped he would be able to throw a little light on the circumstances surrounding my sister's death. But then his next words took me by surprise and led me to believe that he might just be able to help me after all. 'I didn't work at the manor when Cathy was there but, of course, I heard all the rumours that went about – and there was one lady in particular who seemed to know more than anyone else.'

'Who was she?'

He looked thoughtfully into his cup before answering, as if wondering whether or not he should divulge such information. After a moment he looked me straight in the eyes. 'My mother,' he answered. 'It was my mother. For a long time she worked at Foxdale as assistant housekeeper. After my father died we had very little money and she had to find work. The job became available so she applied and was accepted for the position and we both moved into a cottage on the estate. When I was old enough I was given work there and when her health prevented her from working any more we were allowed to remain in the cottage, which is where we live today.'

I thought back over the years. 'I remember your father. He was a clerk in the solicitors' office in Nether Wilmslow wasn't he? I remember your mother, too. She always looked so neat and well dressed.'

'Yes, she still is, although my pay is not a lot to live on. And, yes, my father did work for Bennet, Pendleton and Ludgrove the solicitors in Nether Wilmslow.'

The name immediately struck a chord. 'Did you say "Pendleton"?'

'Yes, why?'

'Is that any relation to Simon Pendleton who was with me when I saw you at Foxdale?'

'Yes, I believe so. It's his uncle, I think. I can't be certain but I believe that's how the Tremaynes and he became acquainted in the first place. Bennet, Pendleton and Ludgrove were Sir Mortimer's family solicitors. Pendleton managed to pull a few strings and succeeded in getting his nephew, Simon, into the same university as Nigel. His uncle is an astute businessman and has a finger in many pies, so to speak. He and his brother, Simon's father, are involved in a great many business ventures, which is how the family came to be quite wealthy. Between you and me, if my father's words are anything to go by – and I don't doubt that he was telling the truth – not all the Pendleton fortune was made by an honest day's work.'

I remained silent. Now, why didn't that surprise me?

After a moment or two I asked, 'Would your mother talk with me; tell me what she knows of Cathy?'

Once again he thought carefully before giving me his reply. 'I don't know. I really don't know. You see, she's scared that if it became known that she had voiced what she believes to be the truth surrounding Cathy I will lose my job and we will both lose our home. She's too old and too ill to be out on the streets or to go to the workhouse and who would employ me and give me a home without a reference and with a sick mother to care for?'

'Please, won't you speak with her?' I pleaded. 'I have to know what happened to Cathy. It doesn't add up. There's something very wrong and I shan't rest until I know the truth.'

'I'll see what she says,' he said, at last, 'but I can't guarantee anything. If she makes up her mind to say absolutely nothing, then there will be no shifting her however persuasive you might be.'

It was as much as I could hope for. I could see that there was very little point in trying to press him further so we changed the subject. I found myself really enjoying his company and it was well into the evening – long after the tearooms had closed – when he finally said goodbye and returned home. I was left with a warm feeling inside as I watched him walk down the road and long after I went to bed he was in my thoughts, not least of all because I hoped desperately that he would persuade his mother to talk with me.

* * * * *

CHAPTER 14

'Come in, my dear. Come in. Let me look at you.' It was two whole weeks before James eventually persuaded his mother that she should talk to me about Cathy. And now, here I was in the small cottage on the edge of the estate not far from the very place where I'd scaled the old flint wall as a young girl in order to wash my mud-splattered hair and clothes in the lake.

'My, you've grown into such a beautiful young woman.' Mrs Bilbrook smiled at me with genuine admiration on her face. 'I remember you as a young, barefooted child,' she mused. 'I remember your mother, too, God rest her soul, and all your brothers and sisters. Life was hard for you then, my dear, wasn't it? But you certainly seem to have done well for yourself now. James tells me you own the little tearooms in the village. How proud your mother would be of you.'

I smiled and knelt down beside her to take her hand. I remembered her well. She had always been so kind to me and other members of my family. There were times when I can remember she gave my mother items of clothing that she no longer needed and occasionally she baked a cake and sent it home for us all. It's funny how little acts of kindness so easily slip your mind but seeing her again, now, brought it all back to me.

She was older, a lot older, and clearly racked with pain and severely disabled from destructive arthritis, but she still managed to smile and have a kind word to say.

'Mrs Bilbrook, I can't tell you how much this visit means to me. Thank you so much for agreeing to see me. Please rest assured that whatever you tell me, I will do nothing to jeopardise your home here or James' position at Foxdale. But it is so important to me to find out exactly what happened to Cathy. I'm quite sure that the information I have is not the whole truth and I'm determined to find out the true circumstances surrounding her death. I have to, for Annabelle's sake as well as for my own, because I believe that, if I don't, one day her life will be in danger. Don't ask me why I believe that. I don't know. It's just some instinct which tells me so.'

'And I think your instincts could be right, my dear.' Mrs Bilbrook took hold of my hand as best she could and looked anxiously into my face. 'I've kept quiet for so long, believing that no one would take notice of me and that James and I would lose everything we have. But the time has come to face up to the truth, for Annabelle's sake, as you say. If anything happened to her – like it did to her mother – I should never forgive myself and I know James agrees with me. For too long I've pushed it to the back of my mind. But you've made me think again and you're right, my dear, Annabelle's life could well be in danger if we do nothing.' She shifted uneasily and thought carefully on what she was about to say. 'First I must tell you what I know.'

* * * * *

I sat in silence for some moments after Mrs Bilbrook had finished her story. In my mind I went over, again, all that she'd said.

If her memory was correct, on the afternoon prior to the night on which Cathy had died Mrs Bilbrook had overheard a conversation between Nigel Tremayne and a man she had never seen before. Quite by chance she came across the pair talking together on the road from the village. They hadn't been aware of her presence because she had taken a short cut across the fields from her sister's house and couldn't be seen from where they stood. As she approached she heard the low murmur of their voices and then heard clearly what they were saying. Only then did she realise that it was Nigel and instinctively she felt that it would not be in her best interests if he were to see her. She crouched behind the hedge and heard every word of their conversation.

In short, the man was asked to pick up a woman and her child from Mrs Gilmore's home in the village. He was to take them to London but was to make a detour some twenty miles along the route. There, he would be met by two masked men who would take the woman and the child but would leave him unharmed. If he kept his mouth shut he would be paid well. At this point Nigel had handed him a large bundle, presumably of gold coins. He promised there would be a great deal more if the job was done well.

'And you have no idea at all who that stranger was?' I asked her.

'None at all, my dear. He certainly wasn't from around these parts. I've lived here all my life and I'd never seen him before. One thing I am quite sure of, though, is that he died that night alongside your sister. When the carriage was found, off the beaten track, it was burned out and the horses were missing. There were two bodies inside, both unrecognisable. They could only have been that man and your sister. It was said that the coach was held up by a pair of dangerous masked robbers. When they discovered nothing of any real value they,' she paused, 'they shot the two occupants, in anger, and then set light to the whole thing. This explanation would have seemed quite plausible to most people at the time – there were some very dangerous highwaymen in that area – but having overheard that fateful conversation, I'm inclined to believe that Nigel Tremayne had organised it from the very start. It was never his intention that the driver should escape with his life. I'm quite certain that it was his intention that the man should die along with your sister Cathy on that night. Thank God that Annabelle wasn't with them. If she had been she, too, would have died.'

'But didn't you tell anyone what you'd overheard or what you suspected?'

'I didn't dare, my dear. I know' – she put up a hand to stem any protest from me, ' you must think I'm a dreadful old woman for allowing such an injustice and for not speaking out. But it's my opinion that Nigel Tremayne is a very dangerous man. He's quite the opposite to his brother, Adrian. In any case, who would have believed my story? There were no other witnesses to the conversation he had with the stranger on the road that afternoon. It would have been my word against his. He would have denied everything and would, I'm sure, have had a good alibi for his whereabouts at that time. In time he would, without a doubt, have made me – and James – pay for making such an accusation against him. His retribution would have been subtle, he's a wicked man, but, believe me, in one way or another he would have got rid of us. If he hadn't arranged for us, too, in time to meet with some terrible accident then the best we could have hoped for would have been to end up in the workhouse in poverty and without references. My health was already deteriorating at that time and I couldn't – wouldn't – put James through such distress. In any case, what would it have achieved except fear, misery, poverty and possibly even death for us both. Believe me, I thought about it very carefully and when I learned that Annabelle was to come and live at Foxdale I made up my mind that I could be of far more use watching over her to make sure that she came to no harm. Of course, it isn't so easy now that I don't work at the house, but James is there and keeps his eyes and ears open all the time. I fear for that child, Anna, I really do. But I still keep in touch with her and see her occasionally. She comes to visit me sometimes.'

'You mean she comes here, to the cottage, to see you?'

'Yes, she does. She's a dear little girl, although there have been times when I've seen her throw quite a tantrum.' I laughed at this. How like Cathy that sounded, as she was as a small child. Mrs Bilbrook went on, 'I like to think that she came to see me almost as a surrogate mother. She had no one else to turn to. I would sit and play and talk with her for hours in my spare time and we became quite close. I'm very fond of her which is more than can be said for Lady Charlotte. She's supposed to look after her and she tutors her but it's all under sufferance. Her only reason for being at Foxdale is because she's fallen on hard times and has no other means of acquiring an income. Not that she would want to work for a living in any case. That would be far too far beneath her. Because she is a cousin to Nigel and Adrian she has privileges which a normal governess wouldn't expect and so her lifestyle isn't too far removed from that which she's been used to. She's also in love with Nigel. At least, that's the way I see it. If I'm right I can't, for the life of me, understand why. He doesn't treat her very kindly. I sometimes wonder if it isn't just his money she's after. If Adrian were the eldest son, and not Nigel, she'd probably be making a play for him instead.'

'How often does Annabelle come to see you?' I asked.

'Not very often, my dear, perhaps once every two or three weeks. Lady Charlotte sees it as an opportunity to go off on her own for a few hours, so it's very much when she wants to arrange it. It's an arrangement that suits us all but I'm not so sure that Nigel knows anything about it. Somehow I doubt that. There again, he spends most of his time up in London. He seems to have no desire at all to spend any time with his daughter.'

'I wonder if I might ask a very great favour of you, Mrs Bilbrook,' I said to her.

'Of course, my dear. What might that be? Although I have a suspicion I know what it is.'

'One day, when you know that Annabelle is coming to visit you, may I be here also. She doesn't know who I am although I have seen her out and about once or twice, but I would so love to speak with her and get to know her.'

'Of course you would. I can't promise anything but when I know she's coming I'll try and get a message to you.'

'I'll be the messenger,' James laughed. 'In fact, I'll come and collect you.'

'You're very kind, both of you,' I told them. James and his mother were two lovely people. I felt so comfortable and at home in their company. 'Believe me, I won't say a word of what you've told me,' I said, turning to Mrs Bilbrook.

'I know that, dear. Do you think I would have told you if I'd thought you would betray us? In any case, it's to all our benefits to remain silent at the moment – for Annabelle's sake.'

James took me home later. I'd enjoyed my afternoon immensely. Half of me felt really happy and content to have been in the company of both him and his mother. The other half felt deeply sad at what I'd learned from Mrs Bilbrook regarding the circumstances surrounding Cathy's death. It was a curious mix of feelings. My mind wanted to be free to dwell on my newfound happiness and a sensation, almost of excitement, when I recalled the occasional look of intense interest on James' face as he'd looked at me when he thought I wasn't aware of him. And yet there was a part of me which wanted to break down and cry for my little sister; to sob my heart out because I hadn't been with her when she had needed me most.

As the horse and cart took us along the narrow, winding country lane towards the village I was aware of a deep sense of contentment sitting up in front with James. We talked all the way. Not about anything specific, just everything and anything. I was amazed at how well we seemed to get on and how much we had in common. In our school days we hadn't taken a great deal of notice of each other. But then, at that age the boys kept together and the girls, too, stayed in their own little groups.

When we arrived back at my cottage he jumped down and saw me right to the door. Muffin greeted me with joyous abandon as I went inside. I hadn't taken him with me, preferring to leave him at home for the afternoon. I gathered him into my arms and turned to find James already halfway back down the path. He was looking back over his shoulder and smiling as he said, 'I'll be in touch. It was lovely being with you this afternoon.'

Unlike Simon Pendleton, he made no attempt to come inside or force his presence on me. I felt totally at ease and unthreatened in his company and it made me like him all the more.

As he set the horse at a trot and waved goodbye I watched him until he was almost out of sight. I knew that in him I had made a very dear friend as was also true of his mother. As I laid my head on the pillow that night I felt truly content, more so than at any other time in my life.

* * * * *

CHAPTER 15

In the days which followed I made sure that I had a good supply of bread and cakes and all that was necessary for the tearooms should I have to go out unexpectedly. I knew I could leave my customers in the capable hands of Jenny and Maevis should James suddenly appear to tell me that his mother was expecting a visit from Annabelle. As it turned out, less than a week later he visited me, briefly, one afternoon to say that Lady Charlotte had asked Mrs Bilbrook if Annabelle could spend the following day with her, so I had plenty of time to make arrangements with the two girls.

'There's only one problem,' James told me as he sat in the kitchen with Muffin at his feet and a plate of sandwiches on his lap. Muffin had taken to attaching himself to James from the moment he stepped through the door, despite all efforts on my part to maintain the rules I'd set which didn't permit him to enter the kitchen whilst the tearooms were open. As on other occasions I found myself ignoring this small oversight. Muffin was so happy with his new-found friend and I loved to see them together.

'What problem is that?' I asked, and for a moment thought he was about to say that tomorrow wouldn't be a convenient day for me to visit.

'I'm afraid I have to work,' he said, disappointment clearly written across his face. It isn't my day off until next Thursday. I'm only here now because it's quiet up at the house and I've slipped out unofficially for an hour or so. Adrian and Lady Charlotte have taken Annabelle out for the day and won't be back until later. Everybody else thinks I've just nipped off home to see me Ma for a short while. Tomorrow is a very busy day. I can't see that I can slip out, unnoticed, even for just half an hour. So you see it does mean that I won't be able to call for you. You would have to make your own way to my mother's cottage.'

'That doesn't matter.' I told him. 'Don't worry, I shall be perfectly alright finding my own way. I shall enjoy the walk. Remember, I had no one to look after me when I was a small child and roamed these hills and country lanes alone.'

'Yes, but things are a little different now,' he said with a smile. 'You're a grown woman and a very attractive one at that. I shouldn't like any harm to come to you.' I blushed at his compliment and at the caring way he seemed to feel responsible for me. 'Will you promise me that you'll stay with my mother until I get home from work,' he went on, 'then I can bring you back here safely. It will be quite late I'm afraid.'

I was happy to make that promise. I have to admit to a twinge of disappointment when I first thought I wouldn't see him. When I told him that I would wait, he beamed and his eyes lit up. He couldn't be called handsome but his kind, gentle and honest nature shone through and gave an attractive, very appealing appearance to his features. He was handsome in a way which had nothing to do with the contours of his face or the colour of his eyes. His good looks came from within, from the beauty of his character and his kind nature.

He left soon after, but the memory of his face remained with me. Long into the night, when I had retired to bed, I lay thinking about him before eventually, I drifted into a more peaceful and contented sleep than I can remember having experienced for many years.

* * * * *

'My dear Anna, we haven't seen you for so long.' Lucille and Graham drifted in the following morning and walked straight into the kitchen where I was giving last minute instructions to Jenny and Maevis before leaving the tearooms in their capable hands for the afternoon. I felt perfectly at ease leaving them in charge. They worked well together and, I know, had my best interests at heart. I had no doubt that, after a job well done, they would clean and tidy up, then lock the cottage door behind them as they left. Jenny, under my tuition, was becoming a first class cook, so in the unlikely event of them running short of any cakes or scones I knew she was quite capable of preparing something at a moment's notice. It was a real blessing to me to have found two such willing and reliable helpers.

'Well, I'm a very busy woman,' I said to Lucille with a smile as she kissed me on one cheek. Tactfully, Jenny and Maevis left the room to get on with their chores. Graham came towards me and took hold of my lower arm before he looked me straight in the eyes and gave me a kiss on the cheek; a kiss which lingered just a little too long for my liking. Thankfully Lucille had turned to look into the garden for Muffin so she didn't notice. How, I wondered, could I ever have been attracted to this man? He was so, so different from James. I recalled my feelings for him when Lucille and I had lived at Cherry Tree Cottage in Lynhead, and my heartache when I discovered that it was she he loved and not me. How thankful I felt, now, that he hadn't returned my affections. Poor Lucille. She was so in love with him and clearly blind to his meandering eyes. I had hoped that, on the evening of his birthday weekend, when he'd called to collect me and looked at me with such blatant attraction and approval, that I'd misinterpreted his expression; or at very least that it was a brief moment of flirtation which he'd regretted. But I saw now that it wasn't. There was no mistaking the look in his eyes and I didn't like it. I shifted away from him, hopefully making it clear from the straight expression on my face that I wasn't interested in his attentions. He was quite unperturbed by my reaction. With a broad grin he went over to his wife and put an arm around her shoulder, giving the impression that he was a devoted, loving husband.

'I'm afraid you've called at a rather inconvenient time,' I told them. 'It's lovely to see you but I wish I'd known you were coming. I'm afraid I was just on my way out.'

'On your way out?' Lucille turned and stared at me in surprise. 'But, what about the tearooms? Are you closing for the afternoon?'

'Not at all. Jenny and Maevis are very capable. Everything will run perfectly smoothly in their hands. I have absolute faith and trust in their abilities.'

'You do surprise me. I was under the impression that your life begins and ends here. You always seem to be working so hard.'

I laughed. 'I do take a little time for myself now and again, you know.'

'Surely Simon isn't down from London, is he?' This was from Graham. He stood behind Lucille and his expression was one of open disapproval.

'I really don't know if he is or he isn't,' I said, tartly. 'In any case, it's of no importance to me if he is.'

'But you both seemed to get on so well when you were with us for the weekend.' There was disappointment on Lucille's face. I was fully aware that she had tried to act as matchmaker and somehow hoped that Simon and I would have more than a liking for each other. 'Didn't you go to the ball at Foxdale with him?' she asked.

'Yes, I did. It was a very pleasant evening. He called on me the following day to invite me to tea there before he returned to London. I'm afraid I declined.'

'You declined? You had the chance of another visit to the manor and you declined?' She stared at me in disbelief.

I felt irritated. 'Look, Lucille. I know that Simon Pendleton is a friend to you and Graham but I'm afraid I have no interest in him.' I thought better of telling her what had actually happened between Simon and myself on the last occasion when I'd seen him. 'I know you mean well, but I really don't need you or anyone else to look for a husband for me.'

She was a little taken aback by my openness and plainly hurt by my inference that she was interfering in my life. I hadn't meant to upset her. She was such a sweet and kind person. I put an arm around her shoulder and would have liked to have told her about James, but something prevented me from doing so. 'Sit down and have a cup of tea with me,' I said to her kindly. 'I don't have to go out just yet.' This wasn't strictly true. I had hoped to leave almost immediately but I couldn't part company with her so abruptly, especially as they'd come all the way from Nether Wilmslow to visit me. I glanced at Graham. There was a smug look on his face. Could it be that he was pleased I had no interest in Simon? I dismissed the thought. I was sure that it wasn't that important to him.

They sat down whilst I busied myself preparing tea and a light lunch for them. 'So where are you going this afternoon?' Lucille asked, after a while. I put the kettle on the hob and was pleased that I wasn't facing her. It made it easier for me to be economical with the truth.

'I'm going to visit an old friend,' I told her. 'She's an elderly lady who isn't too well. I said I'd spend the afternoon with her.' This seemed to satisfy her curiosity and she questioned me no further. We spent the next hour talking and at one point Graham disappeared into the garden. I couldn't help noticing that Muffin paid very little attention to him, unlike his reaction to James. Jenny and Maevis passed in and out of the kitchen and I could see they had everything organised and under control.

Just when I began to think that my guests had no intention of leaving, despite the fact that they knew I was going out, Lucille stood up and said it was time for them to go. I breathed a sigh of relief. I was anxious to spend as much time with Annabelle as I could and already I was late. It would take me at least half an hour to walk to Mrs Bilbrook's cottage.

'Can we take you anywhere?' Graham asked, as I walked with them to their brougham.

'You're very kind, but it's not very far and I'd prefer to walk, thank you,' I told him. In actual fact I didn't want them to know where I was going or who I was visiting. We said our goodbyes and I waved to them as they headed off in the same direction as I was going. When they were well out of sight Muffin and I hurried along the main street and into the country lane that would take me to the Foxdale Estate.

***** *

Annabelle greeted me shyly at first and then she recalled having seen me in the tearooms. From then on she chattered away happily and before the afternoon was over it seemed that I'd known her all her short life. Whether it was because she was so much like Cathy, or whether it was just a natural bonding between us because we were family, I don't know. But I do know that we had an instant understanding of each other even though she was unaware that I was her aunt.

The day was overcast and spitting with rain so we were restricted to staying indoors but that made no difference to our enjoyment of the afternoon. She adored Muffin and he, in turn, thought it wonderful to have a small child to play with and give him plenty of attention. We spent several happy hours playing games and we read books and even did some sums. She was a bright child and was clearly well advanced in her academic abilities. Mrs Bilbrook sat back and watched us for most of the time but she joined in when she could with games such as 'Something in the Room', where one of us chose an item we could see and said what letter it began with. The others had to guess what it was. Another game was 'Beasts, Birds or Fishes' where the only clue given was the type of creature that the caller was thinking of. The correct answer had to be shouted out before the caller could count to six. This brought squeals of delight from Annabelle when she came up with the right answer.

Between us, in those few short hours, there was much fun and laughter. We had tea at about five o'clock and Annabelle even helped me to wash up the dishes. Despite her upbringing at Foxdale where there were servants for her every need, she was a very down-to-earth child and presented no airs and graces. I wondered who had been responsible for this very balanced view she had of life. Surely it couldn't be Lady Charlotte. From what I'd heard and seen of her she appeared to be a very stuck-up, very snobbish individual who believed in keeping those of a lower class than herself very much in their place. It couldn't be Nigel himself. He was just as bad and, in any case, spent most of his time in London, apparently. It didn't strike me that he wanted to have a great deal of involvement in his daughter's upbringing. She was under his roof, not because he wanted her there, but because she had to be, in accordance with his father's Will.

This really left Adrian whom I suspected was, himself, a very down-to-earth individual. Prior to this afternoon, whenever I'd seen Annabelle, she was with him. He obviously felt a certain amount of responsibility towards her, even if his brother didn't, and he clearly had a great deal of influence over her. She, in turn, adored her Uncle Adrian, that was plain for anyone to see. All afternoon she referred to him at odd times; Uncle Adrian this – or Uncle Adrian that. He was never very far from her thoughts and, clearly, she loved him to bits.

'Would you teach me how to make some cakes?' she asked, when we had finished the dishes. I smiled down at her. She was such a lovely child and reminded me so much of Cathy.

'Nothing would give me greater pleasure,' I told her, 'but we'll have to make it another day. I think Lady Charlotte will be calling for you before long.'

Her expression dropped and the smile left her face. 'But I want to stay here with you and Mrs Bilbrook.'

'I'm afraid that isn't possible, my dear,' Mrs Bilbrook told her. 'Much as we'd love to have you stay, I'm afraid that Anna, here, has to look after her tearooms. She has a lot of bread and cakes to make and customers who expect her to be there.'

She thought quietly for a moment then, surprisingly, changed the subject. 'Your name – Anna,' she said, looking me in the eyes, a smile coming to her own, 'that's like my name, isn't it? Except you haven't got 'belle' on the end.'

I smiled back at her and found it hard to suppress a tear. Little did she know that her mother had most likely named her with me in mind; that her name had deliberately been an extension of my own.

'I think I hear a carriage coming up the drive,' Mrs Bilbrook commented, thankfully relieving me of the necessity to reply. 'That must be Lady Charlotte. She said she'd return about now. Perhaps you can make cakes next time,' she said, turning to Annabelle.

The little girl's face lit up. 'Can I come tomorrow?' she pleaded.

'I'm afraid we have to leave your next visit up to Lady Charlotte, my dear. But we shall see. Perhaps it won't be too long before I have the pleasure of your company again.'

Annabelle flung her arms around the old lady's neck. 'Oh, I do wish I could live with you all the time, Mrs Bilbrook,' she said. 'I always have so much more fun here.'

Before Lady Charlotte appeared she rushed over to me and gave me a wonderful, affectionate hug. I felt a lump come to my throat. Never could I have hoped in a thousand years that my sister's child would respond to me in such a way after such a brief meeting. 'I do so hope I shall see you again soon,' she said.

As I released her from my arms, Lady Charlotte appeared at the door. Immediately, Annabelle's whole demeanour changed. She became quiet and demure, unlike the happy child I'd seen all afternoon. She very primly said goodbye to Mrs Bilbrook and myself before adding, 'Thank you for having me,' then made her way out to the carriage. After a few brief words with Mrs Bilbrook, Lady Charlotte followed her, barely acknowledging my presence in the room. Whether she recognised me or not from her visit with Adrian and Annabelle to my tearooms I don't know. If she did she certainly had no intention of referring to it. I didn't like her and instinct told me never to trust her.

When they were gone Mrs Bilbrook brewed another cup of tea. We spent a pleasant evening talking together and were quite amazed at how the time had flown when James arrived home soon after eleven o'clock. It was almost midnight when he took me back to my cottage. He took Muffin and I back in the horse and cart and made certain that we were safely indoors before he left us.

It was some time before I eventually lay in my bed. What an exciting day it had been. I went over every moment of it, again and again, in my mind. It's a wonder I went to sleep at all, but in time I must have drifted off because the next thing I knew, the sunlight was streaming in through my bedroom curtains at the beginning of a wonderful new day.

* * * * *

I became a frequent visitor to Mrs Bilbrook's cottage. Annabelle wasn't always there. In fact, more often than not it was just James, his mother and me. James was always very attentive towards me but never overpowering. There was never a time when I felt threatened in his presence. He was always a perfect gentleman and made no attempt to do anything which would make me feel at all distressed in his company. It was many weeks before he plucked up courage to kiss me and even then it was little more than a brief kiss on the cheek as we said goodnight. I felt a warm contentment inside when he was gone and looked forward to the next time when I should see him. Clearly, Mrs Bilbrook was pleased to see the relationship developing between her son and me and always made me feel most welcome.

The weeks and months passed by and it seemed that I was no nearer to finding any real proof where my suspicions regarding Cathy's death were concerned. I had to be very careful not to arouse any undue attention by asking too many questions locally so I had to bide my time.

Annabelle and I got on wonderfully well. We had such fun together. I don't know if she ever mentioned to Lady Charlotte that I was often at the cottage. If she did, nothing was said. I suspect that she regarded it as her secret and so Lady Charlotte was unaware of my visits and the time we spent together. Probably this was just as well. I didn't want Nigel knowing who I was or suspecting my relationship to Annabelle.

It was Spring when an opportunity arose quite out of the blue. James and I had taken Muffin for a walk one evening when he suddenly turned to me as if an idea had sprung into his head.

'You'd make a good teacher for Annabelle, wouldn't you?'

I laughed. 'I'm not so sure of that. Professor Argyle taught me well but whether I could teach someone else all that I know is a different matter. But I don't understand. Why do you say that?'

'Lady Charlotte had an accident today. She slipped on the steps leading into the garden. They were wet from the shower we had this morning. Needless to say she blamed the gardeners and everyone around her for the accident. She was carried to the bedroom under a great deal of protest and the doctor was called. He said that she's broken her leg and has put it in a splint. She has to rest for several weeks and, of course, can't get about. Someone is needed for just a short period of time each day to be with Annabelle and help her to continue with her studies. It might only be from nine o'clock in the morning until about mid-day. Just until Lady Charlotte is up and about again. 'You'd be perfect,' he said, with enthusiasm, 'and just imagine, I should be able to see you every day.'

'But even if they considered me suitable for the job, you forget that I have a tearooms to run and organise,' I told him.

'Surely Jenny and Maevis could look after it until you get back at lunch time? From what I've seen of them, they're very capable.'

'But it isn't just me being there, James. I have a great deal of preparation each day to ensure that we have an adequate supply of bread and pies and cakes. There's a vast amount more to running a tearooms than just putting the kettle to boil.' Even as I said it, there was an element of excitement building inside me at the prospect of being with Annabelle every morning for several weeks. Already my mind was subconsciously trying to work out a way of making it possible. That was assuming that I was given the position. In the end there was no question about it. I couldn't let such an opportunity pass me by. I'd find some way to organise my life, and the tearooms, so that I could be with Annabelle each morning if I was lucky enough to be accepted for the job. I was sure that I could cope with it all, even if it meant that I was cooking and baking well into the night.

'Very well. But how shall I go about applying for the position?'

He thought for a moment. 'We could say you overheard my mother discussing the situation when she called in at the tearooms with a friend. Mother would be happy to have a word with Annabelle's uncle Adrian and say that you have expressed an interest in the position as it's only for a few weeks. He holds my mother in high regard and I'm sure would be happy to accept her recommendation.' He took both my hands in his own. His face was alive with excitement. 'Please, let me have a word with her,' he urged.

After only a moment's hesitation, I agreed. No doubt he assumed that it was because I was keen to work in the same house, close to him, every day for a short while. In fact my motivation was more to do with the fact that I would be able to spend more time with Annabelle and might also have the opportunity to discover what really did happen when her mother died.

* * * * *

CHAPTER 16

It was all arranged. Almost before I had time to take a deep breath James called on me to say that Adrian had been delighted with the idea and was more than happy for me to look after Annabelle each morning.

'In his own words,' James told me, 'it has relieved him of a great deal of worry. To seek out and interview an appropriate person for the temporary job may well have taken several weeks and then there might not have been anyone suitable. By then Lady Charlotte will, most probably, be back on her feet. He remembers meeting you when he came to the tearooms and is more than happy to take my mother's recommendation that you would be suitable for the job. He wants to see you tomorrow morning with a view to starting immediately.'

'Then I have a great deal of work to do today in preparation for my absence here each morning. I must ask you to leave, I'm afraid, James. I really do have to get on.'

His face fell. 'Can't I sit in a corner and watch you? I won't get in your way.'

'Well, just for a short while. You could make yourself useful and brew some tea,' I suggested.

True to his word he didn't get in my way. In fact, at one point I almost forgot he was there. I was so busy cooking and baking and making a list of things the girls had to do that I became totally engrossed in my chores. He didn't seem to mind, though, and Muffin was only too pleased to have his company. Poor old Muffin; obviously he wouldn't be able to come with me each day so he would, no doubt, wonder where I'd gone. Still, it wasn't for too long, only for a few short weeks and it was an opportunity that I could never have hoped would come my way. In any case, I would be home shortly after lunch and I could spend the rest of the day with him.

* * * * *

It was very plain that James was becoming more than just fond of me. This worried me. Once or twice he intimated that he was falling in love with me but I quickly changed the subject. I had no wish to hurt him but much as I liked him something held me back and I found that I couldn't contemplate the idea of us spending the rest of our lives together as husband and wife. Although he never said as much, I knew that it was on his mind. He never gave me cause for alarm. He was always kind and considerate and never made me feel that he was pushing me into a relationship I didn't want. But I knew what was on his mind and I also knew that Mrs Bilbrook would have been delighted to know her son and I were thinking seriously about each other. In some ways I felt guilty. I loved their company and always felt so at home when I visited them but I knew that the time would surely come when I'd have to dash all hopes James might have of us sharing a future together. In some ways I felt I'd used him and his mother, for without their help I wouldn't have come to know Annabelle; nor would I now be contemplating this temporary job at Foxdale which would, hopefully, lead me towards some answers regarding Cathy.

For the time being I had to let things carry on as they were without in any way raising James' hopes still further by my words or actions. To crush his dreams now would make it very difficult for us both during the time I was to spend at Foxdale.

* * * * *

I stood in the morning room awaiting Adrian Tremayne. It was a beautiful room, softly furnished and with a view out over the terrace and immaculate gardens. My eyes wondered towards where I knew the lake to be. Memories of that fateful day when I'd sought to clean my mud-splattered clothes and hair in the lake came rushing back. The recollection of Nigel Tremayne's hands on me made me feel sick, even now all these years later. Then Adrian came into my thoughts and I remembered how he had saved me from his lecherous brother and how afterwards, for a long, long while, he'd been constantly in my thoughts. Looking back now I wondered, as on other occasions, if it hadn't been just a childish infatuation brought about by the fact that he'd saved me from such degradation and had shown a kindness and concern for me which I'd hitherto not known from anyone.

'Good-morning, Miss Briggs.' I hadn't heard the door open and was brought suddenly from my contemplation of the past. I spun round.

'Mr Tremayne – Good-morning.'

He came forward and held out a hand in greeting. I took it and felt the strength in his fingers as he shook my own. 'I'm delighted to meet you – again,' he said, easily. Because of my thoughts just a moment before, I felt a sudden touch of panic. Did he recognise me from all those years ago? Surely not? And then I realised that he was referring to the day when he'd visited my tearooms and, of course, the night of the ball when I'd been a guest at Foxdale along with Simon Pendleton.

He had a warm smile. On the evening of the ball there had been so many other guests that there really hadn't been the opportunity to speak with him. Nor his brother, come to that. Which was just as well because I was afraid that one or other of them might just recognise me and connect me with Cathy. Having given it careful consideration since, however, I realised that the possibility of them making such a connection was very unlikely. I was far removed from the scruffy, dirty young girl of their first acquaintance. I had matured and was well educated. My name, although the same, didn't necessarily mean I was related to Cathy. There was no possible way they could know who I really was.

Confidently, I sat down on the seat which he indicated. He remained standing. He was tall with extraordinary long legs, well dressed and perfectly groomed.

'I think this meeting is purely a formality,' he said. 'I have every faith in Mrs Bilbrook's recommendation of you and, of course, this isn't the first time that we've met. Perhaps you could tell me a little of your education and what sort of routine you'll have with my niece. I'm quite happy to leave her entirely in your care each morning and open to any suggestions you might wish to make. I had thought Lady Charlotte might want to be involved to a certain extent but she tells me that as soon as she is able she is going away for a short while to convalesce. At the moment, of course, she's restricted to her bed.'

Without telling him that I had once lived in Thursledown and that my initial schooling had been at the village school, I explained how I'd received my education from Professor Joseph Argyle in Lynhead. He responded with surprise.

'Good gracious me! I've heard of the gentleman. By all accounts he was an excellent teacher, a professor at Cambridge at one time, I believe?'

'Yes, that's correct,' I confirmed. 'He was also a very dear friend. Sadly, he died about two years ago.'

'I'm sorry to hear that.' He was silent for a moment, then obviously decided that my education was not an issue. He went on to ask about the tearooms and enquired what hobbies I enjoyed. I felt completely comfortable in his company and realised, then, why, as a young girl, I'd thought I was in love with him. He was totally charming with no airs and graces or delusions of grandeur such as his brother possessed. He had a remarkable quality, despite his privileged upbringing, of making a person feel that they were just as important as he was, from whatever walk of life they came.

When, finally, our meeting was over he shook my hand again. 'We shall look forward to seeing you first thing tomorrow morning,' he said. 'I'm afraid I have some estate business to attend to but I'll get James to take you to Annabelle. I believe you have met her on a couple of occasions at Mrs Bilbrook's home.'

I nodded. I wasn't sure whether or not he knew that Lady Charlotte had left her with James's mother on odd occasions but, clearly, he was aware of the fact. 'She's a delightful child,' I said as he turned to leave the room.

'Yes, indeed,' was his response. 'I only wish she were my own. She's my brother's daughter.' He thought for a moment before saying, 'Her mother died – shortly after she was born.'

With this he obviously thought no further explanation was necessary. 'I shall no doubt see you,' he said, as he opened the door. 'James will be with you in a few moments.'

He marched into the hall and I heard the low murmur of voices before James appeared to take me up to Annabelle's schoolroom. He had a beaming smile right across his face and for a moment I thought he was about to lift me up and twirl me round, such was his excitement. 'I knew he'd like you,' he said. 'He told me what a charming young woman you are. Of course, I already know that,' he laughed.

*****

Annabelle, who hadn't been told of the plans, was delighted and so excited when she learned that it was to be me who would be looking after her for the next few weeks.

The following morning I decided to ease her, and myself, gently into a routine. Before we began I thought it a good

181

idea to take a short walk around the grounds to 'blow away the cobwebs' and to allow the fresh air to waken us up before we settled down to lessons. It was a beautiful day. A soft carpet of dew lay on the grass and it was as if the birds sang as they'd never sung before. We went for a walk through the gardens and I had an overwhelming urge to run and skip just as she was doing. After a while she turned and took my hand in her own. She was such a sweet child and even if I'd been unaware that she was my niece I couldn't have helped but grow to love her. The fact that I knew she was Cathy's daughter endeared her to me even more.

We walked slowly round the gardens and grounds and I pointed out to her all the shrubs and spring flowers and fresh new buds on the trees. She took everything in, eager to learn and know all the names and discover everything she could about nature. I could see she was going to be a pleasure to teach.

Suddenly, her attention was drawn away from me. She let go of my hand and went rushing off along the grassy path. 'Be careful you don't slip,' I called after her, 'the grass is damp from the morning dew.'

She didn't hear what I said. Her whole attention was focused on her uncle Adrian whom she had caught sight of walking towards us. 'Slow down, young lady. Slow down,' he called to her as he swept her into his arms and sustained the bombardment of hugs and kisses which she bestowed on him. When he'd hugged and kissed her in return he set her gently on her feet and, with her small hand in his own, he walked slowly towards me.

'Come and meet Miss Briggs,' she urged him, trying to hurry him along. 'Her name is Anna, like my name but without the 'belle' on the end. You know – I've told you all about her. She sometimes comes to Mrs Bilbrook's cottage when I'm there.'

'I know. We've met,' he said to her with a smile in my direction. 'I can see you two get on very well.' I realised then that he must have been watching us for some time.

She chattered on and he walked with us for a while, asking her what new things she'd learnt from the garden this morning. Even I was surprised by her informative reply. She had obviously listened and absorbed everything that I'd told her. It was a pleasure to watch them together. Clearly, she adored him and, I'm sure, would have followed him to the ends of the earth. Equally clear was the fact that he, too, was very fond of her. They had a lovely relationship which, as Cathy's sister, I was so thankful for. My mind was put at ease to know that at least one member of the Tremayne family cared about her and would, undoubtedly, make sure that no harm came to her.

It was a curious feeling. Far from feeling that I was employed by this man who walked beside me, I felt more as if we were a family group out for a morning stroll. When I thought about it later I realised that this, of course, is exactly what it was. We were related, except that Adrian and Annabelle, herself, were completely unaware of that fact.

After a while I suggested, reluctantly, that it was time for us to make our way up to the schoolroom and begin our lessons. This was met with a certain amount of opposition from Annabelle until Adrian explained that he, too, had work to get on with and would see her later in the day. He walked with us to the foot of the stairs then disappeared through a door into a room which looked out towards the front of the house.

The rest of the morning passed very quickly and in the days that followed I settled into a routine which was both pleasant and rewarding. Of course I saw a great deal of James when we passed in the passageways or on the stairs. It was not permitted for us to stand and talk for long but he seemed more than happy just to see me there and say a brief 'hello', before we both went on with our work. The staff, with the exception of perhaps one or two, were friendly and helpful and even the housekeeper, Mrs Pringle, who was a true matriarch, was pleasant enough.

My days were busy. When the morning came to an end I rushed home and went straight into my work at the tearooms to allow Jenny and Maevis to take a break. They were, as I'd expected, perfectly capable of looking after things in my absence and after a few days I ceased to worry that everything was going according to plan. We all fell into a regular routine and even Muffin accepted that I had to leave him behind for a few hours each morning. He was in good hands. Jenny and Maevis loved animals and I suspect he was given a few too many treats whilst I wasn't there. My evenings were spent cooking and baking in preparation for the next day and it was often after midnight by the time I fell, exhausted, into bed.

A week or two later Lucille came to visit me. Thankfully she was alone. Graham wasn't with her as it was a week day and he was at work.

'You're looking very tired,' she commented, 'Whatever have you been doing. You look as if you could do with a break. Why don't you come and stay for a few days.'

I didn't like to tell her, but the last thing I wished to do was stay with her under the same roof as Graham. I would never have hurt her feelings by telling her so, but I just didn't trust him, not after his behaviour towards me.

'Graham saw Simon a week or so ago,' she said. Simon, there was another one I didn't trust. 'We could invite him to stay at the same time,' she went on, 'You two seemed to get on very well at our dinner party.'

How little she knew. Simon and Graham were two of a kind and the two men I trusted least of all. I considered telling her of my experience with Simon then thought better of it. 'Perhaps some other time,' I said, 'I'm very busy at the moment.'

'Exactly, dear, and that is the very reason why you need a break. I'm concerned for you. You're working far too hard.'

She assumed that the tearooms was at the root of my tiredness. I hadn't told her that I went to Foxdale each morning. Nor had I told her about Annabelle. She was a good friend but I truly felt that the less people who knew of my connection the better. If I told her she would most probably tell Graham and he, in turn, would very likely pass on the information to Simon. Being a friend of Adrian and Nigel, Simon would undoubtedly, at some time, bring up the subject in the course of conversation with one or other of them and that was the last thing I wanted.

'I'll think about it,' I told her. 'Perhaps when things quieten down a little.'

She seemed happy with this and we went on to talk of other things. All the while I was cooking and baking and making bread dough, stopping only briefly for a quick cup of tea. The girls hurried in and out of the kitchen attending to the needs of our customers.

'Mrs Gilbert was just saying she never sees anything of you, Miss,' Jenny said, as she gathered up fresh scones.

'Then I'd best come and say hello,' I told her and left Lucille to hurry into the tearooms for a quick chat to keep my customers happy. When I returned I was surprised to find James seated in a chair opposite Lucille. She'd poured him a cup of tea and he had obviously been there some little while. I hoped and prayed he hadn't mentioned anything about Annabelle.

I needn't have worried. True to form James was as discreet as ever. It appeared that he'd coaxed Lucille into talking about Lynhead and our earlier days together when her father was alive. He very diplomatically told her nothing of my present circumstances and introduced himself to her as an old school friend.

'Well, well. You're a quiet one,' she said, when later she left to return home. You've not mentioned James before.'

'We only met again recently,' I told her, which wasn't strictly true as it was now some months since the ball at Foxdale when I'd met up with him again.

'No wonder you're not interested in seeing Simon again,' she teased with a smile. I let her comment go without response. She could think what she liked, just so long as she didn't try to bring Simon Pendleton and me together again.

James was playing with Muffin when I went back inside. 'So that's Lucille,' he said. I'd told him most of what happened to me after I left Thursledown so he was well acquainted with her name. 'Curiously, I recognise her,' he went on. 'I'm sure I've seen her somewhere before but I can't think where.' He thought hard for some moments but nothing sprang to mind. 'Maybe it will come to me later,' he said.

I finished my chores and we took Muffin for a well-deserved walk. I have to admit that, in that respect, I wasn't as conscientious as I should have been. There were days when I was either too tired or just didn't have the time to take him out, but he was a good little dog and didn't seem to mind so long as he was with me. Sometimes, on the quieter days, I asked Jenny or Maevis to take him for a walk. But no sooner had they left than they were back again, saying that he'd flatly refused to go more than a few yards along the road and wanted to return home. He never liked going far without me.

'I really came to tell you that Nigel is back from London,' he said, as we walked along. 'I thought you'd like to know rather than suddenly meet up with him at the house tomorrow.'

What he said came as something as a shock. I hadn't considered the possibility of Nigel Tremayne returning home during the few weeks I would be Annabelle's tutor. He spent so much time in London and hadn't been back to Foxdale since the ball. I had assumed that I wouldn't have to meet with him.

'I heard him shouting at Adrian in a rage,' he enlightened me. 'Apparently he isn't at all happy that he wasn't consulted about you taking the temporary position as Annabelle's tutor. He wants to see you first thing in the morning so ... be prepared for the summons,' he said, with mock severity.

My heart sank. What if he should tell me I was no longer required? Worse still, what if he should see some resemblance between Annabelle and me or detect a familiarity in my face which made him think of Cathy? What if, in the fullness of time, he suspected the truth?

* * * * *

I needn't have worried. Nigel Tremayne gave no indication of recognising me other than from our brief meeting at the ball. He expressed his disappointment at the fact that I hadn't been able to accept the invitation to tea with Simon on the day after, then he went straight on to discuss his requirements where Annabelle was concerned. From the way he spoke it was clear that neither Annabelle, nor anyone else, had enlightened him to the fact that she and I had come to know each other quite well. This surprised me. I suspected that Lady Charlotte, at least, would have told him that I'd been at Mrs Bilbrook's occasionally when she left Annabelle with her. But then, maybe she didn't want Nigel to know that every so often she went out alone. None of us knew where she went, only that every few weeks she asked Mrs Bilbrook to look after

Annabelle whilst she disappeared, sometimes for a full day at a time.

For the full half an hour of our interview I felt decidedly uneasy in Nigel's company. I didn't like the man. Even if I'd never met him before, and didn't know of his unpleasant nature, I doubted if I could ever have liked him. He was so unlike his brother, both in looks and in temperament. It was hard to believe that they were of the same parents. Whereas Adrian had hair which was dark brown in colour and deep blue eyes which sparkled with kindness and humour, his brother, Nigel, was of a much fairer complexion with mousy coloured hair and harsh, grey-blue eyes which looked almost as if they were made of steel, such was the way in which he stared out at the world around him. There was no hint of softness in his face or compassion for his fellow man. Any act of kindness would have been out of keeping with his entire nature and I doubted that he could ever be capable of showing true love or kindness to anyone. I was both relieved and grateful when he decided, quite abruptly, that he'd asked enough questions of me and that our interview had come to an end.

'I'm sure that for the time you're here you'll have a very positive influence on my daughter,' he said, as I turned to leave. 'I look forward to seeing you around the house each morning.' He was charm itself, but something in his tone made me want to escape from his presence just as soon as I could. At the door, I turned out of politeness to thank him and to wish him good morning. In that brief instant I caught him looking at me. His eyes were appraising my appearance from head to toe in what can only be described as a lecherous fashion. I felt sick. If he thought, for one moment, I'd encourage any attention from him he was wrong, very wrong indeed. I hurried from the room and made my way up to the nursery.

With the exception of Nigel's constant presence I found myself looking forward to my mornings at the manor. I settled into a routine with the running of my tearooms and found I could happily leave Jenny and Maevis in charge whilst I wasn't there. They were very capable and liked by all my regular customers who were, of course, most interested to learn why I wasn't there, myself, until after lunch each day.

James was very clearly delighted to have me working in such close proximity to him. Whenever he could, he stopped what he was doing and sought me out for a few moments. Annabelle and I were both pleased to see him but I did have to warn him that we would all be severely reprimanded if he did it too often.

Occasionally Adrian came to the schoolroom to see how we were getting on. This brought squeals of delight from Annabelle. She clearly loved her uncle Adrian and he, in turn, loved her. He was so kind and gentle, a far cry from his obnoxious brother. In Annabelle's company he was full of fun and I could see why she loved him so much. I felt happy that my niece was, for most of the time, in his care. He, at least, would protect her from harm.

I saw nothing of Lady Charlotte and a week or two later I learned she had left Foxdale to spend a few weeks recuperating by the sea. I settled into a routine which I found both pleasant and rewarding and the days slipped by very quickly. Most of the staff, with the exception of perhaps one or two, were friendly and helpful. Even the housekeeper, Mrs Pringle, who had a reputation for being hard and dictatorial, and who left no one in any doubt that it was she who was in charge, had a warm heart where Annabelle was concerned. The only member of the household who made me feel truly ill at ease was Nigel Tremayne.

The days passed and I heard whispers amongst the staff concerning his length of stay. Most had expected him to return to London within the week, as he always did, but ten days went by and he was still around. What I found more disturbing were his regular visits to the schoolroom each morning just after my arrival. This was, according to Sarah the nursery maid, a habit he'd only acquired since he'd discovered I was there. Another thing disturbed me. If the weather was fine I took Annabelle for a walk in the grounds each morning to give her a brief respite in the middle of her lessons. I often had an uneasy feeling that he watched me from his study window. Did he wish to make sure that I was doing my job properly? If this was the case then he was welcome to watch just as often as he wished. I was confident that he'd not find fault in my handling of Annabelle. But I had an uneasy feeling that this was not the case; that his interest in me was something more than mere concern for his daughter's welfare. Thankfully, when I came into contact with him his conversations were brief but I couldn't ignore the suspicion that his eyes were constantly on me.

My worst fears were confirmed when, having completed my morning's work with Annabelle, I was walking through the rose garden on my way home. Instead of leaving by the main gate I found it was quicker to take a short cut through the gardens and along a path which led me round the lake to a gate on the far side of the estate. The gate led me onto the road into the village and so cut my journey time by a good ten minutes.

The rose garden was a secluded and pretty place with a high hedge enclosing many varieties of rose bush in full flower. I was so engrossed in the wonderful smells that I was unaware of anyone with me until I heard a footfall on the gravel behind. I turned to find Nigel following me.

'I'm so glad I have the opportunity to talk with you alone for a change,' he said. There was a smile on his face but it didn't touch his eyes. They were as cold and grey as ever. 'You don't mind if I walk with you for a bit, do you?'

I felt nervous. There was nothing about this man that inspired my confidence. He took my silence as consent and slowed his step to match mine.

'My daughter seems to have taken quite a liking to you. Are you happy here, Miss Briggs?' he asked.

'Yes. Very happy, thank you.'

He pulled a leaf from a bush and systematically tore it to pieces before saying, 'You know, you're very beautiful for a governess.'

I felt a warmth come to my cheeks, more from anger than anything else. 'Really? Are governesses supposed to be plain and ugly then?' My voice was cold.

He laughed. 'Not at all. It's just that you happen to be a great deal prettier than any I've seen.'

I could feel no respect for this man. 'Mr Tremayne, I should point out that I am not your daughter's governess, nor anybody else's for that matter. I have my own business and am standing in for a short while until Lady Charlotte has recovered from her accident.' I walked on, faster, hoping he'd take the hint and go away. He didn't. I disliked this man intensely and I was far from happy to find myself alone in his company in this secluded rose garden where no one could see us.

'You forget that I pay your wages,' he shouted angrily after me. 'Stop! Right now – or consider yourself dismissed! I haven't finished talking with you.'

I was so angry. At the same time an underlying fear was taking hold of me. This man, I knew, was capable of anything and it wouldn't stop at just dismissing me. He expected women to become subservient in his presence. That one should challenge his authority was unthinkable in his eyes. I took a deep breath, allowing reason to creep into my mind. To make an enemy of Nigel Tremayne would do me no good at all. I would no longer be able to spend happy hours in the company of Annabelle, albeit for only a few short weeks, and my hope of finding out any new information regarding Cathy's death would be completely gone. I swallowed hard and turned to face him.

'I apologise,' I said, sweetly, though the words stuck in my throat. 'I'm afraid I'm in a great hurry to return home.'

'Sit down,' he commanded, pointing to a bench by the path. 'I'm sure you can spare just a few moments.'

I had no choice. I seated myself at the far end of the bench hoping he'd keep some distance between us. He didn't. He sat right next to me.

'You have such magnificent hair,' he said, taking a strand of my hair between his fingers. 'It catches the sunlight and reflects the golden rays of the sun itself.'

My whole body became tense. If I could have moved further along the bench I would have done so, but I was already at the very end. I glared at him icily.

'Come, come, Anna.' He used my Christian name quite freely. 'Don't be unfriendly. I'm sure you and I have a great deal in common.'

Angrily I jerked my head away from his hand. 'I fail to see how that can be possible,' I retorted, bitterly, 'and if you don't mind I would prefer you to call me Miss Briggs.'

The smile left his face. I made a move to stand up again but he caught my wrist in his bony fingers and forced me to sit beside him.

'I'm used to having my own way where pretty young women are concerned,' he snarled, 'don't think, for one moment, that you are an exception.'

I felt sick. Panic took me in its grasp as I recalled how, once before, he'd forced me, unwillingly, to the ground. I tried to remain outwardly calm but every nerve in my body was shouting at me to bite hard on the bony fingers, which gripped my wrist, and run as fast and as far as I possibly could. Still holding me firmly, he placed his other hand around my shoulder and drew me closer to him.

'Please, let me go!' I ordered him, mustering all the calm superiority I could find. A flash of anger touched his steely eyes before he burst into laughter.

'My, we are a challenge,' he said, as his grip tightened. I was about to throw all caution to the wind and hit him hard about the face with my free hand when, with profound relief, I heard Adrian's voice. He was walking along the footpath towards us. I saw it as my means of escape from this hateful man. As Nigel released his hold I stood up and hurried out of the rose garden, vowing that I would never go there alone again.

I have no idea how Nigel explained his behaviour to his brother but one can imagine my horror when, a day or so later, Adrian passed me in the corridor and said:

'I'm sorry if I interrupted your ... conversation with Nigel the other morning. I'm afraid there was a matter concerning the estate which needed urgent attention.'

'It was nothing of importance,' I told him. What else could I say? That his brother had tried to molest me?

He turned to go, then on second thoughts he said, 'I wouldn't take my brother too seriously if I were you, Miss Briggs. I'd hate to see you get hurt.'

I was dumbfounded, completely speechless. He passed a quizzical look in my direction and had disappeared before I had time to ask the reason for his remark. Whatever Nigel had told him, it was clear that he thought I'd met his brother's advances with approval. I felt utterly sick.

*****

CHAPTER 17

I knew that I had the option of walking away from Foxdale; of disassociating myself from everyone who worked or lived there. But I couldn't. To do so would have been like abandoning Annabelle and a betrayal of Cathy. In any event, I'd heard rumours that Lady Charlotte was recovering well and that it wouldn't be too many weeks before she returned home. My services as Annabelle's tutor would then no longer be required. Already I'd been there almost three weeks and apart from the wonderful opportunity it had given me to spend time with my niece, I was no nearer to discovering any clue regarding the circumstances surrounding Cathy's death. But where was I to start? I couldn't go around asking questions. That would raise far too many suspicions.

I was pondering on just what I should do, one morning, when a member of staff, whom I hadn't seen before, approached me as I left to return home. Since my encounter with Nigel I preferred to take the longer route back to the village which didn't involve walking through isolated areas of the estate. It was as I walked back along the drive towards the main gate that she came running after me.

'Anna! Anna! Can I have a word with you?'

I turned to see a young woman, about my own age, hurrying towards me. Her uniform indicated that she was a member of the kitchen staff which was why I probably hadn't seen her before. There was something familiar about her but I didn't know what it was until she introduced herself.

'I'm Sally,' she told me. 'You probably don't remember. We were at school together. Sally Tendersall.'

'Why, yes.' Now that she told me who she was I did remember her. She was a year or too older than I and was in a different class to me. I was at a loss for words. All manner of questions were flying through my mind. If she recognised me she would know that Cathy was my sister. She would know, too, that Annabelle was my niece. Her next words eased my fears a little.

'James said I should 'ave a word with you. 'E told me not to say nothin' to anyone. Not to tell anyone who you really are.'

'When did you speak with James?' I asked.

'This mornin', Miss. I 'ad to go in the 'orse and cart with 'im to the village on an errand. We got talkin' and 'e says I should 'ave a word with you. But to keep it under me 'at, like. Not to say anything to anyone.'

'So, what is it that he wants you to talk to me about, Sally?' I asked, cautiously.

She looked about her as if to ensure that no one else was within hearing distance. 'That coachman – the one who died when Annabelle's mother died?'

'What about him?'

'I was a friend of his girlfriend, Miss.'

'I don't understand, Sally. Why should that be of interest to me?'

'Because I'm sure that she went with 'im on that night, Miss. She told me 'erself. 'E wasn't supposed to tell anyone where 'e was going. Sworn to secrecy an' all that. But 'e said it would be an opportunity for them both to go to London together, cos that's where 'e'd been told to take your sister and 'er baby. 'E promised to marry Letty when they got there. She told me so. They were eloping, you see, because 'er parents didn't approve of 'im. 'E told Letty that she was to be ready an' waiting for 'im just outside the village on the road to Nether Wilmslow. 'E'd pick 'er up there. 'E told 'er not to say a word to anyone but she was so excited, Miss, she was bursting to tell me where she was goin'. All I can say is, in view of what 'appened, thank God little Annabelle wasn't with them as planned.'

'But I was under the impression that only two bodies were found by the burnt out coach. If what you're saying is true, then there should have been three.'

'I know, Miss. That's what's puzzled me for a long time. I even went to see Master Nigel to ask 'im if it wasn't three people they'd found but I never got to see 'im.'

'Why was that Sally? Surely it was important to find out if she was there.' I held my breath as I waited for the answer to my next question. 'Perhaps she didn't meet him after all. Did she return home having changed her mind?'

Sally bowed her head. 'No, Miss, she didn't. No one's seen 'er since. She knew 'er family wouldn't approve and that they'd try to stop 'er so she told them she'd been given the opportunity of work down on the coast. She told them she'd contact them when she was settled but, not being much of a letter writer, they weren't surprised when the weeks went by and they didn't 'ear from 'er. It wasn't until they learned some time later who the driver of the coach carrying your sister was that they began to wonder. By then the funerals 'ad taken place and everyone had assumed that it was your sister Cathy who died that night. Which, of course, it probably was. Who's to say otherwise? The bodies were unrecognisable by all accounts.' Her hand shot to her mouth. 'Oh, Miss – I'm so sorry. That was tactless of me. I didn't mean to upset you.'

I swallowed hard and fought back the tears. 'That's alright Sally, you just didn't think.' I placed a hand on her arm to reassure. She was quite distressed at the insensitivity of her remark.

'There is something you should know,' she volunteered after a moment. I waited for her to collect her thoughts and go on. 'As I said, I was on me way to ask Master Nigel if it wasn't three bodies they'd found when I over'eard 'im and Mr Pendleton talking.'

'Simon Pendleton? What's he got to do with it?'

'I don't know, Miss, but I 'eard them talking about the accident. Master Nigel was in a rage. I distinctly 'eard 'im say, "Why the hell wasn't the child with them?" That's what stopped me from goin' any further. His study door was slightly ajar. I didn't realise 'e 'ad company and I was about to knock before going in. When I 'eard what 'e said I stopped straight away.'

'Did you hear anything else?'

'Yes, I did, Miss.' She hesitated. 'I – 'eard 'im swear. Quite brought the colour to me cheeks, it did. Then I'm sure 'e said that by rights Annabelle should've been in the coach that night and that he "couldn't dispose of 'er now", – as 'e put it – without arousing suspicion. Then after a moment 'e said, "It's of no matter. Anytime before she's twenty-one will do." 'E said after that she'll receive the money in 'er own right and there'd be no way 'ed be able to get 'is hands on it. 'E said what a blessing it was that 'is father used the firm of solicitors that Mr Pendleton works for to take care of 'er finances. It's 'is uncle's business – Mr Pendleton, that is – Bennet, Pendleton and Ludgrove. They've got an office in Nether Wilmslow. I was horrified, Miss an' scared for me life, I can tell you. If 'e'd come out and found me there goodness only knows what 'e might 'ave done. I turned round then and hurried away just as fast as I could, expecting any moment to 'ear 'is footsteps be'ind me. I was frightened, believe me. I'm more than certain that 'e 'ad something to do with that tragic event what killed your sister. What's more, I'm frightened for your little niece. I've only got this job in the kitchens now because I couldn't get work anywhere else. I need to be near to the village because me mum isn't well and needs me close by.' She watched me as I silently took in all that she had said. 'You won't say nothing to anyone, will you Miss? It's more than me life's worth, only James seems to think that I can trust you and that you should know what went on.'

'Rest assured I'll say nothing to anyone,' I told her. 'It's in both our interests to remain quiet for the time being. I'm sure James has told you that it must not be known that I am Annabelle's aunt, least of all to Nigel Tremayne.'

'Yes, Miss. You can depend on me. I won't say a word to no one. Not to a soul. And if I can help you, you know where I am.' With this she turned and hurried away, scouring the area with her eyes to make sure that there was no one else around.

I hurried on, deep in thought. Our conversation had thrown new light on circumstances and confirmed what Mrs Bilbrook had already told me. Nigel Tremayne was most certainly involved in the death of both Cathy and the coachman.

But where, exactly, did Simon Pendleton fit in to all of this?

* * * * *

My business thrived, despite my temporary absence each morning. I was even asked by the proprietor of the Laughing Rabbit Inn if I would supply him with scones and biscuits each day for his guests and for passing travellers who stopped for refreshment and to water their horses. Of course, I was only too happy to oblige. It was a useful source of income, especially on those days when few people stopped by at the tearooms for one reason or another.

Early one morning I took the usual tray of biscuits and scones across to the inn before making my way to Foxdale. As I walked in through the main door I almost bumped into a young girl coming out into the street. She apologised profusely for almost knocking me over.

'I'm so sorry, Miss,' she said, catching hold of the other side of my tray in case its contents should tumble to the floor. She looked into my face and smiled. She was a pretty girl and I immediately recognised her as the housemaid who had come to my room on the first morning I arrived back in Thursledown. As on that occasion, I was struck by something familiar in her features.

'You're Miss Briggs from across the road aren't you?' she asked. 'I remember you staying here before you opened the tearooms. My name is Alice, Miss.'

I nodded and smiled at her in return. 'Yes, I do recall seeing you before,' I told her. 'Forgive me, Alice, but your face looks vaguely familiar. Do I know you from somewhere else?'

'I don't think so, Miss. I've never left the village.' To my relief it was clear that she thought I was a relative newcomer to Thursledown and had no idea that I once lived and grew up nearby. All of a sudden her face became serious. 'Oh, Miss, it couldn't be that you've met my sister at some time, Could it? I heard you'd come from Lynhead on the coast and me sister went that way, years ago. We haven't heard from her since. Ever so many people say I'm the spit image of her, as she was at my age.' She stared into my face, a look of desperate hope on her own. 'She left one day after an argument with me mum and dad, said she was going to look for work on the coast. That was almost six years ago. We've heard nothing of her since. It fair broke me mum and dad's heart, Miss. If you can think back and recall ever seeing anyone who might have looked like me, we'd all be so grateful.'

I looked at her, feeling the sadness in her eyes. Her story was familiar, and then I realised why. Only days before, Sally Tendersall had mentioned something very similar about her friend Letty who had been the girlfriend of the coachman employed to take Cathy to London. 'I'm so sorry Alice.

No one comes specifically to mind. I don't recall having met your sister. Tell me, what is your surname?' I said, at last.

'Kent, Miss. I'm Alice Kent. My sister's name was Letty.'

So, I was correct in my assumption that Alice's sister and Sally's friend were one and the same person. More than that, I recalled the name of Kent from my school days. Of course! Letty had been at school in the same class as Sally, a year or so ahead of me. No wonder Alice looked familiar to me, if she and Letty were so much alike.

Disappointment washed over Alice's face. I was sorry I couldn't be of more help to her. Clearly, her sister was constantly in her mind and hadn't been forgotten by her or any of her family.

'I'm afraid I have to go,' I told her. 'I do hope you find your sister one day.' She gave me a half-hearted smile and continued on her way. I couldn't resist the temptation to turn and watch her as she walked down the street. Her head was bowed and, even from behind, she looked a sad figure. For a moment, there, her hopes had been raised, only to be just as quickly dashed to the ground seconds later. I thought of my own family and how, despite the fact that there were so many of us, we had all lost contact with each other. My previously bright spirits evaporated and for the rest of the day I kept returning to memories of my childhood, happy memories with my brothers and sisters which brought with them sad feelings of deep regret that I no longer knew where they were.

* * * * *

When I next saw Lucille she once again came to visit me alone. She didn't look happy.

'Graham has had to go away on business,' she told me. 'He may not be back for a week or two. I feel quite lonely in the house on my own. I wish you could come and visit me for a few days. It would be such fun to go shopping; to have time for long chats together. I used to enjoy those times we shared when we lived at Cherry Tree Cottage.' There was a touch of nostalgia in her voice, almost as if she yearned to return to the days before her father's death.

'Is everything alright?' I asked her. 'You don't seem quite yourself, today.'

She shrugged her shoulders. 'Yes, I suppose it is. I'm probably just being foolish. Perhaps I have too much time to spare; too much time to ponder on little trivialities.'

'Why do you say that? Is there something worrying you? We've always been such close friends. You know that anything you might tell me will go no further.' As I said these words it crossed my mind that I hadn't told her of my connections to Annabelle, neither had I told her that I spent almost every morning at Foxdale. In fact I hadn't even voiced to her my fears concerning Cathy's death, despite the fact that she and I had been close friends for many years.

'I've always thought I knew Graham well,' she went on. 'We've known each other for so many years, since his mother first arrived to work for my father at the cottage. But just recently I've begun to question whether I truly know him at all.'

'But you're married to him,' I said, in amazement. 'Surely you know your own husband?'

'Yes, you'd think so, wouldn't you? But he's changed Anna. He seems so different since we married. He's not the kind, loving person I used to know. At times he can be so hard, almost cruel. It's a side to him I never knew existed and yet I always thought I knew him so well. I even begin to think that perhaps my father was right in trying to prevent us from marrying. Perhaps he saw something in Graham's nature which I was blinded to because of my love for him.'

I tried to reassure her by saying that she must be wrong; that for some reason perhaps she was tired and overwrought and had got things out of perspective. But deep down inside I had an uneasy feeling that what she said was true. Graham was capable of being charm itself. Hadn't I, before his marriage to Lucille, fallen for his charms and thought myself to be in love with him? The weekend of his birthday party when he had called to take me back to Nether Wilmslow so that I could stay with them overnight, I'd briefly seen a different side to him. He and Lucille had been married for such a short time and yet he thought nothing of showing his admiration for me. I felt sure that if it had been in my nature to encourage him he would not have hesitated. When I thought about it carefully, I realised that it was an instinctive distrust of Graham that had prevented me from talking to Lucille about Annabelle and my own concerns. I knew that she would, in her desire to have no secrets from him, talk openly on the subject believing him to be as much a friend to me as she was herself.

'Where has he gone on business?' I asked.

'To London. He seems to be away so much just lately. I know he has offices in Lynhead and in other places and that there are times when he has to go there to make sure that all his business is being carried out as he would wish, but it seems that more and more I'm left alone in the house, especially during the last month. Sometimes he's away for just a day or so. At others he's away for more than a week, particularly as of now when he has to go to London.' She hesitated, as if contemplating whether or not to tell me something else. After a moment she came to a decision and went on, 'There is something which worries me greatly.' I waited, not wishing to press her into revealing anything she might later regret saying. 'It concerns our finances,' she said, at last. 'When my father died he left my brother, Richard, and I the cottage and quite a considerable inheritance. Of course, when I married Graham he automatically took charge of my share of my father's fortune and that, of course, is how it is when a woman marries. It is her husband's right to take possession of her money and everything she owns. But I fear that he is using it indiscriminately. He says that he invests it in his business and in stocks and shares for the benefit of both of us, but I can't help feeling that he is squandering it in other directions.'

'In what way? Do you have any proof?'

'No, I don't. But when we married I thought he used a considerable amount of my inheritance to buy our house in Nether Wilmslow. You can imagine my surprise when I came across a letter from our bank the other day which indicated that the deeds of our property are in their possession as collateral against a loan issued in favour of Graham.'

'Did you confront him about this?'

'No, I didn't. I didn't dare bring up the subject. The letter was addressed personally to him and in private. It was quite by accident that I came across it. If he were to find out that I'd read it, I think his anger would hold no bounds.'

'Then you must remain silent for your own sake,' I told her. 'Oh Lucille, I do so hope that there is a rational explanation to all of this and that your fears are unfounded. I pray that what you suspect is wrong because, if it isn't, he is deceiving you and could be doing so in many other ways.' My words sounded harsh, even to my own ears. I tried to soften the enormity of such implications by placing an arm around her shoulder. I knew how very much she loved him and how much all of this must be hurting her if it was, indeed, true. 'For the time being remain silent,' I counselled her. 'In the fullness of time all will be made clear and it could be that your worst fears are quite without foundation; that there will be a perfectly plausible explanation to all of this.'

She nodded but I could see she wasn't at all convinced and, I have to say, neither was I.

* * * * *

CHAPTER 18

James was such a dear friend. I was very fond of him. But I didn't love him, which was a shame really because Muffin adored him to bits and he would have made a very good husband to me. Somehow, though, I just couldn't see myself as his wife. We saw a lot of each other, mostly at the cottage on the estate, which he shared with his mother or when he visited me at the tearooms on his days off. Occasionally we'd go for a walk and take Muffin with us but there was nothing more to our relationship. I knew that he would have liked our friendship to become more serious but I felt it unfair to encourage him further in that direction. He was too much of a gentleman to force his attentions on me and so we remained the best of friends with no obligations attached on either side. I told him what had happened when Nigel had followed me into the rose garden and he was deeply disturbed. He suggested that maybe I should reconsider my duties towards Annabelle and ask to be replaced.

'That isn't an option,' I told him. 'It's only for a few more weeks and I want to spend as much time with Annabelle as I possibly can. In any case, I'm sure Nigel won't give me any more trouble. I made it quite clear to him what I felt about his advances. I've no doubt he'll return to London again before long, so there won't be any problem.'

'I hope you're right,' he said, seriously. 'My God, if I didn't work there and he wasn't my employer I think I'd have something to say to him. All I ask of you, Anna, is that you take care. Be on your guard against him.'

I promised that I would, then went on to tell him that Sally had spoken with me, and what she had told me. I also told him about Alice Kent and the fact that she was Letty's sister. Of course, he knew all this. Sally had already confided in him which was why he had asked her to have a word with me in the first place.

'What I can't understand is where Simon Pendleton fits into all of this,' I told him.

'He and Nigel have been friends for years,' he enlightened me. 'It doesn't surprise me in the least to learn that he might be involved. I never have liked the man. He's frequently been a guest at the manor over the years. At one time, when Nigel spent more time here he was almost like a member of the family, he was here so often.'

'But I thought he was a friend of Adrian's.'

'Good heavens, no. If the truth were known I suspect Adrian doesn't much like him at all. He remains civil to him because he is his brother's friend. I think he likes to see the back of him when he returns home as much as any of us.'

'I first met him at my friend's home over in Nether Wilmslow,' I volunteered, then laughed as I recalled the evening. 'I think they had ideas of matchmaking. They introduced me to him and that's how I came to be at the ball on the evening when I first saw you at the manor. He asked me if I would attend as his guest. It very soon became apparent that he was not the sort of person I wished to be acquainted with,' I said, remembering my altercation with Simon the day after the ball.

'You've told me about your friends at Nether Wilmslow. That is Lucille and her husband. She was Professor Argyle's daughter, am I correct?' he asked.

'Yes, her husband, Graham, owns a number of real estate offices and deals in property. I believe that's how he came to know Adrian.'

'Would his name be Graham Fairs, by any chance?' There was a scowl on his face, most unlike James.

'Why, yes. As a matter of fact it is. Do you know of him?'

'Only vaguely. He's been to Foxdale on one or two occasions. But I think you'll find he was a friend of Nigel long before he became acquainted with Adrian.'

How very strange that Graham had never, over the course of time, spoken of his connections with Nigel. It was obvious that he hadn't even told Lucille because I felt sure that she would have mentioned it to me.

James and I changed the subject then and went on to other things, but long after we had parted company I was mulling over our conversation and thinking about what he had said. There was something very strange going on around me, something I didn't quite understand. It made me all the more determined that, sooner or later, I would get to the bottom of it all and find out the truth.

* * * * *

Much to my dismay Nigel didn't keep his distance from me as I'd hoped. For a few days I saw nothing of him and then it seemed that he was around every corner and sought me out at every opportunity under the pretext that it was his daughter he had come to see. It disturbed me that he was taking such an interest in me but I knew that all the time Annabelle was in my company he would do nothing to give her cause for alarm.

For a time I had visions of him leaping out of the bushes in front of me as I hurried down the drive and out onto the road on my way home. But my fears were unfounded and it soon became clear that he had no intention of doing such a thing, probably because the full length of the drive was in clear view of the house and anyone who might be peering from its windows. Part of me wanted to take James' advice and suggest to Adrian that it was no longer convenient for me to tutor Annabelle. The other part of me knew that I wanted to stay on because I had come to love her dearly and I wanted the opportunity to spend as much time with her as I could. I liked to feel that she, too, was fond of me. These precious hours we spent in each other's company would come to an end soon enough when Lady Charlotte returned. After that I'd have to be content with seeing her on the rare occasions when she visited Mrs Bilbrook.

It never occurred to me that Nigel might make an attempt to see me at any time other than when I was at the house with Annabelle, so it came as a great shock when I was out walking Muffin late one evening and I heard the fall of a horse's hooves behind me. I stepped to the side of the lane so that the rider could pass by, but, as I did so, I looked up to see Nigel's pompous face leering down at me.

'I hoped I might come across you one of these evenings,' he said, triumphantly. I heard a low rumble in Muffin's throat. It had taken him only seconds to decide he didn't like this man. I picked him up and held him close to me for fear that he might go for the horse, which carried this objectionable person, and be trampled underfoot. I had no doubt that Nigel was cruel enough to take delight in forcing his horse to kill my darling pet with his heavy iron hooves.

'Is it wise to be out alone at this time?' he asked sarcastically.

'I'm sure nobody would be interested in what little I have,' I replied, facing him boldly. The last thing I wanted to do was to give him the satisfaction of knowing that he frightened me.

'Where are you going?'

'I'm going home. Now if you would let me pass I think it's time I was on my way.'

'At least allow me to escort you back.'

'I'd prefer that you didn't,' I told him coldly.

'Nevertheless I shall,' he said, dismounting his horse. I had little option but to bear his company.

We walked in silence and it occurred to me that, outside the realms of the estate, I was faced with the hard, ruthless, demanding man I knew him to be.

'At last I have you to myself for a while,' he said. 'No prying servants around to see or listen to what I have to say to you.' I quelled the nervous fear I felt inside. Dusk was falling. Unusually, it was late for me to be taking Muffin for a walk or else I would have been safely indoors by now. It occurred to me that he had recently been careful to be seen with me only when I had Annabelle by my side. This was possibly because he was afraid that one or more of the servants, or maybe even his brother, might accidentally witness my rejection of his unwanted advances. He would be totally humiliated and become the laughing stock of the entire household. It was a risk he wouldn't want to take. My step quickened but he adjusted his own pace to keep up with me.

'Why are you hurrying so, Anna? Am I to assume that you are afraid of me?'

I stopped abruptly. The last thing I intended was that he should be under the impression that he frightened me.

'Most certainly not!' I said, with dignity. He placed both hands on my shoulders and held on tightly. Muffin, whom I was still holding close to me, growled and bared his teeth. Nigel's face turned black with anger and I thought he was about to strike my little pet. Instead he released his hold.

'Why are you so intent on ignoring me, Anna? I have so much to offer you. No other woman has ever had the effect that you have on me. From the first time I saw you at my brother's birthday party I've wanted you. Don't be a young fool. You have much to gain by showing me a little kindness. I can offer you everything you've ever dreamed of.'

'I doubt it,' I said, dryly. The arrogance of the man! It was true to his nature that he thought he only had to offer himself, and the promise of wealth, and any woman would fall over herself to be with him. Well here was one who wouldn't!

Before I could stop him he took my face roughly between his hands. 'I want you Anna. Believe me, I shall stop at nothing to have you.' His breath reeked of alcohol and I wanted to heave as I felt his cold, hard lips seeking my own.

'Get away! Get away from me!' I yelled, twisting my face away from him.

'I must have you! I will have you!' he commanded. There was no love, no tenderness in his attempt to kiss me, just an overwhelming desire to possess what he knew he couldn't have.

In the next instant Muffin had clamped his jaws around his bony wrist and was biting him so hard he yelled out. My fury and hatred of the man supplied me with the strength to cling tightly to Muffin whilst, at the same time, I used my free hand to give him a resounding slap across his face.

At first he was startled. Then his cruel lips narrowed into a thin line and his steely grey eyes blazed with anger. For a second I thought he was about to hit me with his clenched fist but then he took his emotions in check and calmed down a little. In that instant I turned on my heels and ran with all the speed I could muster, praying that he wouldn't mount his horse and come after me. I reached the narrow lane which took me past Mrs Gilmore's cottage, between a row of terraced houses and into the main street of the village. I contemplated knocking on her door but decided it was best for me to go straight home. It was only a few hundred yards further on and if I stopped now he might be waiting for me later when I had to return to my own cottage. Far better to get home and lock the doors and windows so that I was safe for the night. As I entered the main street I turned to look behind me. He'd gone. There was no sign of him. I breathed a sigh of relief.

Safe inside my little home I placed Muffin gently on the mat. Only then did my strength weaken. Trembling from head to foot I crumpled to the floor and dissolved into a flood of tears.

* * * * *

Much to my amazement I found myself walking as usual to Foxdale on the following morning. Before going to bed I'd made up my mind that there was no way I would pass through those gates ever again. But with the morning light had come a more rational way of thinking and I decided that Nigel Tremayne wasn't going to frighten me into abandoning Annabelle. In any case, it was only for a few more weeks. Only yesterday I'd heard the housekeeper, Mrs Pringle, say that Lady Charlotte would be returning within a month. When she did, my services would no longer be required. All I had to do in the meantime was to become very vigilant and make sure I was never in a situation where Nigel could find me alone. I just hoped and prayed that he would give up his attempts to win me over and return to London before too long. If I ignored him completely I felt sure he would come to understand that I had no interest in him whatsoever and eventually cease bothering me. Unfortunately it wasn't quite as simple as that.

* * * * *

If Nigel Tremayne was a hard, callous, arrogant brute, then his brother was the complete opposite. It was difficult to believe that they were from the same family. How could two brothers be the exact opposite of each other?

When I arrived at the schoolroom next morning, Annabelle was already there. Her nursery maid was playing with her until I arrived. We settled into our usual routine and before long Adrian appeared at the door. Annabelle ran forward to give him a hug but his eyes weren't on her, they were on me. He looked puzzled.

'Is everything alright, Miss Briggs?' he asked. Only then did I realise that I must have had a frightened expression on my face as he'd come through the door. Before I could see who it was entering the room I believed it might be Nigel. I forced a smile.

'Yes – yes, thank you. Perfectly alright, Mr Tremayne.' My hands were trembling. The door opened again and this time I dropped the rubber I was using on the blackboard and it went crashing to the floor. I needn't have worried; it was only Gladys, the nursery maid, returning.

Adrian stooped and picked up the rubber. He said nothing but there was concern in his eyes.

'I thought, maybe, you and Annabelle might like to accompany me to Lynhead today,' he said. 'I have some business to attend to and it occurred to me that you might both enjoy a day out. It's a long journey so it means we won't be back until this evening.'

Before I had time to reply Annabelle had let out squeals of delight. 'Oh, Uncle Adrian, yes, yes. Please say yes, Miss Briggs,' she begged, hugging me tight. 'Please say we can go.'

I have to admit to experiencing a sense of relief. It would mean that I could get away from Foxdale for today at least, and not spend every moment in fear of coming face to face with Nigel. I nodded and smiled at her enthusiasm. 'I don't see why not. It would make a pleasant change from lessons but I will have to make arrangement regarding my tearooms this afternoon,' I said, looking up at Adrian, 'and, if I could be so bold might we take Muffin, my dog, with us?'

'Of course we can,' he agreed, obviously delighted that I'd accepted his suggestion. I suspected that he was pleased to have his niece to himself for a while. Since Nigel's arrival there had been little chance for him to indulge her. As for myself, my nervous apprehension at coming face to face with Nigel temporarily disappeared. For today, at least, I wouldn't have that to contend with him. I knew that sooner or later I would have to confront him but I would deal with that when it happened. Tomorrow was another day and by then I would, quite possibly, have settled down again and be able to regard his actions of the night before with the contempt they deserved. For now, though, I allowed myself the luxury of feeling excited by the idea of a day out with Annabelle and her uncle. I looked forward to seeing Lynhead again, too.

* * * * *

The carriage, pulled by four beautiful horses, sped along the rough uneven roads to the coast. It all seemed a little unreal. Never in a thousand years could I have imagined myself on a journey such as this. As a child I'd always admired this very carriage as it had passed me by with the family coat of arms displayed on either side; two doves on a shield with the motto 'Peace and Goodwill' inscribed beneath it. And now, here I was, seated inside surrounded by the luxurious comfort of burgundy red, deeply upholstered cushions. It was as if I found myself in another world and the nearest, no doubt, I would ever come to feeling like the Lady of the Manor. Thank goodness, I reflected, I was suitably dressed and had on one of my better gowns. Of course, it wasn't quite what a lady of the manor would wear but it was very neat and attractive and most acceptable. I didn't feel in the least out of place in it. Muffin sat on my lap, as pleased as I to have my company for a longer part of the day. Annabelle showered him with attention and kisses which pleased him no end.

When we had stopped briefly at the tearooms for me to organise Jenny and Maevis and to collect Muffin it occurred to me that he had never seen Adrian before. I was curious to see his reaction to him, bearing in mind his immediate dislike of Nigel on the previous evening. I needn't have worried. He took to Adrian immediately, treating him like a long-lost friend. I could see, too, that Adrian liked and respected animals, quite unlike his brother who appeared to have no respect for anyone or anything.

We had a pleasant journey. The two hours it took us to reach the coast went by so quickly. There were times when we sat in silence, all of us admiring the passing countryside. At other times we talked of all manner of things. In the quieter moments I reflected on my childhood and recalled my first encounter with Adrian and his brother. It seemed so many years ago. I glanced across the carriage. He was a good-looking man and had a kindness in his features which was totally absent on Nigel's face. I wondered what he would say if he knew that I had been the young girl he'd rescued from his brother's clutches on that day so long ago by the lake. I looked out across the fields then back at him again. I could quite understand how I'd fallen for him, in my girlish way. There was an air of gentle strength about him. A nobility and authoritive manner which suited him to his station in life. At the same time it wasn't marred by arrogance or cruelty and I sensed in him a compassion for his fellow man and all creatures around him.

I realised I was staring at him. Then, to my horror, I caught his reflection in the window and realised he was looking at me. He had seen me studying him. He turned his head and looked straight into my eyes, the twinkle of a smile in his own. My cheeks suddenly felt warm. I was embarrassed that he'd caught me so blatantly looking at him and turned aside to watch the scenery pass by hoping that he would think nothing of it. It was too much of a temptation, however, to glance at the reflection in the window on my own side. To my discomfort I found that his eyes were still on me, an expression of deep interest revealed in them. Being the man he was, he had no wish to add to my embarrassment, I'm sure, and so he turned his attentions to Annabelle and the moment passed.

We had a wonderful day. Whilst Adrian attended to his business, Annabelle and I walked round the town and visited the shops. We ended up in the small tearooms where I'd first seen Annabelle from the window. Adrian joined us there later. He asked me, as we were in the area, if there was anyone in particular I should like to visit or any place I'd like to go. I could honestly say that there wasn't but I thought how kind and considerate it was of him to make the suggestion.

We left Lynhead for our return journey in the late afternoon. We were all tired. It had been a busy and exciting day. Even Muffin dozed off to sleep beside me. He slipped lazily from my lap onto the velvet-covered seat and stretched himself out contentedly. This, I felt, was definitely not to be allowed.

'Leave him there,' Adrian said, as I moved to lift him back onto my lap. 'He looks so comfortable. Don't disturb him.'

'You're very kind. Thank you,' I said, and left my adored pet to indulge in his moment of pure luxury.

For a while we sat talking together and Annabelle excitedly told her uncle all that we'd been doing, during the day, in his absence. He showed great interest in all she told him and I admired the way in which he made her feel just as important as any grown up. So often, especially in the upper classes, I'd heard tell that the children had 'to be seen and not heard' and that their opinions were never taken into account. Clearly, Adrian didn't hold with this idea and regarded children as little adults who should always be taken seriously.

After a time, there was a lull in the conversation. Annabelle was sitting next to her uncle on the opposite side of the carriage. Her little face looked tired and she yawned once or twice. I could see she was ready to fall asleep. To my surprise she suddenly moved over to my side and snuggled up next to me, placing her head on my shoulder. Within seconds she was asleep. Gently, I lifted her onto my lap and cradled her in my arms so that she could relax comfortably. When I looked up, Adrian had a gentle, affectionate smile on his face.

'She's very fond of you,' he stated.

'And I am very fond of her,' I told him. 'She's a dear little girl. She reminds me of …' For a moment I almost forgot myself and who I was talking to. I'd been about to say that she reminded me of her mother, Cathy, when she was her age. He didn't pursue the point and I was thankful that he didn't ask me who it was she reminded me of.

With Annabelle asleep on my lap and Muffin stretched out beside me, we lapsed into a very relaxed atmosphere. I found it easy to talk with Adrian. He treated me as an equal, not as someone beneath his own station in life. There was no touch of snobbery about him, no sense at all that he regarded others in any way more or less worthy than himself. As we talked, it was more like talking to a friend rather than to the brother of the person who paid me, albeit temporarily, to look after his child each morning. Our topic of conversation covered many mutual interests. Professor Argyle had taught me well on many subjects and I was able to discuss and voice an opinion on almost anything that Adrian cared to talk about. When I spoke of Professor Argyle he asked me about my life in Lynhead. I was concerned he might ask me how I had come to be living with the Professor. But he didn't pry. Perhaps he assumed it wasn't any of his business.

I was quite surprised when he turned to talking of his own family and flattered that he felt he could do so without fear that I might pass what he said around the village. Unknown to him I already knew a lot of what he told me. The local gossips had never been slow to pass on information regarding the Tremayne household. But it seemed that even their constantly alert ears and eyes were unable to discover all that went on.

To my utmost surprise I learned that the late Sir Mortimer's wife, whom I had always considered to be dead was, in fact, very much alive and living somewhere in London with her fourth husband since her divorce from Adrian's father.

'I only learnt that particular piece of information from Nigel,' Adrian told me. 'When he pursued a more active political career he lived in London for a time and somehow or other he met up with her.'

'Have you no wish to see her yourself?'

'Frankly, no. I don't remember her at all. Nigel and I were very young when she left. She broke my father's heart. When they first met, by all accounts, he fell head over heels in love with her. However, her family wasn't very well 'connected', as they say. His parents, my grandparents, were absolutely against the match but he defied all reason and went ahead and married her anyway. She was, apparently, like a young, wild foal that needed taming. He thought he was the one who could do it.' He fell silent for a moment or two and stared out of the coach at the passing countryside. 'How wrong, he was,' he muttered. 'She wasn't the motherly sort,' he said, after a while. 'She was far too interested in partying and maintaining her social life.' He spoke without bitterness or resentment. 'At the time the whole business was hushed up; made easier by the fact that both my parents had been in London on a whirl of social engagements for several months. For the sake of my father's reputation it was made known locally that she had died suddenly from a viral infection. I didn't really know her, I was very young when she left but, from the rumours and stories that have flown around over the years, I can well imagine that Nigel is just like her as she was then and, from what I've heard, still is now.'

'Don't you ever wonder what she's like?'

His expression hardened just a little. 'I know what she's like. I can't deny the fact that she's my mother but, to be honest, I don't see that we have anything in common other than that. It was generally regarded that I took after my father's side of the family. Nigel bears far more resemblance to her, in many ways, than I do.'

He changed the subject then and I was pleased. Talk of his mother had dampened his previously good humour and left him subdued. It wasn't long, though, before the smile returned to his face and he began to tell me of his reasons for visiting Lynhead.

I discovered that, contrary to my impression that Foxdale was the only property owned by the Tremaynes, Adrian had invested in several large farms both in North Devonshire and in Dorset. These belonged entirely to him and had nothing to do with his brother. All his life he'd been keenly interested in animals and the land. When his father died, leaving him a considerable personal inheritance, he bought the properties because he considered them to be a good investment. A manager and various staff were installed in each of them to ensure that things ran smoothly and, he told me, he visited them whenever it was possible. From what he said it would appear he took a great interest in all the people who worked for him. There was much to do in the way of administration but he enjoyed it enormously. It had been because of an urgent need to see one of the farm managers that he'd been prompted to make this particular journey. In meeting the man in Lynhead he halved his own journey and saved a great deal of time.

He seemed quite happy to discuss all of this with me and I was both honoured and privileged that he felt comfortable enough in my company to do so.

By the time we arrived back in Thursledown it was almost dark. He insisted on taking me to the door of my cottage and waited until I was safely inside before telling the coachman to drive on. By then Annabelle had stirred from her sleep. Bleary eyed, she waved goodbye to me as I watched from the tearooms window.

It had been a wonderful day; interesting and certainly different. All thoughts and fears of Nigel had, for a while, left my mind. But now I was back home again and tomorrow I would, quite probably, have to face him once more. It wasn't an encounter I looked forward to.

* * * * *

James told me, when I saw him, that Nigel had returned to London. When he saw how profoundly relieved I was I had to explain my fears to him and what had happened just a few evenings before when Muffin and I had been out walking. He was furious. I think he would have thrown all caution to the wind there and then if Nigel had been around. He would, I felt sure, have confronted him over his appalling behaviour and risked losing his home, his job, everything he owned and any possibility of a reference to enable him to get future employment. I was touched by his loyalty to me but the last thing I wanted was for him and his mother to be made homeless because of me. I managed to calm him down and make him see sense. Nothing would be achieved by a confrontation with Nigel. I made him promise that if and when he returned he would say nothing. Reluctantly, he agreed.

Life settled back into a calm sense of normality and my routine with Annabelle went on as usual. The only difference, I noticed, was that Adrian stopped to talk with me more often when Annabelle wasn't with me. Sometimes it was for only a few moments. Sometimes we would talk for, perhaps, ten minutes or more. I came to the conclusion that he had enjoyed our conversation on the way home from Lynhead, just as I had, and that he liked to think of me as a friend despite the difference in our way of life. Once or twice I came across him walking casually down the drive when I was on my way home and on several occasions I went into the tearooms of an afternoon to find him and Annabelle sitting at the table by the window. On days when it was busy I wasn't able to give them much of my attention but he didn't seem to mind and gave me the impression that they were there purely for Annabelle's sake.

'She's always asking me to bring her here,' he said. 'She's very fond of you and I think she's fascinated by all the ornaments you have around the tearoom.'

'And I want to see Muffin,' she piped in. This, of course meant that they had to come through into my kitchen because Muffin had to stay out in the back yard, unless it was pouring with rain in which case he remained upstairs in my sitting room. After a few visits, at my suggestion, they dispensed with seating themselves at the table in the window and came straight into the kitchen instead. They had tea and scones while I worked and Annabelle was able to play with Muffin to her heart's content for an hour or so. I was never sure when they would call in for tea but I found myself looking forward to their visits even though I saw Annabelle, and very often Adrian, every morning. The only problem with this was that James often came to see me of an afternoon when he had some free time. Sooner or later, surely, he was bound to turn up when my visitors were there.

Strangely enough he never did.

* * * * *

The time was fast approaching when Lady Charlotte would return home. I knew then that everything would change. I should no longer be needed to tutor Annabelle in the mornings and I doubted that Adrian would be able to bring her to see me quite so often. If they came at all, they would be accompanied by Lady Charlotte and would take tea in the tearooms just like any other customer. I wondered what his feelings for Lady Charlotte were. Did he look forward to her return? Had he missed her presence at the manor?

Why was I asking myself these questions? It was none of my business. I put them out of my mind straightaway. I couldn't hold back a slight feeling of regret, though, that when his cousin returned he would no longer see me as a friend whom he could talk to. He would have no need of me once she was back at Foxdale.

* * * * *

The time came, as was inevitable, when I was no longer needed at the manor. Lady Charlotte returned to Foxdale, fully recovered and apparently no worse for wear after her accident. If anything, she looked as if she'd been away on holiday. For a week after she came back I stayed on to tutor Annabelle but the situation very soon became quite untenable. Her time away certainly hadn't done anything to alter her disposition. If anything, she was even more haughty and supercilious than ever. I felt she was watching me all the time, ready to take fault with anything I might be teaching Annabelle. She spent far more time in the schoolroom than was necessary so that, in the end, I had no option but to speak with Adrian.

'Now that Lady Charlotte has returned and is fit and well again, I think it's time I went back to my own affairs,' I told him. 'I feel I've neglected many of my customers at the tearooms over the past few weeks.'

Was it disappointment I detected in his face? Whatever it was, it was only a fleeting impression before it was replaced with a smile.

'I can't thank you enough for all you've done,' he said. 'I quite understand your desire to get back to your own responsibilities and, of course, Lady Charlotte, I'm sure, is anxious to resume her duties.' I turned to leave and he walked across the room to open the door for me. 'We shall miss you,' he added. 'I know Annabelle will be sorry not to see you each morning.'

'I shall miss coming here,' I told him, truthfully. 'Perhaps I will see you both at my tearooms from time to time.'

'You will, indeed, Miss Briggs. Wild horses won't keep us away,' he laughed, staring deeply into my eyes. I was struck by the depth of colour in them.

'May I call you Anna?' he asked, suddenly.

'Why, yes, of course. I'd be pleased if you would,' I told him. I turned and crossed the hall, conscious all the while of his eyes on me. Out of curiosity I wanted to turn around but before I reached the stairs I heard the drawing room door close as he shut it behind him.

* * * * *

I settled back into my normal routine attending to my own business. Apart from my talk with Sally Tendersall, I hadn't acquired, as I'd hoped, any further information with regard to events surrounding Cathy's death.

Lucille and Graham were together the next time they came to see me. After my conversation with her, a short time before, I half wondered if there would be a strained atmosphere between them. But to the outside world, at least, they were as loving and close as they had ever been. As they came in, Lucille silently implored me with her eyes not to mention her previous visit. Perhaps, then, she had discovered her worries to be unfounded.

We spent a pleasant hour together talking in the main about inconsequential matters of interest to us all. 'We must have a day shopping,' she said, as they left. 'It's been so long since we spent time together and there's much I want to talk to you about.'

I could see that Graham interpreted this as 'women's gossip' but I sensed there was more to her words. Gossip was the last thing on her mind. She had something far more serious she wanted to discuss. No doubt it involved him.

I walked with them to the gate. As I did so a horse and carriage came down the street towards us. It was Adrian with Annabelle and Lady Charlotte by his side. The horse slowed to a sedate walking pace and stopped just a few yards from us. Adrian jumped down and tethered the reins to a ring on the wall. Quite formally, he wished me 'good afternoon' as he helped first Annabelle and then Lady Charlotte to alight. He was less friendly than I had become accustomed to, no doubt for the benefit of his cousin. Annabelle was entirely different. Excitedly she ran up to me calling out 'hello'. As I bent down to speak with her, Lady Charlotte immediately called her to her side and reprimanded her for running ahead. It was clear that they'd not be coming into the cosiness of my kitchen on this occasion.

I turned my attention back to Lucille and Graham. It was then that I was struck by the expression on Graham's face. Lucille had her back to him but his whole attention was on Lady Charlotte. I glanced at her as she walked up the path behind Adrian just in time to catch the brief backward glance she cast in Graham's direction. To my surprise, I saw there was recognition in her eyes. More than that, there was a softness in them that I didn't think she was capable of. It was the briefest of encounters but when she saw that I'd noticed her she turned away. By the time I looked back at Graham he was helping Lucille into their horse and trap.

How strange. If Graham and Lady Charlotte were acquainted, then why hadn't they acknowledged each other? Perhaps my impression had been wrong.

CHAPTER 19

'I miss seeing you at the house each morning,' James told me one afternoon as he sat in my kitchen. 'Ma says you're very welcome any time. In fact she asked me to invite you to supper one evening.'

I thanked him. He and his mother had been so kind to me. I knew how much she cared for Annabelle and while I had been her tutor I'd taken her on several occasions to visit the old lady. Once or twice I'd detected a note of interest in Mrs Bilbrook's voice when she spoke about James and his future. Something in her tone made me suspect she harboured the idea that I might, one day, become his wife. I really didn't regard James in that light. He was a dear friend but I just couldn't imagine that I would one day marry him. I think he suspected how I felt, probably because I avoided all intimate contact with him and kept our conversations very much on general terms.

'I would love to come to supper,' I told him, now. 'Would Sunday be convenient?'

His face lit up. 'I'm sure it would. I'm afraid, because I'm working, I won't be able to join you until much later but I shall be able to escort you home. I'll let Ma know.'

We spent a pleasant hour or so talking. Muffin, always pleased to see him, encouraged him to go into the garden and play a while. I watched them through the window. He was such a nice person, so kind and considerate. Why, then, couldn't I think of him in a more romantic light? It was what he wanted, I felt sure. This impression was confirmed when I visited Mrs Bilbrook on the following Sunday.

She was an excellent cook and we enjoyed a really tasty supper before she broached the subject with me.

'James is very fond of you, my dear,' she began.

'And I am very fond of him,' I told her. Her face beamed. I could see what was going through her mind. 'But I don't love him,' I added, immediately. When I said this her expression changed to one of disappointment.

'I had hoped you might make a match,' she said, after a moment or two. 'He clearly loves you and he'd make a very good husband.'

I placed a gentle hand on her arm in an effort to ease her disappointment. 'I know. I've often thought that of him. He's a dear, kind man but I've always imagined that I'd feel something more for the man I marry.'

'Not all women love their husband on their wedding day, dear. That can come in time.' She paused to study my face. 'Many young women are married long before they reach your age.'

Was she telling me that time was running out; that I should find myself a husband before too long or I would be left on the shelf? It was of no consequence to me. Far better that I should not marry at all than to marry someone I didn't truly love.

'I know what you're saying,' I said, gently, but you see, I don't believe that one should marry for the sake of marrying. When I do take a husband it will be because I love him more than life itself; not purely for convenience sake. I've learnt to stand on my own two feet. I have my business and I don't need to rely on anyone to look after me.'

'Your principles are very commendable, my dear, but such romantic notions have little to do with reality. Few women experience the sort of love you suggest when they first marry. There would be an awful lot of spinsters in the world if they all wanted to fulfil the dream you envisage.'

I felt she was trying to persuade me away from my ideals. It irritated me a little. Nothing she could say would encourage me to consider marriage to James. It occurred to me in that moment that the whole purpose of her invitation to me had been so that she could speak for her son. Did he know what had been in her mind? If so, my opinion of him went down a little. Why hadn't he had the courage to talk with me himself? On the other hand, perhaps he was unaware of her intentions and would, justifiably, be as angry as I that she had brought up the subject and had embarrassed me in so doing.

'I suppose, because Cathy was your sister, he sees much of her in you,' she said, of a sudden.

My anger dissipated and interest took its place. What had Cathy to do with any feeling James' might have for me?

'I don't understand,' I said.

'Well, dear, James was once very much in love with your sister Cathy.'

'But he's never said anything to me. I had no idea.'

'It was long after you left the village. He never speaks of her now because it broke his heart when she died, despite the fact that she had borne Nigel Tremayne's child. When she found she was pregnant, after she'd been raped, James wanted to marry her; to give the child his name. But she would have none of it. She was determined that, in some way, she would make Nigel pay for his wicked deed. When she realised that she had proof that Annabelle was his child she was determined and hell bent on the idea that her daughter would have a better life than she had experienced as a child. She was obsessed with the idea that she should be brought up in the Tremayne household. Once the idea had formed in her mind she became utterly determined. It would appear that the old man, Sir Mortimer, was equally determined that his son should pay for the misery he had inflicted on her.' She paused. 'By all accounts he became very fond of Annabelle,' she added, on a softer note, as an afterthought.

I was silent. So, James had loved my sister. If only she had done as he had asked and married him. Quite possibly she would be alive today.

'Mrs Gilmore told me what happened,' I volunteered, 'but I had no idea that James had asked Cathy to marry him. I had no idea that they even knew each other except that he would have known that she was my little sister.'

'Well, there you are, my dear. I can only tell you the truth. Cathy, I believe, was the only girl he has truly loved in his life – until you came back, of course. I know that his feelings for you are more than just as a friend and I hate to see him hurt again which is why I felt the need to speak with you. But, please, don't mention this conversation to him. He'd be most upset.'

So, James didn't know of her intentions. He was unaware that she was trying to pave the way towards a marriage between us.

'I won't tell him,' I told her, 'but I do think I should go home now.'

'No! No, please don't go. James told me he would escort you home after he finishes his work. Please don't go. He'll wonder why you've left so early.'

I agreed to stay. I also determined, in my own mind, that I would make every attempt to keep James at a distance in the future and not see too much of him, much as I liked him as a friend. Quite how I was to achieve that, I didn't know.

When he took me home later I tried to keep the conversation light and made no mention of the discussion I'd had with his mother. He kissed me warmly on the cheek as we parted and I hurried indoors, excusing myself by saying that I was very tired. In truth, I was anxious not to prolong the time alone with him.

* * * * *

A week or two later I received a message from Mrs Bilbrook to say that Annabelle would be spending the following day with her. She asked if I'd like to join them.

As it happened, it was the same day that Lucille and I had arranged to go into Castleford shopping. Although I would have liked to spend time with Annabelle, part of me was relieved that I had an excuse not to go. Knowing what I did about James's relationship with Cathy, and the fact that he cared for me, the strain of being in his company and trying to maintain our friendship on just that level was beginning to have its effect. He wouldn't be at the cottage when Annabelle was there. At least, I didn't think he would. Even so, I found it difficult to contemplate a day in Mrs Bilbrook's company without either of us making reference to our previous conversation. It wasn't something I wanted to discuss with her any more.

Lucille knew me well. She called for me in the horse and trap early on the following morning. She knew at once that I wasn't myself.

'Are you alright?' she asked, almost before I'd had time to settle myself in the seat beside her. I assured her that I was, but she didn't seem convinced. 'You look a little peaky,' she commented.

'I'm just tired,' I said, and forced myself to give her a bright smile. 'I've been looking forward to today. We haven't spent enough time with each other lately.'

'You're always very welcome to visit us,' she said, as she flicked the reins and the horse moved off at a trot. 'It's been quite ages since you came to Nether Wilmslow.'

How could I tell her that my absence had been deliberate? Since Graham had tried to foister his unwanted attentions on me I'd felt loathe to place myself, too often, in his company, whether Lucille was there or not. The idea of staying overnight, again, at their home was quite out of the question. However, I couldn't tell Lucille that, nor could I tell her my reasons for staying away. I changed the subject and we discussed what shops we wanted to visit in Castleford and the items we each wanted to buy.

By the end of the day we were very tired and our feet ached. Lucille suggested that we go to a small tearooms she knew of in Jassica Road. I followed her, at a loss to know where in the town we were. We passed through a dirty passageway and came out into a narrow lane. There were one or two shops and the tearooms which was about a hundred yards further on.

We stepped inside to the tinkle of the bell over the door and I followed as Lucille made her way to the back of the building where there was another room full of tables and chairs. The tables all had blue gingham cloths on them and a small vase of flowers in the centre of each. They were all prepared ready for afternoon tea. The wide, latticed windows along the back of the room overlooked a park, towards the centre of which was a pretty lake surrounded by footpaths and trees. Beyond the park, the glorious open countryside stretched as far as the eye could see.

We sat down at a table by the window and admired the view. There was a touch of autumn in the air and the leaves on the trees were just beginning to fade. Across the park and fields our eyes were met with magnificent hues of red and gold.

The waitress took our order for tea and cakes. Like everything around her she was immaculate. She was dressed in a white starched cap and apron over a plain black dress. Her shoes, which just peeped out from beneath the hem of her skirts, shone to perfection. I couldn't fault the service we received nor could I fault the tea and cakes which were clearly home-made and quite delicious. We enjoyed a very pleasant hour, taking our time over tea and talking together. It gave us the opportunity to rest our weary legs.

When the time came for us to leave, Lucille insisted on paying. I resisted this strongly and insisted that it should be my treat but she would have none of it. When the waitress presented us with the bill she quickly took it from her hand before I had a chance to do so. Not wishing to create a scene I let her have her own way. It was as well that I did.

'You collect our things together,' she told me. 'I'll go and see to this.'

She found her way to the front of the shop whilst I gathered together all the bags and parcels we'd collected during our morning around the shops. I was about to leave and follow her when I happened to glance out of the window.

Across the park, walking slowly around the lake and coming towards me I saw two figures, a man and a woman. I gave them no more than a perfunctory glance as I turned to make my way to where Lucille would be waiting. Then with a sudden sense of shock I turned back to look at them again. There was something very familiar about them both. As I saw them more clearly it dawned on me who they were.

I watched closely as Graham sauntered slowly towards me, unaware of my presence. By his side, holding tightly onto his arm, was Lady Charlotte Grieves.

It took me only a second to realise that they were making for this very tearooms. I hurried to where Lucille was just tightening the drawstring on her bag.

'Are you ready?' I asked, trying hard not to appear too keen for us to be on our way. She nodded and smiled at me.

'I've really enjoyed today,' she told me as I opened the door. 'It's been so long since we spent a day together like this. We must do it more often.' We both stepped out into the street where, unfortunately, the tea-pots and ornaments in the window caught her eye. I wanted to say, 'Hurry, Lucille, we must get home,' but it would have aroused her suspicion. Instead I moved further along in the hope that she wouldn't linger too long. Thankfully, she didn't and we were, very soon, well away from the area and any possibility of coming face to face with Graham and Lady Charlotte.

We made our way back to the stables where we'd left the horse and trap to be attended to whilst we did our shopping. At last we were on the road home and I breathed a sigh of relief.

'Is Graham at his office, today?' I asked when, eventually, I'd calmed down inside.

'No, he isn't,' she replied, with a smile. 'He had some urgent business in Lissingham. He won't be back until much later,' she said innocently.

I didn't pursue the subject. I knew there was little point. Clearly, he had deceived her into thinking that he was elsewhere. Presumably she hadn't mentioned to him that we would be shopping in Castleford or, I was sure, he wouldn't have taken the risk of being seen with Lady Charlotte. For a while I sat in silence contemplating the situation. Without doubt I'd been right in my assumption that Graham and Lady Charlotte were acquainted when I saw the look which passed between them outside my cottage. This being so, could it be that each and every time she left Annabelle with Mrs Bilbrook, she had arranged to meet Graham somewhere? I would dearly have liked to know what he was doing on those days. I doubted that he was in his local office. Quite probably, like today, he'd told Lucille he had business elsewhere.

Another thought passed through my mind. Several weeks ago, before Lady Charlotte had returned to Foxdale, he had been away on business for several days according to Lucille. Had he been with Lady Charlotte then?

A feeling of depression descended upon me. Not for myself but on behalf of Lucille. If what I suspected was true, her husband was deceiving her. I wanted to believe that there was some other reason for his meeting with Lady Charlotte but everything pointed to the fact that my suspicions were correct. Knowing, as I did from experience, that he was capable of trying to seduce other women, and after what Lucille had told me just a few weeks ago, I failed to see how I could be wrong. But what was I to do? I could hardly tell her what I suspected and why. It would break her heart. Yet if I said nothing, sooner or later she would find out anyway. I decided that, for the time being, I would remain silent. As it happened it didn't, in the end, fall on my shoulders to tell her the truth.

* * * * *

CHAPTER 20

The weeks drifted by and nothing very extraordinary happened. I was careful to take special note of any time that Lady Charlotte left Annabelle in the care of Mrs Bilbrook.

Adrian called to see me on several occasions, much to my surprise particularly as he was alone.

'I do hope you don't mind me calling on you like this,' he said, the very first time he visited me without Annabelle or Lady Charlotte with him. 'I miss our little chats in your cosy kitchen. I'm afraid I no longer have the excuse of bringing Annabelle to see Muffin but if you would prefer me not to visit you I shall quite understand.' How was he to know that my heart had begun to pound furiously beneath my ribs from the moment he'd set foot in the door?

After the formal way in which he had greeted me when I'd last seen him, on the day when Lucille and Graham had visited me, I accepted that it was unlikely I'd see much of him in the future. It didn't stop me missing his company, though, and the cosy, companionable talks we'd had in my kitchen and at other times, in rare moments, at the manor.

'Of course I don't mind,' I told him, truthfully. 'I'm pleased to see you.'

'Are you, Anna?' His eyes held a hidden question and I wondered what was going through his mind. 'I know James Bilbrook comes to see you,' he said, as he seated himself in a chair opposite my table. 'I've made quite sure he's working this afternoon. I wouldn't like him to find me here.' Was that because he was James' employer or because he was aware that James and I were good friends? He watched with interest as I went about my chores.

'I feel so at peace here,' he said, at last. 'So relaxed.'

I smiled. 'I'm pleased to hear that. But, surely, you relax in your own home? Foxdale is such a beautiful place and you have everything you could wish for.' I found myself marvelling at the fact I could talk to him in such a way. Our backgrounds were so vastly different and yet we were at one with each other. We each understood, perfectly, the other's point of view and how the other person felt even though we'd grown up in entirely different social circumstances.

'Not quite everything.' His voice was low. I barely heard his muttered words. What did he mean? Before I had time to boldly ask, his mood lightened and he began to talk of other things. In particular, he spoke of Lady Charlotte and her return to Foxdale. It crossed my mind that, despite what I'd heard to the contrary, maybe it was she whom he hankered after. If this was so then he was in for a disappointment. Clearly, she had no feelings for him if, as I suspected, she was carrying on a covert liaison with Graham. But surely, if it was a secure financial future that she wanted, as Simon Pendleton had intimated, it would, in her eyes, be far more to her advantage to endear herself to Adrian or his brother. Why, then, was she seeing Graham? Admittedly, he had a very successful business and was moderately well off, especially after his marriage to Lucille, but even in her wildest dreams she could never imagine he was as wealthy, or had such social standing as the Tremaynes. Could it be that Lady Charlotte was actually in love with him?

I put aside this puzzling question. Here, in my little kitchen, I experienced a deep contentment talking with Adrian. I wanted nothing to spoil it. It was a contentment which I could never remember having experienced before, not even with James despite the fact that I enjoyed his company so much. The time passed so quickly. I was barely aware of all the baking I was doing as we talked. When, at last, he stood up to leave I experienced a sense of deep regret and wished he could stay longer. He told me that he really had to get back to the manor but he promised faithfully that he'd call again. After he'd gone I found myself looking forward to the next time when it would be just the two of us, together. That night I lay awake for quite some time which was most unusual for me. Normally I was so tired I would fall asleep the very moment my head touched the pillow. On this occasion, however, try as I may I couldn't stop myself from going over and over, again, all that we had talked about during the afternoon. But most of all I recalled the features of his face and the sparkle which lit up his deep blue eyes when he laughed.

My contentment was shattered a few days later when Nigel returned and the very thing I feared most became reality.

* * * * *

I knew he was back. James told me he arrived in a drunken stupor late one evening having lost a small fortune at the gambling tables.

I did hope that I wouldn't see him. After all, now that I no longer had reason to go to Foxdale there was really no need for our paths to cross; or so I thought. I was wrong.

The tray in my hands almost dropped to the floor one morning when I came out of the kitchen and into the tearoom to find him seated by the bay window. It was early and only one or two other customers had arrived. He grinned when he saw me.

My stomach churned as I recalled our last meeting. I wanted nothing to do with him. With only a slight incline of my head to acknowledge his presence I continued with what I was doing. Jenny and Maevis were there to attend to anything he wanted. If only it could have been as simple as that but he was determined to have my attention.

'I've missed you Anna,' he said, in a raised voice as I made my way to the far end of the room with the tray. All eyes turned to look at me. Thank goodness there were only a few people seated at the tables. I suppressed my embarrassment and placed the tray on the sideboard then returned to where he sat.

'I trust you had an enjoyable stay in London, Mr Tremayne,' I said to him, trying to make light conversation. 'Forgive me if I continue with my work, I have a great deal to get on with today.' Without waiting for a response I turned and headed towards the kitchen but he would have none of it. He stood up, scraping the chair along the floor. I, like everyone else, couldn't help but notice that his balance was unsteady. A moment later my suspicions were confirmed when he staggered towards me and I smelt the repulsive odour of alcohol on his breath. Even at this hour of the day, he was drunk.

'Don't go Anna,' he mumbled. 'I came here esh-peshurlly to see you.'

I could see that his words were creating a great deal of interest amongst those present. One lady was even poised with her cup halfway to her lips, waiting for what was to come next.

'I think maybe you should go,' I told him. 'I really have nothing to say to you and you are disturbing my customers.'

'Then I'll come and talk to you out there,' he said, casting his eyes in the direction of the kitchen.

'I don't think so Mr Tremayne. Now if you don't mind, I have to get on.' I didn't wait for a response. I turned and hurried away and, once inside, closed the kitchen door firmly behind me. If I could have bolted it from the inside I would have done so. To my relief he made no attempt to follow. Presumably he decided it was wiser to leave, because a moment or so later when Jenny came to collect an order for a customer she told me he was gone.

Instinct told me that it wasn't the last time I would see him. It was futile to imagine that his behaviour had been a one-off situation and that he'd leave me alone. My fears were proved correct. Almost every day he came to the village for some reason or another. He didn't come to my tearooms, for which I was thankful, but I couldn't shake off the uneasy feeling that he was watching me.

The next time that Adrian came to see me I was in two minds as to whether I should mention his brother's behaviour. I decided against it. No doubt sooner or later Nigel's infatuation with me would be replaced with an attachment to some other poor unsuspecting woman. It wouldn't last, I felt sure, and all the time he didn't actually bother me and make his presence known, I could cope with it.

I very nearly told James what was in my mind but then thought better of it. Perhaps I was being unnecessarily concerned. Nigel didn't actually talk to me again for several weeks and I began to think that, maybe, I had become just a little paranoid about the situation. After all, maybe he did have good reason to visit the village so frequently. Maybe I was reading far more into his actions than was reasonable. I began to settle down again and ignored any sighting of him when he came near to my cottage.

Over the course of time I began to notice a subtle change in Adrian. His visits were less frequent and we seemed to lose the easy going relaxed atmosphere I had so loved in his company. This worried me. Had I done something to offend or upset him? Surely he would have told me if this was the case. I concluded, in the end, that I had to ask him when I next had the opportunity.

Weeks went by and I saw nothing of him. He no longer came to see me on his own and even his visits to the tearooms with Annabelle and Lady Charlotte became less frequent. On these rare occasions when I did see him he was formal and almost unapproachable which at first I took to be expected because of the company he was in. It was only when I realised that he would never look directly at me that I began to suspect the something was very, very wrong and that, perhaps, he no longer regarded me as the friend he had once seemed so keen to know. I was deeply saddened by his attitude. There was, however, nothing I could do about it unless the opportunity arose when I could speak with him; a situation which was becoming less and less likely.

* * * * *

Everything came to a head one evening about three weeks later. I was returning home from a visit to Mrs Gilmore and it was getting quite late. My conscience had got the better of me that day because it had been many weeks since I last saw her and I knew she was always keen to have news of Annabelle. She waved to me from the door and I hurried along the lane to the main street of the village. As I passed between the row of terraced cottages I was aware of a horse's hooves walking slowly behind me. Muffin was walking on ahead so I called him to my side then I stepped back to let horse and rider pass. As I did so I looked up. A gasp of alarm escaped my lips and at the same time I heard a low rumble in Muffin's throat. The horse was almost on top of me but Nigel had no intention of passing. It became obvious that he had known I was visiting Mrs Gilmore and had waited for me to leave her cottage before following me down the lane. I wondered if she had seen him from her sitting room window. I doubted it. Dusk was fast approaching and her curtains would most probably be shut. I remained silent but took hold of Muffin's collar in case he had it in mind to snap at the horse's hooves.

'Leave me alone,' I said, bluntly. 'Go away, Mr Tremayne. I want nothing to do with you. I thought I made that quite clear at our last encounter.'

He grinned, a smirking, supercilious grin. My hands trembled, as did the rest of me. I had an uneasy feeling that he was, metaphorically speaking, about to pounce like a black panther. He was gloating, though for what reason I had no idea. It was as if he knew he had me just where he wanted me.

'Oh yes. I remember our last encounter very well,' he said, 'and I believe I told you then, as I'm telling you now, that I would stop at nothing to have you. I want you, Anna, and I shall have you. I'm used to getting my own way with women and I don't intend making an exception where you're concerned.'

'Then you're about to receive a great disappointment,' I told him. 'I have no intention, whatsoever, of complying with your wishes. I don't like you, Mr Tremayne. I never have liked you. So you can forget any ideas you might have that we could be associated in any way.' Blunt words indeed. I marvelled at my own ability to be so strong, particularly in such circumstances. I was experiencing a feeling of true fear in the knowledge that we were alone in the lane and it was becoming darker by the moment as night-time fell.

I gathered Muffin close to me and prepared to walk, boldly, away. His next words sent a cold chill rippling down my spine.

'I think, when you hear what I have to say, you may well wish to reconsider your decision, my dear. I'm afraid that you leave me no alternative but to give you an ultimatum! – Miss Briggs!'

There was something in the way he said my name. Had he discovered who I really was? Did he know that I was Cathy's sister? I stepped back, shocked and confused. My head was spinning. Clearly, my thoughts showed on my face.

He smiled, a long, slow, twisted smile which gave rise to a triumphant expression. 'You appear surprised, my dear.

Did you really believe that you could keep your little secret indefinitely?'

There was no point in denying it. My legs had become weak and my whole body trembled as I asked, 'H-how did you find out?'

'It was really very simple,' he replied. 'You see, some time ago I happened to meet up with a certain Richard Argyle, the son of a Cambridge University Professor. When you came as tutor to Annabelle for that short time and I learned that you had been taught by the acclaimed Professor Joseph Argyle, naturally I was interested. It took very little research on my part to discover who you really are and how you came to be accepted as a member of the Argyle family. I must congratulate you, Anna, on the way in which you've improved your status. Who would believe that you were once an ignorant little chit of a girl living in squalor not half a mile from the very place in which you now have your own business?'

A new, very great fear suddenly presented itself to me. Obviously he knew who I was and that Cathy was my sister. If, as I suspected, he had arranged her death, then I presented a potential threat to him because he would be forever afraid that I should learn the truth and attempt to do something about it. I looked around me. The lane was silent and empty. There was no one in sight, not even the odd person walking along the main street of the village which I could just see from where I stood. Even the terraced cottages looked deserted. I opened my mouth to speak but the muscles in my throat tightened with fear as I speculated whether he might have plans to dispose of me also. But that was not what he had in mind.

'As I said, I'm offering you an ultimatum.' He was calm and confident now, completely in command of the situation. 'I'm sure that you are fully aware that, as well as being my daughter, Annabelle is also your niece. I was curious, when I first saw you together, at the way you seem to get on so well but, of course, I can now understand why. She's your sister's child. No doubt you feel the need to compensate her in some way for the loss of her mother. I've noticed that you're very attached to her and she obviously adores you which is why I'm offering you the opportunity to watch her grow up with all the benefit of your loving care and guidance.'

I relaxed just a little. It seemed he didn't have thoughts of killing me after all. What, then, were his intentions? I wanted nothing more than to be a part of Annabelle's growing years but I sensed that the penalty for this pleasure would be high. When I didn't answer he stared hard into my eyes, a self-congratulating smirk twisting his cruel features. He was revelling in the blow he was about to strike. At last, he spoke.

'I want you to become my wife,' he said, simply. 'The very first day I saw you I made up my mind that it was you whom I wanted as mistress of Foxdale. No other woman has ever drawn me to thoughts of marriage as you do. I want you to marry me.'

Marry him! The very thought caused my stomach to churn. I felt sick.

'A-and if I won't?'

'Then Annabelle will never – ever – see you again.'

I trembled from head to foot. Just what did he mean? Was it a threat? Was it his intention to send Annabelle right away from Foxdale if I refused him? Or was it in his mind to rid himself of my presence once and for all; to arrange for me to have a 'convenient' accident in the same way that he'd killed Cathy. His face revealed nothing.

'I don't expect you to give me an answer immediately,' he said, 'but think about it for a few days. I'm fairly certain that you'll eventually come to the conclusion that you have nothing to gain by refusing my offer of marriage – and everything to lose,' he added, ominously.

He left me then. With a slow, deliberate motion, he placed one foot in the stirrup and rose up onto his horse's back. I stared at him blankly and was met with a supercilious, self-congratulating grin. Clearly he thought he'd won. Without further conversation he commanded the horse to walk on and, having turned into the village street, rode off at speed towards Foxdale.

I felt completely numb. It was as if every muscle in my body had ceased to function. I wouldn't – I couldn't – marry him. The very thought put life back into my motionless body and caused me to squirm inwardly. But if I didn't marry him it would be impossible for me to carry out Cathy's wish, made to Mrs Gilmore, that I should look after Annabelle and see that no harm ever came to her. Who could say what would become of me if I went against him in any way?

Dazed and confused, a million thoughts crashing through my brain, I turned and wandered slowly back to my home. Only when I was once more in the safety of my cottage did I allow all the strain and tension, which had built up inside me, to be released in a flood of tears. Muffin cuddled up, trying hard to console me as I lay on my bed and wept uncontrollably.

What had I let myself in for when I had returned to Thursledown village?

* * * * *

CHAPTER 21

My mind was in turmoil. At five o'clock the next morning I was up and dressed after a restless and troubled night. My head ached and I was bleary eyed from lack of sleep but I couldn't remain in bed, tossing and turning, any longer. To make matters worse I had Lucille on my doorstep long before Jenny and Maevis arrived.

She rushed in, flustered and upset and in a terrible state.

'Whatever is the matter?' I asked.

'I – I'm so sorry to call on you at such an early hour,' she apologised. There were tears in her eyes and I could see she was having difficulty in holding them back. I made her sit down and put the kettle on the hob to boil. When she'd composed herself a little she began by saying, 'It's Graham. Oh, Anna. We've been married for such a short time and now he says he's leaving me.' At this she burst into a flood of tears. 'Why? Why?' she cried. 'I don't understand. I love him so much and I thought we were happy.'

I was at a loss to find words to console her. Her revelation didn't come as a shock but then I could hardly tell her that I'd had my suspicions and had seen him and Lady Charlotte together.

'To make matters worse,' she went on, 'I discovered various letters amongst his private papers. He is in the most terrible debt. The house we live in, from what I can gather, is almost entirely owned, now, by the bank against loans which he's taken out since we were married. Every penny my father left to me has been frittered away. He took control of all my financial affairs after our marriage. He said it was something I shouldn't have to worry about. My inheritance went towards the purchase of our house at Nether Wilmslow and it was all placed in his name. Almost

everything I own has been taken by him and squandered.'
At this she broke into another outburst of tears and cried
uncontrollably. 'How could he do it to me, Anna? How
could he do it? I thought he loved me.'

I tried to find words to ease her pain. 'I'm sure he does,'
I said, placing an arm around her shoulder. But even to my
own ears I really didn't sound very convincing. 'There must
surely be an explanation for all of this. Have you spoken
with him?'

'No. He left last evening. We had the most terrible
argument. Oh, Anna. It was as if I didn't know him. He was
like a stranger to me. He told me he wouldn't be back.'

'Perhaps after a day or two, when he's had time to think,
he'll come home. I'm sure he'll regret his decision.'

Her eyes were so sad when she looked at me. 'No, I don't
think so. There's more, you see. I also found a bundle of
letters to him, clearly from a lady friend. She speaks to him
of love and waiting for the time when they can be together
for always. She signs herself quite simply, 'C'. There's no
address on the letters so I have no idea who she is or where
she has come from. I only know that he has given her every
indication that their future lies together.' This brought
forth another flood of tears. I wondered if I should tell
her about Lady Charlotte. On second thoughts I decided
against it. It would achieve nothing. 'My father was right,'
she said sadly, with a touch of irony. 'He never wanted me
to marry Graham. I couldn't see why he was so opposed to
our marriage at the time but I'm beginning to understand
now. He was a very wise old man, my father. I do so wish
that I'd listened to him. I suppose I was completely blinded
by my love for Graham and I didn't see him clearly for
the person he really is. There have been times when I've
wondered about things he's said or done but, until now, I've
refused to acknowledge that he isn't the person I thought I'd
married. I've ignored so many misdemeanours on his part

and convinced myself that I must be wrong. Now I have to face up to reality and acknowledge that my father was right. Graham isn't a very nice person.' Once again she went off into floods of tears; heartbreaking sobs which she couldn't control. I let her cry for as long as she needed to. There was little I could say. Nothing could change her situation and nothing I said would make any difference to the emotional pain she was experiencing. For a while my own problems were put aside as I tried to console her grief.

She spent the entire day with me, watching as I made bread and cakes and went about my chores. 'You're so lucky,' she said at one point. 'You have just yourself and Muffin to worry about. You own your own business and have no man to consider or be beholden to.'

How little she knew.

It was much later in the day when she came to the conclusion that she should return home. I told her that she was most welcome to stay with me overnight but she was keen to get back to Nether Wilmslow. By now she had calmed down a little and I was pleased to see a glimmer of a smile on her face as she left. My heart went out to her. She was such a lovely person and she didn't deserve in any way to be treated as Graham had treated her. It would take a long time for her pain to heal. I wondered if she would ever trust another man again.

Back in the kitchen my thoughts turned, once more, to my own problems and for a while Lucille was cast from my mind as the enormity of the decision I had to make overwhelmed me.

At the end of the day I knew that there was only one answer I could give Nigel. To refuse to marry him would not only bring possible danger to me but would also deprive Annabelle of the love and care that only I, as her aunt, could give her. Guilt would lay heavily on my shoulders for the rest of my life because I knew from my conversation with

Mrs Gilmore that it had been Cathy's dearest wish for me to look after her daughter and see that no harm would ever come to her.

* * * * *

It came as something of a surprise to me to learn that Lady Charlotte Grieves was still living at Foxdale. From what Lucille had told me I assumed that maybe she and Graham had run away together. Obviously not. A week or so later I discovered why.

It was Tuesday afternoon; a very wet afternoon which made people want to stay indoors. Consequently there were few customers in my tearooms and business was slack. I decided to leave Jenny and Maevis in charge and go out for a walk because, although it was wet, it was a pleasant enough day. Besides, I just felt the need for some fresh air and to be alone for a while. Naturally, I took Muffin with me.

I found myself walking through the village and out the other side towards Foxdale. It occurred to me that I hadn't seen Mrs Bilbrook for some weeks; not since she had told me of James's feelings towards me and how he had once been in love with Cathy. Presumably she never mentioned our conversation to him because he made no reference to it. He and I had settled back into our easy going friendship and I no longer felt any embarrassment in his presence so I decided that I would pay her an impromptu visit.

As I walked along, the ultimatum that Nigel had given me weighed heavily on my mind. I'd seen nothing of him since that evening but I knew that sooner or later he would be expecting a reply from me. It was a terrible decision to come to and one which I couldn't make lightly. In my heart I knew that there could only be one outcome but even so, I still desperately sought for a different solution to my dilemma. There was none. As far as I could see I had no alternative but to comply with Nigel's wishes and marry him. A heavy feeling of depression engulfed me and a knot tightened in my stomach. I could think of nothing more repulsive than to be married to such a man. But what choice had I? If I didn't marry him I would live, forever, in fear of my life. He wouldn't just let me go, I knew that. If I moved right away he would track me down because I presented a potential threat to him. And what about Annabelle? What did he mean by the words, 'Annabelle will never see you again'? If my life was in danger, then surely her life was even more at risk because she stood between him and the inheritance his father had left to her. In time, if she died, after she came of age and inherited from her grandfather, then everything she possessed would pass on to him as her next of kin. My only hope of protecting her from any future harm was for me to agree to this marriage. As I saw it, I had absolutely no choice.

I found myself outside Mrs Bilbrook's cottage without really being aware that I'd walked the distance from the village. I knocked on her door and after some moments she opened it. She was delighted and a little surprised to see me.

'Come in. Come in, my dear. What a lovely surprise. I'm so pleased to see you. Sit down and I'll put the kettle to boil.'

I sat in a comfortable old chair by the fire. While I waited for her to come back with the tea tray I recalled my last visit. How ironic that I had so steadfastly explained to Mrs Bilbrook that I could never consider marriage to a man unless I truly loved him. Yet here I was on the point of agreeing to marry a man I not only didn't love but whom I actually loathed. How was I to explain that to her? I decided that it might be better to say nothing for the time being. She and everyone else would know quite soon enough of my impending plans. This thought brought Adrian to mind. What would he say? How would he react to the knowledge that I was about to become his sister-in-law? I felt myself slipping even further into a state of abject depression.

Mrs Bilbrook returned with a beaming smile on her face. She was genuinely pleased to see me and glad of my company.

'Annabelle is coming to me for the day tomorrow,' she said, as she entered the room. 'Lady Charlotte sent a message yesterday asking if I could look after her. It's curious; she's left her with me far more frequently just lately. I don't know where she goes. Of course, if you'd like to join us you'll be more than welcome. I'm always pleased to see you, my dear.'

I thanked her and said that I would love to see Annabelle which, of course, was true. There had been few occasions for me to see her in previous weeks now that Adrian so rarely came to the tearooms with her.

Mrs Bilbrook and I spent a pleasant hour discussing all manner of things. Thankfully she didn't mention James or our previous conversation but she did return to the topic of Lady Charlotte.

'I have a feeling that, that little madam won't be living at Foxdale much longer,' she said, after a long silence.

'Who do you mean?' I asked, knowing full well whom she was referring to.

'Lady Charlotte, of course.'

'Why do you say that?'

'Well, it was something she let slip a week or so ago. She happened to mention that she was going to a funeral on that particular day. Apparently it was her uncle on her mother's side. By all accounts he was also her Godfather. James told me that he'd heard rumours that her mother and this uncle never saw eye to eye. He never liked Lady Charlotte's father and some years ago there was a tremendous row in the family. The outcome was that he and Lady Charlotte's mother were estranged. They had nothing to do with each other ever again even when her husband died. On the day of the funeral Lady Charlotte returned looking very pleased with herself. Far from being sad at the loss of her uncle she appeared almost jubilant and if rumours are to be believed she's inherited quite a tidy sum of money from him.'

So that was it. I could see now why Graham had left Lucille. Having fleeced her of all her inheritance and everything she owned he was now in the process of doing the very same thing to Lady Charlotte. On learning of her inheritance from her Godfather he had immediately agreed to leave Lucille, no doubt with far-fetched promises to Lady Charlotte of a wonderful life together once his marriage had been dissolved.

I felt almost sorry for her in that moment. She and Graham were really as bad as each other. No doubt, she must have realised that neither Nigel nor Adrian would ever ask for her hand in marriage. The thought of remaining at Foxdale, forever dependent on their charity and treated as little more than an unpaid governess, probably filled her with despair. When Graham came into her life, by whatever means, she saw him as a very suitable alternative. He wasn't rich but then, thanks to Lucille's inheritance and the success of his business, he wasn't poor either.

I wanted to laugh. It appeared that both she and Graham were really only interested in each other for whatever possible financial gain could come out of their relationship. She had probably seen him as a means to quite a comfortable life, although not nearly as comfortable as the life she'd had before her father died.

Then everything had changed if the rumours were true, she had inherited quite a substantial amount of money from her uncle. No doubt when Graham heard of this he seized his opportunity for fear of losing her, which was why he had left Lucille so abruptly. He had to convince Lady Charlotte that it was she he wanted to be with more than anything else, even to the extent of giving up his wife and home. Of course, it could be that they really did love each other but I doubted that somehow.

'You're very quiet today, dear,' Mrs Bilbrook said, of a sudden. I realised that I hadn't spoken for several minutes.

'I'm just tired,' I excused myself by saying. 'I've a lot on my mind at the moment.' She didn't pry and I was thankful she didn't want to know why I was so distracted. I was glad when the time came for me to leave. Having called on her I didn't feel I could rush away too soon but I was pleased to have the excuse that I would return the following day to see Annabelle.

* * * * *

Annabelle was as delighted to see me as I was to see her. When I walked in through the door she dropped what she was doing and ran straight into my arms. The tears came to my eyes. I'd grown to love her as if she were my own child.

We had a wonderful afternoon and I was able to recapture, for a short while, the feeling of peace and contentment that I'd always found in Mrs Bilbrook's home.

It was my intention to leave before Lady Charlotte returned to pick up Annabelle but shortly after we'd finished tea the doorbell rang. I heard Mrs Bilbrook walk to the front door.

'Well, good evening, sir,' I heard her say. 'This is a surprise.'

My heart gave a sudden flutter. Could it be Adrian? I waited expectantly but my excitement was short-lived when Nigel, not Adrian, walked through into the sitting room. He looked surprised to see me.

'Miss Briggs. This is very fortuitous. I've been

contemplating calling on you for a day or so now.' He turned towards Mrs Bilbrook. 'Perhaps you would allow us to have a word in private,' he said to her. I could see she was puzzled. 'Oh, before you go,' he said, as she turned to leave the room, 'in case you're wondering, I should tell you that Lady Charlotte won't be returning to Foxdale. Hence the reason for my presence now. I've called to collect Annabelle. She left me a note this morning to tell me that I'd find Annabelle here with you and that she's left Foxdale for good. She wouldn't, by any chance, have told you where she was going?'

'No, sir. She said nothing. Although it doesn't …' I knew she'd been about to say that it didn't surprise her, but then she obviously thought better of it. Nigel picked up on her words.

'It doesn't … what?' he asked.

'Oh, nothing, sir. I must get back to my kitchen,' she said, as she hurried from the room. 'I've left some cakes in the oven and they'll burn if I don't take a look at them.' I knew this wasn't exactly true. She'd said nothing to me about making any cakes and there was certainly no smell of baking coming from the kitchen. Nigel appeared not to notice this.

Annabelle was very quiet. 'Get on with what you're doing,' her father said to her. 'I want a word with Miss Briggs.'

'Yes, father,' she replied, obediently. Her smile had gone and she had become very subdued. Was she frightened of him? I certainly was so it didn't surprise me that she might be. I preferred not to look at him but he came to where I sat and stood over me, staring at me in such a way that I couldn't keep my eyes from him. I met his gaze boldly and with all the dignity I could muster.

'Have you thought over my offer?' he ventured after a while.

'Yes, I've given it a great deal of thought,' I answered, not looking directly at him.

'And dare I hope for an answer?'

I got up from where I sat and walked towards the window. My hands were clasped tightly together, almost as if they were glued. Once I told him of my decision there would be no going back. Should I tell him now or give myself a little extra time to think it over more carefully? No – there was no point in that. I could think about it for a hundred years and my answer would still have to be the same.

'Yes – I'll marry you,' I told him, flatly.

I didn't turn to look at his face but, instinctively, I knew that it held a triumphant expression.

'I'm delighted that you've made such a sensible choice,' he said, after a second or two. Then he turned to his daughter, 'Annabelle, do you hear that? Miss Briggs has agreed to marry me. That means she'll become your step-mother.'

Annabelle dropped what she was doing and looked first at her father then at me, her face radiantly happy with a delighted smile.

'Does that mean she'll be my Mama?' she asked.

'As good as,' her father replied.

In the next moment she had leapt across the room and was in my arms, hugging and kissing me as if she would never stop. 'Oh, Miss Briggs! I'm so pleased you're to be my mummy. I love you so very much.'

Tears came to my eyes as I held her close. I knew then that my decision had been the right one.

'We shall also have to see about a new governess for you, Annabelle,' Nigel broke in. 'No doubt you heard me say, just now, that Lady Charlotte will not be returning to Foxdale.'

'But Miss Briggs can teach me, can't she? Can't you Miss Briggs?' she asked, eagerly.

'I don't see why not,' I said, turning to her father. 'There's no reason why I shouldn't be Annabelle's tutor, is there?'

He considered the matter for a second, then obviously saw that I was prepared to remain firm. 'Very well, then, if you insist but we can discuss that another time. Meanwhile, I shall send my carriage to collect you this evening. I insist that you join Adrian and I for dinner so that we can all celebrate the good news together.'

I felt a cold chill run through me. What would Adrian say? What would he do? How would he take the news of my coming marriage to his brother?

As Nigel and Annabelle left, Mrs Bilbrook came out into the hall. He said nothing to her but it was Annabelle who broke the news.

'Miss Briggs is to be my new mummy,' she said, her eyes alight with happiness.

Mrs Bilbrook looked first at me and then at Nigel. Her expression was difficult to define but it certainly wasn't one of joy for us both. 'Is this so, sir?' she asked of Nigel, keeping her eyes focused away from me.

'Yes, indeed, Mrs Bilbrook. Miss Briggs has agreed to become my wife. But you are the first to hear the good news so I would appreciate it if you would say nothing to anyone until we've spoken with my brother.'

'Yes, of course, sir. I quite understand.' But I could see that she didn't. She didn't even offer us her congratulations. I couldn't bear to be left alone with her. She would only pry into my reasons for marrying him and ask me awkward questions, so I said goodbye along with Annabelle and Nigel and hurried from the cottage before she had time to make me change my mind. If I stopped to talk with her I would probably burst into tears and then she would know there was something wrong.

I was halfway to the village before the enormity of what I'd done struck home and the reality of it all began to dawn on me. My decision was made. There was no going back. Cast deep into depression, my face awash with unchecked tears, I wondered what the future would hold for me now.

***** *

The horses stopped at the foot of the marble steps leading to the main entrance. James came down them and opened the carriage door to help me alight. I looked up at him with a smile ready to say hello but his eyes weren't on me. His face was like stone as he stared silently past me.

'Good evening, Miss,' he said, almost as if I was a stranger. I felt hurt by his attitude. I wanted to tell him so. But this was neither the time nor the place to enter into a discussion with him. Instead I said nothing and followed him quietly up the steps and into the vast hall lit by two huge crystal chandeliers.

I wore my lemon evening gown. It was my favourite, indeed the only gown I possessed which was suitable for the occasion. As I followed James across the hall I was aware of unseen eyes watching me. The news that I was to marry Nigel had obviously travelled fast and I didn't doubt that most of the staff were already well aware of why I was here. I guessed that I was the subject of much gossip and speculation below stairs; not all of which would be to my credit. I trembled; not with excitement but with fear. Uppermost in my mind was the thought of coming face to face with Adrian. I dreaded the questions which I knew would be in his eyes. He, no doubt like everyone else, would most probably be unable to comprehend why I was marrying Nigel.

At first, to my surprise, he appeared completely indifferent to his brother's plans. When I entered the drawing room he was already there and alone. He said good evening to me but he made no reference to the matter whatsoever although he was quite obviously expecting me. His manner was pleasant and friendly, as always, but the very fact that he avoided any mention of my intended marriage caused me to believe that he disapproved wholeheartedly. My heart sank. There was a barrier between us that I'd never felt before. Could it be that even though he and I, not so long ago, had discovered a mutual friendship, he considered me to be unsuitable as the future Mistress of Foxdale? I was, after all, nothing more than the owner of a tearooms in the village. There was a strained silence between us. If he could have only shown me some sign that he was pleased to accept me as a member of his family it might have eased the tension between us, but he said nothing.

Probably for the only time in my life I was actually relieved when Nigel appeared. His expression reminded me of a cat that has just tasted fresh cream. He had a broad grin on his face and his whole attitude made me feel as if I was a newly acquired prized possession.

'Forgive me for being late,' he apologised. 'I was looking for something very important. Can I pour you a drink?'

'I've already done the honours,' Adrian replied, quite brusquely I thought. 'Miss Briggs and I already have a sherry.'

Nigel seemed to ignore his tone and poured himself a whisky from a cut-glass decanter. 'You'll have to get used to calling her Anna, you know, Adrian. After all, she is to be your sister-in-law.'

Adrian glanced at me but said nothing. Nigel raised his glass. 'To my future wife,' he said.

Adrian didn't answer at first. I looked across at him to find that he was staring at me with an indefinable expression on his face. After a second or two he lifted his glass to me almost in a mock gesture.

'To your future wife. May you both be very happy.' There was no smile on his face and I detected a slight ring of sarcasm in his voice. I felt a lump come to my throat. Perhaps he believed that I was marrying Nigel purely for the money and social status I would gain. If only he knew the truth. If only I could tell him how I'd been trapped into agreeing to this marriage, the very thought of which made me feel both physically and mentally sick. In that moment yet another thought suddenly came to my mind. I realised, for the first time, that I cared for Adrian far more than I was prepared to admit. If only it could have been him, and not his brother, who had asked for my hand in marriage.

It was as well that I didn't have too long to dwell on this thought. I might just have fled from the room. Whilst all of this was passing through my mind Nigel had drawn a small red, leather case from his pocket.

'I told you I was late because I was looking for something very important,' he said, 'and this is it. It belonged to our grandmother and, since I am the eldest son, you, as my future wife, Anna, are entitled to wear it.'

He lifted the lid of the case to reveal one of the most beautiful rings I have ever seen. It took my breath away. Lying on a bed of deep blue velvet a magnificent cluster of diamonds and sapphires sparkled in the light like a small group of stars. He took it from its case and was about to place it on my finger when Adrian stopped him.

'I don't believe the fact that Miss Briggs is to be your wife necessarily entitles her to wear that ring,' he said, sharply.

Nigel glared at him angrily. 'Of course it does,' he retorted. 'The wife of the eldest son has always worn this ring. It's a family tradition passed down through several generations. I am the eldest son so it is my privilege to claim it for Anna.'

'Is it?' Never before had I seen Adrian's face look so grim. Unless I did something to prevent it, I was sure that the two brothers would come to blows.

'Please, I wouldn't like to be the cause of any disagreement between you,' I broke in, hastily. 'It's a beautiful, beautiful ring but I really couldn't wear it. It would worry me that I might damage it in some way or, worse still, lose it. Couldn't I, please, wear something smaller and a little less grand, Nigel?'

He looked first at me and then at Adrian before he replaced the ring in its case and snapped the lid shut.

'Very well, then, if that's what you want, but I shall expect you to wear it on our wedding day.' Almost defiantly he glared at Adrian as if daring him to dispute his decision. Thankfully, just at that moment, dinner was announced.

We went through into the dining room and I was awestruck at the exquisite way in which it was furnished. Down the centre of the room was a very long, highly polished table surrounded by twelve Regency chairs. Three sets of silver candelabra graced the table and in between these were several crystal bowls of late-flowering, short-stemmed roses. The curtains were Regency striped and made of gold brocade in keeping with the seats of the dining chairs. A log fire blazed in the open hearth and to one side of it stood an enormous porcelain vase which had been filled with a variety of autumn leaves and dried flowers. The floor was as highly polished as the dining table, as were the two long sideboards which stood at either end of the room. It all seemed so unreal. I had difficulty in coming to terms with the fact that, once married to Nigel, it would be my place to dine in such grandeur.

Throughout the meal I tried hard to maintain the conversation but it was a difficult task. Far from being a celebration this was turning out to be quite an ordeal. Both men were sullen and ill-disposed towards talk of any kind.

I was sure that Adrian's apparent disapproval of me as a wife for Nigel was based on the fact that he regarded me as socially unsuitable so I decided that, when I could, I would confront him with it. It was shortly after dinner when, quite by chance, we found ourselves alone together that I decided to broach the subject.

'I'm sorry if you don't approve of your brother's choice for a wife,' I said.

'Whether I approve or not is irrelevant,' he answered. 'I'm not my brother's keeper. He's free to marry whom he pleases.'

'But you'd have preferred it if he had chosen someone else?'

He poured a large brandy into a cut-glass brandy goblet and swallowed it in one go. Then he looked me full in the face, that same indefinable expression on his own. His reply was blunt.

'If you must know – yes.'

'But why? Is it because I live in the village and own a tearooms?'

'That has nothing to do with it.'

'Then why have you changed towards me, Mr Tremayne?' I asked, quietly. 'I had begun to think that we were friends.'

His expression softened, then, and I believe he suddenly became aware that he'd been treating me a little too harshly all evening. He came forward and took both my hands gently between his palms. He had warm, strong hands with long fingers and square-shaped nails. I looked down at them. In that moment I wanted so much for him to put his arm around me. I felt so lonely; so desperately in need of his friendship. I couldn't look up at him. He would have seen too much revealed in my eyes.

'I thought you had dispensed with calling me Mr Tremayne,' he said, softly.

I smiled, still lacking the courage to look into his face.

'Anna – I'm sorry. Of course I don't dislike you. It's just that I know my brother so well. I'm a little concerned that you may not be fully aware of what you are letting yourself in for.'

I drew away from him. 'I think I do. Probably more than you may realise.'

He filled his glass, again, then crossed over to the window where he stood looking out onto the gardens.

'Then I can say no more,' he said, at last. 'You have all my best wishes. I hope you'll be very happy.'

The matter was closed. Clearly, Adrian had no wish to pursue the subject any further. For a while he turned his attention to admiring the gardens and remarked on the efficient way in which the gardeners looked after the grounds. When Nigel re-appeared he seemed eager to be alone and excused himself by saying that he ought to exercise his horse before it became too dark.

It was late when Nigel's carriage eventually took me home. To the best of my knowledge, when I left, he still hadn't returned.

* * * * *

CHAPTER 22

'So, you're to marry Nigel Tremayne?' Mrs Gilmore shook her head sadly. It was a day or so later and Muffin and I were taking our usual morning walk. Mrs Gilmore was on her way to the vicarage to see her brother, Reverend Mead.

'How did you find out?' I asked.

'You should know by now that news travels fast through the village,' she said. 'Oh, Anna, what are you thinking about, my dear? I wasn't born yesterday. I can't believe that you love him.'

I stared down at the ground, avoiding her eyes. 'How could I love a man who did such a dreadful thing to my sister?'

'Then why are you marrying him? Tell me, Anna, why?'

I could trust her. I knew that. She'd done so much for Cathy and she was one of the few people whom I felt I could talk to.'

'Do you remember, when I first returned to Thursledown, Reverend Mead brought me to see you?' She nodded. 'You told me that it had been Cathy's wish for me to look after Annabelle and I vowed, then, that whatever happened I would try and do so. Somehow, Nigel has discovered that Cathy was my sister and that I am Annabelle's aunt. He knows that I've become very fond of her and he's told me that if I don't marry him she will never see me again.' I didn't tell her that I also felt threatened by him; that I feared for my own life if I didn't comply with his wishes.

Her hand went to her mouth. I could see she was deeply shocked. 'My dear child,' she said at last, 'you simply cannot go through with it. You're jeopardising your whole life's happiness for the sake of one small child.'

'My sister's child,' I broke in.

'But Cathy wouldn't want or expect you to ruin your whole life in such a way. Don't you see? Annabelle has been perfectly alright until now. She's well clothed and fed; she'll have an excellent education and her family on her father's side is exceedingly wealthy so she'll, no doubt, marry a man of equal standing. She's assured of all the comforts and financial security that life can offer. When she's grown up and has a family of her own to love, you'll be left to reflect on the empty, wasted years of your own loveless marriage. When she is no longer the centre of your life you may well secretly envy her for the happiness which we hope she'll find. She has her whole life ahead of her. You will be wasting yours on a man you don't love.'

'But is that justification enough to deny her the love which is so desperately important to a growing child? Is her happiness, now, any less important than my own? I made a promise to take care of her; a promise I cannot break. I love her as I would my own child. If I were to turn my back on her now I would be plagued with guilt for the rest of my days. My life would be no less miserable than it would be as Nigel's wife.'

'How can I convince you that you're making a terrible mistake,' she said. 'Annabelle has many people around her who love her dearly, not least of all her uncle Adrian. He adores her. I'm quite sure he wouldn't let any harm come to her.'

'But Nigel has told me that I'll never see her again, whatever he means by that. I wouldn't even be able to watch over her from a distance.'

She stared at me in sudden realisation of what his words might mean. I knew from her expression what was going through her mind and, like me, she was well aware that he was capable of almost anything.

'This mustn't be allowed to happen,' she said, angrily. 'There must be something that can be done; someone who can help you. He cannot be allowed to blackmail you in such a way.'

But there was no way, as far as I could see, in which anyone could help me.

We talked for a while longer then said goodbye and parted company. I was almost at my front gate when I saw James coming down the street towards me. Unusually, he didn't smile when he saw me. I stood and waited for him.

'Hello.' I tried my best to sound cheerful. 'Have you come to visit me?'

'That wouldn't be right under the circumstances, would it?' I could see the hurt in his eyes. 'I'm just on my way with a letter for Mrs Gilmore,' he added.

'I saw her a moment ago,' I told him. 'She was making her way to the vicarage to see her brother. Won't you come in for just a short while and have a cup of tea with me, James. I need to talk to you.'

He hesitated. For a moment I thought he was about to refuse but then he agreed and followed me into the cottage.

'I thought we were friends,' he said, as he followed me through into the kitchen.

'We are, James. Of course we are. Your friendship is important to me.'

'Then why didn't you tell me about Master Nigel and his proposal of marriage to you. What in God's name are you doing, marrying him, anyway?' I'd never heard James speak so vehemently or with such anger. 'After all he did to Cathy! I don't understand, Anna. I feel as if I don't know you any more.'

I found myself telling him just what I'd told Mrs Gilmore. It was a relief to talk with him. For the past two days I'd thought of nothing else but my decision to marry Nigel and I'd descended deeper and deeper into a state of depression. His reaction was the same as Mrs Gilmore's.

'Don't be a fool, Anna. You can't go through with it.'

I could see that he really didn't see the sense in my decision. Perhaps he, too, thought I was only interested in becoming lady of the manor because of all the trappings of wealth and status associated with such a title.

I made tea for us both and sat down at the table opposite him. It was important that he didn't go away with such an opinion of me. Very slowly, I told him all that had happened between Nigel and me since my few weeks at Foxdale as Annabelle's tutor. He listened in silence as I spoke but I could see something akin to rage building inside of him.

'We must stop this at once,' he said, when I came to the end of my story. 'It really cannot go ahead.'

'But I'm frightened James. I'm frightened that he might harm me in some way if I don't comply with his wishes. He's a hard, cruel man. Who knows what he might do?'

He could see there were tears in my eyes. Next minute he was by my side with an arm around my shoulder. It was all too much. He was such a dear, kind friend. I found myself sobbing my heart out in a release of all my pent-up emotions. I was so grateful to be able to talk to someone of my fears. When, at last, my tears subsided his face was grim.

'You're not married to him yet,' he said. 'A lot can happen between now and then. I'll come and see you again as soon as I am able to. In the meantime I really must deliver this letter to Mrs Gilmore and get back to the manor before they begin to wonder why it's taking me so long.' He took a letter from his pocket which I could see was written on fine parchment. The seal, which held it down, had on it the Tremayne coat of arms.

He left me then, anxiously reassuring me that all would be well and that I must try not to worry too much. What he meant by these words I didn't know but as far as I could see there was no solution to my problem. I wondered why he sounded so convinced that everything would be alright. I wondered, too, who had written the letter which he needed to deliver so urgently to Mrs Gilmore.

* * * * *

It was foolish of me to believe that life would carry on as usual. I wanted nothing more than to organise and run my tearooms with the help of Jenny and Maevis but even that pleasure was denied me. The number of our customers increased to the point where we were run off our feet. Of course, there were those who regularly visited us but in addition there were many people whom I'd never seen before. It very soon became apparent that they were only interested in taking a look at the tearooms' owner who was to become the future Lady of Foxdale. I created something of a stir. Most of them couldn't believe that Nigel Tremayne would have chosen someone away from his own social circle. I found myself hiding away in my kitchen, reluctant to be seen by them and embarrassed by the constant attention.

Totally wrapped up in my own distress I completely forgot that Annabelle was without a governess now that Lady Charlotte had left Foxdale. If I thought that Nigel would allow me to continue with my life on the same basis as before, until our wedding, then I was completely wrong. He came to see me and pointed out in no uncertain terms that it was not appropriate for the future lady of the manor to be running a tearooms. He insisted that I was to move myself to Foxdale immediately, adding that I wouldn't be in need of any clothes other than bare essentials because he'd arranged for a dressmaker to provide me with a complete new wardrobe.

'Apart from which,' he added, 'Annabelle is without a tutor. If, as you say, you want to take over that particular task then I would suggest that you begin immediately. I shall arrange for the sale of this property straight away.'

I was angry. How dare he? This cottage, with the tearooms, was mine. I had no intention of letting it go.

'You have no choice,' he said, when I objected. 'Once we're married your possessions become mine and you will have no say in the matter.'

I was incensed. I would rather give my cottage away than have him dictate to me what I should do with it. But I knew that he was right. Once we were married he would have complete control over my affairs.

'And you can get rid of that dog,' he said, pointing to Muffin. 'I won't have any animal wandering around the manor house.'

I looked at my little pet. He stared back at me with such loving eyes and gave a flick of his tail. I couldn't bear the thought of parting with him.

'No!' I said, stubbornly. 'Muffin comes with me.'

He stared at Muffin and I heard a low rumble coming from the doorway where he sat. Man and dog didn't like each other.

'If you bring him with you,' Nigel told me, 'I shall shoot him at the very first opportunity.'

I gasped. How could he be so cruel? How could he, so callously, deprive me of my little companion? I was unable to say anything. I just wanted to cry or, better still, to run as far away from this brutal man as I possibly could. I knew that wasn't an option.

Before he left he told me that he would send someone to collect me at the weekend. He broached no argument. I had no choice.

The following day my prayers, in part, were answered. I received a letter from Lucille. It was postmarked Lynhead and read as follows:

My dear Anna,

It is with a very sad and heavy heart that I'm writing to you. In the weeks since we last met I have lost my home and almost everything I owned. It would appear that Graham has built up a tremendous amount of debt which he has not attempted to repay. The bank, therefore, has foreclosed on the monies which he owes to them. Our house at Nether Wilmslow was used as collateral and so now has to be sold to cover those debts. I'm left with nothing, which is why I have returned to Lynhead and am living back at Cherry Tree Cottage with my brother Richard. It's not the best of situations but I have no alternative. Forgive me for not coming to see you before I left. I was too distraught and didn't want to burden you with my worries. Richard has been a wonderful support to me. In our younger days we didn't always see eye to eye but he's mellowed as he's become older and we find we have much more in common, now, than we had as children.

I should perhaps tell you of one more piece of information that has come my way though I am loathe, in many respect, to do so. My dear Anna, when you read this you may wish to have nothing more to do with me and if this is the case then I would hardly blame you for it.

I have learnt through Richard that that wretched man whom I thought I loved, may well have been involved in the death of your dear sister Cathy. I have no proof, but Richard tells me that he was in London many years ago and met up with Graham. At the time Graham was with a certain Nigel Tremayne. They were both worse for drink and were not careful of what they discussed. No names were mentioned but reference was made to the unfortunate 'accident' in which your sister died. Richard cannot be sure, but his suspicions lead him to believe that Graham may well have been implicated in the events which took place that night. It is only now that he has mentioned it to me. He never liked Graham which is why he rarely visited us at Nether Wilmslow. Without proof he didn't like to talk to me of what he'd overheard and, with the passing of time, he came to the conclusion that he must have been wrong and had misheard the conversation which took place. Even now I cannot believe that my husband would have done such a thing but I do know that his greed for money might well have led him to contemplate it.

This letter comes with my love, dear Anna, but if I should receive no reply from you then I'll understand your reluctance to maintain our friendship in view of the information I've imparted to you. Please take care of yourself.

Your friend, as always,

Lucille.

I read and re-read the latter part of her letter. Was it possible that Graham had been involved in Cathy's death? If so, how? It was no secret to me that he'd become acquainted with both Nigel and Adrian through Simon Pendleton, but surely he wouldn't have stooped so low as to kill for possible monetary gain. I thought of his mother, Mrs Fairs. She'd been so kind to me in my days at Cherry Tree Cottage. Surely she couldn't have produced a son who would contemplate such evil intent. I felt deeply sorry for her.

Whatever Graham had or hadn't done, I needed to reassure Lucille that we would always be friends. She was one of the sweetest people I had ever come across. We had become so close over the years, almost like sisters. I certainly wasn't going to abandon our friendship now, whatever her husband may or may not have done. Besides, I needed her as much as she needed me. I sat down and wrote a letter back to her immediately.

In the course of my writing I found myself opening up my heart to her, telling her all that had happened to me. Because we had both had our troubles in the weeks gone by there hadn't been the opportunity for us to talk together and confide in one another. Now was the time to put that right.

As I wrote an idea began to form in my mind. I reached the point where I was telling her of Nigel's visit and all that he'd said about me relinquishing my tearooms and getting rid of Muffin. It suddenly occurred to me that Lucille was the solution to my problem. I suggested to her that she might like to take over my cottage and my business. I would gladly give it to her. It had been her father's money, after all, which had given me the means by which to buy it. I knew that she liked animals and that Muffin liked her. If she came to live at the cottage Muffin could stay here with her and I would be able to see them both when time permitted. I would miss him terribly but at least he'd be safe and well looked after. Lucille had never been one for cooking but then that wasn't a problem. Jenny and Maevis were perfectly capable of running the tearooms by themselves as I'd discovered when I spent the mornings at Foxdale teaching Annabelle. If any additional help was needed I felt sure that Lucille would agree to taking on an extra pair of hands to do the baking.

As I wrote I prayed that she would jump at my offer. I needed her agreement to the idea as quickly as possible so that I could contact a solicitor and arrange for the cottage and the business to be transferred into her name before my marriage to Nigel took place.

Within an hour I had written and sealed my reply to her and sent it on its way. I arrived outside the inn just in time to catch the mail coach which only passed through once a day.

As I walked back to the cottage I experienced a profound sense of relief. Here was a solution to at least one of my problems if only Lucille was agreeable. No doubt it would be several days before she would confirm her intentions and even then I might not receive the answer that I was hoping for. But at least, for the time being, I could put that particular worry aside.

My thoughts turned to the coming weekend and the fact that I was expected to take up residence at the manor. It wasn't a prospect that I relished. I was beginning to feel that Nigel wanted me there so that he could keep an eye on me; almost as if he was afraid I might disappear without trace. The thought of going to live at Foxdale was akin to being locked up in prison. I had an uneasy feeling that, once I was there, Nigel would watch my every move and I wouldn't be allowed the freedom that I'd like.

* * * * *

CHAPTER 23

Lucille replied to my letter immediately. She was over-whelmed by the fact that I wanted to give her my cottage and the tearooms and told me that the prospect of a new life in Thurseldown gave her hope for the future and filled her with excitement. At the same time she begged me to think again about my decision to marry Nigel. Just as Mrs Gilmore and James had done, she put forward all the arguments against me going ahead with such a rash and foolhardy decision. But none of them knew how I felt. None of them really knew how frightened I was at the thought of what might happen if I refused to become Nigel's wife.

Without a moment's hesitation I sat down and wrote to Mr Carrington, my solicitor in Farlington. The sooner I put the matter into his hands and transferred the property to Lucille the happier I'd be. I realised time was short. It would be difficult for me to receive correspondence from him at the manor so I arranged for him to write to me at the cottage. James, I knew, would help me by collecting any letters if I was unable to call for them myself.

* * * * *

There was no opportunity for James to call on me again because I was installed at Foxdale before he had another day off and the time to visit me. Of course, once I was living at the manor he had to maintain his position in the household and treat me with all the deference he would show to the mistress of the house. Not that I was yet mistress but all the servants had been instructed to treat me as such. Many of them, particularly the younger girls, conveyed their best wishes to me when I passed them in the corridors. I could see from the expression on their faces that they wondered why on earth I was contemplating marriage to Nigel of all people but, nevertheless, their good wishes for my future were genuinely meant.

The only person I came across who outwardly showed her disapproval of the situation was Mrs Pringle, the housekeeper. Her cold, calculating expression conveyed her innermost thoughts and it was plain to see that she didn't approve of the marriage. Clearly, the prospect of me becoming mistress of the manor was even more displeasing to her. I decided that her opinions were of no consequence and dismissed all thoughts of her to the back of my mind.

It was difficult for me to have a word with James without anyone overhearing. There always seemed to be someone around. In the end I realised that if I could get to see Mrs Bilbrook I could pass a message on to him through her.

An opportunity came the day after my arrival. It was late afternoon and the house was relatively quiet. I slipped quietly out into the gardens by a side door and made my way across the vegetable garden and along a small path which I knew to be a short cut to Mrs Bilbrook's cottage.

I don't know whether she was surprised or angry to see me. Her expression lead me to believe that I wasn't exactly welcome, on the other hand her attitude towards me softened after a moment or two and she asked me, hesitantly, if I would like a cup of tea. I was relieved that she didn't just shut the door in my face. Had James told her of my predicament? I was none too sure. But clearly, if he had spoken with her, she was decidedly unimpressed with my decision to go ahead and marry Nigel. There was a strained atmosphere between us which I tried to dispel but I found it difficult to break down the barrier which she insisted on putting up between us.

'I really came to ask you if you'd mind giving James a message from me,' I told her.

'And what might that be, Anna?' she asked. I wondered

from her tone if she was contemplating whether or not she wanted to pass a message on to him.

'It's very important. I think he'll understand the urgency of my request,' I said. 'Do you have something I could write on? It might be better if I give you a letter for him.'

She found me pen and ink and paper to write on. I scribbled a few words to him, outlining my request and the need for strict secrecy. If Nigel discovered my plans he would undoubtedly put a stop to them. I had to transfer the cottage and business to Lucille with all haste so that he could have no say in my decision.

I knew that Mrs Bilbrook was curious to know what it was I was asking her son to do so, when I'd finished the letter, I gave it to her to read. I was quite sure I could trust her. When she'd finished reading it her expression softened.

'I really don't understand all of this,' she said, at last, with a sigh, 'but I am willing to help you where I can. That isn't to say I agree with what you're doing. I think you're a fool, Anna. James has told me a little of what has been going on and, in view of all you said to me not so very long ago about truly loving the man you would marry, I think you are out of your mind – or scared to death,' she added. I stared at her. She was watching me very closely to see what response her words drew from me.

I couldn't hold back the tears. I tried hard to put on a brave face so that she wouldn't ask too many questions but she was a very intuitive lady. She came closer and placed an arm around my shoulder. 'Oh, Anna, my dear, Anna. What are we to do? You can't go through with this. You mustn't go through with this.'

I found myself talking to her, then, telling her of all my fears for Annabelle and for myself. I could see no way out of my predicament and I told her so.

'And when does Nigel intend this marriage to take place?' she asked, as I dried my tears.

'I have no idea. It's not something we've discussed yet. He told me the other day that he would make the arrangements. It would appear that I have no say in the matter.'

She was thoughtful. 'We can only hope that it won't be too soon,' she said, after a moment's silence. 'Now, dry those tears, my dear. All is not yet lost. I believe you have more friends who will help you than you may realise.'

I thought about her words as I made my way back to the manor house. What could she have meant? I could see no way in which anyone could help me, however many friends I might have.

Before we said goodbye she told me that she, herself, would ensure that any letters from my solicitor would be collected from the cottage if James was unable to find time to go into the village. She would give them to him so that he could pass them on to me. I was so grateful for her kindness and understanding. I knew what an immense disappointment it was to her that I didn't regard James as more than just a friend, but she was prepared to stand by me nevertheless.

*****

I walked back a different way to the way I'd come. I was so deep in thought and so low in spirit that I didn't really care where I was going. What I did feel, though, was that I couldn't bear the idea of returning to the house. It was almost like walking back to prison. This was, in some ways, a foolish concept because I was in fact free to come and go, just as I had done this afternoon.

Before I knew where I was I came across the lake, the very lake where as a young girl, so many years ago, Nigel had tried to rape me and Adrian had saved me from his monstrous intentions. I sat down on an old tree stump, lower in morale than I had ever been in my life. When I'd told Nigel that I would marry him the whole situation had seemed a little unreal, as if it couldn't possibly be happening to me and as if sooner or later I'd wake up from this nightmare. But now it was dawning on me that, by my own decision, I was about to tether myself to a cold, miserable, existence with Nigel, succumbing to his every whim until he no longer found me interesting or attractive and perhaps, eventually, devised a cunning method by which to dispose of me without drawing attention to himself.

I thought of Mrs Gilmore's words. In many ways she was right. Annabelle did have all the material things she could wish for. In years to come she would have her own family to love and, when that time came, she would neither need nor indeed want me to become too emotionally involved in her life. I would become just a kindly, middle-aged aunt who had helped to bring her through the undulating, twisting, turning path of childhood years.

I thought of Adrian. I loved him. For the very first time I truly acknowledged this thought. It occurred to me that, for some unaccountable reason, I must have loved him since that day when he'd rescued me from his brother. For years I'd put him to the back of my mind, believing that to love him was an impossible dream. Our lives and backgrounds were so entirely different. And then our paths had crossed again and quite by chance, for a short while, we'd become the closest of friends; that is until Nigel had fallen in love with me and put paid to all my future happiness. But what foolish thoughts; I doubted that Adrian would ever regard me as anything more than a friend. What senseless spark of hope could lead me to believe that he might one day love me in return? Even if I weren't now promised to Nigel, women of my class were not for Adrian. He would pick his wife from the gentry; a beautiful woman, well educated in the more refined ways of living. The thought of such a woman on his arm caused a pang of sadness to shoot through me. If only I could be that woman.

Dejectedly, I peered into the centre of the lake. How deep was it? Deep enough for me to drown? I'd heard tell that drowning was a painless way of ending one's life. Right at that moment I lacked the courage and strength of purpose to face up to the future that lay before me.

I stood up and moved towards the edge of the lake. The cold water seeped through my shoes and lapped gently round the skirts of my dress, as if it was beckoning me, urging me to walk in still further. It seemed to be encouraging me to end my life; to lay myself gently on the soft bed of mud beneath the gentle ripples and let the pure white swans glide gracefully over me whilst the weeping willow trees bent their swaying boughs to touch the surface of the water.

The more I thought of it, the more I felt the urge to walk in still further, to put and end to my life once and for all and escape this predicament I found myself in. Even my promise to look after Annabelle didn't deter me. As Mrs Gilmore had said, she would be perfectly alright. No harm had come to her yet and, no doubt, no harm would come to her in the future. As for Muffin, his future lay with Lucille now because, whatever happened, I had left my wishes with my solicitor and Lucille was to inherit all I owned. The water rose higher and higher about me. I had but one purpose in mind.

'Anna!' There was fear in the man's voice as he ran through the trees towards me but I only saw him as a blurred figure. It was as if I was in a trance. I didn't care any more. Life had no meaning. In a short while life would be no more. I would be at peace.

The water closed in around my head and engulfed me within its peaceful, beckoning depths. And then I was no longer aware of the cold seeping through my clothes or the pain in my heart. I was oblivious to all things.

The next thing I knew strong hands had taken hold of me and I was no longer in the lake. I had no idea who had denied me that escape from life but whoever it was held me close to him; so close that I could feel his heart pounding against his ribs.

'Anna! Darling, Anna. You young fool,' I heard him say.

I coughed and spluttered and threw up what seemed to be a gallon of water but which, on reflection, couldn't have been such a vast amount because I'd only been beneath the surface for a short while, or so I thought. Everything became a hazy blur of unfamiliar shapes and I made no effort to see who the man was before I slipped, once more, into the depths of unconsciousness.

* * * * *

I have no idea how long I was ill but I do know that it was many days before my head cleared and I became less disorientated with my surroundings. During this period I was vaguely aware of shadowy figures in my room and gentle hands taking note of my pulse. Most of the time I rested peacefully in the timeless abyss of unconsciousness. I learned later that I'd been heavily drugged. Dr Moreland called every day to see me and very soon he had me well on the road to recovery. He was a jovial, round-faced man with a mass of long, grey whiskers. He did a great deal to lift my melancholy.

Strange as it may seem, life took on a new appearance and I was no longer possessed of the single thought to put an end to it. I had time to think over my situation more rationally and to realise that there could be far worse things than marriage to Nigel. Had I not been dragged from the lake I would, most certainly, have drowned and this realisation that I'd come so close to death made me appreciate how precious life is whatever the hardships.

It soon became apparent that everyone was under the impression that I'd fallen into the lake by accident. In many ways I was glad that it was thought to be accidental. It spared me the loathsome task of explaining what had really happened. But there was one person who knew the truth. That person must have seen me walk into the lake of my own accord and rushed to rescue me. I wondered who he was.

During my time of convalescence James and his mother were able to call in and see me. Mrs Bilbrook brought with her, on one occasion, a letter from Mr Carrington which she'd collected from the cottage. It was a most important document regarding the transfer of my property into Lucille's name and I was able to sign it without anyone else's knowledge and give it back to her so that she could return it immediately to my solicitor.

I was surprised by Adrian's concern for me. He made a point of calling into my room almost every day to see how I was progressing. I saw more of him than I did of Nigel. Sometimes he would sit with me for almost an hour and we were able to recapture the happy, relaxed moments we'd shared in my kitchen at the cottage. I treasured every one of those moments he was near. It never once crossed my mind to question why he should want to spend so much time in my company. I was so happy to have him there and I assumed that he was just being kind.

* * * * *

Ten days after my 'accident' I had a surprise visitor. The door opened one afternoon and a very elegant lady was shown in. She was introduced to me as Lady Isobelle Grant. I'd never met her before but I certainly knew of her. She and her husband owned a large estate some five miles away. As I understood it, they were longstanding friends of the Tremayne family.

'I'm so pleased to meet you, my dear,' she said, 'I do hope you don't mind me calling on you like this but Adrian assured me that you'd have no objections. If you'd prefer not to have a visitor I'll call on you another day.'

I was only too pleased to have company and I told her as much. I liked her immediately. She was so kind and considerate and I soon discovered that she had a warm-hearted disposition and a natural concern for those around her. I felt so at ease with her and found myself talking to her as if we had known each other for a lifetime. She appeared not to be in any great hurry so I rang for the maid and asked for tea and cakes to be brought to us. It was a lovely afternoon and I found myself hoping that she wouldn't rush off too soon. She told me a lot about the Tremayne family and I deduced from what she said that she was none too keen on Nigel although she was far too polite to put her feelings into words particularly as she was aware that I was about to become his wife. Her attitude towards Adrian was so different. She spoke of him with warmth, affection, one could say. It was clear that she and her husband regarded him as a friend but the same couldn't be said for his brother.

She made no reference to my 'accident' although I presumed Adrian or someone had told her that I hadn't been well. Why else would she call on me at this time? I reassured her that I was feeling very much better and that I'd almost completely recovered.

'Then you'll be well enough to travel?' she asked. I could see she had something in mind. 'How would you like to come away from here and stay with me for a few days, my dear?'

Her invitation appealed to me, more than she might have realised. 'Oh, that would be wonderful,' I told her, 'but I can't see that Nigel will allow me to go very far.'

'Then we'll ask him,' she said. 'I shall tell him that you need a change of scenery to help you convalesce. Surely he won't object to that?'

Oh, how I hoped that he would not. Away from him I'd have a chance to think more clearly; to convince myself that I'd made the right decision and to resign myself to life with him, to being his wife.

'I'd love to come,' I told her. A sudden feeling of excitement overcame me and I burst into tears, laughing at the same time. It was just what I needed. Inwardly, I prayed that Nigel wouldn't prevent me from going.

As luck would have it he came to visit me before Isobelle left. Curiously, Adrian was with him. It was rare for them both to visit me at the same time. I noticed that Isobelle took Adrian's hands warmly in her own but acknowledged Nigel with only the merest inclination of her head.

I decided to tell Nigel there and then of her invitation and that I planned to go away for a short while to recuperate after my ordeal. At first he was angry. He was suspicious of my intentions, as if he imagined that I was trying to escape and wouldn't come back. I thought he would forbid me to go. Isobelle came to my rescue. She explained that the idea had been hers and not mine. Indignantly, she told him that she took exception to his implication that there was an ulterior motive for her friendly invitation.

'Just what you think we'll be doing, I really don't know,' she told him angrily, 'particularly as Anna has not yet recovered from her distressing accident. No doubt you are of the firm opinion that I shall be throwing wild parties every night with scores of eligible young men eagerly awaiting the chance of a few words with her. Well, have no fear Nigel, that is not my intention. The idea is for her to rest and relax as much as she can. Perhaps a little selfishly, I also thought it would be an excellent opportunity for me to have some female company for a change.' It was plain for anyone to see that she wasn't intimidated by him. She stared at him so coldly that I could almost feel the room temperature drop. It was quite clear that she didn't like him one little bit.

'I think it's an excellent idea,' Adrian put in. 'It will do Anna a great deal of good to spend some time getting to know Isobelle. They are to be neighbours after all. If you wish, Nigel, I shall accompany her to Spindleberry Grange and see that she arrives safely. I have to go away on business for a few days. It's on my way so it will be a pleasure for me to escort her there.'

Nigel calmed down. For some minutes he paced up and down the room. His hands were clasped firmly behind his back; his lips were pursed tightly together. He was deep in thought. I wondered just what was going on inside that devious mind. In the end, faced with the three of us, he relented.

'I have an idea,' he said, at last, his anger giving way to a more condescending mood. 'If you're agreeable Isobelle, I suggest that Anna remains with you until the day of our wedding. He turned towards me. 'Now you've almost recovered from your most unfortunate ordeal, my dear, I can see no reason to delay our marriage plans any further. I have to go to London in a day or so and I shall make the necessary arrangements before I leave.'

A cold, icy unseen hand seemed to grip at my heart. It was almost as if it actually stopped beating. I was unable to respond. Fortunately he didn't wait for an answer and Isobelle spoke before I was forced to make a reply.

'Anna is very welcome to stay with my husband and I for as long as she wishes,' she told him.

'Splendid!' The smile on his face was far removed from the angry expression he'd shown only minutes before. 'Then I shall arrange the ceremony for three weeks from today. I shall commission the best dress-makers in the west of England to come to you in order to make your wedding gown and your trousseau,' he added, as he opened the door to leave.

My stomach churned. My hands were trembling. Reluctantly, I agreed.

CHAPTER 24

Marriage to Nigel, it seemed, was inevitable. The date of our wedding was coming upon me far sooner than I'd anticipated and I was suddenly engulfed in an overwhelming feeling of desperation. A day or so later, as I packed my bags in readiness for the journey to Spindleberry Grange, I began to wonder if Nigel might have more pity in him than I gave him credit for. Was our marriage so inevitable? Perhaps I'd allowed my imagination to run a little wild. There were times when, despite his harsh, cruel manner, it was difficult to believe that he could have been capable of arranging Cathy's death. Would he really be prepared to kill me also if I refused to marry him? He'd never actually said that he would, only implied it – or so I thought. Surely, deep down inside him, there had to be a more compassionate, understanding nature that would realise the pointlessness of our marriage. Maybe if I went to him and explained how I felt he would release me from this promise I'd made.

With new hope I hurried down the stairs and eventually found him in the library. He turned as I closed the door behind me and a smile came to his face.

'Ah, I was just about to send for you,' he said.

I ignored him, eager to discuss my reasons for being there.

'Nigel, I have something very important to ask you.'

'Let it wait, my dear. I've just received your engagement ring by special messenger. Come here and let me place it on your finger.'

I took a step backwards. The ring was beautiful – a large solitaire diamond which had been made especially for me – but I had no intention of wearing it.

'No! Please – let me say what I have to.'

Surprise flashed across his face followed by a fleeting moment of anger before his mood changed yet again. He shrugged his shoulders.

'Very well then. But I can't see why I shouldn't put the ring on your finger.'

I looked at him boldly, summoning all the courage I could muster. 'I don't love you,' I blurted out. 'You are aware of that, aren't you, Nigel?'

His reply was bitterly resentful. 'Yes, I'm only too well aware of it. Your treatment of me doesn't exactly lead me to believe otherwise,' he said, with a touch of sarcasm.

'Then why, oh why, do you insist on forcing me into a marriage I don't want? Please, Nigel, release me from this promise and let me remain here so that I can look after Annabelle for you and act as her tutor. Marriage can bring neither of us any happiness.' I waited in silence for his response. It was a long time coming and when it did, I knew that my words had drawn no pity from him. My courage slowly began to wane as I looked up into his eyes and saw a blaze of fury kindled in them.

He took me roughly by the shoulders and in that instant it flashed across my mind that there must surely be a streak of madness in him. I cried out in pain as his nails dug deep into my flesh. Instead of releasing his hold he tightened his grip and pulled me closer.

'You're mine, Anna,' he almost growled in a low, threatening voice. 'Do you hear? You're mine! Have you no idea how much I love you? I want you for my wife, and my wife you will be. I'd kill you rather than see you in the arms of another man.'

He pulled me, savagely, towards him and kissed me brutally until my lips were bruised and sore. There was no way I could escape his grasp. Clearly, he had no intention of cancelling our wedding under any circumstances. I wondered if there was any compassion at all in this man. Dazed and trembling, I stood motionless whilst he slipped the ring onto my finger. He stood back and admired it. Then, as fleetingly as a changing wind, his mood became gentle again.

'It's beautiful, and most becoming,' he said as he held my hand towards the light. The diamond sparkled like a brilliant star. Obviously he considered the matter closed.

I knew that it was a futile hope but, even at the risk of his anger, I had to make one last attempt to get him to see sense.

'You and I are so different, Nigel. Our lives are worlds apart. We have nothing in common.'

His laugh echoed around the room. 'That's where you're wrong, my dear. We have more in common than you may appreciate.'

'How can that be? I was born on the moors; a poor wretch of a girl eking out an existence in what was little more than a mud hut with nine other members of my family and barely a stitch of clothing on my back. I was ignorant and illiterate until providence took a hand and changed my way of life. You, Nigel, were born into a wealthy family, the son of gentlefolk. You wanted for nothing. When did you ever go hungry for food, or anything for that matter?'

His mouth slowly curled into a twisted smile. 'It's true. I am fortunate to have been born into a wealthy family. But what most people are unaware of is that my paternal ancestors do not bear the name of Tremayne.'

It took some moments for the meaning of his words to sink into my mind. He watched the changing expressions on my face with an element of amusement on his own.

'Are you telling me that ..?'

'That my father was not Sir Mortimer Tremayne.'

Silently, I slipped into a chair and sat digesting his words.

'Sir Mortimer was never aware of the fact,' he continued, 'but I have a vague idea that the old rogue suspected as much. He never did like me, even as a small child.'

'Then ...?'

'My real father? A man who passed himself off as a wealthy farmer but who, my mother later discovered, was a virtually penniless philanderer with nothing more than a mere scrap of land. He was one of my mother's many 'admirers' but not the sort of person who could keep her in the way to which she had become accustomed nor take her to the elegant places she so loves to frequent.'

I was quick to pick up his use of the present tense. 'Then your mother is still alive?' I had to give him the impression that I knew nothing of his mother despite what Adrian had told me on the day we'd gone to Lynhead.

'She is indeed, and living in London,' he replied.

'But what of your real father? Does she still see him?'

He laughed loudly, clearly more than just a little amused. 'Such an idea is farcical. No, indeed not. My mother has had many lovers; both before and since Sir Mortimer secretly divorced her. She is a most attractive woman even now, but in her younger days she was devastatingly beautiful and loved the company of men. She loved handsome men just as I love beautiful women. We are alike, my mother and I, in many ways.'

The words echoed through my mind, for hadn't Adrian said the very same thing?

'So you see, my dear,' he went on, 'you are wrong when you say we have nothing in common. Your father worked on a farm and mine was a virtually penniless farmer.'

There was little point in enlightening him to the fact that, by all accounts, my father wasn't the person he supposed.

'But don't you understand?' I pleaded, 'whatever or

whoever our fathers were, we were brought up in entirely different ways. You are used to grand living and accustomed to mixing in the highest social circles. I have much to learn. Please Nigel, release me from this bethothal and find yourself a more suitable wife.'

'Never!' he bellowed. 'I told you just now, Anna, I'd kill you rather than see you go to someone else. You're mine! And mine you'll remain. Always!'

There was nothing more to be said. Clearly, all my pleading had done nothing to make him change his mind. It had served only to strengthen his determination to have me for his wife. He was hard, selfish, unrelenting and totally uncompassionate. He gave little thought for the feelings of others. His only care was for what he, himself, wanted.

I ran from the library in despair, knowing full well that my last and only hope had failed, taking with it all my pride and self-respect, because it had taken a great deal to plead with him as I had just done. In the hall I ran straight into Adrian. He could see I was distraught.

'You're in a hurry, whatever has happened to get you into this state?' he asked.

He was so kind, so gentle, so different from Nigel.

I shook my head, unable to reply. How could I tell him what had just transpired between his brother and me?

With gentle hands he pulled me closer to him and I felt his arm slip around me as I leaned on his shoulder. When all was said and done we were friends. It felt a natural thing to do and, in any case, I was beyond caring what anyone might say.

'Won't you please tell me what's troubling you?' He tried to coax an answer from me.

'I can't,' I managed.

'Come now. Is it really as bad as all that?'

I was suddenly, very acutely, aware of his closeness. Embarrassed, I drew away from him and with a muttered apology turned to go upstairs. Before I could reach the bottom stair he caught hold of my wrist.

'You really have nothing for which to apologise,' he reassured me. 'You're quite obviously distressed over something. As your future brother-in-law surely I have the right to help you if I can? Won't you tell me what has disturbed you?'

I shook my head again. 'It's nothing, really,' I lied. 'I'm just being foolish. Pre-wedding nerves, I suppose.' I laughed, half-heartedly, in an effort to make light of the situation and allay any suspicions he might have. I could hardly tell him that his own brother had threatened to kill me if I didn't marry him. He would either disbelieve me completely or, if he confronted Nigel with such an accusation, Nigel would, without doubt, deny it as positively outrageous. Either way I would be made to look a fool and achieve nothing by it.

He released his hold of me but there was still concern in his eyes. I had the impression that he didn't really believe my excuse. On the floor above I looked down into the hall. He stood quite still, deep in thought. A moment later I heard the main door slam hard behind him as he let himself out.

*****

I was looking forward to my stay with Isobelle at Spindleberry Grange but I was to be denied even that short time away from Nigel. The following morning he declared, in no uncertain terms, that he had changed his mind.

'I can see no plausible reason for your visit to Spindleberry Grange,' he declared. 'You have everything you could wish for here at the manor. I've sent a messenger to tell her that you won't be going after all.'

I could do nothing except sit and stare at him. I was

speechless. Was I to be allowed no freedom at all? Was I to be kept a prisoner at Foxdale? Perhaps he believed that Isobelle and I had conjured up some plan to whisk me away to a secret hiding place where he wouldn't be able to find me.

Adrian, who had also joined us for breakfast, paused between mouthfuls, his fork poised in mid-air between his plate and his mouth. First he looked at me, then he looked at Nigel, and then he looked back at me again.

'I was under the impression that it was all arranged,' he said, curtly.

'Well your impressions were wrong, dear brother,' Nigel replied. 'I've decided that it's better for Anna to remain here.'

'And why, might I ask? Doesn't Anna have any say in the matter?'

'Damn you, Adrian. Do I have to explain my actions to you? It's none of your blasted business so kindly keep your nose out of my affairs. When I want your advice I'll ask for it.' He rose sharply from the table dragging his chair aside as he did so. He left the room abruptly, leaving his breakfast half eaten. Adrian turned towards me, waiting for me to speak. I was unable to meet his enquiring eyes.

'My God!' he said, after several seconds had ticked by, 'either you're a fool Anna or, in your case, love is well and truly blind. There can be no other reason for you tolerating such treatment.' He rose from his chair. 'Excuse me,' he said, as he threw his napkin onto the plate. Then he, too, left the room.

I was near to tears. Somehow I managed to check the lump which came to my throat. It was no use crying. No doubt there would be many situations such as this and I just had to learn to cope with them; to harden myself against the disappointments and disillusionments that I would undoubtedly encounter as the reluctant wife of Nigel Tremayne.

* * * * *

In my room, the clothes which had been packed ready for my visit to Isobelle had already been taken from the trunk and returned to the closet and drawers. Nigel had been thorough in his instructions. All my plans for the day had been destroyed and my excitement at spending a while away from Foxdale with Isobelle was completely dissolved.

Faced with nothing better to do I made my way to the nursery where I knew I'd find Annabelle. I needed a distraction. What better way than to resume her lessons and to spend time with her.

I had almost reached the nursery door when James came hurrying along the corridor. He looked about him before taking a note from his pocket. 'Mrs Gilmore asked me to give you this,' he said, 'I have to go. Are you alright?'

I assured him that I was before he turned and hurriedly went back the way he'd come. The note was scribbled and brief. It read:

My dear Anna,

Urgent I see you. Surprise visitor. Please come today if you can.

Amy Gilmore.

I wondered who her surprise visitor could be. I wondered, too, how I could possibly get away from Foxdale without being seen because I knew that I couldn't just casually walk out the front door and go into the village. In the end I slipped out by a side door. I didn't walk through the gardens and across the open expanse of grass for fear that I might be seen from one of the windows. Instead, I took a longer route and crept through the shrubbery and trees which ran parallel with the high flint wall that bordered the estate on the southern side. Some way along it there was a narrow opening where the wall had crumbled. From there I found myself on the road leading into the village. I could have taken a pony and trap from the stables but I didn't want anyone to know where I was going, least of all Nigel. In his present mood he would almost certainly prevent me from leaving the grounds of the estate for fear that I might have some plan never to return. I laughed aloud to myself; not with amusement but from utter despair. If only it were that easy. If only I could just run away.

It was good to be on my own, away from the tense atmosphere which had built up at the manor. I derived a certain amount of pleasure in knowing that at that very moment there wasn't a soul who knew where I was. By the time I arrived at Mrs Gilmore's cottage I'd almost forgotten that, by rights, I should have been on my way to Spindleberry Grange. I was curious to know who was waiting for me; who her surprise visitor was.

As I reached the gate she came rushing out to greet me, as if she'd been watching for my arrival.

'My dear, I'm so glad you've been able to come. I have a wonderful surprise for you. There's someone here whom I know you'll be delighted to see. Come in. Come in.' She ushered me in through the door and led me towards the sitting room. 'You go in. I'll brew some tea,' she said, and left me to discover for myself who her visitor was. I opened the door and peered into the room.

'Lucille!'

Lucille rushed forward with outstretched arms and I found myself embraced in a warm and friendly hug. She was the last person in the world I expected to see in Mrs Gilmore's sitting room but, oh, how glad I was to see her. At the same time, my little Muffin leapt towards me with squealing barks of sheer joy at the sight of me. He leapt up at me until I took him into my arms and cuddled him close amidst a bombardment of wet, sloppy kisses in the form of his tongue licking my face all over.

'What are you doing here?' I asked Lucille. 'Have you heard from Mr Carrington? Have you signed the papers?'

'Not yet, dear, but any day now the cottage and the tearooms will be in my possession,' she told me, ' – if that is what you really want?'

'Oh, yes, yes. The sooner it's all transferred into your name, the better. I can't wait to see Nigel's face when he realises he has no say in the matter.'

She took hold of my hand. 'I've come because I'm concerned about you,' she said. 'When I arrived Jenny and Maevis told me that you had already left your home and gone to Foxdale on Nigel's instructions. When I saw that you had left Muffin behind I was certain that something was wrong.' She stopped and waited for me to respond. When I didn't say anything she continued. 'You've spoken to me of Mrs Gilmore and how kind she was to both you and Cathy, so I thought I'd call on her to see if she could tell me what was happening. Being the sister of the vicar it wasn't difficult to discover her whereabouts. The dear soul has made me so welcome since my arrival. She insisted on me staying here with her, at first, but I declined. I thought it better for me to remain at the cottage, especially as Muffin needs me to look after him. It was Mrs Gilmore who suggested that we surprise you with my visit.'

'Such a wonderful surprise,' I told her. I was near to tears. She placed an arm around my shoulder and kissed me affectionately on the cheek. She was so like a sister to me. I didn't want to burden her with my distress but we had been close friends and known each other for so long that there was little to be gained by trying to deceive her into believing all was well. I twisted the sparkling diamond nervously on my left hand. She took hold of it and held it out to admire the beautiful stone.

'Very nice,' she said, without much enthusiasm, 'and I can see you're absolutely ecstatic about the arrangements,' she added with a touch of irony. 'I'm concerned about you, dear, and I'm not the only one. When you first came in, you smiled but there was no laughter in your eyes. Your cheeks are hollow and there are dark shadows beneath your eyes. What has happened to that air of happy contentment that surrounded you not so very long ago? I know you've been ill. I also know from your letter that this marriage is wrong. You've being forced into making a commitment against your will. It can't be allowed to take place, which is why I've made the journey to come and see you. I beg you to reconsider your decision.'

I couldn't remember all that I'd told her in my letter. In any event it would only have been a very vague outline of events so I decided to tell her the full story from the very beginning. Much of it she knew, I was aware of that, but it helped me to talk of it and unburden myself to her, as I'd not previously been able to do. I told her about Annabelle and the fact that she was Cathy's child; I told her all that I'd learnt in connection with Cathy's dubious death and of Nigel's constant and unwelcome attentions. When I mentioned about the two masked robbers who had supposedly held up the coach in which Cathy travelled to London, there was sadness in her eyes.

'So, that seems to confirm what Richard told me about the conversation he overheard between Graham and Nigel some years ago,' she almost whispered. 'Graham must have been one of those masked robbers. I can't believe it, Anna. I loved him so much. I must have been blind. It wasn't until after we married that I realised there was an entirely different side to his nature. But to think that he may have been responsible for your sister's death and the death of the coachman ...' She paused to take a handkerchief from her pocket. There were tears in her eyes. 'Even now, I don't really want to believe it.'

I tried to ease her sadness by saying that Richard might have been wrong. Maybe Graham had nothing to do with the events of that tragic night but, even to my own ears, the words sounded hollow. The evidence was all there. He must have been involved. There was no other explanation for what Richard had seen and heard.

'I wonder who the other highwayman was?' Lucille said after a moment. It was not a question we'd thought to ask until now. 'Whoever it was, it must be someone that Graham knows. Someone known to Nigel as well.'

We sat in silence, contemplating this thought for several minutes. 'Perhaps we should make our suspicions known to the authorities.' I put a voice to what was going through my mind.

'No!' Her reaction was immediate and adamant. I realised, then, that she was still in love with Graham, despite all he had done. She couldn't bring herself to be the instigator of his downfall. For the time being I thought it best to let the matter drop. Sooner or later he would get back what he had put into life. He would pay for his misdeeds without any help from us. Life would be as cruel to him as he had been to those around him.

I brought the conversation back to my reasons for marrying Nigel and how he had learned of my early life and of my growing affection for his daughter. I told her of the threatening manner he had used when he'd told me that Annabelle would never see me again and what he would do if I didn't accept his proposal.

'His insinuations frightened me and I know, now, that my life is in danger if I don't comply with his wishes. Only yesterday, I went to him, belittled myself and cast aside all pride in an attempt to beg him to release me from this bond. He told me, quite clearly, that he'd kill me rather than concede to my pleadings.'

A gasp of horror escaped Lucille's lips. 'This marriage must not take place,' she said, angrily. 'Such deplorable blackmail cannot be permitted. You must go right away from here, Anna. I know it will grieve you to leave Annabelle but you must think of yourself and your own safety. Get right away from that brute who dares to try and subject you to such misery. Go far, far away where he can never find you.'

'He'll find me, wherever I go, I know he will. He won't rest until he has hunted me down to the ends of the earth and then who knows what price I'll pay to avenge his wrath. He would surely kill me and in the meantime I would live in perpetual fear. At least there is a certain amount of safety in becoming his wife.'

She shook her head in despair. 'And just how long do you think that will last?' she asked. 'From what I've learnt he is the type of man who will soon tire of you once he finds he no longer has to fight for you. When he discovers that there's no pleasure in having a reluctant wife he will soon realise his mistake in marrying you against your will, and what then? It seems to me that you're doomed whichever way you turn; far better that you take your leave now with more chance of a total escape. He can't hunt you down forever, nor will he probably want to. He'll grow tired of the search and find another woman to amuse him. Change your name, Anna. Go to Paris. I have friends there who will gladly help you. Even the cleverest of Nigel Tremayne's associates would find it difficult to track you down there. Only please, please, dear Anna, don't remain here.'

For the first time a flicker of hope stirred in me, but I still hesitated. 'Is there someone else you love?' Lucille's intuition astonished me. I nodded, silently but I had no intention of telling her of Adrian. 'Then who in heaven's name is he?' she asked. 'Maybe he can help.'

Helplessly, I shook my head. 'He doesn't know I love him. Probably, he never will,' I enlightened her.

'Can't you tell me who he is?'

Once again I shook my head. 'It's of no consequence and far better that no one, not even you dear Lucille, knows his name.'

Before she could press me further Mrs Gilmore struggled into the room weighed down with a heavily laden tea tray. For the time being, at any rate, the subject was closed. It was quite by chance that I saw the glance which passed between the two women. Only then did it occur to me that Mrs Gilmore might have been listening at the door; an action I would not normally have accredited to her but she had taken an unusually long time to prepare the tea.

Our conversation turned to other things. Mrs Gilmore poured out the tea and I noticed that her hand was more than a little unsteady. She passed me the delicate cup and saucer made of bone china and embossed with a floral design. I'd seen it before, tucked away in her tall glass cabinet along with other selected items which she prized. It was the first time that she'd ever used it in my presence. Perhaps it was in honour of Lucille's visit that it had now been brought into use. I was about to lift the cup to my lips when there was a disturbance and loud commotion outside. The sound of a horse's hooves galloping at speed along the narrow, uneven lane broke the peace and quiet of the morning. We heard a pathetic, screeching whinny as its rider pulled hard on the reigns and brought it to a sudden halt outside the cottage gate. We all turned to peer out of the window.

The cup remained halfway to my lips. I froze on the very spot where I sat. Every nerve in my body became like the taut catgut of a violin. I could feel all colour drain from my face as Nigel stormed up the path. His face was as black as thunder. My hands began to shake violently and, had it not been for Lucille's swift action, my tea would have spilt all over the fine wool rug.

'You don't need to tell me who this is,' she scowled as Mrs Gilmore rose to open the door. I remained quite dumb. The only thought that passed through my mind was how on earth he could have discovered my whereabouts. I thought my departure from the estate had gone unnoticed.

Seconds later his tall frame filled the doorway as he brushed past Mrs Gilmore and came in search of me. He stood glaring at me furiously, his leather riding crop grasped firmly between his hands. He neither acknowledged nor, indeed, appeared aware of Lucille's presence as he came towards me and clamped his long, bony fingers around my wrist. I heard the low, warning rumble in Muffin's throat as he growled at this man he so obviously hated. With a snarl, he leapt forward. Just in time I came between them because I knew Nigel would show him no mercy. I snatched my arm away from Nigel and gathered Muffin into my arms. Before anyone could object, I took him into the kitchen and shut the door on him. As I returned to the sitting room I could hear him frantically pawing at the woodwork, whining in distress. He wanted to protect me.

'So, I wondered where I might find you,' Nigel said, as I closed the door behind me. 'If it hadn't been for Mrs Pringles' sharp eyes and loyalty to me I might never have known. Quite by chance she happened to see you walking through the village earlier. She watched to see where you were going and came straight to me when she returned to the manor. You'll return with me immediately and in future I shall expect you to inform someone when you go out. On no account are you to set foot in this house again. Do I make myself clear?'

As he said this, he once again grabbed hold of my arm. His fingers dug deep into my flesh, pinching the skin until I could no longer bear the pain. I begged him to release his grip.

He glared at me with eyes which were almost wild. Even at this time of day I could tell from the smell of wine on his breath that he'd been drinking heavily. Both Mrs Gilmore and Lucille looked on in horror as he dragged me, unceremoniously, towards the door. That was as far as we got.

'Just what do you consider gives you the right to be so vilely ill-mannered?' Lucille's demanding voice rent the air in cool, commanding tones. Never before had I heard such anger from her. Nigel stopped and turned towards her as if seeing her for the first time. Slowly his steely, grey eyes took in her appearance then, in his most scathing voice, he said:

'Madam, I know not who you are, nor do I have any wish to – and I'll thank you to mind your own business.'

With these words he closed his fingers even more firmly round my wrist and strode angrily down the path towards his tethered horse. Still gripping me tightly so that I couldn't get away he put one foot into the stirrup and rose up into the saddle before hoisting me up in front of him. With little care for me or my clothes he yelled at his horse to move and we rode off at speed towards the manor.

We were within sight of the gatehouse when, for no apparent reason, he turned off the road and headed across the open moors. By this time I felt bruised all over. It was hard and uncomfortable sitting across the saddle in front of him. His arms held me tightly round the waist. I was petrified. My heart pounded so hard I could feel it thumping beneath my ribs. I felt sick with fear. Where on earth was he taking me? It was as if something had snapped inside his devious brain and he'd gone completely out of his mind. He rode like a madman. The wind blew through my hair, whipping out the pins so that each strand was pulled apart and separated until it blew in a tangled mess about my shoulders. Desperately, I clung to the horse's mane; straining away from this hateful man so that my body came no closer to him than was really necessary. On, on we went, scattering wild ponies in all directions as we came upon them grazing on the open land. Rivulets of perspiration ran from Nigel's brow and his breathing was hard from the exertion of the ride. Even the pungent smell of heather and bracken couldn't disguise the foul smell of stale wine which wafted from his mouth into my nostrils.

We rode like this for what seemed an age until, without warning, he slowed down and reigned in the animal before jumping to the ground. As on other occasions his mood suddenly took an abrupt and merciful change. He turned to assist me out of the saddle but, defiantly, I pushed his hand away and told him I could manage.

'Just as you wish.' His voice was calmer now and his temper was more subdued. No doubt the long, hard ride had done much to abate his anger which was more than it had done for me. Trembling and shaking from head to foot I jumped to the ground.

The pain that shot through my left foot was excruciating. I'd landed on a large, jagged stone and twisted my ankle. I tried to steady myself and clung to the horse's neck for support, determined not to give him the satisfaction of seeing me grimace. I had my back to him and, as I stared down at the ground, my attention was drawn to the mud from his riding boots which had dirtied my dress. I was reminded of a time once before, so many years ago, when my dress had been smothered in mud and I'd met Nigel Tremayne for the very first time. I bit my lip – in recollection of that occasion and because of the pain still throbbing through my foot.

'I apologise,' he said, abruptly. He was standing a few yards away, his feet apart and his back towards me with his hands clasped firmly behind him. I said nothing. No apology could right the hurt he had caused to me and to my friends. He was vile. I detested him.

'I said – I apologise.' He turned towards me when he got no response. I still didn't reply. I knew that by ignoring him I was setting light to an already smouldering fire but nothing would induce me to answer.

With slow, purposeful strides he came towards me and swung me round to face him. 'My God, I'll break that spirit of yours in time; you see if I don't,' he growled at me through gritted teeth. 'In fact,' he said, 'why shouldn't I take now what will legally be mine in three weeks' time? Who or what is there to stop me? I've been patient with you, Anna. I've been far more patient and shown far more respect for you than I would normally have done to one of your upbringing. It isn't customary for me to beg for the favours of a village girl; far less so for me to wait until she comes to me.' His eyes slipped over me appreciatively. 'So many times I've longed to hold your slender body close to mine; to run my fingers through that silken hair and unleash the wild, tormenting passion which runs through me whenever I see you. But for some, senseless reason I've been loathe to class you with those village sluts; loathe to claim you outside the bonds of marriage for fear of spoiling you – but not any more. I can see that, even on our wedding night, you won't come to me of your own free will so what point is there in waiting?'

I was terrified. He left nothing to my imagination as to what he was about to do. I couldn't run. The pain in my ankle was too great. In any case, where could I run to? All around me stretched the vast expanse of open moorland. He would easily catch me. There was no Adrian to come to my rescue on this occasion.

On my one good foot I turned back towards the horse and clung fearfully to its damp, perspiring neck. 'No! No!'

I screamed. 'Not here; not now, please Nigel, I beg of you. Please don't degrade me in this fashion.' I pleaded with him in desperation because I knew that there was no escape from him out there on the wild, open moors with no person in sight for miles around.

'Save your pleadings. I've waited too long.' There was no compassion in him at all. He swung me round to face him. The pain wrenched at my injured ankle and I cried out in agony as I tried to fight him off and felt his lips hungrily searching for mine.

After that I knew nothing. Everything went black as I slipped into unconsciousness. I knew no more until I found myself back in my room at Foxdale.

CHAPTER 25

The day was heavy and overcast and the air was stormy. My ankle, though very swollen proved to have sustained only a minor sprain and now that it was tightly bound in a firm bandage I could walk on it with the minimum of discomfort. Doctor Moreland had told me to rest it as much as possible for a few days and to walk no more than was really necessary. Despite Nigel's insistence that I should be cosseted on the couch in the drawing room, I stated very clearly that I would much prefer to remain in my bedroom.

At first I refused to allow myself to dwell on the horrifying events that had occurred but with little else to do but read I found my mind returning time and time again to the events of the day before.

It would seem that my injured ankle had saved me from Nigel. By all accounts he hadn't carried out his evil threat, though I only had his word for it. Shortly after I regained consciousness he came to my room to enquire how I was. As he came close to the bed I recoiled from him. I must have had the one question, to which I was loath to hear an answer, written clearly on my face. A half-hearted smirk twisted his cruel mouth as, bitterly, he told me what I wanted to hear.

'You have no need to worry,' he said, 'your virtue is still intact, my dear Anna. Half the pleasure in claiming you will be in your complete awareness of the fact. Your injured ankle has only postponed the moment. Very soon you'll be my wife and then I shall expect you to uphold your marital duties as a good wife should.'

I glared at him with all the loathing that I felt. 'You may be able to force me into marriage but one thing you'll never get me to do is respond to your love-making.'

He said no more. With a deep sigh of annoyance he stormed out of the room with his lips buttoned tightly. The door slammed behind him.

I lay back on the pillows and thought about what he'd said. I wanted to believe him and from the expression on his face, I was almost certain that he'd told me the truth.

My thoughts returned again to the hazardous ride across the moors. I felt nothing but contempt for the beady eyed, sharp-faced Mrs Pringle for having divulged my whereabouts to him. At the same time I couldn't help but wonder why he had been so angered by my friendship with Mrs Gilmore. Why had he ordered me never to visit her again? Even the fact that Cathy had lived with her for some time was, surely, not justification enough for him to ban my presence in her home. It puzzled me greatly. So much so that I was unaware that someone had quietly entered the room.

'Anna?'

Adrian came and sat on the bed beside me. He took both my hands in his own. There was deep concern on his face. 'Are you alright?' he asked.

I nodded. 'It was only a minor sprain,' I explained.

'That's not what I meant.' His deep blue eyes held mine. 'I think it's time you and I had an honest chat.' He waited for me to respond. He was still holding my hands and I could feel the warmth of his palms. I felt myself trembling at the nearness of him. 'There are a number of people who are very concerned over you, Anna, not least of all myself.'

I didn't know what to say to him. How could I tell him that his own brother had threatened to kill me if I didn't marry him? Would any man want to hear that of his brother? Even if he listened to me and believed what I said, Nigel would never admit to it being the truth. He'd come up with some excuse or other which would make my accusations look absurdly ridiculous.

'You have to talk to me, Anna. I can't help you if you don't,' he urged. 'We're friends, remember?'

'I thought you no longer wanted my friendship. You've seemed so distant lately,' I told him.

He gave a half-hearted laugh. 'Then we've both been wrong,' he admitted. 'Do you remember the day that I came across you and Nigel in the rose garden – when you came here each morning to give Annabelle her lessons?' I nodded. How could I forget? 'Later that day he told me that he was in love with you. He also told me that you returned his love and that he had every intention of marrying you. At first I didn't want to believe it. I thought he must have been lying; that it was just wishful thinking on his part. But then, several weeks later, he told me you had accepted his proposal of marriage. His words were confirmed when you arrived for dinner later that evening to celebrate your engagement. When I learned, for sure, that you were to become his wife, I knew there could be no place in your life for me other than as your brother-in-law. I kept my distance because I felt that it was wrong for you and I to maintain our previous friendship under such circumstances.'

I gasped. 'It isn't true! I've never loved him,' I blurted out.

He was silent as he watched the changing expressions on my face. 'Then why are you marrying him?' His voice was gentle, coaxing. When I didn't reply, only stared at him in confusion, he said, 'Amy Gilmore, and Mrs Bilbrook and her son are extremely worried about you. They believe that Nigel has some hold over you. Is that correct?'

I was frightened to answer. What would Nigel do if he confronted him with my story? And what of Annabelle? Was she really as safe from harm as Mrs Gilmore and everyone else seemed to think? When I didn't give him an answer, he said: 'I know that Annabelle is your niece.'

I stared at him, wide-eyed. 'H-how? How do you know?'

'I think you know that Amy Gilmore was once nanny to me and Nigel? He never liked her, probably because she was very strict in a loving sort of way. I was always very fond of her and we've stayed in touch over the years. When she wrote to me recently and asked me to visit her as soon as I could I knew there was something wrong. At the time I had no idea that it would involve you. I sent James with a message for her to say that I would go and see her that very afternoon.' He paused for a moment, as if gathering his thoughts. I waited for him to go on. 'I already knew who Annabelle's mother was and the circumstances surrounding her birth. I have to say, I was deeply suspicious when I learned of your sister's sudden death. It all seemed far too convenient at the time, especially as Annabelle should have been with her, but on the night that it happened Nigel was with me. There are many things I don't like about my brother but I would never have discredited him with accusations of murder. Not until now, anyway.' His last words were almost a whisper. He got up from the bed and walked over to the window. 'It was Amy Gilmore who told me that you are Annabelle's aunt. She told me, also, of the promise you made. How you vowed to see that no harm would come to Annabelle.' I nodded. 'She's my niece too, you know,' he went on. 'That's where you and I have the same purpose in life. I love her dearly. When she first came to Foxdale I could see why my father was taken with her. Her own father didn't seem to want to know and I vowed that I would make it my duty to look after her and see that she wanted for nothing.'

'She adores you,' I told him, managing a hint of a smile. He didn't say anything for a long time, just stared out of the window across the lawns and gardens. Eventually, he turned back to me.

'Amy confided in me all that you have told her. She told me how Nigel has learned of your relationship to Annabelle and the threat he has put over your head. I had hoped you would tell me yourself but I can see you're too frightened to do so. I don't have to ask if it's true.'

Suddenly all my pent up emotions were released. I let the tears fall unchecked and found myself sobbing my heart out. It was such a relief to have him to talk to and to know that someone in the household, other than James, was on my side; someone I could trust. He hurried over to me and took me in his arms, saying nothing at all until I'd given vent to my feelings.

'My dear, sweet, Anna,' he said, 'This marriage must not take place. I realised your despair when I saw you walk into the lake just a few weeks ago.'

I wiped away my tears with the edge of the linen sheet. 'It was you who pulled me from the water?'

'Yes, it was I. I've tried twice since then to get you away from here,' he said, at last.

I looked at him quizzically. 'I don't understand.'

The first time was when Isobelle Grant came to see you. She's a very dear friend. She agreed to take you back to Spindleberry Grange. Unfortunately, those plans were thwarted. The second time was yesterday.'

'Yesterday?'

'Yes. Your friend, Lucille, turned up in the village quite out of the blue. She went to see Amy Gilmore and it was then that we saw a way of taking you right away from here. The plan was for me to escort you both back to Lynhead yesterday afternoon. From there Lucille suggested that you could travel to Paris and stay with her friends there, for a time at least. It wasn't intended that you should come back to Foxdale. Unfortunately Nigel arrived before you could be told of our plans and I was too late to stop him riding off with you as he did.'

'You were at Mrs Gilmore's yesterday?'

'Yes, I was. I arrived shortly after Nigel had taken you away. I followed but I couldn't find you anywhere.'

Once again the tears welled into my eyes. 'Oh, Adrian, what am I to do? I feel so trapped.'

'We have to get you away from here,' he said. Whatever happens you mustn't marry Nigel. Don't worry about Annabelle. I shall look after her and see that no harm comes to her. My main concern at the moment is for you. Nigel's health over the last few years has not been good, either physically or mentally. I've had my doubts for some time about his state of mind and certainly over the past year or so he's shown signs of mental instability. Who knows what he might do whether you marry him or not.'

I felt a cold chill run through me. He was right. Hadn't I thought, myself, that there were times when Nigel appeared to be just a little out of his mind?

'You can't just leave right now,' Adrian went on. 'The ever watchful Mrs Pringle will no doubt be ready to inform him of your movements before you have time to get to the gatehouse. Now, listen carefully. I shall send James to you this evening when the house is quiet. He will lead you through a part of the house that is rarely used then out through a side door. When he's quite certain that there's no one around he'll take you through the orchard and up along the wooded area until you get to the southern boundary of the estate. From there you can get onto the road which leads out of Thursledown. I shall be waiting there for you with my carriage and we'll be miles away from here before Nigel wakes up in the morning and has time to realise that you're gone. He hasn't seen me today. I told him this morning that I'd be away on business for a few days. He thinks I've already left so it won't even occur to him that you'll be with me.'

I clutched at both his hands. 'Thank you Adrian. Oh, thank you so much.' There was hope for me at last. He left me then.

'Get as much rest and sleep as you possibly can this afternoon,' he said. It will be a long and difficult journey tonight. I'll tell your friend Lucille to be ready for us to collect her this evening.'

He paused at the door and looked out into the corridor to ensure that no one was around. After a moment he disappeared leaving me trembling, both from excitement and from fear. This seemed to be my only chance but it was a long, long time between now and the strike of midnight.

* * * * *

I was restless. The minutes and hours seemed to pass painfully slowly. I hobbled up and down my room. Sometimes I sat on the bed. Sometimes I looked out of the window. At one point I tried to read a book but it was no good, my mind was too distracted. Every time I heard a footfall in the corridor I lived in fear that it would be Nigel and that he had somehow learned of my plans to escape. In the end I decided to put on some clothes and, despite my injured ankle, go for a walk in the garden. I couldn't bear it any longer in my room. Even if he saw me he could hardly object to me walking within sight of the house.

For more than half an hour I wandered through the gardens and relaxed a little in the fresh air. I experienced a feeling of profound relief in the knowledge that I would soon be far away but with it came the knowledge that I would also be unable to see Annabelle again. A feeling of guilt overcame me. Hadn't I made a promise to look after her? I pondered on this for quite a while, tussling with my emotions. And then I thought of Adrian's words and was reminded that he would take good care of her. She could never be in better hands. At the thought of Adrian I realised that I would probably never see him again, either, after tonight. This realisation brought with it a sense of deepened sadness. I couldn't deny that I was in love with him, but for my own safety I couldn't stay. There was certainly no question of him coming with me, not that he would have wanted to. Adrian and I were the best of friends but I doubted that he saw me as anything more.

After a time I decided to return to my room and at least try to rest in preparation for the long journey later that night. I walked slowly back in through the main entrance and then up to the first floor to my bedroom, hopefully for the last time.

* * * * *

'Why haven't you been resting that foot as the doctor ordered?'

As I opened the bedroom door Nigel bellowed the question at me. How long he'd been there waiting, I had no idea. He was clearly displeased.

'What do you mean by wandering off without telling a soul where you're going?' he asked, angrily. 'I came up here to speak with you, only to find that you were gone and not one of the servants could tell me where you were. Kindly explain yourself!'

'No! I will not explain myself,' I retorted. 'You have no right to expect me to give an account of all my movements during the day. I'm not a prisoner, neither will I become one.'

'When you're my wife you'll do just as I say.' He was seething; angry that I should dare to oppose him. 'Which brings me to the reason I wish to see you. I've decided that I don't wish to wait any longer until our marriage. It will take place the day after tomorrow. The arrangements were finalised this morning.'

I was speechless. Thank God that Adrian was taking me away tonight. 'H-how can that be? My gown won't be ready,' I said at last.

'Ah, but it will. I've ensured, with the aid of a little bribery, that your dressmakers will have the garment finished by tomorrow evening. All other arrangements have been taken care of.'

There was a note of satisfaction in his voice. He waited for my response with a self-congratulating smile on his face. When I remained silent his expression changed.

'Very soon we'll put an end to this trifling nonsense, my dear Anna, and you'll settle down to being a good and obedient wife.'

'Never!' I shouted, adamantly. 'Never in my life will I be made to bow down to your wishes.'

'But you already have, my dear, in agreeing to marry me.'

'Agreeing, yes. But until the ring is on my finger, Nigel, I'm not your wife.'

Too late, I realised the stupidity of my words.

'There are no doubts in my mind that you'll become my wife,' he said, walking towards the door. 'But, in the meantime ...' he slid the key from its keyhole, 'I shall take steps to ensure that no foolish notions enter your head, such as making an attempt to run away. Mrs Pringle can attend to you. I can trust her. The remainder of the staff will be told that you are unwell and that you're not to be disturbed.'

He left the room, locking the door behind him. I stood, staring blankly at the closed door. It was just like some terrible dream. Who would ever believe that anyone could be treated in such a way? Firstly to be forced, through fear, into agreeing to marry him; then to be locked up like a prisoner to await the day of the wedding. I couldn't believe it was happening to me. It just didn't seem possible.

I have no idea how long I stood there, staring at the locked door. I felt numb, unable to move a muscle in my body; unable to believe that my last chance of escape had passed me by. All hope of escape had gone completely with the turning of that key. Frantically, I ran to the window, only to discover that escape by that route would be impossible also. There was no way out. I was trapped in my room until the time came for me to be taken to the village church where I would be bound for life, by marriage, to Nigel Tremayne.

* * * * *

CHAPTER 26

Thunder crashed across the heavens as night turned into day and dawn brought with it the most violent storm of the season. As if in sympathy with my predicament, lightning flashed, thunder roared and driving rain beat down relentlessly from an angry sky whipped up by gale force winds. My wedding day had arrived.

As the pale morning light filtered slowly into my room I sat on the edge of the window seat and looked out. Despite the storm the air was very hot and sticky but even so, I felt a cold chill run through me as I thought of the day ahead.

For two days I'd been held a prisoner in my room. The only visitor I had was Mrs Pringle who brought my food, most of which I left untouched. She treated me with disdain, as if I was a naughty, disobedient little child who needed to be punished. I was very aware that she disapproved of me as the future mistress of Foxdale.

It had always been my assumption that she didn't care too much for my presence at Foxdale but her obvious pleasure in keeping me locked away came as something of a surprise. I could see she enjoyed the power of her role as jail-keeper and it became perfectly obvious that she knew why I wasn't permitted to leave my room. She had no sympathy for me and whilst I didn't doubt that she would have been very happy to see me leave – and, indeed, would have helped me to do so under any other circumstances – Nigel was, higher by far, in her estimation than I could ever be. For him she would have done anything, even to the point of discrediting her own kith and kin if she felt it necessary. In his presence she was forever dipping her skirts in a gratuitous curtsey and every sentence she uttered was finished with a very respectful, over-emphatic, 'sir'. Respect and courtesy are one thing but her perpetual bowing and scraping in his presence was quite nauseating and singularly distasteful.

A deep sigh escaped my lips. Two nights ago I should have met Adrian and by now would have been well away from Thursledown, but our plans had been thwarted. I'd watched the minutes tick slowly by as the small hand of the clock approached midnight. How long had he waited, I wondered? Did he know I was a prisoner? He hadn't attempted to come and see me. Somehow Nigel had managed to prevent anyone from coming to my room, other than Mrs Pringle. What had he told them? Surely Adrian hadn't just abandoned me to my fate; not after all he had said. There was James, also. As far as I knew he'd made no attempt to come for me as Adrian had said he would. Perhaps by then he knew it would be a futile exercise. There was no way he could have secured my release without being seen.

With the passing of the hours the storm showed no sign of abating. In a strange, comforting sort of way I was pleased that it wasn't brilliantly sunny or a wonderfully warm day with clear blue skies; that would have belied the fact that it was anything but a happy day for me. The small carriage clock on my bedside table struck eight o'clock. I heard footsteps approaching along the corridor and then the key turned in the lock. Mrs Pringle brought in my breakfast tray. She seemed confused and flustered as she set it down on the small Queen Anne table near the foot of my bed.

'If you've any sense you'll eat it!' she said, sharply.

I didn't reply. My silence angered her still further. She gave me a scathing look. 'He's a fool!' she spat at me.

I remained cool. If I was to become the mistress of this house I couldn't allow her to treat me with such contempt. In my most superior voice, I said, 'I beg your pardon?'

'Master Nigel. He's a fool,' she repeated. 'You'll bring him nothing but trouble. Why he has to marry the owner of a tearooms is beyond me. I've told him – this storm's an omen. No good will come of this marriage. You mark my words. His troubles have already started. As if the weather isn't bad enough, he now has to find himself another best man before the ceremony.'

'Why?' I questioned. 'Surely his brother is to be best man?'

'Not any more. He's disappeared. No one seems to know where he's gone. He was expected back last night but he didn't arrive. Master Nigel is furious, I can tell you.' She cast a cursory glance at me 'Eat your breakfast,' she said, with no hint of respect in her voice, 'the maids will be here soon to help you with your preparations. No doubt once you're mistress you'll be wanting your own personal maid but in the meantime I've chosen two of the more reliable members of staff to attend you – on Master Nigel's instructions,' she added, as if to make it quite clear to me that had the decision been left in her hands she wouldn't have supplied me with help of any kind. As she turned towards the door a thought suddenly came to my mind. I put out a hand to prevent her from leaving.

'Mrs Pringle, please – if you dislike me so much why don't you help me to get away from here? I have no deep desire to marry Nigel Tremayne.' Having made up my mind to go with Adrian I was now prepared to escape under any circumstances despite Nigel's threats.

Surprise flickered across her face, just for a moment. Perhaps, after all, she wasn't entirely aware of my reluctance to become his bride. Perhaps he'd spun some outrageous story to condone his actions in keeping me locked in my room.

'I'll not do anything that's against Master Nigel's wishes,' she said, coldly, and within seconds had left me alone again but not before she'd locked the door securely behind her. That faint glimmer of hope at which I'd clutched was gone just as quickly as it had come. I was left to resign myself, once and for all, to the life ahead of me.

*****

The church clock struck eleven. I stepped down from the carriage and waited whilst my gown was arranged. It was beautiful and had been created with such expertise in such a short time. Made of white moiré silk, it fitted closely in to my waist and had bell-shaped sleeves which came to my elbows. The multiple flounces of the skirt fell gently away to the ground, looped up here and there with white ribbon bows. Over my head I wore a long veil of delicate Honiton lace held in place by one small sprig of orange blossom from the chaplet of orange flowers that I carried in my hands.

The diamond and sapphire ring which had once belonged to Sir Mortimer's mother, had been sent to me earlier in the day with instruction from Nigel that I was to wear it for the ceremony. It still lay, untouched, on its bed of blue velvet back at the manor. I had no intention of wearing it – ever. It was a Tremayne family heirloom and Nigel, himself, had admitted that his father wasn't Sir Mortimer. I could understand, now, why Adrian had so adamantly declared that I wasn't entitled to wear it, nor ever would be. I could well imagine Nigel's displeasure when he came to realise that it wasn't on my finger.

The rain had ceased falling in torrents from the dull, grey sky. Just a few, small drops fell gently on my face as I stood in the church porch and took the arm of Sir Richard Grant, Isobelle's husband. Since I had no father or near relative to give me away it was suggested that he should assume the responsibility as he and his family were old and trusted friends of the Tremaynes. I was in no position to argue. The decision was made without reference to me and my first meeting with Sir Richard had been as we left Foxdale on our way to the church. He was a nice man; pleasant and friendly. I took an instant liking to him in much the same way as I had Isobelle.

Behind me, Annabelle skipped about in excitement. She had no knowledge of the drama surrounding this marriage, nor did she realise her own part in my decision to marry Nigel. To her it was a fairytale day even though the weather was appalling. She was my only bridesmaid and had talked of nothing else since being told of the honour which had been bestowed upon her.

I wiped the tiny drops of rain from my face. It was as if those few small pearls of water on my cheeks had fallen to replace the tears from my own dry eyes. I was beyond tears, completely devoid of all feeling. I felt neither fear nor contempt for the man who stood waiting for me at the altar. It was as if I walked in a trance; a strange, unearthly feeling, like a dream and yet not a dream. There was no spark of hope in me at all that life might, even now, take a different course. I was resigned to what was to be.

As we stepped inside the church the cold chill of the stonework reached out to clasp hold of me. I barely saw the unfamiliar faces of the people who turned to watch as I walked down the aisle. At the altar I refused to look at Nigel. I kept my head bowed and my gaze fixed firmly on the ground. Even when, after what seemed an eternity, Reverend Mead at last began the service, I kept within my sight one single spot on the floor by my feet. His voice came to me from a distance through a haze of unreality.

He'd only just begun the words of the marriage ceremony when Adrian's voice suddenly rang out from the back of the church. I was abruptly shaken from my state of insensibility.

'Stop!' he yelled. 'This wedding cannot take place!'

Nigel spun round and I knew, instinctively, that there was a dark, thunderous expression on his face. 'Just what is the meaning of this?' he questioned his brother, angrily.

'This wedding cannot take place!' Adrian repeated. By this time he had walked the full length of the aisle and stood between Nigel and me.

'Indeed it can, and surely will,' Nigel told him. 'Carry on Reverend Mead. My brother's remark is of no consequence.'

Reverend Mead waited, his eyes on Adrian. Was that an expression of relief I saw in them? Had he been waiting for Adrian to appear? Was that why he'd been so slow in commencing the ceremony?

'I think not,' Adrian persisted. 'You see, Nigel, I have very good reason to believe that you will be marrying your own sister!'

For a full five seconds there was a shocked silence amongst the guests, then a loud gasp went up from the congregation. Only then did I look up, in disbelief, at the kind face of Reverend Mead. I saw there not an expression of surprise but the merest hint of a smile as if he'd known what to expect. I felt my legs become weak and would have slipped helplessly to the floor if Adrian hadn't caught me in his arms.

*****

There was no question of the marriage taking place until Adrian's accusation had been proved or disproved. We left the church and went straight to the vicarage leaving the bemused and curious guests behind us. Reverend Mead and Mrs Gilmore came with us, closely followed by Lucille who took charge of Annabelle and disappeared with her into the kitchen so that we could talk. The rest of us went quietly through to the sitting room.

Nigel was seething with anger. 'Well, what proof do you have to back up this ridiculous statement?' he said, angrily, to Adrian.

Adrian produced a document from inside his cloak stating that its contents had been signed and verified by their mother, Sir Mortimer's ex-wife. He handed it to his brother. In silence Nigel flicked angrily through the sheaves of paper.

'I think you'll see that this document states, without doubt, that Sir Mortimer wasn't your father,' Adrian told him. When certain information came to her knowledge our mother agreed to sign it in order to prevent your marriage to Anna. In it she states very clearly that you were the result of a union between herself and a certain Charles Oliver Gatsby. The indisputable evidence for this confession lies in the identical birthmark which you and the man Gatsby both possess on the back of your necks just behind the right ear. Indeed, it is the same birthmark that you passed on to Annabelle.'

I sat in silence as Nigel flicked angrily through the papers. His hands began to tremble before, ashen faced, he slammed the evidence down on a small table.

'So, this is why my mother didn't honour us with her presence today,' he snorted. 'I wondered why she wasn't here. There's no denying that these papers are written in her own hand and signed by her but, my dear Adrian, you've not revealed anything to me of which I am unaware. I am more interested in this outrageous statement of yours that Anna is my sister. What proof do you have to uphold such a suggestion?'

It was here that Reverend Mead broke his silence. 'We have my sister, Mrs Gilmore, to thank for bringing the matter to light,' he said.

Nigel's face contorted into a look of sheer hatred. 'Damn the woman!' he growled, venomously.

Until now I'd remained silent but, slowly, the truth began to dawn on me as I put all the facts together and came to the only possible conclusion. The very man who had attacked my mother before my birth, Charles Gatsby brother of the local farmer, was, by the signed admission of the late Sir Mortimer's ex-wife, also the father of Nigel.

'But what does Mrs Gilmore have to do with it?' I asked, still a little dazed.

Reverend Mead cleared his throat, straightened the ornaments on the mantelshelf, and then went on. 'It was probably quite by chance that she overheard Mabel Gutheridge the local gossip recalling the scandal that surrounded your mother at the time of your birth, my dear. It was only then that she, herself, brought to mind a piece of information imparted to her in confidence many years ago. You see,' he said, turning to Nigel, 'it was greatly alleged that Anna, here, was illegitimately fathered by Charles Gatsby. If, indeed, it was true she would be your half-sister.'

Nigel's face turned the shade of pure white parchment as he looked first at Reverend Mead, then at Adrian and finally at me.

'But what proof is there?' he demanded, at last.

'There is no real proof,' Adrian answered, 'but you have only to consult the older members of the village to discover for yourself that there is, very definitely, an element of doubt as to who her father was. I think that most will be inclined to say that, as a child, she bore very little resemblance to her brothers and sisters, either in looks or in ways. She'll tell you herself that her mother's husband threw her out of their home because he denied the very fact that she was his daughter. No doubt you'll agree that, because of the uncertainty over her parentage, there can be no question of her marrying you now.'

His words sent a wave of relief surging through me. Whatever happened now it was impossible for me to become Nigel's wife. I could hardly believe it was true. Nigel was defeated. There was nothing he could do about it. With a final outburst of angry words he stormed furiously from the vicarage.

I was in a daze. Everything had happened so fast and I still couldn't really believe that I was under no obligation to marry him. The true consequences of this revelation were yet to be seen and, in truth, I gave no thought as to what he might do. I could only go over Adrian's words again and again in my mind, slowly digesting the implication of what he had said. After a while Lucille and Annabelle came into the room closely followed by James and Mrs Bilbrook. Lucille put her arm around my shoulder and all of them expressed their delight and relief that the marriage had been prevented in time.

'But if you knew that it was possible I might be related to Nigel why didn't you say sooner?' I asked.

It was Mrs Gilmore who answered. 'Without the signed document from Nigel's mother we could do nothing, my dear, and that, as you know, only arrived barely half an hour ago with Adrian and James.'

'With Adrian and James?' I was puzzled.

'When we realised there was no way of getting you away from Foxdale and that Nigel had you held almost like a prisoner with the formidable Mrs Pringle standing guard, we knew that it was imperative to get the only proof he would acknowledge,' Adrian told me. 'We knew my mother was staying with friends in Plymouth and although she was expected to attend the wedding we couldn't take the risk that she might not arrive on time. So James and I travelled day and night to get to her. Whilst we were there a messenger came to say that your wedding had been brought forward and was to be today. In the event it turned out we were right to go to her. She had no intention of coming to the wedding whether it had been today or in a fortnight's time. She said she had always loathed Foxdale and never, ever, wanted to see it or Thursledown again under any circumstances.'

'You have some very dear friends who have been so worried about you,' Lucille put in. 'Mrs Gilmore and Mrs Bilbrook and James just didn't know how to help you. When I came to the village and discovered from Mrs Gilmore what was happening we decided it was time to talk to Adrian about it. It was on his suggestion that Lady Isobelle Grant became involved and we did our best to get you right away from Foxdale. Unfortunately it didn't work.'

James laughed. 'We all became pretty desperate,' he told me. 'I went to the home of Nigel's mother, in London, with a letter from Adrian only to find that she wasn't there. That was how we learned she had left to spend a few weeks in Plymouth with relatives.'

The events of the past few weeks were all falling into place now. 'So that is why I saw nothing of you for several days?' I said to him.

He nodded. 'It's also why I didn't come to collect you at midnight, as arranged, the other evening.'

At this point, Adrian took up the story. 'As soon as we realised Nigel had no intention of allowing you to leave the house we set out immediately for Plymouth. It had been my intention to bring my mother back with us to confront Nigel but she flatly refused to come. We needed proof from her own lips before confronting him and when she learned that the girl he was about to marry was, very possibly, the daughter of Charles Gatsby, she was only too eager to declare openly that he had fathered Nigel in order to stop the marriage taking place.'

I looked up into his face and saw, for the first time, how very tired he looked. He and James could only have had the minimum of sleep in the last week. Tears came to my eyes. All of this was going on without my knowledge. 'It must have come as something of a shock to you to learn that you and Nigel don't share the same father?' I said to him.

'Not entirely,' he admitted. 'I did hear rumours many years ago but I didn't wish to hurt my father by bringing up the subject. He preferred to believe that Nigel was his son. However, I've since learnt that when Mrs Gilmore was nanny to Nigel and me she overheard indisputable evidence from my mother that indicated who his real father was. That is why, as you may recall, I was so adamantly against him giving you the family heirloom as an engagement ring. I didn't feel it was rightfully his to give.'

I glanced at James who, I realised, looked equally tired. 'How can I thank you both for all you've done?'

'No thanks are necessary, Anna,' he told me. 'I only hope you'll forgive us for not telling you of our intentions sooner. While you had given up hope of ever extricating yourself from this marriage, we were all racking our brains for a solution to the problem. A solution which, thankfully, was brought to light by the wagging tongue of that woman Mabel Gutheridge in the village with nothing better to do than talk about other people.'

'What will you do now, dear?' Lucille asked me. 'The tearooms and cottage are still yours. I've purposely held back from completing the transfer into my name because I hoped this would all be resolved long before now.'

It was a difficult question to answer; one which I had to give much thought to. I had to consider Annabelle. At last I gave her my reply.

'I shall go and see Nigel,' I told them all. 'If he bears no grudge against me I would like to remain at Foxdale as Annabelle's governess. She is, after all, my niece and I feel I owe it to Cathy to look after her.'

All of them, without exception, stood staring at me with a blank expression on their faces. It was Lucille who opened her mouth, at last, to speak.

'But how on earth can you consider such a possibility after all that Nigel has done to you?' she exclaimed, aghast. 'Do you forget that he threatened to kill you?'

'No, I haven't forgotten, but that was before he discovered that I am his half-sister,' I said, with confidence, blindly and naively believing that this new revelation would make a great deal of difference to his thinking.

* * * * *

CHAPTER 27

When we emerged from the vicarage some time later all the wedding guests had disappeared and the carriage, which should have taken Nigel and me back to the reception, was still waiting outside the church. I was glad that the Reverend Mead had told everyone that the wedding was cancelled and that they had all departed. I couldn't bear the thought of everyone staring at me with curious eyes. Right now, all I wanted was to change out of my wedding gown, beautiful though it was, and find Nigel so that I could talk with him. Lucille had taken charge of Annabelle and it was agreed that everyone else would remain at the vicarage whilst Adrian and I returned to the house.

'I'll go on ahead and find Nigel,' he said, as he mounted his horse. 'I'll see you back at the house.'

I settled back into the seat and the coachman cracked his whip and set the team of horses at a steady pace along the road towards the manor. As we passed through the village I was careful not to peer out of the windows and sat well back into a corner so that I wouldn't be seen. News travels fast, especially in a small village, and I didn't doubt that there would be a number of curious eyes on the coach as we went by.

I hoped and prayed that when I spoke with Nigel he'd be reasonable and allow me to stay on at the manor as governess to Annabelle. If he didn't, then I would return to my cottage and the tearooms. Lucille and I could live there together. She had been so excited when I'd first suggested she might like to take it over that I didn't feel I could disappoint her now. I could still see Annabelle. Adrian would never be very far away and I felt sure he would see that I had as much contact with her as possible. Nigel would, without doubt, still be very angry but I had to see him straight away in order to put things right with him. Despite the loathing and hatred he inspired in me I couldn't suppress a feeling of deep pity for him and, in view of what had been revealed, I was convinced that I had nothing to fear from him any more. How wrong I was.

As the team of horses turned in through the big wrought iron gates a rider emerged from the trees a little way along the drive. I put my head out of the window to see why we had slowed down and saw that it was Nigel who approached. His horse cantered slowly forward and he ordered the coachman to stop, then asked me to step down. When I had done as he asked he gave another brisk command to the man and told him to continue to the house.

I noticed that he still wore his fine tailcoat which had been made especially for the wedding. His trousers were spattered with mud, kicked up from the wet, muddy ground by the horse's hooves. Slowly, my courage waned as the expression on his face kindled in me a fear far greater than I'd experienced in his presence before.

'I – I was coming to see you,' I stammered.

He said nothing; just glared at me with that same indescribable expression seeming to pierce every bone in my body. I wished then that someone had accompanied me. I looked first one way then the other along the drive but the coach had gone and we were some distance from the lodge house. There was no one in sight.

'I – I'm sorry that everything has gone so terribly wrong for you,' I faltered, nervously. 'I – I hope you won't hold it against me Nigel. In fact I – I was coming to ask you if I might take over the position as Annabelle's governess now that Lady Charlotte has gone away.'

Still he remained silent. The horse champed restlessly at the grass while his master sat motionless in the saddle. His silence was almost unbearable.

'Please – Nigel, say something,' I pleaded.

He did – but the words that he uttered were not the words I wanted to hear. Very slowly, very deliberately, with meaning in every syllable, he said:

'I – am – going – to kill you!'

Panic struck at me then. I picked up my skirts and turned to run in the direction of the lodge house. There was no doubt in my mind, whatsoever, that he meant what he said. Within seconds he was by my side and had lifted me, kicking and screaming, onto the horse's back, then he dug his heels firmly into the animal's flank so that it set off at a gallop in the direction of the lake. Slung helplessly across the saddle in front of him, I was tossed about like a rag doll and barely had enough wind in me to breathe let alone scream for help.

At the lake he dismounted and dragged me crying to the ground. As he loosened his grip I tried, desperately, to get up and run but he caught me again before I'd covered more than a few yards.

'I'm going to kill you,' he repeated, again, and dragged me sobbing and struggling towards the lake. 'I'll not see you live to go to any other man. I love you Anna. Do you hear me? I love you!' His voice was raised and his face was contorted with misery. Slowly, but surely, it seemed that he was going out of his mind. His nails dug deep into my flesh as he pulled me ruthlessly to him and stared into my eyes, his own, deep pools of utter misery and dejection. 'What cruel world is this that can make me love you then calmly let it be known that you are my half-sister?' he screamed at me.

'Nigel, please,' I pleaded, 'don't be a fool. If you kill me you'll be casting away your own life. When my body is discovered you'll be charged with murder and strung up on the gallows for your crime. You can gain nothing. I beg of you! Let me go!'

'Do you not think that I can explain away your death as I did your wretched little sister's?' he sneered. 'It would be simple enough to make it known that, for the second time, you walked into the lake with the very purpose of taking your own life; the first time, only a short while ago – and now. The only difference will be that this time you'll succeed.'

'So you did kill Cathy!' I cried.

'No, it wasn't I, my dear Anna. You may as well know, since I have nothing to fear from you. It was the husband of your dear friend Lucille, Graham Fairs, and that good-for-nothing hanger-on, Simon Pendleton. I paid them well to do the job for me but no one can prove that I was involved.'

'I wouldn't be so sure,' I told him, remembering the conversation overheard by Mrs Bilbrook years ago and also the suspicions of Richard, Lucille's brother.

'If by that you mean you will tell the authorities, then I hate to disappoint you,' he sneered. 'I said that I'm going to kill you and I have every intention of doing so.' He took me brutally by both arms.

'Let me go! Let me go!' I screamed and screamed until, with one swift movement, he forced me down beneath the murky waters of the lake. My mouth and nose filled with the filthy water. My heart was pounding against my ribs. My head throbbed savagely within my skull. I didn't want to die! 'Oh God!' I prayed, 'please don't let me die!'

As if in answer to my silent prayer, Nigel was suddenly flung from me, with all the force of a whirling tornado, and gentle hands lifted me up into the clear, welcome air where I could breathe once more. I coughed and spluttered, then coughed again before I realised that it was James who was sitting on the wet grass beside me. Some distance away Adrian was mercilessly pounding into Nigel with his bare fists; relentlessly throwing out blows which I thought would surely put an end to his worthless life. My fear, however, was not with Nigel but with Adrian.

'Adrian! Adrian!' I screamed when, at last, I regained my breath. 'Don't Adrian! He isn't worth it! You're putting your own life in jeopardy.' For, indeed, if he were to kill Nigel, then his own life would be forfeit.

Panting breathlessly, he gave way to my pleas and stood back from a bruised and defeated Nigel who moved away from him and leaned against a tree, nursing his sore and bleeding face. Adrian appeared unscathed. He came over to me and held me close, his eyes deep with concern.

'Thank God we were in time,' he whispered, hoarsely.

'How did you know?' I asked.

'Intuition, call it what you will. But somehow I didn't have your confidence that Nigel would no longer see any point in carrying out his threat to kill you. In fact, the more I thought about it, the more I realised there was a far greater danger that he would kill you if, indeed, he had the will to do so. James came with me to the house where we found the coachman in some distress. He told us that Nigel had stopped the coach along the drive and taken you from it. My first thought was that he might have brought you here. It's as well for you that I was right in my assumption.' He stood up and helped me to my feet. 'Come now, we must take you to the house so that you can change out of those wet clothes before you catch a chill.'

I looked down at what was once my beautiful wedding gown. It was wet and torn and covered in mud. The ribbon bows which had so delicately looped up the multiple flouncing of the skirt now drooped sadly, intertwined with grass and soggy leaves. My white shoes had gone forever and the beautiful Honiton lace veil had also disappeared. A sigh escaped my lips as I thought of all the painstaking work that had gone into making the gown. I wondered just how the dressmakers would feel if they could see it now.

Adrian and James stood, one either side of me, and held onto my arms whilst I regained my balance. I was still trembling violently from the effects of my ordeal. For a while I was unable to support my own weight. As they helped me towards the waiting horses the thundering sound of hooves brought our attention to Nigel who had stealthily mounted his own animal and made his departure. He rode like a madman; crashing through thin, low branches as if they weren't there.

'Let him go,' Adrian said, as we stared after him. 'If he kills himself he has no one but himself to blame.' He mounted his horse then, with James' help, he lifted me gently into the saddle in front of him. As we rode towards the house he was quiet, deep in thought.

'Something will have to be done about Nigel,' he said, at last. 'I've a shrewd suspicion that a close medical inspection will reveal that he's gone insane. There are a number of people who will be prepared to testify that he's suffered varying degrees of mental imbalance since the death of your sister. It was never proven at the time but there are those who believe, and not without justification, that it was he who arranged that murderous encounter. If it's true, and he's had it on his conscience all these years, then the guilt of it may well have turned his brain.'

I told him how Nigel had already admitted his part in the crime and what he had said to me.

'Then an extensive examination by doctors will prove whether or not he has, indeed, gone out of his mind,' he said. 'I, for one, will be most surprised if they prove otherwise.' There was a sadness in his voice, after all he was speaking about his own half-brother.

We arrived back at Foxdale to find the house in a state of uproar and confusion. Every member of the household had learned that the wedding had been cancelled and the reason why. When the coachman had returned to tell them that Nigel had stopped the coach halfway along the drive and ordered me to step down, their tongues were set wagging still further; even more so when Adrian and James rode off at speed towards the lake after enquiring what had happened to me.

As we stepped into the big hall a hush fell on those nearby. They looked, first at me, aghast expression on their faces, and then at Adrian and, finally, at James. Mrs Pringle pushed her way forward with a stern look of disapproval on her face.

'That storm was an omen,' she declared. 'I knew no good would come of this day. I told him, but he wouldn't listen to me.'

Adrian became impatient with her. 'Get out of our way woman. Can't you see that Miss Briggs is in need of clean, dry clothes? Fetch one of the maids to help her change.'

For a moment I thought she was about to oppose him. I could see she didn't like Adrian, any more than she liked me. After a moment's hesitation she called to a chamber-maid who was standing at the top of the stairs. The girl came down and with Adrian's help supported me as I went up to the floor above. We'd barely reached the top when there was a sudden, loud commotion outside. The main door burst open and one of the gamekeepers, ashen faced and clearly distressed, came running into the hall.

'It's the master! It's the master!' he cried. 'Master Nigel, he – he's dead!'

Both Adrian and I turned in shock. We could do nothing save stand and stare, incredulously, at the man in the doorway.

"E fell from 'is 'orse,' he told us. 'I saw it happen. Ridin' like a lunatic 'e was. Then suddenly the 'orse stumbled and Master Nigel went straight over the top. He landed right on his 'ead. I got to 'im as soon as I could but he weren't breathing. He was dead!'

'Where is he?' Adrian asked the man.

"E's out here, sir.'

I followed slowly behind as Adrian hurried after the gamekeeper to where he'd left Nigel. At the door I had to push my way through the inquisitive servants who were barring my way. When I eventually reached Nigel he'd been taken from his horse and lay lifeless on the ground. His arrogant features were already becoming pinched and white from death's hand. It seemed impossible. Only a short time ago he'd stood waiting for me at the village church. I felt no emotion. Neither jubilation, as one might have thought, nor sorrow at the loss of his life. I felt nothing.

I looked up to find that Adrian was staring, silently, down at the motionless figure of his brother. He stood perfectly still and I could discern nothing from the expression in his eyes. The events of the day had taken their toll. So slowly that I was almost unaware of it, I became engulfed in a state of shock, brought on by my traumatic experience at the lake and subsequent events. I began to shiver violently. Everything became a hazy blur as perspiration ran freely down my face. I placed a hand on Adrian's arm to steady myself. He took one look at me and, the dead man on the ground apparently forgotten, he lifted me into his arms and carried me into the house. As he carried me up the stairs he gave a sharp order that the doctor was to be sent for immediately. After that I knew no more.

* * * * *

For almost three days I was suspended in a state of delirium with a raging fever burning through my whole

329

body. In my wild, disordered mind I relived those tortuous moments by the lake. Worse still, I saw again the lifeless form being lifted from the horse's back to be laid, face up, on the wet, muddy ground. Each time, in my troubled mind, I looked down to see not Nigel's face but Adrian's lifeless features. And then quite suddenly, his eyes would open and he'd lift himself up from the ground and look at me as if I wasn't there. Then he'd turn his back on me and walk away; far, far away into the distance. Again and again in my delirium, I called his name, begging him not to go away; not to leave me. But each time I had this nightmarish vision he seemed not to hear me at all and only walked still further into the distance until he finally disappeared. The pain of his going was unbearable and the hot, burning tears which stung my cheeks felt very real.

When at last my fever broke, I returned to a more stable state of mind to discover that Nigel's funeral had already taken place. His body had been placed in the village churchyard, along with other members of the Tremayne family, at Adrian's request.

The house settled down into a state of relative peace and quiet once more and everyone was anxious to forget the events of the past weeks. One afternoon, feeling considerably better than of late, I dressed and took myself down to the drawing room where I found Adrian sitting quietly reading a book. When he saw me he smiled warmly and placed the book on the hearth. I noticed that he showed no signs of grief over his brother's death. The only indication that there had been a bereavement in the family was a black armband which he wore around his left arm. Other than that he showed no outward signs of sorrow.

'Come and sit down,' he said, kindly. 'It's good to see you up and about again.'

I did as he suggested and sat on a high regency chair by the window. It was a brilliantly warm, autumn day and the sun was throwing golden shafts of light across the beautiful rose patterns on the carpet.

'I'm glad of this opportunity to speak with you alone,' he said. 'In a way I feel responsible for all the misery my brother caused you. It wasn't until Mrs Gilmore brought the situation to my attention that I realised what was going on. Had I known sooner I would have done something to prevent it but, as it was, I did my level best to avoid coming between you and Nigel because ...' he paused, 'because I was under the impression that you really loved him. That is what he led me to believe.'

'I've never loved him,' I admitted. 'I was obliged to pretend that I did for the sake of appearances. You're his brother so perhaps I shouldn't say it, but I loathed and hated the sight of him. I agreed to marry him because I was afraid of him. I was afraid of what he might do to me and of what he might do to Annabelle.' I hesitated for only a moment before saying, 'She is my niece. For my sister's sake I felt that I had to be around to look after her.'

He nodded. 'I know,' he said. 'Amy Gilmore told me as much. I've known her all my life and we have a very close bond. As Governess-cum-nanny-cum special friend to Nigel and me she earned a very special place in my heart. Unfortunately, Nigel never saw her quite as I did. Possibly because he was constantly getting himself into mischief and trouble and so, therefore, felt the firm slap of her hand far more often than he need have done. Don't get me wrong. I was by no means angelic in my childhood. I had my fair share of spankings, just like any normal child, but it seemed that Nigel was never happy unless he was doing something that he knew he shouldn't be doing. Invariably he was caught and any punishment had to be administered by Amy Gilmore. So he grew up regarding her as a fly in the ointment, spoiling his fun. He never liked her. Personally, I regarded her as a mother figure since my own mother wasn't around. She used to get cross with us at times but it was always tempered with a loving quality and a gentle manner. I've always been very fond of her and we haven't lost touch over the years. Which is how I came to learn of your predicament. She and James and Mrs Bilbrook didn't know what to do to help you. James gave me a message asking me to go and see her. I went almost immediately because I knew that it had to be something important troubling her. At first she felt she was being disloyal to you in speaking with me but she really had no choice. She told me all that had been transpiring between you and Nigel and the hold he had over you. Apparently, only that morning you met near your cottage and you told her that Nigel had discovered you were Annabelle's aunt.'

He rose to his feet and stood admiring the beautiful oil painting of Foxdale which hung suspended over the fireplace. His hands were clasped firmly behind his back.

'It was she who told me of your connections in the village and that you are Annabelle's aunt. Quite by chance she overheard that dreadful woman, Mabel Gutheridge, the gossip in the village, relating the suspicions surrounding your own birth. It was this which prompted her to recall something my mother had told her years ago. One evening after Nigel was born, my mother had consumed far too much wine. She was relaxed and her tongue ran away with her. Amy learned that it was very likely that Nigel wasn't Sir Mortimer's son but the offspring of an affair with Charles Gatsby. She was sworn to secrecy over it but she believes that, the following morning, my mother didn't even remember telling her.

When I went to see her she'd put two and two together and realised that you and Nigel could possibly have the same father. As you know, we tried to get you away from him; firstly with Isobelle's help and an invitation for you to stay at Spindleberry Grange. When that didn't work it was arranged, as you know, for me to take you to stay with

Lucille at Lynhead. Unfortunately Nigel became suspicious and prevented us from doing anything. I knew there was no choice but to obtain proof from my mother that Charles Gatsby was Nigel's father. We learned that she wasn't in London and that she'd gone to stay with friends in Plymouth. James and I rode like the wind to get to her and come back as fast as we could with the evidence.

Time was short, and when we arrived in Plymouth we learned it was even shorter. My mother received a note from Nigel, sent by special messenger, to say that the wedding would take place sooner than previously planned. We only just arrived back in time. Thank God we did.'

I silently agreed with him. For several minutes he said nothing, then he went on, 'This estate has been in my family for almost two hundred years. The masters of Foxdale have always been Tremaynes through and through, to the very last drop of blood. Had Nigel lived, his heirs would have inherited the estate since he was, supposedly, the eldest son. Foxdale would have been lost to the natural heirs of the Tremayne family forever because, although he bore the family name, he could never in a thousand years claim to be a true descendant. I'm sorry that he's dead. There were so many occasions, as children, when we had a great deal of fun together. But I'm thankful that it will be my heirs who will, eventually, take possession of this family home.'

'I know how you must feel,' I told him. 'Even though I've lived here only a short while, I've grown to love it. To you, connected with all its ancestry, it must mean a very great deal.'

'It does,' he said, simply. 'It's my life; my inheritance. I could never leave it. That's why I have to be certain that the person who is to become my wife feels the same way as I do.'

It was as if a bucket of cold water had been thrown over me. Was he telling me that he had plans to marry in the near future? If so, who was the lady in question? I was well aware that he'd been seen with a number of lady friends but it came as a shock to know that he was seriously contemplating marriage with one of them.

'Then you're to be married?' I asked.

'I very much hope so.'

I dared not look at him. If I did he would undoubtedly see from the expression on my face just what was passing through my mind.

'What about Annabelle?' I asked. 'Will I be needed here as her governess or will you have other plans for her once you're married?'

'I wouldn't dream of parting you from her,' he said, kindly. 'She adores you nearly as much as I – adore her. Who better than her aunt to take care of her?'

I breathed a sigh of relief. So, I was to be permitted to stay. But now that I had the choice, and in the knowledge that Adrian was to be married, I asked myself if I really wanted to live permanently under the same roof as him. Could I bear to see him every day with his new wife? Maybe it would be better for me to live in the village, to stay at my cottage, and return to the manor each day to give Annabelle her tuition, just has I had done when Lady Charlotte was away?

'Perhaps I could have a little time to think about it,' I said, in a daze. 'I still have my cottage and my tearooms to consider. It was my intention to pass it all over to Lucille but although she has all the documents ready for her to sign, I don't think she has yet completed them and returned them to my solicitor. It may be that she'll decide it's better for her to return to Lynhead and live with her brother.'

Did I detect a touch of disappointment in his face? If so, I was flattered to know that he was so keen to have me as Annabelle's governess. However, I knew that if I remained in his company much longer it would become increasingly difficult for me to hide my feelings concerning his marriage. This man whom I'd loved since I'd been rescued by him as a young girl and whom I still loved, even now, had no idea of the way I felt about him.

I excused myself by saying that I was very tired, having not quite recovered from my illness, and I escaped to my room as quickly as I could.

* * * * *

In the days to come I learned of many changes. I discovered that, on the day of Nigel's funeral, Mrs Pringle had left Foxdale without a word to anyone. She'd been replaced by Mrs Felbridge who was a kind woman, efficient at her work and well liked amongst the servants. When, on one occasion, I sent my dinner back, uneaten, she came hurrying to my room to discover what was wrong and wanted to know if there was anything else that I'd prefer. I assured her that the food was delicious but that I had very little appetite.

'We'll soon have you well and strong again, my dear,' she said, kindly, 'but you must try and eat if you're to regain a nice healthy glow in those pretty cheeks.'

I couldn't. Despite her words of encouragement I was unable to enjoy even the smallest morsel. The time was drawing near, inevitably, when I would have to make a decision. I loved Foxdale and I didn't really want to leave. Neither did I want to leave Annabelle although I knew that Adrian would always take the greatest care of her. But now, knowing that he was contemplating marriage, I was slowly beginning to realise that my most sensible course of action would be to go right away from Thursledown, right away from him and Foxdale. I needed to try and start a new life somewhere else and put him out of my mind. Even if I remained in the village instead of at the manor and continued as governess to Annabelle, it would be impossible for me to avoid the misery of seeing him happily married to someone else. I would envy every moment she shared with him. I had no fears where Annabelle was concerned. She loved her uncle Adrian and I didn't doubt for one moment that both he, and his future wife, would amply make up for the lack of parental love she had received so far. She would be well taken care of. As soon as I was strong enough I would discuss it with Lucille. Maybe she would like to start a new life, away from Thursledown, with me. The more I thought about it, the more the idea appealed to me and I hoped that Lucille would feel the same way.

As I became stronger, my desire to get away from Foxdale increased. In the short term I longed to go back to my cosy little cottage so that I could begin to put the traumatic events of recent weeks behind me.

During my time of convalescence I was never short of visitors. James came to see me at least once every day and his mother, too, was a frequent caller. Lucille, who had remained at the cottage in my absence, was in constant contact and brought my darling little Muffin with her whenever she came to see me. Amy Gilmore and, indeed, her brother the Reverend Mead, kept in close contact and were anxious to know that I was recovering well. I had so many dear and valued friends who were all concerned for my welfare. I knew I had every one of them to thank for the fact that my marriage to Nigel had been prevented. At the same time I discovered there were many other people in the village, some whom I hardly knew, who were thinking of me and held me in their prayers. I received so many flowers and kind messages of support, wishing me well and hoping that I would soon make a speedy recovery. A number of my regular customers at the tearooms expressed the hope that they'd see me back there before too long. I was totally overwhelmed by all their kind thoughts and good wishes for my future.

The one person whom I wanted to see more than any other, however, seemed never to be around. Adrian did seek me out occasionally but it was always with Annabelle, – never on his own. Somehow, in her presence I felt that we lost a little of the closeness he and I had once known as friends. Both of us tended to give her all our attention so that any more personal conversation between us was lost. I realised that he had a lot of estate business to deal with but it seemed that he was never to be seen. He was always out or away on business for a few days. Perhaps he spent much of his spare time with the lady he intended to marry? Which reminded me, who was she? But then, did I really want to know?

* * * * *

CHAPTER 28

With James' help, life returned to normal and I went back my cottage in the village. On the day that I left Foxdale, Adrian was about to go away for a short while to his property in Cornwall.

'Won't you at least stay until I return?' he asked, when I told him of my plans.

'I need to return home,' I told him. 'There are many things I have to think about and discuss with Lucille, but I do hope you'll permit me to visit Annabelle occasionally.'

He turned his back to me and stared out of the window. 'Of course. You're her aunt. You'll be very welcome here at any time. But am I to understand from your decision that you don't wish to be involved in her schooling?'

'I'm sorry, much as I'd like to be, my answer has to be no. I'm planning on possibly leaving the village for good. It will be better for me to start afresh. There are too many memories here.' As I said it I heard the catch in my own voice.

He swung round. For a moment his eyes held mine and I saw in them an expression of surprise, almost shock, then resignation. 'Well, if your mind is made up there's probably nothing I can say to change it, but – we'll all miss you. Not just those at Foxdale but in the village, too. There are many people who regard you very highly. You've made a lot of friends since your return from Lynhead.'

I thanked him for his kind words and for all that he'd done for me. I had to get away from him before I let myself down by allowing unshed tears to fall.

'I have to go,' I said, and put out a hand for him to shake. What he did next took me quite by surprise. Instead of shaking my hand in farewell he looked at it for a moment and then he lifted it to his lips and gently placed a kiss on my fingers. It was all too much. I turned and hurried from the room, unable to hold back the tears any longer.

Within an hour I was back at the cottage. It was good to be home. Muffin was so excited to see me that I thought he would do himself an injury, twisting and turning and jumping up at me. I felt sure that he'd have a very sore throat by the end of the day; such was the high pitch of excitement in his welcoming bark. Jenny and Maevis didn't stop chattering and it was some time before Lucille and I were able to sit down with a quiet cup of tea together. I could see that the cottage and the tearooms hadn't suffered in my absence. Both had been well looked after and there was no shortage of customers coming and going.

'Of course, there's no question of me taking possession of the cottage and tearooms now,' she said, as if to put my mind at rest. 'I shall miss living here and I've enjoyed running the business in your absence but it's time I returned to Lynhead. I've agreed to keep house for Richard. He's away most of the time so he'll be glad to have someone there to look after the place.'

I felt the smile slip from my face. 'I was hoping that you might be interested in moving to somewhere new with me,' I told her. 'We could sell all that I have here and buy something similar, but perhaps larger, in another part of the county. It will do us both good to start afresh.'

Her eyes lit up. 'You mean we could run the business together as a joint venture?'

'Of course. It seems only fair. All this came about because of the generosity of your father towards me, now I can help you by sharing what I have.'

I saw the tears spring to her eyes. 'There's nothing I'd like more,' she told me, and placed her arms around me in an affectionate hug. 'I haven't exactly been relishing the idea of returning to Lynhead. I spent years looking after my father. The thought of going back there to spend the rest of my life doing the same thing for my brother doesn't appeal to me. I've hoped so much that you might ask me to stay here with you, but I appreciate that it isn't a terribly large cottage and there isn't really enough room for two of us.'

'Well then, we shall have to look for a slightly larger investment,' I told her. After that we spent the next few hours engrossed in our plans for the future. It was the right thing to do. I knew it was. Lucille and her father had given me so much in the past. Now it was my turn to repay her and put something back for all the kindness they had both shown me.

* * * * *

Life settled back into a pleasant routine with the exception that I now had Lucille as my companion. She wasn't the best of cooks but then it didn't matter. Jenny and Maevis had always been very good at standing in for me if I needed them to do any cooking and baking but most of the time it was I who took charge of the kitchen and left the two girls to attend to the customers. Lucille took responsibility for the books and the ordering of any supplies we needed. It all worked out very well. In some ways it was a shame that we were considering leaving Thursledown to start our business elsewhere. Now that I was away from Foxdale there no longer seemed to be the urgency to leave the village.

Adrian brought Annabelle to see me several times in those few weeks. Always, he came into the kitchen where I was working and, as time passed, I slowly began to feel that the rapport which had once existed between us was beginning to return. He obviously regarded me as a good friend whom he didn't want to lose. He never mentioned his plans of marriage and I never asked, partly because I couldn't bear to listen whilst he spoke of this other woman in his life.

No doubt he thought it more tactful to say nothing and I was glad because I didn't want to spoil the few precious moments I had with him.

James seemed to believe that now my life had returned to normal, so could our friendship. I saw a great deal of him. Whenever he could he would come and see me and I was invited to have dinner with him and his mother at least once a week. I knew he was very fond of me. I knew that he would have liked to ask me to marry him. But for me it would have been second best. I loved him dearly as a friend but nothing more. Even so, I could tell that Mrs Bilbrook hoped things might change. I didn't have the courage to tell them that Lucille and I were considering the possibility of moving far away. I knew how much it would hurt them both.

It was Tuesday morning, about three weeks later. As it happened it was my mother's birthday. I decided to go to the church and take flowers to place on her grave. I never thought of her without experiencing an overwhelming sense of sadness at the tragedy of her relatively short life. She'd done her best for all of us and had worked hard in difficult conditions. I wondered what she'd think of me now, if she could see how far I'd come.

I took the path which ran close to the side of my cottage and went into the churchyard by a side gate further along. It was a bright day in early December and there was a cold chill in the air. My mother's place of rest was out of sight as I went through the small gate in the low flint wall and made my way between the gravestones. I had with me a small bunch of winter flowers and berries picked from my own garden. As I turned the corner of the church I was aware of three people standing near to my mother's grave. At first, I took no notice of them. I was so deep in thought that I paid little attention to them. It never occurred to me to wonder what they were doing or who they might be. I assumed that they were visiting a grave close by. However, as I drew nearer I realised it was my mother's grave they were standing around. My heart began to beat more quickly. I was sure that one of the women was familiar to me. Another woman was kneeling by the grave, the hood of her cloak pulled well over her head. There was a man whom I didn't know but it was the woman beside him who drew my attention. She had her back half turned to me but she was, undeniably, familiar.

'Mary!' At the sound of my voice they all turned but it was Mary that my eyes were focused on. 'Mary!' I cried again, and hurried forward with my arms outstretched. I couldn't believe it. Here was my little sister, Mary, whom I hadn't seen for so long. She was older, of course, but there was no denying who it was. With only a moment's hesitation she ran into my arms and clung to me, tears streaming down her pretty face. For several moments neither of us was able to speak, we were both so full with the emotion of seeing each other after so long.

As I held her in my arms, I became aware of the other woman who had been tending the grave. As she rose to her feet and turned around I gasped. I was so shocked that the tears in my eyes ceased to fall and I began to tremble; so violently that I thought my legs would collapse beneath me and I would slip to the ground. In shock and confusion I opened my mouth to speak. Nothing came out. As she walked towards me she, too, was crying, the tears running unchecked down her face.

'Anna!' she sobbed, and then I knew I wasn't just imagining what I saw. I knew it was her. It was a voice I thought I would never hear again. It was the voice of my darling sister, Cathy!

I couldn't move. I couldn't say anything. A thousand questions crashed through my mind as she rushed towards me and I held both her and Mary so close that it was a wonder they could breathe. Of a sudden we were all talking at once through tears of sheer happiness and joy. There were so many questions to be answered, so much to tell each other.

In the excitement the man behind us was forgotten. I realised he was standing quietly to one side, watching the reunion with a kind and gentle smile on his face. When at last we parted from each other, Mary turned to him and held out her hand so that he came towards us.

'This is Tom,' she told me. 'We've been married for almost five years.'

He acknowledged me with a beaming smile and said how pleased he was to make my acquaintance. I liked him immediately. Mary had done well. He was obviously a good and loving husband. He placed an arm around her and gently brushed her tear-stained face with one of his large, work-worn hands. She smiled lovingly into his eyes and I could see they were happy. Clearly, they had a very special relationship.

There was so much to tell each other; so many years to catch up on. When at last we all returned to my cottage I decided to give Maevis and Jenny the rest of the day off and close the tearooms for the afternoon. I wanted to know all that had happened to both Mary and Cathy. Most of all I wanted to hear how Cathy had escaped on the night it was intended she should die.

Lucille was amazed and delighted when I introduced them all to her. I could see that, like me, she was keen to know of the circumstances surrounding Cathy's escape. At first she said she would leave us all to talk. We were family and she had no part of it.

'Over the years you've been just like a sister to me,' I told her. 'You have as much right to be here as any of us. Please stay and hear what they have to say.'

'Very well. But first I shall put the kettle on the hob and make tea for us all,' she said, and disappeared down the stairs to the kitchen

We were all seated in my cosy little lounge above the tearooms. I couldn't take my eyes off my sisters. It all seemed like a dream. I wanted to pinch myself to see if it was truly happening. I could see they were as interested in me as I was in them. They were keen to know how I'd improved my status in life but first and foremost I wanted to know about Cathy.

'I don't understand,' I told her. 'Everyone thought it was you, along with the coachman, they found in the burning coach that night. If it wasn't you, who was it? And how did you escape?'

She took a deep breath, sipped at the cup of tea Lucille handed to her and then told me her story.

On the night that she was supposed to go to London the coachman called for her, as arranged, at Mrs Gilmore's cottage. Annabelle was supposed to go with her but at the last minute Cathy decided not to take her. 'Call it premonition, what you will,' she said, 'I just had this awful, uneasy feelin' that I shouldn't take 'er with me, so I left 'er with Mrs Gilmore.'

She went on to say that a mile or two outside the village the coach and four stopped. A young girl was waiting for them by the roadside. She had with her a rough, hessian bag filled with her meagre possessions and Cathy soon learnt that she was the coachman's girlfriend.

' 'er name was Molly,' Cathy enlightened me. 'They was running away together to get married in London.'

I gasped. Hadn't that been the name of the girl who had gone missing about the same time? The girl whose parents thought she had gone off to look for work elsewhere and whom they had never heard of again? That would explain her disappearance. 'Go on,' I said to Cathy.

She continued with her story and I learned that after travelling for about twenty miles the coachman brought the horses to a standstill. For all of ten minutes, they waited by the roadside in a remote part of the country. Cathy couldn't understand why they had stopped and asked the man if there was any reason why they shouldn't continue their journey. He was non-committal and more interested in paying undue attention to his girlfriend who was seated up on the box with him.

After a time, she decided to make the most of the situation and took the opportunity to relieve herself behind some bushes. It was a long journey ahead of them and she wanted to be comfortable. She stepped down from the coach and disappeared into the dense shrubbery so that she couldn't be seen. She was on the point of returning when there was the sound of horses' hooves galloping towards them and then a terrible commotion nearby. Instinct warned her not to show herself. She kept well hidden. The sound of angry voices came to her ears and she heard Nigel's name mentioned more than once. And then, amidst the yelling and shouting, a shot rang out.

'I 'eard the girl, Molly, scream,' she told me. 'It was a terrible, petrified scream. An' then I 'eard another shot and everything went quiet. Me 'eart was beating so 'ard. I was terrified. I thought that any moment they'd come in search of me. I crouched down and kept as still and as quiet as I could. Then I smelt the smoke and 'eard the crackling of wood. Through the bushes I could see the two men who'd done that terrible thing. They was dressed like 'ighwaymen, but when they thought there was no one else around they took off their masks. They un'itched the 'orses and then set light to the coach. One of them said it was best to put the bodies inside then they'd burn with it and no one would recognise them.'

I could see the distress in her face as she related these gruelling details to me. I gave her a moment or two to compose herself and then she told me the rest of the story.

When they were quite sure that the coach was ablaze, the two men had ridden off, taking the four horses with them. In a state of shock, shaking and trembling, she stayed well hidden for what seemed an eternity. It didn't take her long to work out that it should have been she who was lying dead in the burning wreckage of the coach. From what she'd overheard in the angry confrontation between the coachman and his two assailants, he'd been expecting their arrival. What he hadn't expected was to be shot along with his passenger. She'd heard him angrily telling them that Nigel had agreed he should go free and paid him well to keep quiet. That was just before the first shot rang out.

Eventually, dazed and traumatised, Cathy left the safety of the bushes. The coach was well alight and she could just make out the bodies of her travelling companions as the flames licked around their lifeless forms. She thought she would faint. Instead, she threw up the contents of her stomach across the ground in front of her.

At first her whole body felt so weak with fear and shock she was unable to move far. Then she knew what she had to do. She had to allow Nigel to believe that his plan had succeeded. Her first thought was to disappear completely, but then she remembered Annabelle and the fact that she should have been with her on that fateful journey. She had to return to Thursledown, without drawing attention to herself, and collect her daughter from Mrs Gilmore. Then the two of them would go right away from Nigel and Foxdale, right away so that he could harm neither of them. Meanwhile, she just wanted to get as far away from the scene of the crime as she could. She turned and ran. Unaware of the direction in which she was going, she ran and ran as fast as she could, falling and stumbling over rocks and tree roots in the dark. Suddenly, she felt herself falling – falling – falling, and then knew no more.

'She fell over a cliff,' Mary put in at this point. Apparently, we don't know how many hours later, a gypsy couple came by and saw her lying there. They thought she was dead at first. They managed to get to 'er and rescued her but when they eventually brought 'er back to consciousness she could tell them nothing. An' that's the way it was for several years.'

'So how is it that you're all together now?' I asked. Tom took up the story here.

We were travelling in France. You might 'ave guessed that I'm a gypsy; me family goes back generations and generations. We all meet up now and again at a pre-arranged site.'

I nodded and smiled. 'Yes, as a matter of fact the Reverend Mead did mention that Mary had gone off with a traveller.'

'Well,' he continued, 'that particular year we all met up in France. We were makin' our tea one evening when who should arrive but me cousin Alf and his wife Sal. It was great to see them. I told them to come over to our's and eat with us. It was then he told me they had an extra person with them. At first I thought 'e meant they'd had a child since we last met but, no, this was a grown woman.'

'You can imagine my surprise when I saw Cathy,' Mary put in. 'I couldn't believe it. But the worst thing of all was that she didn't recognise me.' Cathy took hold of her sister's hand and gave it a squeeze.

'They wouldn't hear of me staying with Alf and Sal. They insisted that I should live with them. If we hadn't met again, as we did, I might never have come to remember my past. I couldn't remember anything. As it is, with Mary's help I slowly began to recall bits of our childhood and places we both knew. It's really only over the past few months that I've completely regained me memory. Some of it didn't come back until we returned to England and I saw all the familiar places of our childhood. As it would 'ave been Ma's birthday today we decided to visit 'er grave and – and – I thought I'd try an' find out what 'appened to my Annabelle.' There were tears in her eyes. I placed a hand gently over her own.

'She alright,' I told her, gently. 'She's well and grown into a lovely little girl.'

Her face lightened. 'Where is she? Does she live in the village?'

'She lives at Foxdale,' I told her. Her face fell.

'You mean with 'er father.'

'Not any more. He died a few weeks ago. But she does have a very doting uncle to look after her and he adores her.' It was then that I told them everything that had happened in my own life. How I'd met Lucille and her father and how, through his generosity, I'd been able to return to Thursledown with my own business. I told them all that had happened subsequently and how my marriage to Nigel had been prevented by, ironically, the doubt over who my father really was. It was good to talk of all the traumatic events which had occurred in my life over recent months, especially to my sisters. I told them of my many friends in the village and of James, especially, who had stood by me. When I mentioned his name Cathy became more than interested. It occurred to me then that maybe – just maybe – there was a faint flicker of a flame still burning for James inside of her. Time would tell. I knew without a doubt, that he'd take her back into his life without a second thought. Even though he had professed to love me – or so his mother had said – I knew that Cathy had been his one true love and that only she could make him happy in the future.

What a wonderful day it had been. One of the happiest I'd known in a long, long while. We sat for hours talking and talking; so many things to catch up on. There was one thing that Lucille was anxious to know. When she thought the time was right she asked Cathy a question which was burning in her mind and had been since Cathy told us she'd seen and heard the two men who had waylaid the coach and four on the night of the tragedy.

'What did they look like?' she asked, at last, and I could tell from the note in her voice that she was hoping against hope that Cathy wouldn't describe Graham.

My little sister described the two men quite graphically. Obviously their faces and their voices were imprinted on her mind for all time, albeit they had been pushed far back in her memory for a number of years. When she told us what she remembered of them there was no doubting who they were. She painted a vivid picture of both Graham and Simon Pendleton.

'They must be brought to justice,' Tom said angrily. 'Now that we know who they are we must go to the authorities.'

I could see the look of horror on Lucille's face. Even though he'd left her and treated her abominably, she was still loyal to him. We had to explain, then, who Graham was and the part he'd played in our lives admitting, ultimately, that we hadn't a clue where he was. Nor did we know of Simon Pendleton's whereabouts for he, too, seemed to have disappeared. It occurred to me, only then, that during my first few months in Professor Argyll's household, I had asked Graham to go in search of Cathy when he was next in Nether Wilmslow. Clearly, he had never connected my little sister – whom at that time I thought worked at Satchfield House – with the girl he had been commissioned to murder on her journey to London.

It was almost midnight when Tom took my two sisters back to their Romany caravan which they'd left just outside the village. I wanted them to stay but they acknowledged that there was little room for all of us and promised to return very early, for breakfast, the following morning.

I was so happy after they'd gone. I still didn't know what had become of Joey and Harry, Jimmy and Benje, but both Mary and Cathy were again part of my life and I was eternally thankful. For the time being, at least, that was enough to be getting on with. It did, however, make me reassess my plans for the future. I lay on my bed, with Muffin snuggled close to me, and contemplated the fact that if Lucille and I had already moved from the village, I might never have met up again with Cathy and Mary, and Mary's dear husband, Tom. Perhaps one day, one or all of my brothers might return with their families, if only to take a look at the place where they were born. I knew then that I couldn't leave Thursledown. All the time there was hope we might be re-united I had to remain in the village where I belonged.

* * * * *

In the coming weeks only one thing marred my happiness. I couldn't deny that I was in love with Adrian. When I thought about it I suppose I'd always loved him. There had been months, years, when I'd put him to the back of my mind in the belief that he and I were from different social spheres and so could never hope for a future together. But that didn't prevent me from thinking of him. I didn't know how I was going to cope with his forthcoming marriage but, in all events, I had to. There was no choice. I'd made up my mind I didn't want to leave the village. I would just have to cope with it in the best way that I could. I still didn't know who the lucky lady was but then it wasn't any of my business. He still came to see me with Annabelle and I began to feel that we were slipping back into the close friendship we had almost lost. We got on so well together. There was a wonderful rapport between us which I'm sure even he was aware of. He never mentioned the lady in his life, at least, only very obscurely. Once or twice he told me what a wonderful person she was and how she was the only person he had ever truly loved. He never mentioned her by name though.

When he learned that Annabelle's mother had returned and I told him how this had come about he was so angry with his brother, even though he was now dead. At the same time he was delighted to know that Cathy was still alive for my sake but, mostly, for Annabelle. He was quick to suggest that they should see each other and he wanted to arrange a meeting straight away.

Tom and Mary and Cathy decided to remain in the village for the time being. Tom found himself a job on a local farm and was well pleased to discover that his employer was a kind and considerate man. He was offered a cottage on the estate but he said he preferred to live in the caravan. It was a way of life he'd known since the day he was born and it would take a lot of adjustment to get used to living in a house. So the beautiful, painted wooden caravan and the horse were placed in a nearby field and he went off to work early each morning. Mary confided in me that she thought she might be expecting their first child. It was a wonderful, wonderful surprise for her. After many years of hoping to start a family they had both accepted they might never have children. If she was, indeed, carrying their first child, she said that Tom would almost certainly change his mind about the cottage and settle in Thursledown. The cottage would undoubtedly give them far more room than they had at present.

As I'd expected, James couldn't believe that Cathy was still alive. I had to break the news gently to him because I knew it would come as a great shock. When I told him he stared at me in disbelief. At first he thought I was joking.

'But I saw them put her body in the grave in the churchyard,' he said. 'She's buried there. Her name is on the tombstone.'

'It may be her name on the tombstone but it isn't she who is buried there,' I told him, and then went on to relate all that Cathy had told me. His first reaction was to give me a warm, friendly hug. There was so much emotion in his face. To discover that the one person whom he'd loved so much was still alive, after so many years of believing she was dead, was clearly difficult for him to come to terms with. His next thought was to rush out and see her. He had to see her with his own eyes before he truly believed anything I said. I laughed at his impatience as he took me by the hand and we hurried from his mother's cottage. Mrs Bilbrook stood at the door and watched us go. There was an expression of such joy on her face to see her son so happy.

As we neared the place where Tom and Mary and Cathy were living, I saw her outside the caravan washing a few clothes. James didn't wait for me. He ran towards her, calling her name, unable to hold back all the tears he'd bottled up for so many years. There was a sob in his voice as he reached her and she held out her arms to him, tears streaming down her own, pretty face. They clung desperately to each other unaware of anyone else around them. As I walked quietly away I smiled to myself. It wouldn't be long, I was sure, before they announced their intentions to marry. I was happy, so very happy for both of them.

* * * * *

I was busy in the kitchen one morning when Adrian's face appeared at the door. He was alone which was very unusual. There was no sign of Annabelle. When I asked him where she was he shrugged his shoulders and said, 'Oh, James and Cathy have taken her out for the day. They've all gone on a picnic somewhere. She was so excited. You know, she can't believe her mummy is still alive; and they get on so well together. But then, you and she are very close. Suddenly she has her mummy and her aunty and ...'

'... and her uncle,' I reminded him.

'Yes,' he said. 'I've spoken with Cathy and she has absolutely no intention of taking Annabelle away from Foxdale. As she says, Annabelle has spent most of her life there. She could never offer her the same way of living. It wouldn't be fair on her. Of course, she inherits a considerable amount under the terms of my father's will but Cathy wants none of it. She just wants her daughter to be happy. I've told her that she must spend as much time with her as she can. As far as the money goes, I think my brother owes your sister more than any one can put into words for all the misery he inflicted on her. Despite her protests, I'll see that she never wants for anything again.'

How kind he was. There were only a handful of men, born into the luxury of his class, who would be so considerate towards those less fortunate than themselves. It was one of the qualities which made me love him so dearly.

'I called by to tell you of some news I heard earlier,' he said, changing the subject. 'I'm afraid it isn't happy news. At least, it won't be for Lucille.'

Lucille was upstairs and he thought she should hear what he had to say so I called her down.

'I'm afraid your husband, Graham, is dead,' he told her as gently as he could.

To my surprise she didn't shed a tear. She didn't even look unhappy. 'H – how did it happen?' she asked, after a moment or two. By this time we were all seated round the kitchen table and I'd left what I had been doing before he arrived.

'I'm afraid he was leaving the country. He and my cousin, Lady Charlotte, were on their way to Liverpool where they had every intention of boarding a ship to America. Simon Pendleton was also with them. We can only assume that after Cathy told the authorities what happened on the night she was supposed to be killed, and gave a description of them both, it came to their ears that they were wanted men. Obviously it was their intention to make their escape to America where they hoped they could disappear and would never be found. Unfortunately, I think my cousin was totally unaware that she was travelling with two murderers. I've since learnt, from the maid who attended her whilst she was at Foxdale, that she was under the impression that Graham Fairs was an extremely wealthy man. He, apparently, made all sorts of wild promises to her. Sadly, she believed him.' He paused for a moment. 'There's a touch of irony in this situation,' he went on. 'They were well on their journey, by all accounts. Escape must have seemed just around the corner. In order to be sure of reaching Liverpool in time to catch their ship they had to travel overnight. They travelled through unsafe country where there is an abundance of masked thieves who kill and rob lonely travellers. They were no exception. They obviously put up a fight but in the end they lost their lives. Whatever valuables they had with them were stolen, along with their money, and all three were shot in the head.'

We sat in silence. Lucille and I were stunned by his words. 'So ... ' she said, after a while, 'justice has been done.'

Both Adrian and I looked at her. There was absolutely no emotion on her face. We couldn't disagree. By some quirk of fate both Graham and Simon had got their come-uppance. It was true justice indeed. The only person I felt sorry for was Lady Charlotte though I don't suppose Lucille would have agreed with me. I'd never liked her but I didn't feel she deserved to die in such a manner.

Lucille told me she wanted to be by herself. She needed to be alone, which was to be expected. There was much she wanted to think about, not least of all the fact that she was now a widow. She excused herself and went upstairs, leaving Adrian and I alone again.

'There is something else I've learned since Nigel died,' Adrian said, after she'd gone. 'He and Simon Pendleton set up a bogus charity with themselves as Trustees; Nigel being the Chief Executive. Under the terms of my father's Will all the money placed in trust for Annabelle was to be paid to a charity, known only to her solicitors, in the event of her death before the age of twenty-one. As it happened the solicitors were Bennet, Pendleton and Ludgrove, a firm owned in part by Simon's uncle. He managed to secure a position with them and I don't doubt that if anything had happened to Annabelle before she received her inheritance the money in trust would have found its way into that charity. Simon Pendleton had taken over responsibility for Annabelle's financial affairs and between them, he and Nigel thought up a way to ensure that it all came back into Nigel's pocket. No doubt Simon Pendleton was to be paid well for his loyalty to my brother. My God!' he said, after a moment. 'It's only now that I truly appreciate the danger Annabelle has been in during her young life. He could have attempted to kill her at any time. What I've learned recently has enabled me to place all the pieces of the jigsaw together. My brother intended for Annabelle to die that night along with your sister, Cathy. When he discovered that she wasn't in the coach, but had remained back in Thursledown with Amy Gilmore, I can imagine he was incensed. It meant that he had to wait a substantial amount of time before he could get his hands on the money which was rightfully hers. It would have looked very suspicious if she'd also met with an accident soon after Cathy's death. It meant that he had to wait, possibly years, before he could attempt such a thing again. He obviously realised that you were suspicious which was why he so desperately wanted to marry you. He knew that, as his wife, you would be unable to give evidence against him. Having said that, I do believe that he truly loved you, strange as it may sound.' His head fell into his hands. 'When I think of what might have happened to Annabelle – and to you – I can't bear to contemplate it.'

For a long while the atmosphere was subdued. We sat in silence, each of us thinking over the events of the past few months and contemplating the fate which had come, not only to Nigel, but to Graham and Simon and Lady Charlotte. After a while I realised that Muffin had crept, unnoticed, into the kitchen and was sitting between us. He knew it wasn't really allowed but I was loathe to send him out again. I put a hand down under the table to stroke his back. As I did so, Adrian must have had the same idea and our hands touched. I was about to draw mine away but he held onto it. I looked up to find his deep blue eyes staring into my face. There was a question in them.

'Anna,' he said, 'please – don't leave the village.'

I told him that I'd already decided to stay and my reasons for doing so.

'Are those your only reasons?' he asked. Why did he want to know? Was he afraid of losing our friendship? If so, then whether I stayed in the village or not would make no difference.

'Does it matter to you?' I asked. 'Once you're married we won't be able to have these cosy little chats in my kitchen. I'm sure your wife would be most upset. I can't see that she'd allow you to visit me any more.'

'My wife?'

'Yes. Didn't you tell me that you hope to be married?'

He was silent for a moment then with a smile he shook his head several times. 'Yes, I did say I hoped to be married,' he answered. Why was he looking at me like that? Why did he find it so amusing? I didn't find it amusing at all.

'Oh, Anna. Don't you know, there is no other woman in my life? It's you I love and have done for a long, long time.'

Had I heard right? Had he really told me that I was the woman he was in love with?

My hands were trembling. The very words I'd longed to hear him say were on his lips. 'I love you,' he said again. 'When you became engaged to Nigel I stood back from you. Until then I'd hoped you might feel the same way about me. But when he told me you'd agreed to marry him and that, furthermore, "you were ecstatic about the arrangements," I believed – wrongly as it turns out – that you were in love with him. I can't tell you what it did to me. I was devastated.'

'But I do love you, Adrian,' I said, between my tears. 'I've always loved you.'

He kissed me gently on the lips and it was as if I sank into a warm pool of glorious, unending contentment. When we parted he took from his pocket a small red leather jewellery case. Inside, on a bed of deep blue velvet, was the magnificent diamond and sapphire ring which had been passed down through his father's family from generation to generation.

'I am the only true son of Sir Mortimer,' he told me. 'As such, it is my wife, and my wife alone who is entitled to wear this ring. Please Anna – say you will marry me.'

* * * * *